Lovers and Sinners

LOVERS AND SINNERS

Linda Sole

ROWAN

A ROWAN BOOK

Published by Arrow Books Limited
20 Vauxhall Bridge Road, London SW1V 2SA

An imprint of the Random Century Group

London Melbourne Sydney Auckland
Johannesburg and agencies throughout
the world

First published in Great Britain in 1990 by the Random
Century Group
Rowan edition 1991

Filmset by Deltatype Ltd, Ellesmere Port
Printed and bound in Great Britain by
Cox & Wyman Ltd, Reading

ISBN 0 09 984470 2

Prologue

They sit like two black crows presiding over the carcass of a dead sheep. Watching. Always watching me. Why? Are they afraid that the steel bars of the condemned cell will not be strong enough to hold me? Perhaps they think I shall turn into a beautiful canary and fly away.

I have been called a canary. A beautiful singing bird; but that was in the days when the newspapers were kind to me and people bought my records in their thousands. Now they call me an evil woman . . . Betty Cantrel: the woman who murdered her lover in cold blood.

What do they know, all these faceless people who condemn me without hearing my story? How can they guess at the torment in my mind? No one but me knows the whole truth, because I have not spoken. I have not denied my guilt, nor shall I. I shall not beg for my life, nor will I bare my soul to the curious. I will pay the price they demand of me, no matter what it is.

Laurence was here a little while ago, begging me to tell him my story. He is an intelligent young man, with bright eyes and an enquiring mind. He is convinced of my innocence. If I let him, he would appeal against my sentence.

'If only you would speak, Betty,' he said. 'Your silence is taken for guilt. Your refusal to answer the judge made him angry. Please, I beg you, tell me what really happened. Let me demand a retrial. You were torn to pieces by the papers. It wasn't a fair hearing.'

'What really happened?' I smiled at my lawyer. He was so earnest, and, I thought, a little in love with me. 'But

5

you know,' I whispered, my voice mocking and soft. 'Everyone knows that I took a knife and stabbed my lover. I plunged that blade deep into his heart and laughed as I did it — isn't that what they say? Surely you know that, Laurence?'

He stared at me, puzzled and hurt by my attitude. 'It's what they say, Betty,' he agreed. 'But I can't believe it. There's something you're not telling me. Why would you do such a thing? Why . . .' There was a kind of agony in his eyes. 'Why, Betty? If you did it, you must have had a reason.'

'A reason?' I stared at him. 'Yes, there must have been a reason, mustn't there?'

'Then tell me. At least give me the chance to save you!'

He was so intense. For a moment I wanted to speak, to tell him everything, but then I knew, as I had from the start, that it was impossible. My secret would go with me to the grave.

I smiled and shook my head. 'Don't be too sad,' I said. 'I don't think it will be too hard to die. You see, I don't want to live now.'

'But you have so much to live for!' he exclaimed desperately. 'You're rich and famous — and people still love you . . .'

'There was once one person who really loved me . . .'

He looked at me eagerly, hoping for more, but I merely smiled.

'I am already in hell, Laurence,' I murmured. 'Nothing can change that.'

He has gone now. I am alone with my wardens. Two stone-faced women dressed in black. They never smile. I think they are afraid of me, afraid that they might learn to like me. We shall be together for a while yet.

I wonder how long it will be before they come to take me from this cell for the last time? If there is no appeal it will not be too long. I wonder how long it takes to die?

No, I mustn't think about that. It cannot be so very terrible. Hanging is quick. I've seen people die slowly. At least it will be quick . . . And then there will be no more pain . . . no more wind . . .

I have always hated the wind. The sound of it howling about the chimneys frightens me, and the sight of tall trees bent double fills me with a nameless terror. There is something evil in the way it springs up so suddenly, coming like an unseen devil to wreak havoc and destruction upon the land. It is a force beyond human control, claiming lives both at sea and on land. Perhaps it is that lack of control I hate so much, the feeling of being helpless in the face of such absolute power.

Even as a child I was determined to shape my own destiny, to take what I wanted from life. Yet just as a straw is caught in the wind so was I caught by emotions and desires that swept me on, out of control. When I think back now, I realise the wind was a sign that day . . .

PART ONE

Chapter One

The wind was bitterly cold as it blew across the flat sweep of black fenland. It tore at my hair and the chill of it ate into my bones. I wiped the back of my hand beneath my dripping nose, rubbing the wetness surreptitiously on my coat.

'Use your hanky, Betty,' my mother said sharply, glancing up at the threatening sky. 'By the looks of it, there'll be snow tonight.'

As we stood in the gathering gloom of that chill November afternoon in 1945, I sensed the hesitation in her. For a moment she seemed unsure, as if wondering whether to go on. I seized on that moment of uncertainty to renew my protests.

'Let's go back. Please! I don't want to go to The Willows. I want to stay at home with you and the others.'

'We've been over this a hundred times, Betty.' Mother frowned and I saw the moment of hesitation had passed. 'You're going and that's final. You're a selfish, thoughtless girl. If you knew what I'd had to do to get this chance for you . . .'

There was an odd expression in her eyes; I thought it was somewhere between elation and guilt, as though she'd done something that both pleased and frightened her.

'What did you do, Mum?' I stared at her curiously, sensing a mystery.

'Don't ask questions. Whatever it was, it was for you; to give you a better life. Do you really want to work on the land or in a factory?'

Silenced, I gazed into her face, seeing the pinched, slightly sullen droop to her mouth and the signs of premature ageing. Life hadn't been kind to her. Years of penny pinching and make-do-and-mend had taken their toll. There were still traces of prettiness, but disappointment and hardship had etched lines about her eyes and mouth, making her look older than her thirty-three years. Her thick hair was scraped back under an ugly, felt hat, and her coat was a dark shapeless thing that bore the Utility label: a mark of drabness imposed on clothing by the years of war we had all so recently endured. It had taken ages to save the coupons for it, and she was still paying the tallyman at the rate of two shillings a week.

Clothing coupons were just a part of the rationing system that had come into being with the outbreak of war in September 1939. Many other things were rationed too, like petrol and food. Everyone had a card that had to be clipped or marked every time they bought something, and the amount they could buy varied depending on whether or not they were a special case. Diabetics were entitled to more fruit, but most people got just two ounces of butter a week and one of cheese. Some things like bananas and oranges were almost impossible to find. We had all thought rationing would end once the war was over, but it hadn't happened yet. I wondered if my mother had perhaps bribed Mrs Crawley to give me a job with some of her clothing coupons, but that didn't seem likely, though the family at Willow Farm were well-off and I knew that women who could afford it often did buy the coupons their char-women couldn't afford to use.

Mother had been watching me, a wry smile on her mouth. 'Well,' she said as I frowned. 'Do you want to end up like me?'

I flushed. 'You're not so bad.'

She laughed, and for a brief second I caught a glimpse of the woman she might have been if she hadn't made the mistake of marrying Robert Cantrel, but perhaps with me on the way, she'd had little choice. It needed great courage to bear a child out of wedlock. A hasty marriage was better than nothing.

'You've more sense than I ever had, Betty. You've ambition and the courage to go after what you want – that's why I've given you this chance. I want you to have all the things I threw away when . . .' She stopped herself, shaking her head. 'I can't make you go, but two pounds ten shillings is a lot more than you'll get on the land at your age.'

'They're offering twenty-five shillings at a dress shop in Ely.'

'There'll be your bus fares, and I'll want half.'

'I can give you more if I go to the Crawleys.' I sighed, wishing I didn't have a conscience. 'But I'll be a servant!'

'You'll be Frances Crawley's companion; I've told you that over and over.'

'It's the same thing. I'll have to fetch and carry for her – and be polite all the time.'

'Is that so terrible? Frances is a semi-invalid and often has to stay in bed. Mary Crawley worries about her. She's her only child – and she's never been to school! You're so lucky. You've always been healthy. Is it so much to run a few errands for a girl who can't do them for herself?'

'You make me sound awful.' I looked at her resentfully. 'You're going to miss me. Vera can't manage the mangle, and she hates cooking. And Joey won't sleep if I don't read him a story from his *Nipper* annual.'

'Don't do this to me.' Mother was desperate. 'I can't bear it when you look at me like that. You know why you have to go.'

Biting my lip, I turned away. She was reminding me of something I would prefer to forget. Something I felt was shameful.

It was unfair that I should be sent away, and I felt angry. Angry with God or Fate, but mostly with the man who had caused all our troubles. If Robert Cantrel had spent less time drinking and more working, I might still be at home toasting bread over the fire.

13

There was anger against my mother, too. She had told us often enough that she was the daughter of decent folk, brought up in a big house with servants, in a town not far from our village.

'It had ten bedrooms besides the servants' quarters,' she'd told me once. 'There were velvet curtains at all the windows and Persian carpets on the floors – like the one the vicar has only bigger and better. We had a carriage and plenty of money . . .'

'Then why are we so poor now?' I'd asked.

'Because your grandfather was a mean-minded bastard who cut your mother off without a penny when she married me.'

Mother had flushed with pain when my father's voice cut in brutally, and she wouldn't talk any more. I was annoyed with him for upsetting her, and I'd tried to imagine the house that should have been my birthright: mine, Vera's and Joe's.

I imagined how it would feel to live in a house like that, with plenty of money, cosseted and loved. Since then I'd often pictured the scene on nights when we hardly had enough coal for the fire and the wind howled about the chimney of our cottage. It was a church cottage, old and dilapidated, with stone floors that ran with moisture in the winter, and a smoking chimney. It made me wonder what my mother had seen in Robert Cantrel that made her throw away so much for him.

She said it was love, but it was that thing between his legs she loved. The walls in our cottage were paper thin, and I'd learned from an early age how she loved what he did to her in their room. Many a night when money was short she'd started on at him, but she always ended on her back, whimpering and begging him to love her.

I'd seen it once, that thing Father was so proud of. He was doing something to it with his hand. I saw it grow thicker and longer and begin to quiver, and I felt sick, yet I couldn't look away. Then he glanced up and saw me.

'You're like your mother, Betty,' he taunted. 'Lizzie

14

was a hot little thing when I first met her. She'd been guarded like the crown jewels by her father, but when I beckoned she fell into my arms like a ripe peach. You'll be the same. The first man to get between your legs . . .'

I couldn't listen. My heart hammered wildly as I fled from the room, the sound of his laughter following me.

I told my mother that afternoon. Her face went white and then red. Grabbing my shoulders, she shook me until my teeth rattled.

'Did he touch you? Did he do anything to you?'

'No! No, I told you. He just laughed.'

She went for him that night. It was the worst fight they'd ever had, and he hit her. When I heard her sobbing, I wished I'd kept my mouth shut. I felt guilty, as though I'd caused their fight. Then there was silence, and that was worse. When the bed began to creak, I knew she hadn't been able to resist him. How could she let him – after what he'd done to her?

It was a few days after their quarrel that she disappeared for a whole day. When she came back there was mud on her shoes and an odd look of triumph in her eyes, but when I asked her where she'd been, she only shook her head.

'You'll find out soon enough. I want to talk to your Dad first.'

As soon as he came in that night, she took him into their bedroom. They spoke in whispers, tantalising me, but then my father exclaimed aloud.

'But that's blackmail, Lizzie!'

'Hush, Rob. Keep your voice down or the kids will hear.'

'But how do you know?' he said, loudly enough for me to hear. 'All right, I'll whisper – but tell me . . .' As he lowered his voice, I turned on the wireless. Why should I want to know their secrets?

A voice was going on about a woman called Edith Thompson who'd plotted with her lover to murder her husband in 1922 and had been hanged in the following year. I listened, fascinated, despite the shivers it sent down my spine. It seemed that they'd had to drug her with morphine and carry her to the scaffold.

Shuddering, I shut my eyes and tried to imagine what it would be like to know that you were going to be hanged. The worst bit would be the waiting, I thought. I felt very odd as I listened to the voice on the wireless. It was all so cold and emotionless – but it wouldn't be like that! I could almost feel poor Edith's fear. I could hear her screams as she begged for mercy.

Feeling sick, I switched off the wireless. What were Mum and Dad doing in there? It was several minutes before they came out, looking pleased with themselves.

'I've found a job for you, Betty,' Mum announced. 'I went to see Mary Crawley today. The Crawleys own that big farm in the fens – you've heard me talk of them. Mary and I met at school. We both went to a private school, and she didn't have many friends. We stayed at each other's houses during the holidays.'

'You promised I wouldn't have to work on the land!'

'You're not going to.' Her eyes glittered with excitement. 'You're going to be a companion to Mary's daughter.'

'Live in the fens?' I was horrified. 'I'll never be able to go to Guides or choir practice.'

'You're old enough to earn your keep. I'd send you to your grandfather in Chatteris if he'd have you, but he won't. He's never forgiven me for marrying against his wishes. He was gentry, Betty. You come from good stock – and this will give you a chance to make something of yourself.'

'I don't want to live with the Crawleys,' I said stubbornly, and I'd gone on saying it, but now, as I looked at my mother in the fading light, my anger melted. It wasn't her fault I had to leave, it was my father's.

'Yes,' I said. 'I know why I have to go.'

She nodded and smiled. 'Look on the bright side, Betty. You'll be living in the sort of house you belong in. You'll make friends with Frances, and you'll meet the right sort of people. When you're older, you might meet a decent man — a gentleman. Someone who'll treat you right. Someone who'll give you the things I've never had. Someone gentle, kind and good.'

I nodded, looking at her thoughtfully. 'Do you ever wish you'd married someone different — a man of your own class?'

She stared at me, seeming to hesitate, then shook her head. 'It may seem strange to you, Betty, but I've always loved your father. When I first met him he was in uniform and he was so handsome! I knew he was the one. I didn't care that he wasn't an educated man, but my father was furious. I thought he would be happy that I'd found someone I could love, but he wouldn't even talk about it. He said I had to choose between him or your dad — so I ran away.'

'Didn't you mind giving up the pretty clothes and the money?'

'I was so much in love it didn't occur to me. Your father was different then — before it all started to go wrong. And we both thought my father would come round in the end. When your grandmother was alive she used to send us money to help out. She sent you a gold bracelet for your christening, but we had to sell it when Rob had his accident . . .' She sighed.

'What was she like — your mother?'

'She was a real lady.' Mum's face brightened. 'She had a gentle voice and beautiful manners. If she hadn't died maybe Father would've come round . . .'

My heart softened as I saw her sadness. The first flakes of snow had begun to fall as our hands clasped in a rare moment of understanding. 'What's Mrs Crawley like then?'

'She's a good woman. She works for the village and the Church.'

'But what's she really like? Why did you ask her for a job for me — and why doesn't Dad like the Crawleys?'

17

She looked at me oddly. 'What did he say?'

'Nothing much. Just that he doesn't like Eben Crawley.'

'Eben turned your father off his land once. I think they had a fight and Eben won. Rob couldn't stomach that.'

'Was it before Dad's accident or after?'

Her face lit with pride. 'After. Before Rob fell off that haystack there wasn't a man in the county could have stood up to him. I wish you'd known him then, Betty. All the girls were after him when I married him.'

I tried to understand, but it was difficult to imagine my father as anything but the often unshaven, bleary-eyed man that I knew. At thirty-nine, he was stooped and he limped heavily on the leg that had broken in two places during his fall. Because of it he had been unable to join up when the war came, and it added to his bitterness.

'It must have been hard for him, I suppose.'

'Don't hate him, Betty. He'd been drinking the other day, that's what made him . . .'

'Please don't,' I begged. 'It will be all right. I don't like changes, that's all.'

'It's a good place, Betty.'

It was a good place. Eben Crawley was the most important landowner in the district, and in the old days would probably have been thought of as the Squire. He'd come to the fens as a young man in the 1920s, buying land when other farmers were going bankrupt and seeing their farms come under the hammer for a fraction of their worth. Somehow he had made a success where others had failed, acquiring more and more land over the past twenty-odd years and becoming rich and respected. If some people whispered that he'd got his start by making Mary Benson pregnant, it was whispered and not in his hearing. Most people had forgotten, but Dad remembered the tale.

'Eben Crawley was a lucky devil,' he said bitterly when he knew I was to work at The Willows. 'Instead of throwing her out, Mary's father gave her a generous start . . .'

'Now then, Rob,' Mum said. 'No need to talk like that. We don't want Betty getting ideas, do we?'

I remembered the word blackmail and wondered about the secret they shared. The secret I wasn't to be told.

I was still resenting their attitude when I looked at Mum that cold November afternoon. My nose was running again, but this time I wiped it with my hanky. Mum was walking slowly now, and clutching my hand as if she needed comfort from me now that we were nearly there.

I could see the ugly square house that Eben Crawley's money had built. It sat like a great, squatting spider on that flat landscape, unprotected by a park or gardens. Behind it the roofs of the barns had a gentle, mellowed look, as if they somehow belonged there, which they did, having stood there for a hundred years before Eben's arrival.

The house was an intrusion on that sweeping scene of black earth and glowering sky. No attempt had been made to soften its environment. It was simply there, raw and ugly, defying the elements. To reach it we had to follow a muddy, winding track that cut away from the river bank, stretching on endlessly so that we had to trudge on and on down a path beaten flat by the wheels of many tractors and carts. I could smell the sickly sweet scent of sugar beet, and the warm, strong odour of a cow byre. The cold was biting into my flesh now and my hands were so numb that I could scarcely hold on to my small suitcase.

I felt miserable, and I longed to be back in the cottage. It might be poorly furnished, with few modern conveniences, but it was home. Every step down that track was taking me further away and closer to a future I dreaded.

At the end of the track the lane widened out and we found ourselves at the front of the house. Now that we were closer, I saw that there was a gravel drive and a few pitiful flower beds beneath the windows, as if someone had made an effort to cheer the bleakness.

'We'll go round the back, Betty.' Mum sounded nervous and I was surprised. She'd been so elated, what had made her change all of a sudden?

'Why?' I asked. 'You said I'm not a servant.'

She frowned at me. 'Our shoes are thick with mud. Besides, there's a light at the back.' Her face was anxious. 'You won't let me down, Betty?'

'Oh, Mum! Don't fuss so.'

'You're too proud,' she said ruefully. 'You remind me of your grandfather. I hope you won't grow up to be as bitter and unforgiving as he is. I'm only telling you for your own good. Mary can be generous. If you impress her, she might do something for you.'

A dog was barking wildly in one of the outhouses, as if to warn of our arrival, but, despite the noise, Mum had to knock twice before the door was opened. The woman who stood there had a sour expression. She was tall and thin with iron-grey hair, a beak of a nose and pale lips. Dressed all in black, her only concession a collar of white lace, she looked formidable. My heart sank. If this was Mary Crawley I didn't think I could stand being in the house.

My mother's chin went up. 'Good evening, Mrs Jackson. Would you be kind enough to inform Mrs Crawley of our arrival please?'

The woman's gaze became even colder and she looked as if she would like to slam the door on us. She stepped back. 'You'd best come in then.' Her strangely flecked eyes flicked to our muddy shoes. 'Wipe your feet first. This floor is trouble enough as it is.'

Obediently, we scraped the soles of our shoes on the black iron fixture outside the door, making sure every scrap of the fine soil had gone. I trod gingerly on the floor of gleaming red quarry-tiles, fearful lest I leave a trail of mud for this hawk-eyed woman to pounce on.

'You can wait while I tell my sister-in-law you're here,'

she muttered. 'There's tea in the pot if you want something to warm you.'

'Thank you, but we won't for the moment,' Mum said, putting on what Dad called her lady-like airs.

'You didn't tell me about her,' I grumbled as she left.

'Eben Crawley's sister?' Mum frowned. 'She's just a poor relation. Don't worry about her, Betty.'

I nodded. It wasn't unusual for women in her circumstances to live almost as a servant in their relatives' home. While she was away, I seized the opportunity to look round. The kitchen was a large, square room with a huge, black cooking range as well as a cylinder-gas stove and an open fire. There was a large, white cabinet, which I thought must be a refrigerator, though I hadn't seen one quite like it before. Not many people in the village had one, and you weren't supposed to use them because we all had to save electricity. Beneath the window were two deep, stone sinks joined by a ridged, wooden, draining board, and a friendly clutter of flowering plants jostled for position on the windowsill. At one end of the room was a tall, pine dresser set with blue and white china, and a scrubbed, pine table occupied the centre of the floor. Just now it was covered with the produce of a baking session, and the smell of spicy bread and cakes made my mouth water. I wondered how it had been possible to produce all this marvellous food, and I realised for the first time how different life at the farm might be. It seemed that money made all things possible!

From somewhere deep inside the house there was the sound of music. I couldn't quite hear the words, but I thought it was Vera Lynn, singing one of the songs that had made her the darling of the forces during the war.

As Mum and I huddled close to the fire, the outer door opened again and a man came in, stamping his feet and shaking the fast-melting snowflakes from his hair. 'It's cold enough for a foot of snow,' he said, tramping mud as he came to join us by the fire. 'You'll be Betty Cantrel, I reckon. I'm Joe Morris,' he said offering his hand to

Mum and then to me, 'Mr Crawley's foreman. If you want a lift on your day off, Betty, you just ask me.' His hand enveloped mine and I felt the scrape of rough skin.

He was a man of perhaps thirty, taller than average, heavily built, with coarse features and a ruddy complexion. A man who had spent most of his life in the fresh air, working on the land. He was wearing khaki trousers tucked into his Wellington boots, and I guessed that they were a part of his Home Guard uniform. I'd never met him before, but Dad had mentioned his name a few times.

'You used to train at the Vicarage Hall with Dad, didn't you?' I asked. 'He said you were one of the best with a gun.'

'That was right nice of Rob,' he said, a twinkle in his eyes. 'He's not a bad shot himself.'

'Why weren't you in the army, Mr Morris?' I asked. 'Dad wanted to join but they wouldn't have him because of his leg.'

'I volunteered, but they said I was needed on the land.'

'And quite right,' Mum said quickly. 'Growing food was, and still is, an important job. Don't be rude, Betty.'

'Let her speak as she likes,' he said. 'It's best to be open about these things – and call me Joe, everyone does.' He grinned at me.

'I've a brother called Joe. He's four and I read to him from his comics every night. It wouldn't seem right to call you Joe. May I call you Joseph instead?'

'Well, lass, I reckon you can call me what you want.' He chuckled and I thought how gentle his smile was.

The door from the hall opened, and I realised that the music had stopped. Mrs Jackson came in. She glanced at the mud on the floor and her lips tightened but she said nothing. Clearly she had more respect for Joe than for my mother or me.

'You're to come with me.' She shook her head as Mum started forward. 'Just the girl. Mrs Crawley said there's no need for you to wait.'

Mother's face went white, then her eyes began to

glitter. She looked at me and I guessed that she was about to insist on coming with me. I shook my head.

'It doesn't matter,' I said. 'If you go now you'll be home before the snow settles.'

'I wanted to see things were right, Betty.'

'Maybe it's for the best.'

We gazed into each other's eyes and it was as equals. I think she sensed then that I was no longer a child; that that line had been crossed somewhere on our long walk. Perhaps because I was the eldest I had never really been a child. I'd been forced to grow up before my time, learning things that a girl of my age shouldn't know. The war, too, had made us all older than our years.

'I'll come home on my day off,' I said.

'Take care then,' was all she could manage. I wished that just for once she would kiss me or show some affection.

'She'll be just fine,' Joe said. 'Shall I run you home in the shooting brake, Mrs Cantrel?'

'Oh no. If I walk quickly I'll be home before dark.'

'Then I'll walk part of the way with you. All the droves look the same at night.'

I watched as they went out.

'Come along, Betty.'

I turned towards Eben Crawley's sister. 'Yes, Mrs Jackson. I was just saying goodbye to Mum.'

'You call me, ma'am,' she said with a frown. 'Come on now, we mustn't keep your mistress waiting.'

'I'm to be Frances's companion,' I said, glaring at her. 'I'm not a servant.'

'Oh, aren't you,' she said. 'Well, I'll tell you something, Miss high-and-mighty Cantrel, you'll keep a civil tongue in your head or you won't stay in this house long. My brother isn't fond of the Cantrels.'

'I wasn't being rude,' I said sulkily.

'That's a matter of opinion, miss.'

She was standing impatiently by the kitchen door. I followed her into the hall, glad that my mother had gone before she heard the exchange between us. Perhaps I had been rude, but I hated the way Mrs Jackson looked at me, as if I were dirt. Why couldn't she be friendly, like Joe Morris? I was pleased he was walking Mum part of the way home. It would start to get dark long before she got there, and even though the war was over and the blackout was finished, there were no street lights in the village.

The hall leading off the kitchen was narrow and gloomy. Not until we reached the upper landing did I begin to notice my surroundings. A thick carpet in a Persian design ran the length of the passage; it looked very expensive and I thought Eben Crawley must be very rich. My grandfather was also rich, and I thought his house must be like this one with quality furniture and rugs, but I hadn't really understood what that meant until now. For the first time in my life, I was truly aware of my own poverty. It gave me butterflies in my stomach.

Mrs Jackson walked so fast that I had difficulty keeping up with her. I was out of breath when she finally stopped, and from the gleam in her eyes, I guessed she'd done it on purpose. It didn't help that she was also breathing hard. She looked at me as if I were something the cat had dragged in.

'Don't speak until Mrs Crawley invites you to,' she said. 'When she dismisses you, come back to the kitchen.'

I nodded, feeling scared now that I was about to meet the mistress of the house.

I knocked and then opened the door, my heart banging like a tin drum. I was so scared that I could hardly breathe and my feet felt as if they were glued to the floor. I took two tiny steps inside, looking about me with wide eyes.

My first impression was of a room crowded with things; little occasional tables, hard chairs with stuffed seats of horsehair covered in a plush velvet, and cabinets crammed with china knick-knacks, silver oddments, and a large case of beautiful stuffed birds next to a modern wireless in a walnut case. But my eyes were drawn to a

24

large wing-backed chair by the fire and to the woman who sat there.

She had been reading before I entered and the book was still open in her hand. I noticed that her fingers were long and slender and the nails were neatly manicured. She had a plain, almost ugly face. Her black hair was drawn back into a tight knot at the nape of her neck, but though it was plainly styled, it was thick and glossy. My mother's hair might have looked like that if she'd taken more care of it. Mrs Crawley's dress was a dull brown that did nothing for her sallow complexion, but it didn't look like the cheap Utility dresses most women wore these days, and I suspected it had been bought before the war. When she looked at me, I saw her eyes were curiously bright, and when she smiled she was no longer ugly.

'Come in, Betty,' she said in a low, musical voice. 'I want to talk to you for a few minutes, then I'll take you to meet my daughter. She's resting just now. She hasn't been well today.'

Encouraged, I took a step forward. 'Is she very ill, ma'am?' I asked, forgetting Mrs Jackson's instructions.

'Frances is often unwell. You may find her a little difficult sometimes, but you must be patient with her. She is almost a prisoner of the house in winter and it makes her restless.' Her bright gaze lifted and I was aware of an intelligent mind behind that unremarkable face. 'Your mother tells me you are a clever girl.'

'I passed all my exams at school. My teacher wanted me to go to college, but my father said I had to leave and find a job.'

'So your mother said.' Her mouth tightened. 'I'm giving you a chance to prove yourself, Betty, but if you don't fit in here . . .'

'Mum said I was to be Miss Crawley's companion.'

Annoyance showed in her eyes. 'Yes, well, we'll see. You will be Frances's companion in a way, but I'll expect you to wait on her when she's in bed. You'll be expected to look after her clothes, perhaps some dusting – things of that nature.'

'So I am to be her maid after all.'

My dissatisfaction must have shown in my face. She frowned again. 'If you're not happy with the arrangement, you may leave at the end of the month. It's hardly my fault if your mother led you to expect more than I agreed.'

I had the feeling that Mary Crawley didn't really want me in her home, and I remembered that word 'blackmail' again. Had Mum got some kind of hold over her? I wondered. But my employer was frowning and I realised I must apologise.

'I'm sorry. I didn't mean to be rude.'

'I don't want to be harsh with you, Betty. I do realise that you didn't ask to come here. That was your mother's idea.' She nodded as I agreed. 'If you make Frances happy, you won't go unrewarded. There are those in this house who think she's spoilt. They don't understand. I can't make her well, but she is to have whatever she wants, even if it seems selfish to you.'

'I understand, ma'am.'

'Good. You may well be an answer to my prayers. Now then, we'll go to see Frances. I warn you, she's feeling sorry for herself today.'

'What's wrong with her?'

'When she was five she had rheumatic fever. It left her with a weak chest and she catches cold easily.'

'There was a girl at school like that,' I said. 'She was away a lot in the winter, but she came nearly every day in summer. Why doesn't Frances go to school when she's well?'

'Because I prefer to teach her myself. This is really none of your business, Betty.'

I blushed, realising I'd gone too far. 'No, I don't suppose it is – but if I don't ask, I won't know why she's ill, will I?'

Mary laughed softly. 'At least you say what you think

26

to my face. That's more than I can say for some in this house.'

I dared not say any more. I was on trial, and I could be sent home in disgrace. If that happened, Mum would go wild!

Frances Crawley's room was on the other side of the house. At first glance, everything in it seemed to be made of lace. There were creamy lace curtains at the window; the bedcover and drapes around the bed were of the same lace, as were the dainty tablecloths. I counted four tables in that room, each one crammed with knick-knacks. I saw that she had a gramophone of her own as well as stacks of jigsaw puzzles, books and games.

Jealousy surged in me. Why should she have so much when my family had so little? Then I saw the girl propped up against a pile of pillows and the resentment ebbed away. Her hair was the same black as her mother's, but much thinner, hanging lifelessly about her pale face. Mrs Crawley's eyes gave her an air of vitality, but Frances's were dull and seemed to stare blankly in front of her.

Mrs Crawley moved towards her, laying a hand on her brow. 'How are you now, my darling? Is your headache better?'

'A little, but now I feel sick,' Frances whined. 'No one has been to see me all afternoon. May I have supper in bed? I feel too ill to get up.'

'Of course.' Mrs Crawley dropped a kiss on her head. 'Betty will bring it for you. From now on she will look after you.'

Frances looked at me, and I looked at her, noting the sudden gleam in those dull eyes.

'How old are you?' she demanded.

'I was fourteen last summer, Miss Frances.'

'I'm fifteen. You look older than me; you're so tall.'

'People do say so.'

'And you're fat.'

There was a glint of malice in her eyes. I was angry but determined not to show it. She was testing me, seeing

27

how far she could go. Besides, there was truth in what she said. Mum insisted my heaviness was caused by a diet that consisted almost entirely of potatoes or bread dipped in dripping, and that I would grow out of it. Compared to Frances, I suppose I was fat.

'I expect I am,' I said carefully. 'But Mum says I'll grow out of it.'

'You sound like one of those common village children.' She looked at her mother sulkily. 'Do I have to have a common girl as my maid, Mother?'

Mary Crawley frowned. 'Betty will learn to talk as we do in time. Besides, she'll be much kinder and more helpful than Polly or your Aunt Hilda.'

Frances gave me a calculating look. I guessed that she was weighing up the advantages of having a servant of her own, whom she could order about at will, against my commonness.

'Well, I suppose she can't help being fat, and I can teach her better manners . . .' Frances suddenly smiled at her mother. 'You're so kind to me.'

'You know I want you to be happy, darling.' Mrs Crawley stroked her hair. 'Now I'll leave you together. You can get to know each other. Betty is to be a companion as well as a maid, Frances. It will be nice for you to have someone your own age to talk to.'

'I suppose so.' Frances pouted. 'Can't you stay with me for a while? Sometimes I think you don't care for me at all.'

'You know that isn't true. I've been busy, that's all. Now I have to dress for dinner. Your father will be home soon, and you know how he hates to be kept waiting.' She smiled, nodded to me and left the room.

Immediately, I noticed a change in Frances. She sat up and her air of apathy fell away. It had been put on, I suspected, purely for her mother's benefit. Frances obviously used her frequent illnesses as a way of getting exactly what she wanted. She was very spoilt!

'I'm delicate,' she announced, and a gleeful smile

curved her lips. 'That means I have to be waited on all the time. You've got to do everything I want. You can start by bringing me that bag of Milk Tray chocolates from the table by the window – and I want my pillows made comfortable.'

I gritted my teeth. Now I was seeing the real Frances and I disliked her. I would have loved to give her the shaking she deserved, but that would have meant instant dismissal. I could see that she was enjoying the sensation of power, and I sensed that she was watching me with an odd eagerness, as if she would have liked me to lose my temper. I answered meekly.

'Yes, Miss Frances.'

I fetched her sweets. They were still rationed, so someone must have gone to considerable trouble to get them for her. Taking them from me, she leaned forward while I shook and rearranged the pillows.

'Not that way,' she grumbled. 'I need one behind my head.'

I tried again, hitting the pillows hard and pretending they were her.

'That's better.' The dark eyes glittered and I was sure she guessed what was on my mind. She wanted me to do something she could report to her mother. 'Now, fetch me that copy of Daphne du Maurier's book, *Frenchman's Creek*. Over there. I suppose you can read?'

'Oh yes.' I picked up the book. 'I've read this and *Jamaica Inn* and *Rebecca*. I'm reading Defoe's *Moll Flanders* at the moment.'

She stared at me. 'My mother would never allow me to read that. It's a disgusting book.'

'How do you know if you haven't read it?'

'Because it's about . . . Well, I know it's disgusting. Only common girls read books like that. I suppose you've read *Lady Chatterley's Lover* as well?' Her eyes challenged triumphantly.

'As a matter of fact I have.'

'Liar! You can't have; it's banned.'

'Well, I have. A friend of my father's got hold of a copy when he was in the army. Dad had it hidden in the shed, but I found it and I read it. Every word.' I was defiant. 'It's only rude in bits.'

She eyed me in awed silence, then: 'You're not a judge of what's rude – you're not a lady, are you?'

I took a deep breath and counted to ten. 'Shall I fetch your supper now?'

She looked disappointed at my self-control. 'I suppose so.' Her fingers scrabbled in the bag of chocolates. 'Just some soup and a scrambled egg. I'm not hungry.'

I made no comment, but I thought it was hardly surprising if she ate sweets all the time. It seemed to me that her mother was too soft with her. It was worrying that she took cold so easily, but that was surely no reason to pamper her every whim.

'Very well, miss,' I said, my mouth watering as she devoured a chocolate orange cream. I was so hungry!

'Don't call me miss all the time. It sounds silly. You can call me Frances.'

'Your mum might not like that.'

'She lets me do as I like because it's her fault I'm an invalid.'

'That's not a very nice thing to say about your mum.'

'It's true – and she's my mother. Please try not to be so common.'

'I'll try, miss . . . Frances.'

'That's better. Do as I say and I might let you stay.'

My cheeks flamed and my hands itched to slap her, but I held my head high as I left the room. I stood outside for a moment, getting my bearings before retracing my steps the way I'd come. No wonder Mrs Crawley said people thought she was spoilt.

Smothering my annoyance, I began to look about me. Although there was electricity in the house, the upstairs passages were lit by oil lamps. I guessed there must be a small generator somewhere that was not powerful enough to supply all the needs of the household. Most of

30

the houses in the village now had some electricity, but only the bigger ones had more than a few lights, and points for the wireless and a cooker. I liked the yellow glow of the lamps. Because of the war, many people used them to help save electricity for industry.

Descending into the lower regions of the house, I was not certain which of the three doors into the hall led to the kitchen. Then I saw a chink of light from beneath one of them, and, approaching it, I heard voices coming from inside.

'You're being too hard on the girl. I thought she was a bright lass.'

That was Joe's voice. They must be talking about me! I hesitated, wondering what to do.

'Too bright for her own good.' Mrs Jackson, of course!

'That's unfair. Give her a chance.'

'She's a Cantrel, isn't she? They're a bad lot. Her father's a drunkard — and his father was a thief.'

'Old man Cantrel poached a few rabbits and a pheasant or two. There's a good many more have done that these past few years; it's not such a terrible crime.'

'Other people managed,' Mrs Jackson grumbled. 'What was he doing when the rest of us were digging for victory, I ask you? Sitting in the pub when he should have been growing vegetables.'

'Mum always said poaching was a poor man's privilege.' A third voice joined in; the voice of a young woman. 'What's she like then, Joe? I mean, I've seen her in church — but what sort of a girl is she?'

Trembling with indignation, I pushed open the door before they could tear me to pieces as they had my father.

All eyes turned on me. Mrs Jackson was slicing bread at the table; Joe sat in the rocking chair by the fire, and a girl of about eighteen was stirring something in a pan on the range. She was plump and pretty and as curious about me as I was about her. I admired her dark chestnut hair and blue eyes, then turned my gaze on Mrs Jackson.

'I'm to take a tray up for Miss Frances. She wants soup and a scrambled egg.'

'Does she indeed?' Her mouth thinned. 'Why can't she have the same as everyone else?'

'Because she isn't very hungry.'

'And we all know why, don't we? Mary takes everyone's sweet ration for that girl. Well, as long as you don't expect me to get it ready. I've enough to do without pampering to Frances. I came here as a favour to Eben when Mary wasn't too well, but I'll not be treated as an unpaid housekeeper. The cooking is one thing, but running up and down stairs all day after a girl who could . . .'

'I'll prepare the egg if you'll show me where the tin is.'

'We don't have that powdered rubbish here,' the girl laid down her spoon and laughed. 'Only real eggs for us.' She came towards me. 'I'm Polly Baxter. I'm glad you've come, Betty. We've enough to do without running after Miss Frances. And she's not really ill half the time . . .'

'Stop gossiping and look after that soup,' Mrs Jackson warned.

'It's not hurting. Betty should know the truth. She'll be looking after Miss Frances now.' Polly smiled at me. 'The eggs are in the pantry, and everything else you need is in the dresser or by the range.' She pointed to a row of pans. 'Can you manage the range? The cooker's temperamental; we don't use it much.'

'I'm used to a range at home. I can see to it now. Thank you, Polly.'

I soon had the tray set, and, as a last minute thought, I asked for a thin slice of bread and butter, spreading Marmite on it.

'She'll not eat it,' Mrs Jackson grumbled.

'Our Joe likes his bread cut into soldiers. I thought it might tempt Miss Frances.'

'Just be sure to come straight back for your own supper.'

I nodded and picked up the tray. It was a long way to

Frances's room. Despite the silver covers, the food would be getting cold. I could hear a dog howling somewhere in the distance. It didn't sound as if it came from the farm, but further away, deep in the fen. It was a mournful, haunting sound.

I hurried on towards Frances's room. She had her bedside lamp on and she was reading *Frenchman's Creek*. I placed the little table that fitted across her lap on the bed, removing the covers.

'Don't go,' she said as I turned away. 'Stay with me while I eat. You can sit on the edge of the bed.' I did as she asked, thinking regretfully of my own supper. She swallowed a mouthful of soup and then pushed it away. 'Too much salt.'

'I'll see if yours can be put aside before the salt is added next time. Why don't you eat the egg instead?'

She didn't answer, but she picked up a finger of bread and butter. She ate a forkful of egg then bit the bread. I waited for some comment but none came. I smiled inwardly as one by one the Marmite soldiers disappeared.

When she had finished I was at last allowed to leave. My stomach was rumbling; it was hours since I'd eaten and then it was only bread and jam. Remembering the mouth-watering smell of the food cooking, I walked as quickly as I could. It was ages since we'd had any meat at the cottage. Because of the war meat was scarce and expensive, but Polly had definitely been stirring something that smelt good.

As I approached Mrs Crawley's sitting-room, I saw that the door was slightly open and I could hear raised voices.

'You had no right to bring the daughter of that man into my house, Mary,' a man was saying. 'You know how I feel about him.'

'Her mother is respectable, Eben. Elizabeth Chilton came from a good family. We were at school together. I felt obliged to do something for her – and the vicar speaks well of Betty.'

'She's a Cantrel. I caught her father going after the chickens and threw him off my land. He made some excuse about the war and starving children, but I wouldn't take any of that nonsense. I vowed I'd shoot Cantrel if he ever came back, and I meant it.'

'He won't come, nor will her mother. Please don't be difficult, Eben. You know something had to be done. After Frances was rude to Polly she threatened to leave. It's so hard to find girls who are willing to live in the fens these days – why should they when they can work in the factories? If Polly goes I don't know what we'll do. It's all the fault of the wretched war, of course.'

'Can you wonder that Polly threatened to leave after the way Frances behaved? You've ruined her with your spoiling.'

'It's unfair of you to criticise me. Frances is delicate.'

'Delicate be damned! The girl is ungovernable and it's your own fault.'

'Perhaps if you'd been a little kinder to her . . .'

'Damn it, Mary! Now you're being unfair. I've never been unkind to the girl. I don't like the way you keep her wrapped in cottonwool, but I've never laid a finger on her – have I?'

'But you don't love her and she feels it.'

'I wanted a son. I almost lost you because of her.' A softer note had come into his voice. 'In some ways I have lost you. She's poor compensation.'

'Please don't look at me like that.' I heard the distress in Mrs Crawley's voice. 'It's hardly my fault if I can't be a proper wife to you.'

'I know the doctor said it would be dangerous for you to have a child too soon after Frances's birth, but you're much stronger now.' There was a short silence, then, 'Mary. Mary love. I miss you in my bed . . .'

Hearing the throaty, pleading note in his voice, I felt a shiver go through me. It wasn't right that I should hear these private things, but I was frightened to go past that door.

'Oh, for heaven's sake, Eben – don't!'

Mary's voice was raised in an angry protest. I heard an odd, strangled groan and then the door was pushed to with a bang. Breathing a sigh of relief, I began to creep past the door, but then a voice spoke suddenly from behind me, making me jump. I glanced over my shoulder, my heart thumping wildly as I saw the man standing there. Now I was for it!

'Eavesdroppers always hear ill of themselves,' he said, his eyes bright with mockery. 'It serves you right, Betty Cantrel.'

'I – I was afraid to go past,' I said defensively. 'I didn't want to listen.'

I stared at him, feeling sick with fright. Who was he? He obviously knew my name. As I stood there, unable to move, he came towards me and I caught the faint tang of Brylcreem. As I gazed into his face, I felt my knees tremble. He had such an odd expression just then. At first glance he wasn't really handsome; his nose had a little bump in it as though it had been broken at some time, and his mouth was thin and slightly cruel. Or perhaps it was only the taunting smile that made me think so. I couldn't decide what colour his eyes were. At one moment they could have been green, but then they became the colour of woodsmoke as they narrowed into an intense stare that caused my pulse to jump. A lock of straight dark hair had fallen across his brow. As he reached up to brush it back, I instinctively recoiled.

'Are you afraid of me?' he asked. 'What a timid creature you are.'

'No, I'm not!'

'Aren't you?' His soft laughter seemed to threaten me. He had a brooding air about him, a haunting look in his eyes that I found intimidating. I was immediately aware of a capriciousness about him, and I felt that he was unpredictable and might be capable of anything. 'Shall I put that bold statement to the test, kiddo?'

My skin prickled with tension as I gazed up into his

35

eyes, and I felt as if I were walking on the edge of a precipice. I'd heard about men like him, and I knew that in what Dad called the 'bad old days', many a girl had lost her place through the unwelcome attentions of a member of the household. I stood poised for flight, yet somehow I suspected that he was testing me and I decided to call his bluff.

'If you touch me I shall scream. I don't know who you are, but . . .'

'The black sheep – or perhaps I should say ram?' One fine brow arched wickedly as he looked at me. 'Don't tell me no one has warned you to beware of the evil Nathan Crawley?' He saw my puzzled expression and pursed his lips in a soundless whistle. 'You surprise me. I thought one of them would've done it by now. Well, Betty, now you know. Eben is my uncle – my dear, fond Uncle Eben.'

There was mockery in every line of his face and bitterness in his voice.

'You're making me nervous. I'm sorry if I listened to something I shouldn't. May I go now? I haven't had my supper yet.'

'And I'm delaying you – what a brute I am.' His smile was still faintly sardonic though not as disturbing. 'How old are you?'

'Fourteen, sir.' He must be about twenty-one or two, I thought. He had the look of a man who'd been in one of the armed services during the war. It was something in his eyes.

'You're a big girl, Betty.' His gaze was disturbing. 'Are you sure you're only fourteen?'

'Yes, sir. Miss Frances says I'm fat.'

'Ah, my cousin.' He grinned. 'She's a spoilt brat, but you mustn't let her get you down. Her illness makes her restless and sometimes cruel. She needs someone to be kind to her. Will you be kind, Betty?'

'I'll try.' I shifted from one foot to the other, trying to balance the tray. 'May I go now?'

'Impatient, aren't you?' He inclined his head

imperiously. 'Go then. We'll meet again – unless you've already decided to flee this house of iniquity?'

'I don't know what you mean.'

He laughed. 'If I'm honest nor do I. Take no notice of me, kid. In this mood I'm not fit company for a child of your tender years. Away to the kitchen, Betty. You amuse me – and that's when I'm at my worst. Go quickly, before I change my mind and gobble you up!'

As he spoke, he made a move with his hands as if to grab me. I jumped back, squealing with fright, and set off down the hall as fast as I could.

I could feel those strange, chameleon eyes watching me as I fled. Clearly I wasn't going to be made welcome in this house. Mr Crawley didn't want me here. Both he and his sister had called my father a wastrel, and because of Dad's behaviour they despised me. It was unfair and it made me angry. It wouldn't be easy to keep my place here, but I was determined to do so. I'd decided that I wanted to stay – and no one was going to drive me away. Not even Nathan Crawley!

A seed of ambition had been planted in me that night. I was going to make something of my life. My mother had thrown all her advantages away, but the world was changing. Things would be different now the war was over. Once we'd had time to lick our wounds, we'd build a new world – and I was going to find my place in it. I wanted to be like Frances Crawley, only better.

Chapter Two

Everyone had finished eating when I got back to the
kitchen. Mrs Jackson glared at me as she took my supper
from the oven and banged it down on the table in front of
me. The vegetables had turned brown and the gravy had
dried round the edges, but it was a real meat pie! They
certainly didn't seem to be suffering too badly at The
Willows. It smelt wonderful and I began to eat as fast as I
could. I was hungry and I hadn't tasted anything this
good since before the war.

'Anyone would think you were starving,' Mrs Jackson
said. 'I expect some manners at my table – I don't know
what your mother's been thinking of, letting you eat like
that.'

'Sorry. I've had nothing since breakfast and there
wasn't much of that.'

'I've seen pigs with better manners.'

'Oh, leave her alone,' Joe said. 'She'll not be so hungry
another day. Give her the last of the treacle tart.'

I stared at the tart in disbelief. All the sugar and treacle
that had gone into that! Someone must have been getting
stuff from under the counter.

Mrs Jackson scowled, but she placed a small plate in
front of me. That tart was so moist it just melted on my
tongue. I thought for a moment that I'd died and gone to
Heaven, and I smiled gratefully at Joe. He winked at me
and I felt a glow inside. I had at least one friend in the
house.

'When you've finished I'll take you upstairs,' Polly
said, wiping her hands. 'I can finish the washing up later.'

'There's the uniforms to sort out — and her dutie[s]' Jackson agreed. 'Go on then. Bring her down after[...] and we'll all have a cup of tea. My feet are killing[...] Sometimes I don't think Mary appreciates all I do in th[e] house.'

'She must do,' Joe said appeasingly. 'She couldn't manage without you. All those meetings and charities — she'd never have time if it weren't for you.'

'It's nice to know someone appreciates me. I think I'll just sit down for a while . . .'

'Come on.' Polly smiled at me. 'Where are your things?'

'In that case.'

She picked it up. 'It's very light. Haven't you come to stay then?'

I blushed hotly. 'I didn't bring much. Mum said Mrs Crawley would provide me with clothes and things.'

'Uniforms, yes. You'll need a nightdress, though.'

'I sleep in my petticoat at home. Mum didn't have enough coupons to buy new underclothes for all of us, so we make do and mend.'

'Well, never mind. I think I've got a nightie that might fit you. I've got a new one a friend gave me the other week. It's made of parachute silk. Jean got it from a friend of hers in the Air Force.'

'That's a likely tale,' Mrs Jackson said. 'You'll land yourself in trouble one of these days, Polly. For one thing it's illegal to use parachute silk for underclothes. Your friend's friend could be court-martialled for stealing it in the first place.'

'Oh, they all do it,' Polly said, grimacing. 'You should hear the girls rustle as they dance up at the Vicarage Hall on Saturday nights. You can always tell when someone's wearing them.'

'It's not patriotic, that's what I say.'

'Well, the war's over now,' Joe grinned at us. 'Ask your friend if she knows any Americans, Polly. She might get you some nylons then.'

I think I'd kill for a pair of nylons. Jean
th Americans, so I suppose I'll have to
e-up on my legs instead.'

' Mrs Jackson grumbled. 'And don't
in Polly's head, Joe Morris. She's got
Silk nightdresses indeed!'

, was laughing as she pushed me out into the hall.
Joe's not a bad sort. Fancy him saying that about the
nylons. I wouldn't dare wear them in Sutton if I had them.
Everyone knows you've been with Americans if you do,
and that's the end of your reputation. You know what
they all say then.'

I laughed and nodded, remembering all the talk there'd
been about girls in the village who had dated the
American servicemen who'd been stationed in the nearby
towns. We'd had New Zealanders and Australians
billeted in the village, some of them living in the house
right next door. They were pilots flying the bombers from
Mepal Aerodrome and we'd known them all by name. At
nights, when they went out on a mission, Vera, Mum and
I had gone to the aerodrome, crouching in the ditches at
the end of the runway to count them out and count them
back in again just after dawn. We were always happy
when the same number came back as flew out, but that
was not often the case.

In the passage I turned towards the stairs, but Polly
pulled me back. 'Not that way. Didn't Mrs Jackson show
you our stairs?' She opened a door at the end of the hall.
'These lead to our bedrooms. And it's a shortcut to Miss
Frances's room, too. You go through a door at the first
landing, then you don't have to pass Mrs Crawley's
sitting-room.' She saw the look on my face and giggled.
'No wonder it took you so long.'

'I was delayed.' I bit my lip. 'Is Nathan Crawley really
wicked, Polly?'

'So you met him, did you? Watch out for him, Betty.
He was in the Navy until he was demobbed in October –
and I wish he'd stayed there!'

'Why?'

'He was bad enough before the war, but you know what they say about sailors. Well, in his case it's all true!'

I laughed. 'I'm glad you're here, Polly. Mrs Jackson doesn't like me.'

'She's not so bad underneath. She's had a bit of a rough time herself.'

I was curious but I didn't ask questions. Polly might have been cross.

'Here we are then.'

Polly stepped out onto the upper landing, leading me to the second door down the hall. I followed her inside. There was a double bed, a wardrobe with a full-length mirror, a chest of drawers and a floral carpet square that covered most of the floor. But what drew my attention was the china wash basin with hot and cold taps. Fancy having running water in the bedrooms! This was real luxury after the cottage. Beside the bed was a chair with a nylon nightdress flung over it, and the chest was strewn with Polly's personal things. I saw a magazine about film stars with a picture of Clark Gable in *Gone with the Wind*, lipstick and rouge. The whole room smelt of her perfume, which was very strong and like roses. I felt I was intruding.

'Do you mind sharing with me?'

'I wasn't too pleased when Mrs Jackson told me, but now I've met you, I don't mind.' She pulled two faded nighties from the chest. 'There you are, Betty. They're old but there's still some wear in them. Your uniforms are new; they were made specially for you.'

She opened the wardrobe and, taking out two thick blouses and a skirt, laid them on the bed. Then she reached for a dark blue wool dress and several aprons. 'The skirts are for everyday, and the dress for Sundays.'

I looked at the clothes. I was resentful that Mrs Jackson had called them uniforms, but at least they were new. I was so tired of having to patch, turn collars and generally make do. The newspapers were always praising women

41

for their efforts, but I was secretly thrilled by the thought of my new clothes.

'They're almost as fine as Miss Frances's things.'

Polly laughed. 'Not quite, though it's good stuff. Better than you can buy these days. Mrs Crawley was clever. She guessed things would be short when the war came and she bought bales of material and stored them in the linen chests. That wasn't all she tucked away either.'

'That wasn't very patriotic of her was it?'

'Patriotism is for the poor. There's always a way of getting luxuries if you've got enough money. If you've got more than twenty hens you're supposed to sell your eggs to the Ministry of Food, but there's many an egg and a chicken finds its way into Mrs Jackson's larder, not to mention the sides of bacon that have never seen a blue stamp. She doesn't complain about that though.'

I held the blue dress against me in front of the mirror. 'Do you go to church on Sundays, Polly? I used to belong to the choir, but I don't suppose I'll get to practise now.'

'You like to sing, don't you? I've heard you in church. Not that I go every week.' Polly looked at me. 'Mrs Crawley always goes. If you asked, you could go with her I expect. Mrs Jackson mostly stays behind to cook the dinner.'

'What about Miss Frances?'

'Her mother says prayers with her before she leaves. Sometimes in the summer she takes Frances with her.' Polly pulled a face. 'Mr Crawley hardly ever bothers. He says his wife does enough praying for the both of them. Don't you let on I told you, will you?'

'No, of course not. What's Mr Crawley like?'

A faint blush crept into her cheeks. 'Some folk think as he's a hard man, but I like him. Joe says he treats the men fair, though he's a rough tongue on him. He's always been decent to me. I know they say Madam married beneath her, but I think she had the best of the bargain.'

'What do you mean?'

Her eyes slid away from mine. 'Never you mind. I talk too much. Try your things on. Let's see if they fit.'

The blue dress fitted perfectly. I glanced at myself in the mirror. Mum's mirror was spotty and I'd seldom bothered to use it. Now I could see that my dark brown hair was thick and glossy, and where the light from the lamp fell on it, it seemed to turn red. I could also see that Frances was right. I was too fat. The buttons were stretched tight across my breasts; I had hardly any waist and my hips were too wide.

'You look a treat in that,' Polly said encouragingly. 'It's a pity you have to save it for Sundays. Now change into a skirt and blouse. You can keep your own clothes for going home in on your day off.'

I hung my old dress in the wardrobe. It looked so shabby beside Polly's things that I felt ashamed. It hadn't seemed so bad being poor until I came here. It was no wonder that Mrs Jackson had looked down her nose at us. If anything, my mother's clothes were worse than mine.

It didn't take long to unpack my possessions. I changed hurriedly and went downstairs with Polly. The kitchen table had been cleared, apart from a large brown teapot and four blue and white cups and saucers. There was a relaxed atmosphere, as if the cares of the day had been put away. Joe gave me a welcoming smile and pointed to a stool at his side. I took my place there, feeling grateful.

'How did it go today then, Joe?' Mrs Jackson asked as she settled down with her tea. 'I mean with Nathan. Will he settle to it, do you think? Now that the war's over, I mean?'

Joe took a pipe from a rack beside him and filled it with a rich, dark tobacco, reaching towards the fire to light a taper. Only when he had drawn a deep, satisfying puff did he reply.

'I have my doubts. He can work when he's a mind to it – and there's none better with the horses or the tractor – but he's no heart for it. You can tell his mind's away somewhere. You can hardly expect it after the fancy education he's had.'

'He'd have been at university if it hadn't been for the war. Do you think he's a mind to go back?'

'I've wondered about that.' Joe puffed on his pipe and the pungent smell of the tobacco wafted past my nose. It was quite pleasant and I liked it. 'I somehow don't think any four walls could contain our Mr Nathan for long now he's had a taste of freedom. It surprised me that he came back when he was demobbed. He's never made any secret of the fact that he dislikes the fens.'

'Eben wanted him back. The men are coming home slowly, but some of them never will.'

'Aye, that's true. Still, I can't see Mr Nathan being happy here long. He's got restless feet, that lad.'

'Maybe he thinks he owes Eben something. If it hadn't been for him . . .'

'That's long gone,' Joe said, taking out his pipe to blow on the bowl. 'If he hadn't been sent to all those schools when he was a boy he might have settled to the land.'

'We all know why that was – Mary couldn't stand him in the house after . . .' Mrs Jackson snorted. 'As you say, the least said about that, the better. He's always been wild that one. They threw him out of two boarding schools. Hanging the headmaster's wife's knickers on the flagpole – I never heard the like! And there was that girl when he was only sixteen . . .' She glared at me. 'None of this must go any further. Do you understand me, Betty?'

'I'm not a tittle-tattle.'

'It's no secret that Mr Nathan was thrown out of his last school for seducing the daughter of one of the local big-wigs,' Polly said laughing slyly. 'I dare say a few of the local girls know our Mr Nathan!'

'I hope you've the sense to keep your distance!'

'Nathan's no worse than the Yanks,' Joe said. 'Besides, things will be different now. Nathan's not a boy any more. He's been to the war. He'll have more sense.'

'Not that I've seen,' Polly quipped. 'But I've better prospects in mind.'

'And what might they be?' Mrs Jackson frowned at her.

'Never you mind. That's my business.'

'You watch your tongue, miss. You'll come to a bad end if you're not careful, my girl.'

'Don't squabble,' said Joe, knocking his pipe against the fire. 'I'll have another cup of tea if you don't mind, Mrs Jackson. Then I'm away to my cottage and bed.'

'And I'll not be long before I'm on my way. My bunions are killing me. I'm a martyr to my feet.' She looked at me sharply. 'It's time you were upstairs.'

'Let her drink her tea,' said Joe. 'She can go up with Polly for once. It will be a bit strange for her. She'll be missing her family.'

Again I was grateful to Joe. He'd taken me under his wing, and that was to be the first of many nights that I sat by his side, listening to them all discussing the business of the farm and the family.

I wasn't to have my first glimpse of Eben Crawley until I'd been at the house for almost a week. It was early in the morning, and I'd been sent to fetch a jug of milk from the dairy. The night had been frosty and the mist was slow to clear. Ice crunched under my shoes and the ground was hard and slippery.

He came towards me out of the gloom. A tall, thickset man with short, wiry hair speckled with grey. He wore riding breeches and a thick tweed jacket patched at the elbows. His boots were of stout leather and fastened with double brass buckles just below knee height. Square faced, he had a high colour and his nose was long and hooked. In no way could he be called handsome, but there was something powerful about the manner in which he strode through the yard. I'd no idea who he was, and yet he couldn't have been anyone but the master. He looked like a military man, and he'd taken an active role in the local Home Guard during the war, though he was too old to serve in the army.

Nervously, I smiled as he looked at me, and I fancied I saw lines of disapproval about his mouth. I knew that he was thinking that I was a Cantrel and unworthy of notice. Pride made me lift my chin.

'Good-morning, sir.'

He made a growling sound that might have passed for a greeting, his stride lengthening as if he couldn't wait to put a distance between us. Anger stirred in me. He had no right to dismiss me as trash. My grandfather was as good as him if not better. Pricked by hurt pride, I stuck out my tongue.

'I'm as good as you, Eben Crawley,' I muttered fiercely. 'And one day I'll prove it!'

'And how do you intend to do that?' A soft chuckle made me jump with fright. 'I admire the sentiment if not the action.'

I swung round, feeling hot and bothered as I saw the amusement in Nathan Crawley's eyes. 'I didn't see you there, sir,' I said, blushing. 'You had no right to creep up on me that way.'

The amusement faded. 'It's not my habit to creep up on anyone. Had you been less concerned with your own pride, you would have seen me.'

I stared at the ground, knowing he was right. If he were to report me, I should be instantly dismissed. Eben Crawley wouldn't stand for rudeness from his staff. Especially from a girl he despised.

'I – I'm sorry, sir.' I raised my eyes slowly.

Nathan took a cigarette case from his inside pocket, extracted a cigarette and lit it with a silver lighter. His action was so deliberate that I knew he was doing it to make me nervous.

'And so you should be, young Betty. Rudeness is a waste of time. However angry someone makes you, keep your temper. Once you've learned to control your emotions, you'll have the advantage over those who're ruled by them.'

I wasn't sure if he was mocking me or giving me good

advice. Looking up at him defiantly, I asked, 'Are you the master of your emotions, Mr Crawley?'

'Not always.' A smile flicked at the corners of his mouth, and I saw that he was amused by my cheek. 'Sometimes it's difficult, but I try, kid, I try – and so should you. We're kindred spirits, you and I.'

'You're teasing me now.'

'You guessed!' He quirked his brow. 'My sense of humour is not always shared by others.'

'Then you were kidding me when you said we were kindred spirits?'

'No.' His eyes were brooding now. 'We share my uncle's censure. I'm here because he needs me, though the truth is that he keeps me tied to the land because he knows it's the last place on earth I want to be. And you're here because it pleases the sainted Mary, and she's his Achilles heel . . .'

'I don't understand.'

'Every strong man has his weak spot. In most cases it's a woman. If you know which side your bread is buttered, you'll keep on the right side of Mary – but don't push your luck too far. Even Mary can't rule Eben when his temper's up.'

'So you won't tell on me?'

He stared at me for a moment and I saw that he was trying not to laugh. 'I'm tempted to wring some advantage from this,' he murmured, eyes glinting. 'What would you give me to keep my mouth shut, I wonder?' He laughed out loud as he saw my shocked look. 'Hey, don't look so scared, kid. I'm not that much of a heel. Just remember your debt to me, young Betty. I may collect, one of these days.'

As he strolled away, I drew a sharp breath. My knees were trembling. He'd done me no harm, but his manner was threatening, and there was something about his eyes . . . some secret brooding as though he were haunted by his own private devils. To me he had the aura of a film star. I couldn't quite decide between Ronald Colman,

Gary Cooper and Laurence Olivier. Maybe he was all three rolled into one. I hadn't actually been to many cinemas, but I read every magazine I could get my hands on.

I shook my head, laughing at my own imagination. Nathan Crawley wasn't a romantic figure, nor was he a man who would be haunted by his own conscience. Sensual, selfish and ruthless, he was no better than my father and I should stay out of his way.

Even without the complication of Nathan's games, my life at The Willows wasn't easy, nor was I sure what my position really was. Sometimes Frances forgot to play the mistress and then she would talk to me as an equal, but at other times she seemed to think I was her slave. When she was sulking she could be very difficult. She was restless, and if I didn't do exactly as she wanted she would be spiteful and cruel. No matter what I did it was never enough. It was as though she just had to take her frustration out on someone, and I happened to be there. In a way I understood why she did it. She was lonely and unhappy. I knew she resented it because her father had not bothered to visit her even once while she was confined to bed.

Mrs Crawley visited regularly every day. She spent an hour with Frances in the morning, discussing the books Frances had read. Mrs Crawley believed that her daughter's education would be broader for having had the advantage of unlimited books, and the library she had collected for that purpose was extensive. Providing that at least a part of the day was devoted to studying, Frances was allowed to do much as she liked and she often played her records or listened to the wireless. She liked Sandy Macpherson, 'Music While you Work' and 'Music Hall', though she did tune in to the school services when her mother came.

Frances was often sulky with her mother. I thought it was because she felt Mary spent too much time with her committees and too little with her. She resented it, and I'm sure that's why she often pretended to feel worse than she actually did. It was to punish her mother for neglecting her.

I was determined to make a good impression on my employer. I hadn't needed Nathan's warning about that. Since overhearing the argument between Mr and Mrs Crawley, I believed that Mary ruled the household. He was undoubtedly the master of the land, but within the house Mary's wish was law. He was dominated by a love and passion for his wife that she seemed not to return.

It seemed strange to me that Eben Crawley should have to beg where my father commanded. For all his faults, Dad must have some quality that Eben lacked. If only Mum had a little of the Crawleys' money, she would be the happiest woman alive. There would be no more rows and maybe Dad would give up the drinking. Yet despite all she had, there was always a secret sadness in Mary's eyes.

What was it that haunted both Mary Crawley and her nephew? I'd become aware of an atmosphere in the house, a shadow from the past that still affected the lives of all those who lived at The Willows. Somehow I didn't think it was just the aftermath of the war.

It wasn't my business to pry into the lives of those I served, but they intrigued me. I was fascinated by the hint of tragedy I sensed, yet they hadn't lost anyone in the war. So why did I sometimes feel that it was a house in mourning?

The days slipped into a routine. Every morning I rose at six. After an early breakfast I got out the Bissell carpet sweeper and helped Polly clean the three reception rooms on the ground floor. Then I laid the table in the breakfast-room. While the family were eating, Polly and I cleaned the bathroom. How I envied the Crawleys that gleaming white bath with its shining taps! I often opened the jars of Grossmiths' bath salts and sniffed the perfume, imagining what it might be like to soak in a bath with such expensive salts. Then we tidied the bedrooms. Eben and Mary had separate rooms. After that it was time for me to see to Frances, who always had breakfast in bed.

I wasn't forced to help Polly. Mrs Jackson suggested it, but if I'd objected I doubt she would have insisted. It was no hardship. I was young and strong, and full of energy. Besides, Polly was my friend and she had so much to do. I sometimes wondered how she managed it all, but she never seemed tired and she never complained.

Polly usually cleaned Nathan Crawley's room, but one morning when I'd finished my dusting more quickly than normal, I hurried along the passage to help her. I thrust open the door without thinking, gasping in surprise as I saw Polly struggling to free herself from Nathan's arms. He was laughing and trying to kiss her, but she was resisting determinedly.

'Just you stop it,' she cried. 'If you don't let me go this minute, I'll tell your uncle.'

'Polly, Polly,' he chided. 'You're fooling yourself if you think . . .' He broke off as he saw me. 'Why are you always where you shouldn't be?'

'I – I'm sorry . . .'

'Of all the bedrooms in all the towns in all the world, she had to walk into mine,' Nathan drawled and rolled his eyes.

I stared blankly.

'Oh no,' Polly groaned. 'He's doing his Humphrey Bogart impression again. Tell him it's awful, Betty.'

The penny dropped and I laughed. 'But it was good, Polly,' I cried. 'I remember now, I saw that film – *Casablanca*, wasn't it? But he said of all the gin joints, not bedrooms.' I looked at Nathan. 'Do some more. Go on, please!'

He grinned and puckered his lips. 'Here's looking at you, kid.'

'Oh Lord, now you've done it!' Polly said. 'He'll never stop now. Mr Nathan likes his little jokes.'

I remembered I was in disgrace for bursting in and blushed. 'I came to help you . . .'

Nathan's mouth twisted wryly. 'Didn't it occur to you that I might be standing here naked, Betty? Or were you hoping to surprise me?' His smile was positively wicked!

I went bright red and Polly frowned. 'Now, don't you start on her, sir.'

'It was my fault. I shouldn't have burst in like that.'

'He's just trying to shock you, Betty.' Polly pulled a face. 'It's all those bad ways he learned in the Navy. Come on, I've finished in here.' She pushed me out of the room in front of her, giggling as she closed the door. 'That will teach him! In future we'll do his room together. He's always messing about – but that was the nearest. And he only does it to spite me.'

'What do you mean?'

She shook her head. 'It doesn't matter. What you don't know won't hurt you, that's what my Mum always used to say and she was right. I don't know how he found out – but he always seems to know everything.' She shuddered and crossed herself. 'Sometimes I think he's sold his soul to the devil.'

I stared at her, feeling a chill run through me. So Polly thought there was something sinister about Nathan Crawley, too!

'What do you mean, Polly? Can a man really sell his soul to the devil?'

She blinked and then laughed. 'Course not! I've been to too many movies. It's just that he seems to think that because he wants something, he has the right to take it.'

'Oh, I see.' That wasn't sinister. My father was just the same.

It wasn't until later that I wondered what Polly had meant about Nathan finding something out. What could he possibly know that made him think he could force her into doing what he wanted?

I'd been at the house for almost a month when I

accidentally discovered Polly's secret. Frances had a headache. She was in one of her sulks again, and she'd sent me away so that she could sleep. I went to look for Polly. She'd promised to show me how to iron Frances's silk blouses. When I got to the kitchen, Mrs Jackson was baking, her sleeves rolled up to the elbows as she kneaded the dough.

'Run and find Polly for me,' she said. 'I sent her for some eggs half an hour ago.'

Taking my coat from a hook behind the door, I went out into the yard. A gust of wind caught me, nearly sweeping me off my feet. Shivering, I pulled up my collar. How I hated the wind! It seemed even worse here, where there was nothing to break its force.

The barn door was banging as the wind got behind it. I looked at it, wondering who'd left it open. If someone didn't shut it, it could twist off its hinges. Hesitating, I stared at it uncertainly. It wasn't my job; I was searching for Polly. I checked the hen house and drew a blank. If the men collected any eggs they left them in the dairy, but there was no one there. Where had Polly got to?

As I left the icy chill of the dairy, my eyes were drawn back to the barn. My instincts told me to carry on to the kitchen, but my feet seemed to have a will of their own. I walked slowly, unwillingly. Yet my curiosity was aroused.

Where was Polly? Why was that door open?

I stood outside, hovering. Should I go in? Then I heard Polly laughing and my blood ran cold as a man spoke, chiding her.

'Lie still, you little bitch. I've not done with you yet.'

'You've had me once, Eben Crawley. Is there no satisfying you?'

Polly was doing it with the master! I'd heard that tone in my father's voice often enough to know exactly what was going on in the barn.

I'd guessed that Polly was up to something, but I hadn't dreamt of anything like this. She'd laughed over the gossip about the girls who seemed to jump out of their knickers as soon as a Yank looked at them, but now she was doing it with Eben Crawley. No wonder Nathan thought he could get her into his bed!

I wanted to see what was going on. I pressed my face to a tiny crack in the door, but it was too dark inside and I couldn't see anything. I couldn't see, but I could hear. Eben was grunting and groaning like one of his own pigs and Polly was laughing. My first reaction was one of elation. Eben Crawley was no better than my father. He should be exposed to the village for what he was, a hypocrite and an adulterer. Everyone looked up to him and he wasn't worthy of respect. I wondered what the Vicar would think if he knew, and I realised that this was my chance of revenge. If I told Mary . . .

My triumph was short-lived. It wouldn't be Eben Crawley who would suffer if this became known. Polly would lose her job, and everyone would whisper about her behind her back. They'd say she was cheap and make her life miserable.

A surge of bitterness went through me. It was always girls like Polly who were the victims. It seemed to me then that men were all brothers beneath the skin, their lives ruled by that thing between their legs. The only difference between Dad and Eben Crawley was that one of them was poor.

I moved away from the barn, knowing I had to keep my mouth shut. Polly was my friend. I wouldn't tell on her. Collecting some eggs in my apron, I took them back to Mrs Jackson.

'Where's Polly?' she demanded.

I shrugged. 'She's busy.'

I got a glare from Mrs Jackson for my rudeness, but she thought me a mannerless Cantrel brat anyway. So what did it matter?

Already, at the age of fourteen, I was becoming a cynic. I was too young to evaluate the superficial knowledge I'd gathered about men, women and the passion between them that was called love. I believed men were all the same, taking what they could from their women. Saints and sinners. Winners and losers. Polly was a sinner. Ma was a loser. Mary Crawley was a saint and it seemed to me that she had won as much as any woman could reasonably expect of life. I wasn't quite sure about Frances. She changed so often that I couldn't make up my mind.

It occurred to me then that the easiest way of getting on in the world was to marry a rich man. Remembering what Mum had said about finding a decent man, I thought that he would have to be kind and gentle. Handsome, of course, and cultured, not rough like my father. Suddenly I laughed at myself. I wanted the moon and the stars! The man of my dreams didn't exist, and if he did he wouldn't marry a girl like me.

Polly had a lot of pretty things. Watching her hunt through her drawers, I thought I knew how she'd got them and I wondered if she thought it was worth it.

Suddenly, she found what she'd been looking for and pounced on it with a cry of triumph. It was a crimson chiffon scarf.

'There you are, Betty,' she said. 'Take it for your mum.'

'It's lovely, but you've given me so much already.'

'It's a present. It's your first pay day. Go on then, Joe's waiting.'

I hugged her, took the scarf and ran. In many ways she had such a generous nature. The scarf wasn't a bribe. She didn't know I'd heard her with Mr Crawley.

Mrs Jackson had packed some of the previous day's cakes in greaseproof paper. 'Take these for your brother and sister,' she said. 'I'll be baking fresh today and they'll only be wasted.'

I thanked her and went out into the yard. Joe had a large wagon loaded with sugar beet he was taking to the railway station in Sutton, to be shipped to the factory in Ely. He would be carting three loads in all during the day and he'd offered to take me into the village and call for me after his last load in the afternoon.

'It will save you the walk,' he'd said. 'And it's no trouble to me.'

I'd accepted gratefully. I liked Joe; he was so good-natured and I'd never yet heard him raise his voice to anyone. I had my wages tied into a handkerchief in my pocket. Ten pounds was more than I'd ever seen in my life. Far more than I would have earned on the land. Some of the women could earn two, three or even as much as four pounds a week if they did piece work, but only if they were very quick. Potato picking was very hard work. You had your back bent all day and you had to claw the muddy roots into a wire basket that gradually became heavier and heavier as the day went on. Then you had to empty your basket into sacks left at intervals through the field, and if you didn't keep up with the others you would soon find yourself out of a job. In comparison running errands for Frances was like being on holiday. I knew now how lucky I'd been.

Joe grinned as he helped me up beside him at the front of the wagon. 'Your mother will be pleased to see you, I reckon?'

I nodded, a thrill of anticipation running through me. Because the weather had been bad, I hadn't bothered to go home before, but I was looking forward to giving Mum most of my wages. 'I expect so,' I said. 'She'll be pleased with the money.'

Joe didn't glance at me as he steered the horses into the drove. 'How much have you to give her then?'

'Mrs Crawley gave me ten pounds for the month,' I said proudly. 'Mum said I can keep two for myself.'

'Two pounds . . .' He nodded to himself. 'Well, that's not so bad. I'll be going into Ely tomorrow. Will you be wanting anything from the market?'

'I need some things for Christmas,' I said. 'Can I give you my list tomorrow?'

'Of course you can. What sort of things will you be

wanting then?' He winked. 'Don't worry about coupons too much. There's a few friends of mine can wangle a thing or two from under the counter.'

'Oh, Joseph!' I laughed at him. 'You're wicked, you are!'

He grinned at me. 'It's wonderful how powerful a few eggs can be now and then.'

'I've been saving my sweet coupons for Christmas, but I could take the children up the street today – if you can get me some more?'

'That's the easy bit.'

'Do you think you could get some plain hankies? I'd like to embroider one specially for Polly. She's been so good to me.'

'I'll find you something, don't you worry.'

'You have so much to remember. Do you ever forget anything?'

'I mind one Christmas when I forgot the almonds for Mrs Jackson's cake – it was just before the war. I'd been celebrating in the Cock and Feathers and it went right out of my head. Lor! She did take on something cruel.'

I laughed as I listened to Joe's stories, feeling glad that he was the foreman at The Willows.

This year would be the first I'd spent away from my family. Mum always made an effort at Christmas. Somehow she found the money to put an orange, a few nuts and a packet of Rowntree's pastilles or a sherbert dip in our stockings. Sometimes there would be a little present, like a game of lexicon for me, some colouring pencils for Vera or a toy for Joey. Usually, though, our presents were items of clothing, often bought from the secondhand stall in the market. This year she would be able to buy more for the children, perhaps even a goose for Christmas dinner. She wouldn't be able to cook it in the tiny oven in her range, of course, but she could take it to the bakehouse at the end of the lane as many others in the village did. The thought of my family sitting down to a roast goose for their Christmas dinner warmed me as we drove through the chill of a damp, misty December day.

There is nothing lonelier than a fen drove when the mist settles over it like a blanket. The land is so flat, with scarcely a tree to be seen, and the hedges are miserable scrawny things in winter, picked bare of their berries by the birds. The stillness is all-enveloping, cutting off the surrounding land as if it did not exist, and it seems as if there is in all the world only that narrow track before you. It was a slow process, for the horses had a heavy load to pull.

When we left the droves behind and began to climb the hill that led to the village, I felt a sense of relief. I should soon be home. Mum would have the kettle on the fire and I'd soon be warm. I touched the coins and notes in my pocket to make sure they were safe. They were still there and I was reassured. It would have been a disaster if I'd lost them.

At last I could see the cottage, which was at the edge of the village, its thatched roof still white with frost. The mist had lifted as we came up from the fen, though it was still a dull grey day. I did not envy Joe his constant journeys back and forth with the loads of sugar beet. As we drew up outside my home, the door opened and Vera came running out, followed by little Joe.

'Betty, Betty, you're home,' Vera cried and I felt my eyes misting. I jumped down from the wagon, hugging and kissing them both in turn, while Joe Morris looked on benevolently.

'So that's your Joe,' he said, nodding and smiling. 'A fine boy – and two lovely girls. Enjoy yourselves. I shan't forget you tonight, Betty, so don't worry about getting back.'

'Bye, Joseph,' I called, waving as the wagon moved off.

Mum was waiting for me inside. The kettle was just beginning to boil as I entered with the others hanging about me. 'Well, Betty, so you're home,' she said. 'How was it then?'

'It's fine,' I said, seeing the anxiety in her. 'It's a good place.'

She was clearly relieved. 'So you've not been miserable then? They've treated you all right?'

There was no point in telling her that it was not quite as she'd promised. I'd made up my mind to stay, and the alternatives no longer appealed to me. 'No, I've not been miserable,' I said. 'I'll tell you all about it in a minute. I'm that cold.'

'It's a bitter, raw day. Sit by the fire while I make the tea.'

I sat down in the armchair with its wooden arms and sagging upholstery seat, rubbing my hands in front of the flames. 'Mrs Jackson sent some cakes,' I said, unwrapping them. 'They're a bit hard but you could soak them with milk and make a pudding.' Even as I spoke little Joe reached for a cake and ate it hungrily. Vera followed suit.

'Can we finish them?' Joe asked. 'They're good.'

I'd forgotten how good any food can taste when you're hungry. I'd forgotten other things, too. Glancing round the room that was both kitchen and living-room, I realised how small it was. Not half the size of the kitchen at The Willows. It was much shabbier than I'd realised, and it smelt of washing and stale cooking. The legs of the table were bruised and cut, and the rugs on the floor were threadbare. The old sofa in the corner was lumpy and the springs were showing through, and everywhere was very untidy.

'Can we, Betty?' Joe was tugging at my sleeve. 'Can we have the cakes now?'

'Leave one for Mum.'

'Let them finish them,' she said. 'I'm not hungry.'

'Well, this will help.' Proudly I spread the money on the table. 'Eight pounds. I've kept the two you said I could have to buy things I need.'

'I thought it was all found?'

'I need soap and things. I've been sharing with Polly.'

'I should've thought of that.'

'It doesn't matter. Polly's my friend. Look what she sent you.'

I produced the scarf with a flourish, waiting for her cry of pleasure. She stared at it, then shook her head. 'I couldn't wear that, Betty.'

Disappointment churned in me. I picked it up and looked at Vera. She was singing to herself about the 'Boys in Blue' and looking at a *Daily Mail* annual someone had lent her.

'If Mum doesn't want this, you might as well have it.'

'Can I?' The delight in her face cheered me up. I watched as she wound it around her neck and ran to look at herself in Mum's tarnished mirror. She was smiling when she came back. 'It's lovely, Betty. Are you sure I can have it?'

'Of course. Polly gave me a blue one to go with my Sunday dress. She's got lots of things. You'd like her, Vera.'

She squatted at my feet. 'Tell me about her, Betty. What's it like at The Willows? Is it very posh?'

They were all eager to hear what I had to say, even Mum, though she'd been there herself. She put a mug of tea in front of me and poured one for herself. I held the mug in both hands, letting it warm me. Then I began to describe the house, its contents and the people who lived there, bringing it all to sparkling life for Vera's benefit. I wanted to share the excitement of my new world with my family.

'When I went to Frances's room for the first time, I couldn't believe it,' I said. 'It's so pretty, Vera. Her curtains and bedspread are all made of lace, and you should just see her clothes. I've got a new dress, too. It's blue and it has lace collars.'

'You are lucky,' she said, her mouth twisting with envy. 'I wish I was old enough to work at The Willows.'

'Mum couldn't manage without you. Besides, Polly has to work very hard. I don't think you'd like that. Anyway, things will be better at home now I'm earning some money.' I looked at Mum. 'Where's Dad then?'

'He's helping out at the garage for a few days. Jason Darby has gone down with a fever and your father's looking after the pumps. It's not hard work and it suits him. He hasn't been drunk for a week.'

'Has he given you any money?'

'He gets paid today.'

'Don't tell him I have too. You'd best hide what I've given you or you won't get a penny from him.'

'Betty!' She looked surprised and upset. 'I don't know what they've been teaching you up at the farm, but I won't have you speak of your father like that.'

I flushed. 'I'm sorry, but I earned that money for you and the children – not for Dad to waste on beer.'

Her eyes challenged mine for a moment, then her shoulders sagged. 'I'll spend it on the children, don't worry.' She gathered the money, taking it into the bedroom and returning. 'There, it's safe now.'

I wished I could believe her, but I knew Dad would wheedle his share out of her somehow.

When we'd had our tea, I put my coat on again and took our Joe up the street to buy some sweets. I asked Vera to come but she shook her head.

'I daren't, Betty. I stopped off school to help Mum and I'm supposed to be ill.'

'I'll bring you something back then. What do you want?'

'A sherbert dip or some licorice pipes.'

'I'll see what they've got,' I said, taking my brother's hand. 'Come on, Joe. Let's see if they've got any Cremona toffees. You like those, don't you?'

His pale face lit up. He clutched my hand, skipping happily as we walked up the High Street. It was a cold day and people hurried by me, nodding and calling out as they passed.

'Hello, Betty. How does it feel to be a working girl then?'

'Fine. It feels fine. I'm taking Joe to the shop.'

'Going to spend all them hard-earned wages then?'

As we passed the pub, I saw Joe Morris's wagon pulled up outside and I smiled to myself. The horses were tucking into the oats in their nose-bags, and Joe had obviously popped in for a quick one – or two.

It was warm inside the shop, which smelt of spices and hot bread. Despite the shortages brought about by the war, it was well stocked with tins of golden syrup, jars of boiled sweets and biscuits in big square tins. There were a few luxuries like tinned salmon and fruit, but they were put right at the back and you had to have enough points to buy them. With my sweet ration, which I'd saved for weeks, I was able to buy a large bag of treats for my brother and sister. I let Joe choose just what he wanted, waiting until he'd finished before buying some Kolynos toothpaste for myself. I bought threepence worth of broken biscuits, too. They were cheaper that way and Joe tucked into them as we walked home.

Just after we left the shop, I heard someone shout my name. I looked across the street, frowning as I saw the youth who had called to me. His name was Zac Jarrold and he'd come to the village as an evacuee at the start of the war. He lived in the Row with his mother, who spoilt him rotten, and he was well known for his cheek. It came of him being a Londoner, so everyone said.

'Where've you been then?' he asked, coming over to stand in my way. 'I haven't seen you around lately.'

'I've been working,' I said. 'Not that it's any of your business what I do.'

'Don't be like that, Betty,' he said, grinning at me. 'I was going to ask you to come to the pictures with me in Ely on Saturday.'

'What's on then?'

'It's a musical – with Betty Grable and Robert Young. It's called *Sweet Rosie O'Grady*.'

I stared at him, torn between my desire to go to the pictures and my dislike of him. Then I realised I wouldn't be able to go anyway. I could never walk all the way from The Willows and back. Besides, if you wanted to get the bus into Ely on a Saturday afternoon, you had to start queuing at half-past two, then you were lucky if you got on by four o'clock. I was never free until after supper in the evenings. I shook my head.

'No, I can't,' I said. 'I'm working.'

'You can't be working all the time. You must get a Saturday off sometimes.'

I knew I could have a Saturday if I wanted to change with Polly, but now I'd had time to think about it, I realised I didn't want to spend my free time with Zac Jarrold.

'No, I don't,' I said. 'And if I did, I wouldn't go out with you. Come on, Joe. It's time we were home.'

I walked past Zac with my head in the air. 'Stuck up bitch,' he called after me. 'You're not the only girl around. There's plenty that will jump at the chance.'

I didn't bother to look round. When I got back to the cottage, Mum had bowls of hot soup waiting for us. We ate our meal, then I shared the sweets between Vera and little Joe.

'You should have kept them for Christmas,' Mum said.

'Joe Morris is going to get me some more.'

'Talk of the devil . . .' She glanced out of the window. 'He's just stopped outside. You'd best get your coat on. You don't want to keep him waiting.'

'No.' I swooped on our Joe, kissing him on both cheeks. Then I smiled at Mum. 'I'll be over before Christmas.'

'Come when you can.'

Joe was waiting outside for me. He smiled as he saw me come out.

'Had a good day then, lass?'

'Yes, thank you. We went to buy some sweets. Little Joe was so excited. I bought him five shillings' worth to himself.'

'He'll make himself sick.'

Joe helped me up on the wagon and I caught the stink of whisky on his breath. He must have spent more than just a few minutes in the pub. Yet he wasn't drunk, and I couldn't blame him for wanting something warming inside him on such a day.

'Don't forget to give me that shopping list tomorrow,' he said.

'I won't.' I smiled at him. 'I've still got thirty shillings left.'

'You can buy a lot with that if you're careful.'

'Most of it is for the children.'

We lapsed into silence. It was dark by the time we reached the last drove, and the mist was gathering around us. Our lantern shed a yellow glow in front of us, but it wasn't much help. Not that it mattered. The horses were following their instincts rather than seeing their way; they'd get us home without any direction from Joe. He was crooning Bing Crosby's songs from *Going My Way*, and sounded happy. At last the house loomed up in front of us. I jumped down as soon as Joe stopped.

'That's it,' he said. 'Run into the kitchen and get warm. I'll be in as soon as I've seen to the horses.'

I gladly did as I was told. Polly was at the deep sink, preparing vegetables. 'Did you have a good time, Betty?'

'Lovely,' I said. 'They were all pleased to see me, and Mum was that thrilled with her scarf. Mind you, Vera will have it off her if she can.'

Polly looked pleased and I was glad I'd told a white lie. I ran up to my room to change. I wasn't due back on duty yet, but I thought I'd see if there was anything Frances wanted before supper.

Chapter Three

As I approached Frances's room, I saw that her door was open and I could hear voices and laughter coming from inside. A little chill went through me as I realised that one of the voices belonged to Nathan Crawley. What was he doing in her room? I'm not sure what was in my mind as I went in, but I stopped in surprise as I saw him sitting on the edge of her bed. She was lying there fully clothed with just a light blanket thrown over her legs. Even at first glance I could see that she was enjoying herself. He was teasing her with a piece of Fry's chocolate, pretending to put it in her mouth and then snatching it away just as she went to bite it. It was a childish game but it obviously amused her.

'Oh, there you are, Betty,' she said, her eyes still sparkling. 'I didn't expect you back yet.'

It was clear that she didn't care either. I was a little piqued as I looked at them, feeling shut out. 'I'm not due until after supper, but I thought you might need something?'

'Nathan's been looking after me.' She pouted at him with the ease of familiarity. 'I've been scolding him for neglecting me. He doesn't visit me often enough.'

'I thought you wouldn't need me now that you have Betty,' he replied, his eyes glinting with mischief. 'I expect you've got lots of female chatter that you wouldn't want me to hear. Besides, if you want to see me, you can get up and eat your dinner downstairs.'

'I would if I were sure you would be there – but I can't bear it when you're not. Father is always so cross when you go out.'

'And when I stay in. Your mother has almost forgiven me, but Eben never will.'

'Oh, Nathan!' Frances clung to his hand, her eyes clouding. 'They can't still blame you after all these years.'

My ears pricked. Was I about to discover Nathan's story?

'Bless you for that, kid.' His smile was caressing. 'I sometimes think if it weren't for you I'd leave the farm.'

'Don't!' she cried. 'I couldn't bear it.'

I watched them together, envying the affection between them. Nathan was different with her, and she seemed different too. I hadn't realised he visited her in her room sometimes. After he'd gone, she explained.

'You won't tell Mother? She doesn't approve. Nathan usually sneaks in when everyone's busy.'

'Why shouldn't he? He wouldn't – I mean . . .' I finished lamely as she laughed.

'Of course not! I know all about his reputation, but he's like my own brother . . .' The smile faded. 'He's even better than a brother. No matter what Father says. Nathan isn't wicked. He couldn't have . . .'

'Couldn't what, Frances?'

Frances's eyes flew to mine in alarm as her mother walked in. There was such an obvious appeal in her look that I jumped in to help her.

'I was telling Miss Frances how my brother ate four of Mrs Jackson's stale rock cakes, ma'am.'

'I see.' Mrs Crawley's face was expressionless. 'I thought this was your day off?' She placed a cool kiss on Frances's brow. 'How are you, my love?'

'I thought I might get up.'

'Your father has a business friend to dinner this evening. Perhaps tomorrow you can join us.'

'You're always telling me I should get up, then when I say I will, you say you've got guests.'

Mary frowned. 'Don't be silly, Frances. You'd only be bored.'

'I've been alone all day,' Frances complained. 'I hate

being alone. If I can't come down to dinner, then I want Betty to have hers with me.'

Mrs Crawley frowned. 'I'm not sure you can ask her to carry all that extra food up here. The tray would be too heavy for her.'

'Oh, I could manage . . .' I faltered as she looked at me. 'I know it's not for me to say, but I wouldn't mind.'

Mary was silent. If she gave permission now she wouldn't be able to retract it later. It would be a step up for me, a step closer to being a part of the family.

'Very well,' she said at last. 'Betty can eat with you in your room, but you mustn't make a habit of it. You know your father likes you downstairs for lunch.'

'Thank you, dearest Mother.' Frances winked at me behind her back. 'Perhaps tomorrow I shall be well enough to stay downstairs all day.'

'That would please me very much.' Mary bent to kiss her.

'I knew I'd get my own way,' Frances said when her mother had gone. 'She can't bear to refuse me anything, because she knows it's her fault I'm so delicate.'

'You shouldn't say things like that.'

'I'll say what I like,' Frances muttered, a flicker of pain in her eyes. 'Perhaps she does care about me a bit, but if I'd been a boy both Mother and Father would've loved me. It's because I'm a girl that he hates me — because he wanted a son so badly.'

There was pain in her eyes and something else that faintly worried me. It wasn't the first time I'd realised she resented the way her father ignored her.

'What makes you think that, Frances?'

She seemed to come back from far away, a malicious smile on her lips. 'Wouldn't you like to know, Betty Cantrel!' She scowled at me. 'We'll have our meal on the table by the fire. Clear it first, then go and fetch the food. I'm hungry.'

'I'm not a slave, you know,' I said. 'I can leave any time I like.'

Her eyes gleamed. 'But you won't, because you like it here, don't you?'

'Not when you're in one of your moods. Sometimes I could hit you, Frances Crawley . . . Oh!' I was dismayed as I realised what I'd said. To my surprise, she began to laugh.

'At last,' she crowed. 'Oh, don't worry, I'm not going to tell on you. I like it much better when you don't pretend to be so meek and mild. I'll keep your secrets, Betty Cantrel, as long as you keep mine.'

I stared at her, then nodded. 'All right. It's a bargain.'

She leaned forward, her eyes glittering with excitement. 'You've got to promise,' she said. 'You've got to swear on pain of death that you'll always be faithful to me; you'll always be my friend and never betray me.'

Her eyes held mine and I was caught in a kind of spell. For a moment I was afraid of her, then I nodded solemnly, and I felt as if I were making a holy vow as I said, 'I swear I'll never betray you, Frances. I swear it on my life.'

As I opened the kitchen door, I heard Joe's voice. I caught only the tail-end of a sentence but it sounded like, 'All but two pounds, poor lass . . .' There was an awkward silence as I walked in and then they all started talking together.

'Miss Frances wants me to have supper with her tonight,' I announced into the midst of the babble. 'I know it isn't right, Mrs Jackson, but she's feeling lonely – and Madam said it would be permitted this time.'

'It will save your supper getting dried to a cinder every night,' she said, sniffing. 'As long as you don't go giving yourself airs and graces.'

'I shan't do that. Besides, you said I need to learn some manners. Maybe eating with Frances will teach me how things should be done.'

'I can teach you all the manners you need,' Mrs Jackson said sharply. 'Just because I choose to eat in the kitchen, don't you go thinking I wasn't brought up properly. I'm as good as Mary for all her fancy ways.'

'Why don't you ever join the family when they've company?'

She looked indignant. 'I could dine with Eben and Mary whenever I like, but I'm more comfortable in my kitchen and that's a fact. I never had much schooling. My mother kept me at home with her until I married, and I don't care to be made a fool of in front of Mary's friends. I'm a plain woman and I say what I think, and there's an end to it.'

'But surely . . .' I began, faltering as Joe shook his head at me. 'Well, it's none of my business.'

It was obvious from Joe's expression that I'd put my foot in it. I thought she was hiding something, but I couldn't expect her to tell me everything.

'It certainly isn't your business, Betty,' she said. 'But I shan't scold you since it was meant kindly. Now, about this supper tray – do you think you can manage it?'

'I'll take up the first course and come back for the pudding,' I said. 'Vera and Joey ate all your cakes. They asked me to say thank you.'

They hadn't thought of it, of course, but I wasn't above a little flattery if it would win a few treats for my family. I could see by the slight softening of her mouth that I'd said the right thing.

'Well, it's nice to know someone appreciates my cooking,' she said. 'Supper won't be ready for a few minutes. Why don't you sit by the fire? We're about to have a cup of tea.'

It was the first time I'd felt she had really accepted me. I suspected it was something to do with what Joe had been saying earlier. They were feeling sorry for me because I'd had to give most of my wages to Mum, but they didn't understand how much pleasure it had given me.

'Mum was that pleased with the money,' I said as Mrs Jackson gave me my tea. 'I'm glad to help her a little. She's worked so hard for us children.'

They glanced at each other and I hoped they understood. I neither wanted nor needed their pity.

I gave my shopping list to Joe the next day, and he came back with several parcels, which I smuggled up to the room I shared with Polly, hiding them in the little cupboard beside the bed. I wanted to work on my embroidery in secret and surprise her. It would soon be Christmas, but I had plenty of time before she came up in the evenings.

Christmas was a time of celebration at The Willows and, as the great day approached, more and more visitors came to the farm. Mr Crawley had a brother who lived in Ely, and he drove over in his Hillman Minx to bring presents for the family. Frances was in the back parlour when he came in, and she ran to greet him with a cry of pleasure. During the war he'd worked for the War Office in London and she hadn't seen him much. He swept her up in his arms and kissed her.

'How's my favourite girl then?' he asked in a big, hearty voice.

'I'm much better for seeing you, Uncle Henry. You should come more often.'

'And I would if it wasn't for your father,' he said, frowning. 'Eben and I don't get on, and that's the truth of it. I wouldn't come to this house at all if it weren't for you and Hilda.'

Frances looked at him curiously. 'Why don't you like Father? I've never known why you quarrelled.'

'It was a stupid thing.' He shook his head. 'Nothing for you to worry your pretty head over . . .' His eyes flicked to me. 'And who's this then? I haven't seen her before.'

Frances looked at me, then, 'Her name is Betty and she's my friend. She looks after me when I'm not well.'

'That's nice of her,' Henry Crawley said. 'If I'd known you were here, Betty, I'd have brought you a present. But you can buy something for yourself.' He put his hand in his pocket and took out five pounds.

I hung back, blushing, but he thrust the money into my hand. 'Thank you,' I stammered. 'I – it's very kind of you.'

'It's Christmas,' he said. 'The time for giving. Now I'm going to have a glass of sherry and a mince pie in the kitchen with your Aunt Hilda, Frances. She won't come into the parlour so I'll have to go to her. I've told her she's a fool to stay here; she can come to me any time she likes. I might not be as rich as Eben, but I can afford to give her a home.'

I looked at Frances as he went out of the room, making it feel suddenly empty. 'He's nice,' I said. 'I didn't know you had an uncle.'

'He only comes now and then,' she replied, a wistful look in her eyes. 'If Father's here they won't speak to each other. I don't know why, but I think it's something to do with Nathan. Nathan's father was the youngest of the family, but he made a lot of money very quickly. Nathan will be rich when he comes into his trust. He won't have to stay here then.'

'When will that be?'

'Not for a while. He was only a baby when his father died and there was a clause in the will that made Father his guardian until he was twenty-five, that's when he gets his money.'

I frowned. 'That seems odd, doesn't it?'

'I think Uncle Harry and Father quarrelled over the will, but I don't really understand it.'

'He's a generous man, your uncle.'

Frances nodded. 'What will you spend your money on?'

'I don't know yet. I'll probably give most of it to Mum.'

'You should buy yourself a pretty dress, Betty.'

'Maybe I'll get some shoes . . .'

'I want lots of things for Christmas. I've given Mother a long list.' Frances smiled happily. 'Oh, I do love Christmas!'

Her mood continued during the next few days. Several

visitors came to the house, many of them bringing brightly-wrapped gifts for Frances, but Henry Crawley was the only one who gave me anything. Although I was usually with Frances, Mary's friends did their best to ignore me. They thanked me politely as I handed round the plates of mince pies, but their eyes never made contact with mine. I resented it at first, but then Frances started winking at me behind their backs.

'Take no notice,' she said. 'You're my friend now and they're not important to us.'

In the front parlour there was a tall Christmas tree decked with candles and glittering glass balls. As Christmas drew nearer, the pile of parcels around it grew into a huge mound. I'd never seen so many presents, but I didn't feel jealous. With the money that Henry Crawley had given me, I'd bought bars of Fry's chocolate and packets of Callard and Bowser butter sweets for Vera and Joey, wrapping them in the pretty paper Frances had shared with me.

She had a small tree in her room, and we decorated it together. She received many cards, which we strung about the room, giving it a festive look. She was excited about the big party her mother was giving on Christmas Eve, and I guessed that she wouldn't have one of her headaches that day.

I'd noticed her eyes sparkled more often now, and she complained less of her headaches, which I suspected had been mostly imaginary. Sometimes she dined with the family, but on other days I carried a tray for two up to her room.

Joe cut armfuls of holly and mistletoe and we all helped to decorate the house. There was an air of furtive excitement in the kitchen now. Everyone was hiding something from the others. I knew it was their custom to exchange gifts, and by working at my sewing every night in bed, I'd managed to make something for everyone. For Polly I'd embroidered two handkerchiefs with her name in the corner. I'd done a similar one for Joe. For Mrs

71

Jackson I'd bought a bookmark and a box of Meltis Newberry Fruits. It was more difficult to decide what to give Frances, but in the end I made her a pencil case and embroidered her name on it.

My pressing need was for a new pair of shoes. The ones I wore every day were badly scuffed and constantly needed mending. Joe had promised to do it for me, but I wanted a pair of sling-backs from Tru-Form. I was not forced to spend any of my own money on them though, for Mrs Crawley had asked me what I would like for Christmas. During the war it had been almost impossible to buy women's shoes, but Joe had seen some in the shops in Ely that sounded just what I needed. I told him my size and he'd promised to do his best – and that meant I would get what I wanted. Joe had a flair for supplying the household's needs, whether we had coupons or not.

For a week before Christmas Mrs Jackson never seemed to stop cooking. She was at it from early in the morning until late at night. Her feet swelled up and she wore slippers most of the time, so perhaps it wasn't surprising that her temper was short. Neither Polly nor I could do anything right.

'Out of my way the pair of you,' she shouted whenever we appeared. 'I can't cope with people in my kitchen.'

The Christmas Eve dinner was a tradition. It meant a lot of work for Mrs Jackson, Polly and me, but we all enjoyed it. The stockman's wife came in to help out on the day; she was a plump, jolly woman who made light of all the washing-up, and it all added to the general excitement.

I discovered that there was to be another party on Boxing Day. It was Eben's custom to invite all the families of the men who worked on the farm. Polly, Joe and Mrs Jackson would be there, as well as the family. I was to go too this year.

I wasn't invited to join the guests at the Christmas Eve dinner, but I hadn't expected it. I felt a bit envious when I saw Frances in her new dress of blue velvet, but I cheered up when I thought of the party to come. Besides, I knew I should be needed in the kitchen.

The preparations had begun early in the morning. Joe brought in piles of wood, and I helped where I could, though most of my time was taken up with Frances, who was in a fever of excitement.

Polly was in a good mood, too. Her brother had been to visit her, bringing a box full of presents from her family. He had stopped to drink a glass of sherry and gossip with Joe, telling us all the news from the village. Although he lived in Mepal, which was just over the hill – though you had to go right round it because the Air Ministry had closed the road when they built the airfield – he courted a girl from Sutton and he often called in to see his sister. He was a fine-looking man in his early twenties, with broad shoulders and strong legs. His name was George and there was a warm affection between him and Polly. He told us how he'd boxed the ears of a lad from Sutton for cheeking his girlfriend.

'That Zac Jarrold has been spoilt by his mother,' he said heatedly. 'It's time he went back to London where he belongs. I know he lost his father in that bombing raid on the East End, but that's no reason to let him run wild.'

'London wasn't the only place to get bombed,' Mrs Jackson said. 'Do you remember the night that bomb fell on the house at the end of the High Street? That young New Zealander went in to see what he could do and the second bomb went off and killed him.'

George nodded his head. 'That was when the plane crashed through the roof, wasn't it?' He glanced at me, frowning. 'You want to warn your Vera about that Jarrold boy, Betty. I saw her hanging about with him the other night when she ought to have been at home safe in bed. She'll get herself a bad name if she isn't careful.'

'Vera?' I stared in surprise. 'She's only eleven.'

'All the more reason for her to be at home. I wouldn't want a sister of mine to be hanging about outside a pub with that lad.'

'I should think she was looking for Dad. Vera's just a little girl.'

'Well, mebbe you're right,' he said, but I could see he wasn't convinced.

'You take this wood into the dining-room,' Polly said, pushing some logs into my arms. 'I want you to see how pretty the table looks.'

I thought about Vera as I obeyed. Could she really be hanging about with boys when she should be helping Mum? I didn't like the idea of her talking to Zac Jarrold. I remembered the way he'd reacted when I refused to go to the pictures with him, and I decided to warn Vera when I next saw her.

Walking into the dining-room, I caught my breath as I saw how it had been decorated. No wonder Polly wanted me to see it! The long table had been highly polished and set with crystal glasses and silver, and there were two heavy candelabra spaced between the epergnes of fruit and flowers. I could imagine how the glass would gleam and sparkle once the candles were lit. The very best china had been brought out; it looked fragile and delicate, and I hoped I wouldn't be asked to help with the washing-up. I should die of fright in case I dropped a plate. Napkins of fine white linen were rolled and slipped inside engraved silver rings, and in the centre was a magnificent arrangement of roses – roses in the middle of winter? They must have been sent specially from a heated greenhouse and obviously cost a fortune.

Dumping my logs in the grate, I crept across to the table, wanting to touch the deep red petals of those wonderful flowers. Leaning forward to sniff them, I was disappointed that they had no perfume. My hand reached towards the engraving on one of the epergnes.

'Stealing Turkish delight from the table carries a penalty of instant dismissal.'

I swung round at the sound of Nathan Crawley's voice, my cheeks flaming. He was grinning at me, those strange eyes of his seeming to burn with green fire.

'Oh, you did startle me,' I cried. 'I wasn't stealing. I just wanted to touch the silver epergne.'

'A fine excuse,' he said loftily. Then he reached out and took a chocolate-covered nut from the dish. 'No one will notice. Open your mouth, Betty.'

I shook my head. 'I don't want it.'

'Stubborn girl.' He advanced on me menacingly. 'Open your mouth or I'll force it down you.'

Reluctantly, I obeyed. He popped the nut between my lips, but before I could bite it, he was kissing me and biting the nut at the same time. I gave a cry of alarm, almost choking as the hard nut stuck in my throat. He laughed and then thumped me on the back to make me cough it up.

'Foolish Betty,' he chided. 'Don't you know how to behave when a gentleman gives you a nut?'

'You nearly choked me,' I cried. 'If you were a gent you wouldn't do things like that.'

'And you'd know, of course.' He laughed mockingly. 'Don't look so annoyed, kiddo. I was only teasing you. You should learn to enjoy life.' His hand reached out to stroke my cheek. 'I'd like to teach you . . .'

I jumped away as though I'd been stung. 'You just leave me alone, Nathan Crawley. I'm not one of your . . .' I gasped as I realised what I'd been about to say. 'I – I didn't mean to be rude.'

'Oh, but you did.' His eyes brimmed with laughter. 'It's not fair, is it, Betty? You know you're as good or better than me, don't you? Why should you have to be polite when I can say what I like to you? I can see the indignation in your eyes – I can read your mind like a book, and such a devious mind it is, too. I think you like me, Betty. You tell yourself I'm wicked but underneath you rather like me – don't you?'

What could I say? If I denied it, he would be insulted, but if I agreed, he would take it as an invitation to continue his games. It amused him to torment me, just as it amused him to flirt with Polly. It was as though he had a little devil sitting on his shoulder, prompting him.

75

I'd remained silent too long. The laughter vanished from his eyes, and he was angry. He flung away from me, staring moodily out of the window, a nerve flicking in his taut cheek. For a moment I stood perfectly still, not knowing what to do, then I began to edge towards the door.

'I haven't told you to go,' he said harshly.

'Mrs Jackson will be looking for me.'

'Let her wait,' he said coldly. 'They've told you, haven't they? That's why you despise me.'

'I don't know what you mean.' His manner had changed so abruptly that I was startled. 'I know you've a reputation for – well, that you like girls.'

He laughed bitterly. 'Are you sure that's all? You haven't heard anything more sinister?'

'No, sir.' I stared at him, feeling peculiar as I met his intense gaze. 'I – I've sensed a mystery, but no one has told me anything.'

For a moment his eyes blazed at me and I was frightened. He seemed to be fighting a battle within himself, and I believed he was on the verge of telling me something important; then he shrugged, laughed and waved me away.

'Go on then,' he muttered. 'Why should I force you to share my nightmares? I'm a fool. Take no notice of me.' As I still hesitated, he glared at me. 'I told you to go!'

I shrank away as if he had threatened to hit me, turning to flee from the room. He was laughing now, bitter, harsh laughter that sent ripples of fear running through me. I ran without stopping until I reached the kitchen.

We exchanged our gifts in the kitchen after dinner had been served in the parlour. Polly gave me a pretty brooch with red stones. She laughed as I went into raptures over it.

'It's only glass, Betty, not rubies.'

'It's just as good to me.'

'I prefer the real thing – one day I'm going to have real

diamonds and rubies.' She seemed to be bursting with happiness.

'You'll end in the gutter if you talk that way,' Mrs Jackson said darkly.

'Open your other presents, Betty.'

Mrs Jackson had given me two pairs of Wolsey stockings, and Joe had bought me a warm wool cardigan in a Fair Isle pattern in a mixture of heather, blues and beige.

'I thought it would go with your Sunday dress,' he said, looking pleased as I gave a cry of delight.

'It's lovely,' I said, slipping it on straight away. 'I couldn't have asked for anything better. I don't know how to thank you – all of you.'

'Just be yourself,' he answered gruffly. 'I think we're all agreed that you've proved yourself a good girl.'

'Betty helps me no end,' Polly said. 'I'm glad she's come to work here.'

Polly had opened her present from Joe a few minutes earlier. She screamed with glee when she saw that he'd given her two pairs of nylon stockings.

'Where did you get them?' she asked. 'How did you manage it? They're like gold dust.'

Joe tapped his nose. 'It all depends on who you know,' he said smugly. 'Does it deserve a kiss under the mistletoe?'

Polly giggled. 'You never know,' she said coyly. 'It just might.'

Mrs Jackson sniffed, casting an eye over the remains of our supper on the table. 'Well, if everyone's had enough, we'd best clear this away. We'll make a start on the washing-up before they start ringing for the tea-tray.'

It was Mary Crawley's habit to send for a tray of tea before she retired for the night. In the kitchen we preferred a mug of Ovaltine made with milk and water. Eben Crawley usually made himself a night-cap with brandy, sugar and hot water from Mary's kettle. Tonight, as there were guests, the tray would be too heavy for Polly to carry so she would use the wheeled trolley. I set the trolley for her before going to help with the washing-up, beginning to yawn.

'Tired, Betty?' Polly gave me a sympathetic smile. 'Never mind, it will soon be all over. It's a good thing the master doesn't entertain every week or we'd all be worn out.'

Mrs Jackson was talking to Joe. I looked at Polly, speaking in a low voice. 'I thought Mrs Jackson would go to the party,' I said. 'She's family but she hardly ever seems to eat with them.'

Polly glanced across the room to make sure we weren't overheard. 'She's only herself to blame. I know for a fact that Mary asked her to join them. She grumbles all the time about the way she's treated as an unpaid house-keeper, but it was her choice.'

'It seems a bit odd to me. It's almost as though she goes out of her way to avoid company.'

'It's her pride,' Polly whispered. 'She hadn't a penny to bless herself with when she came here. They'd a cook then but when she left, Mrs Jackson took over. She said it was because she didn't want to be beholden to her brother. I think they quarrelled about something years ago and she's never quite forgiven him. I don't really know much, Betty. Joe's the one to ask.'

'But surely . . .'

'Shush! She's looking at us. We'd best get on.'

Polly presided over one of the deep stone sinks, washing the precious china carefully in warm water and soda crystals and rinsing everything in cold water. The stockman's wife and I wiped the dishes equally carefully before placing them on the table for Mrs Jackson to put away. It was a long, tedious procedure, and it was past midnight before we had finished. Even then, Polly had to clear more glasses and dishes from the front parlour after the family had retired.

'These will wait until the morning,' she said with a yawn as she brought in a loaded tray. 'I think we've done enough for today.'

Mrs Jackson agreed. I could scarcely put one foot in front of the other as I climbed the stairs. I was so weary that I let my clothes drop where they would and tumbled into bed, my eyes closing. I was tired and yet I didn't immediately fall asleep. Feeling the side of the mattress move, I struggled to open one eye. Polly was putting something under the mattress. Even though I was on the point of falling asleep, I wondered why she should do that.

In the morning I'd forgotten the small incident. Everyone was going to church, except Frances.

'But it isn't right she should be left alone today,' I said.

'She won't be alone,' Polly said. 'Mr Nathan will keep her company.'

I'd been about to volunteer to stay behind, but I knew Frances would prefer her cousin's company, and I was glad to have the outing. I always liked the Christmas service in church. It would be decked with holly and we should all sing carols. I loved the singing, and I had a good voice. The vicar said I was the pride of his choir, and since I'd been going to church with Mrs Crawley, she too had commented on it. But as much as the pleasure of singing in church was the chance that I might see Mum and the children when the service was over.

I was lucky. Mum had brought both Vera and our Joe, and I managed to snatch a few minutes with them afterwards. Because everyone was in a festive mood, they all stood about in little groups in the churchyard, spilling down the slope to the path below. Mrs Crawley was talking to the vicar, so I knew I was safe for the moment.

'Oh, you do look smart,' Vera said, looking with envy at my dress and the cardigan Joe had given me. 'You are lucky, Betty.'

I noticed that she was wearing the crimson scarf Polly had sent for Mum in her hair, and that her eyes kept straying to a small group of girls and youths in the street. They were making a lot of noise and I saw several women frown in their direction. I was glad Vera wasn't with them, and I hoped that George Baxter had been wrong. I was about to say something to her when Mum spoke.

'Thank you for your presents and the extra money, Betty. Your friend Joe Morris brought us a big pork pie and a side of bacon. He's a good man.'

'Yes.' I smiled at her, forgetting about Vera. I couldn't scold her in front of Mum on Christmas Day. 'Joe gave me this cardigan. He's so generous with everyone.'

'It's very pretty. What did Mary Crawley give you?'

'I'm to have some shoes tomorrow.'

'Shoes?' She frowned. 'I thought she might give you money?'

'She asked me what I wanted. There's only a week to my next pay day. Surely you can manage until then? I gave you three pounds out of the money Mr Henry Crawley gave me.'

There was guilt in her eyes and she glanced away. 'I was in deep with the tallyman, Betty, but we'll manage, we always do.' She looked at me suddenly. 'Your father's been in a bad mood. He made me give him the three pounds you sent.'

'Oh, Mum . . .' I sighed but I couldn't reproach her. She was shamed enough as it was. 'I have to go. Mrs Crawley is getting into the car. I'll see you next week.'

She hesitated and I knew there was something on her mind. 'I may have some news for you when you come.'

Was that an anxious note in her voice? I might have paid more attention if I'd guessed what she had to tell me, but my thoughts were already back at the farm. I kissed Vera and swept Joe up for a big hug, then I was running back to the station wagon. I was the last to scramble in, and I heard Eben Crawley make an annoyed sound in his throat, but he didn't say anything to me, though I saw him glance at his wife.

I couldn't wait to get back to the house. While the others were still rubbing their hands in front of the fire, I hurried up to Frances's room. She was sitting propped up in bed against a pile of pillows. Torn wrapping paper on the floor was evidence of the gifts she'd received that morning, and I could see bags of Milk Tray, Mackintosh's toffees, writing paper, books, records and various trinkets strewn across the coverlet. She was wearing a pretty new gold bracelet on her arm and I knew that Mary had already given her a new velvet dress and a pair of shoes. Nathan was sitting on the side of the bed and they were laughing. Frances frowned as she saw me.

'Oh, are you back already?' she said. 'What do you want?'

'I came to see what you wanted for lunch.'

'This lazy creature is about to get up and come downstairs,' Nathan said.

She pulled a face at him. 'Mother said I was to rest this morning. I was up late last night.'

'Nonsense! You're not in the least tired. Admit it, Frances, you feel perfectly well. Quite well enough to get up and play Monopoly with me.'

'I suppose I shall have to.' She pretended to scowl. 'Go away while Betty helps me dress.'

He turned his quizzing gaze on me. 'The wind has brought some colour to your cheeks. It must agree with you to be out in the air.'

'The air was very fresh, sir. I don't like the wind; it frightens me.'

'Indeed?' His brows lifted. 'You told me you were not easily frightened.'

'I'm not, sir. It's just the wind I hate.'

'One day we'll put that to the test, won't we?' His gaze flicked back to Frances. 'Don't keep me waiting, wretch – or I'll come and tear you from that bed!'

I would not let myself look at him as he left the room. The memory of our last meeting was still fresh in my mind. He had been moody and bitter towards me then, and I would not let myself be swayed by his charm now. He thought he could get his own way too easily, did Nathan Crawley. Still, he was a good influence on

Frances, even I could see that. She was always more alive after his visits.

'Isn't Nathan wonderful? I never feel so ill when he's with me.'

'It's a pity you can't spend more time with him.'

Her face clouded. 'I don't know what I'll do if he goes away.'

'Is he thinking of leaving soon?'

'He hates the fens. He says they're damp and dismal, and he wants to live in London.' A wistful look came into her eyes. 'He says when I'm older I can go and live with him – at least until I marry, but I don't suppose I shall – marry that is.'

I fastened the buttons at the back of her frock. 'Why not, don't you want a husband?'

'I'm not sure. I like it when Nathan teases me, but how could I be sure my husband would be like him?' She gave a little shudder. 'He might be more like Father.'

There was a look of such disgust on her face that I could only wonder at the thoughts behind it. What had she seen or heard that she should look like that? I recalled the argument I'd heard between Eben Crawley and his wife on my first night at the house. If I'd heard them quarrelling, it was more than likely that Frances had heard them at some time, too. Had she gone to her mother's room for some reason, standing in the darkened hall as I had, to hear things that would better have remained private? Was that why she had convinced herself that her mother felt herself to blame for her ill health?

'Your father must be disappointed that Nathan doesn't want to work on the land?'

A strange expression came into her eyes. 'He thinks he can make Nathan do as he wants. He doesn't know what my cousin is planning. You won't tell anyone, Betty?'

'Not if you don't want me to. I haven't forgotten our bargain. Shall I brush your hair now?'

She nodded, moving to sit on the stool in front of her

dressing-table. Holding up her arm, she invited me to admire her new bracelet. 'It's gold,' she said. 'And I can add more charms to it when I like. Nathan gave it to me. Do you like it?'

'It's very pretty,' I said, feeling a pang of envy though I knew I shouldn't. 'I had a gold bracelet once. My granny sent it for my christening.'

'Your granny?' Frances frowned as she turned her head to look at me. 'Oh, I suppose you mean your Granny Chilton. Doesn't your grandfather still live in Chatteris?' As I nodded she stared at me. 'Haven't you ever seen him?'

I shook my head. 'He hasn't spoken to my mother since she ran away to marry Dad. My granny used to send presents until she died, so Mum says. She was a real lady, kind and gentle – I wish she was still alive.'

Frances nodded. 'My granny's dead, too. I've only seen pictures of her.'

'Let me finish your hair. Nathan will be waiting for you.'

'Wait a minute.' She picked up two parcels from the table. 'I'd almost forgotten. This is my present to you – and Nathan left this for you.'

I was surprised. I certainly hadn't expected a gift from Nathan. I hadn't even been sure that Frances would give me one. She laughed as I hesitated, pushing the parcels at me.

'Go on, then. Open them.'

My fingers trembled as I opened hers first. Inside was a leather-bound journal with a brass clasp. It was a beautiful, expensive book, the kind of thing she used herself. I stroked it reverently.

'I'll always treasure it.'

'I thought you'd like it,' she said smugly. 'You can keep your accounts in it – or write down all your secret thoughts.' She laughed as I looked startled. 'Oh, I know you have them. You're not as meek and innocent as you make out.'

'Frances, what can you mean?'

'Nothing. I have my secrets, too.' There was a sly expression in her eyes. 'Finish my hair now. You can open Nathan's parcel later.'

Never had I obeyed more willingly. When she departed in search of her cousin, I took my precious book and the present from Nathan up to my bedroom. Sitting on the edge of the bed, I stared at it, almost reluctant to see what was inside. If Nathan had given it to me himself, I might have refused it, but as I untied the ribbon, I began to smile. Inside was a box of the chocolate nuts that I'd seen in the dining-room. They were exactly the same as the one he'd thrust into my mouth, and I knew he'd chosen them deliberately. His note was brief but typical of him.

'They will not taste as sweet as the one we shared, but I hope you enjoy them. Forgive me, Nathan.'

He was a man of extreme contrasts. At times bitter and cruel, he could be charming and thoughtful when he chose. I wasn't sure how I felt about him. His moods disturbed me, yet in a way I liked him.

I knelt down to put my presents in the cupboard by the bed. As I leaned forward, I saw that the sheet was hanging untidily at the side of the bed. Without thinking, I slid my fingers beneath the mattress to tidy it. As I did so, a jeweller's box fell to the floor. In that instant I recalled Polly hiding something the previous evening. I stared at the box for several seconds, knowing I should replace it.

It was wrong of me to pry into Polly's affairs, and yet I couldn't stop myself. I suddenly had to know what she had hidden. Opening the box, I caught my breath as I saw the exquisite pendant and chain. Even to my ignorant eyes its value was obvious. The chain was gold, I was certain of that. It was very like one Mrs Crawley sometimes wore in the evening, but slightly finer. The pendant was gold, too, and set with rubies and what looked like a diamond in the centre. I couldn't be sure the stones were real, of course, but I couldn't see any difference between this and the pieces of jewellery Mary sometimes wore.

Remembering Polly's words the previous evening, and her look of excitement, I felt certain the pendant was genuine. How had she come by such a valuable thing? The answer seemed easy enough when I thought about it. No wonder she had hidden it! She would never dare to wear it in the house.

I replaced the box, feeling guilty. I'd had no right to pry, yet I was concerned for my friend. I'd already noticed that she had lots of pretty things. How long would it be before someone else put two and two together?

There were too many wives and children for the servants' party to be held in the house, so one of the barns had been cleared. Mrs Jackson laid out a spread of cold meats and pies that rivalled those for the Crawleys' own dinner-party. Besides all the food, there was a cask of cider, beer and lemonade for the children.

Since the labourers' wives helped clear up afterwards, it meant little extra work for Polly and me. The family paid a short visit before departing to eat their own supper of cold meats, and then we all began to enjoy ourselves. By eight o'clock in the evening, someone had begun to play the fiddle and several of the men were singing. The plates were looking empty about this time, and Mrs Jackson sent me to the kitchen for a dish of mince pies she had kept in reserve.

'Be careful,' she warned. 'Don't you drop anything.'

'I won't,' I promised.

I could still hear laughter from the barn as I made my way across the yard to the kitchen. It was a cold night but the moon was bright and I could see my way clearly. I was in a hurry to get back to the party and I flung open the kitchen door without any thought of what I might find. Shock held me rooted to the threshold as I saw Polly and Nathan beneath the mistletoe. They were kissing: a passionate embrace that made me cry out an apology at the intrusion.

'I'm sorry,' I said as they broke apart. 'Mrs Jackson sent me for the mince pies.'

Nathan looked annoyed, but Polly only laughed. 'It doesn't matter. It was just a bit of fun.'

Well, she'd certainly changed her tune! I looked at her suspiciously, wondering why she was suddenly willing to kiss Nathan. Any softening of my feelings towards him halted right there. He might have found a way to get round Polly, but I wasn't having any of it. I glared at him and picked up the pies.

Chapter Four

It was my pay day again. I was glad to be going home, though not as excited as the first time. The children were out of the door and Mum had the kettle on as soon as I got there. I took little Joe on my knee as he presented his *Pip and Squeak* annual for me to read him a story, jigging him up and down until he squealed with laughter.

'Did I hear a car just now?' my mother asked.

'Yes. Joe Morris is taking Mrs Jackson to Ely to stay with her brother Henry for a couple of days. He dropped me off on the way and he'll pick me up when he comes back this afternoon.'

'That's nice for you, Betty.'

'Yes.' I gave her my wages, and when she took the money into the bedroom, my brother tagging at her heels, I questioned Vera about Zac Jarrold, asking if what I'd heard was true.

She pulled a sulky face. 'I didn't do anything wrong. I can talk, can't I? There's no law against it. Besides, Mum sent me to get a packet of Woodbines for Dad.'

I thought she was lying. Her expression was sly and I felt she was hiding something. My mother came back then and I could see she was worried when she sent our Joe next door to borrow the *Daily Mirror* from the neighbours. Looking at the dark shadows beneath her eyes, I sensed trouble.

'Are you ill, Mum?'

There was a bothered look in her eyes. 'I haven't been feeling too good; that's why I kept Vera off school again.'

She glanced away at the fire. 'There's another baby on the way.'

'Oh no, not again!'

Although there were only three living Cantrel children, my mother had had two miscarriages over the past seven years. It made me angry to think of her having to suffer all the months of pain and ill health again.

'Betty, don't look at me like that. You should be pleased for me.'

'Should I? I'm pleased if you are.'

A glint of pride was in her eyes. 'Well, I've told you now.'

She'd told me and there was no more to be said. We both knew that it was my father's selfish ways that were to blame. I felt resentment stir in me, but then I saw how tired she was.

'Never mind, Mum,' I said. 'Vera will help you as much as she can, and I'll help with the baby clothes. I'll buy some wool and knit you some new coats.'

'Thank you.' She sighed wearily. 'You're a good girl. You remind me of my father sometimes. You even look like him when you're cross.'

I leaned towards her. 'Wouldn't he help you, Mum?' I asked. 'Supposing I went to see him on my next day off?'

'No!' she cried. 'I've asked him often enough myself. If you go he'll only hurt you. We'll manage.'

'But why did he turn his back on you? He must have loved you once.'

'Oh, he loved me,' she said. 'I was his little girl. He didn't want me to grow up. I think it would've been the same whoever I married. Now, my mother, she was different. She knew he was unfair and she tried to persuade him to let go – but he was that stubborn.'

'So you've told me before,' I said and smiled.

'There's a packet of Mazawattee tea in the pantry, Betty,' my mother said. 'Make the tea and give me that bottle of cod liver oil, will you?'

Grimacing, I handed her the small square bottle and a

spoon. I didn't know how she could swallow that stuff, but I supposed it would do her good. I made the tea and we drank it, then I washed up.

I spent the rest of the day cleaning the cottage. Despite all my efforts, there was an air of tension between Mum and me. It made me feel that it was hardly worth visiting, and when Joe Morris came to fetch me, I asked him if I could go into Ely with him another week. He said I could and I decided I would, but then I began to feel guilty again. Mum wasn't well. She could do with a hand whenever I could manage to get home. I supposed I'd go home on my day off after all, but in the event, I was saved from making the decision. Snow had fallen, blanketing the fens in a crisp, cold whiteness that cut us off from the outside world.

Everyone was talking about the skating championships on the washes at Sutton Gault. The snow had cleared but the ground was still frozen hard. For days Joe and Polly had agonised over the weather, worrying that the thaw would come too soon for the event to be properly organised. It was a big occasion and skaters would come from miles around to compete against each other. According to Joe, the rivalry was fierce, and, weather permitting, carried on from year to year. Even during the war skating had been popular, and Joe told me a tale about some youths who had gone skating on the washes one moonlit night.

'They saw the plane go over,' he said, 'but they took no notice. Then it circled round and swooped low, firing at them. They scattered pretty fast then I'll tell you.'

'Was anyone hurt?'

'No.' Joe grinned. 'The Jerry pilot just wanted to put the wind up them.'

Polly's brother George had been the local hero for the past two championships, beating competitors from as far away as Wisbech and March. Polly was a keen skater herself, and she promised to lend me a pair of skates she had outgrown.

'I've never tried to skate,' I protested. 'I don't think I could stand up on them.'

Despite my protests, I was dragooned by a determined Polly and Joe into joining their party in the wagon. They were taking the wagon rather than the shooting brake because several of the men wanted to go, and we could all climb in together. Mrs Jackson had promised to look after Frances for once, adding her weight to the argument.

'It might be years before the ice is thick enough to hold the races again,' she said. 'I remember when I was a girl the ice lasted for three weeks. My father was a keen skater and he took me every day.'

So, on the Sunday afternoon, I climbed into the wagon with Polly and Joe and half a dozen of the young men who worked on the farm. Just as we were leaving, I heard a shout and someone sprinted towards us, leaping into the back at the last minute. I glanced round as an odd hush fell over the others, surprised to see Nathan squatting in the straw.

'I thought we should present a united front,' he said with a grin. 'We'll show these foreigners, eh, lads?'

'You nearly missed the boat there, Lieutenant Crawley,' one of the men said. 'What's the matter, can't you get up in the morning?'

Nathan laughed. 'You're right there, Ted,' he said. 'I nearly missed my first watch on the *Connaught* through over-sleeping. I had to make a dash for it and escaped being put on a charge by the skin of my teeth. After that, the Olympics would be a piece of cake.'

His little joke eased the tension, and soon they were swapping war stories. They went on to talk of the championships, bragging about the prowess of the local men. According to general opinion, the outcome was a foregone conclusion. George Baxter would beat all comers with his eyes shut!

We were not the first to arrive by any means. I'd never expected such a crowd. People were skating on the frozen

90

washes and there was a huge, crackling bonfire on the bank. We'd brought our food in a big hamper, but one enterprising man was selling potatoes to bake in the fire. He seemed to be doing a roaring trade.

The championships were due to begin at two o'clock. It was now half-past one: time enough for me to have my first lesson on the ice. And that's where I spent most of it, sitting on my bottom. I was very wobbly and every step I took was a danger to others. Joe and Polly tried to keep me upright, but I very nearly brought the pair of them down on top of me.

'I don't think you'll be racing this year, Betty,' Polly said, laughing as I went down yet again. 'It's easy once you get your balance.'

Easy or not, I was glad when the racing began and I was allowed back to the safety of the bank. Watching other people skate was far more satisfying, especially when they were so skilful. So many eager contestants had turned up that they had to divide the contest into six heats of eight men, only the two fastest finishers from each race going on to the final.

The excitement was intense right from the start. Polly's brother was in the first heat, and he won it easily. We cheered and cheered, jumping up and down in excitement and hugging each other. Three of The Willows' men were in the second heat, and one of them came in second. Joe managed to win his heat by the skin of his teeth, and then we were suddenly at the last heat. I was surprised to see Nathan Crawley lining up with the others at the start, and even more surprised to see the skintight breeches he was wearing. They appeared to be made of a fine elasticated material that clung to his thighs and ankles, and looked a bit like dad's flannel long-johns. Most of the other men were wearing their normal trousers, simply tying them round the ankles to stop them flapping, though some had cut them to fit tighter.

I asked Polly why they did it and she said it cut down on resistance from the wind as they skated; her own brother's trousers were quite narrow, now that I looked closer, but not quite like Nathan's.

'Trust him to have all the right things,' she said crossly. 'Just look at those skates!'

'They look sleeker and longer,' I said. 'What sort are they?'

'Norwegian. All the best skates are Norwegian – but those must have been expensive. Still, it doesn't mean he can skate.'

As we talked the race began, and immediately Nathan went into the lead. I wasn't sure if it was his skates or his clothes that made him stand out from the others, but there was definitely something different about his style. It was more aggressive for one thing, and there was something about the way he held his arms very straight, something almost professional that made most of the others look like the amateurs they were. His body leaned foward at an angle as he shot into the lead and stayed there, moving with a wonderful ease. He was exciting, magnetic, powerful. A strange hush greeted his victory, and though there were a few belated cheers, no one seemed really enthusiastic. I thought I heard a few disgruntled mutters about cheating and it made me angry. Just because he was so much better than the others!

There was a distinct atmosphere of tension. It was as if the crowd sensed a new champion was about to be born, and the idea wasn't popular. George Baxter was the local hero, whereas Nathan Crawley was an unknown quantity. He'd been away to school and he was gentry. Rumours had been circulating about him ever since he got back from the Navy, and they were being remembered now. I could sense a strange hostility towards him and I thought it was unfair. I couldn't see that it was cheating just because he could afford a superior pair of skates. Later, when I asked Frances about it, she told me that one of his friends from the Navy was from Norway, and it was Hans who had taught him to skate so brilliantly; but standing on that river bank in the biting cold of that Sunday afternoon, I was aware only of the tension around me.

My loyalties were divided. Standing next to Polly, I could hardly cheer for Nathan, but I had a sneaking desire to see him win. Everyone else was against him, so, perversely, I wanted to see him come out on top. My heart was beating wildly as the men began to line up. Then Nathan happened to glance straight at me. I waved, hoping that he would know I was rooting for him and he grinned. Somehow I was sure that my message had got through and I was glad. Suddenly I was longing for him to show them all.

There were twelve men in the final race, but as they lined up we all knew that it was between just two of them. Nathan seemed to get off to a bad start this time, and George went into an early lead. He was certainly very fast, but he didn't have the same strange beauty on the ice as Nathan. Polly was screaming in delight, jumping up and down in her excitement as she urged her brother on. I held my breath, my eyes on Nathan. My nails were digging into the palms of my hands and my heart was beating wildly.

'Go on. Oh, go on, Nathan,' I murmured beneath my breath. 'Show them all!'

The race wasn't over yet. Slowly but surely Nathan passed all the others, moving with that lithe, animal grace that I found so enthralling. Now only George was ahead of him. I was so excited that I could scarcely breathe. I was silently urging him on, willing him to win. As they rounded the beacons and began the return stretch, Nathan began to gain on George Baxter. Gradually, he was closing the gap between them and a ripple went through the crowd. I heard a muffled groan from Polly as she realised what was happening.

'Don't let him win, George,' she muttered. 'I was counting on you to teach the bastard a lesson.'

I shot a shocked glance at her. The last time I'd seen her

in Nathan's arms, she'd seemed quite content to be there – so why should she feel that way? Hearing an odd sigh go through the crowd, I turned my attention back to the race. Nathan had caught George and was about to pass him. As I watched, holding my breath, he suddenly shot straight across in front of his rival, causing George to swerve and then to fall. He was up again in a matter of seconds and had started back after Nathan in a desperate attempt to regain the lead, but it was obviously too late. No one could catch Nathan now. The race was all over bar the shouting. From all sides I heard boos and cries of shame and I had a terrible feeling of disappointment that something wonderful had ended that way.

'Did you see that?' Polly cried indignantly. 'He did that on purpose. He made George swerve, hoping he would fall.'

I couldn't deny what I'd seen with my own eyes. I felt let down personally. I had so wanted Nathan to be a worthy champion and now he had spoilt it all. For a short while I'd felt really proud of him, but now I was ashamed of what he'd done. If I hadn't been there, I would never have believed Nathan capable of cheating. It was as though he had to win at any cost, and the stupid thing was that he would have won anyway.

It was ridiculous but tears were burning behind my eyes. I turned away, not wanting to watch the finish. How could Nathan do it? How could he?

For a few seconds I was so upset that I didn't notice the sudden silence. Then all of a sudden I heard shouting and yelling and I turned round. Nathan and George Baxter had taken off their skates and they were on the bank yelling at each other.

'That's it, George,' Polly shouted. 'You tell him!'

Everyone was watching, some in silence, others murmuring about it being a shame. Then George made a sudden lunge at Nathan and suddenly they were pushing and shoving each other. I heard Nathan saying something about George being a bloody fool, then their voices were drowned by shouting from all sides. George hit out at Nathan and missed, taking a blow himself on the chin. He staggered back, steadied and then threw himself at Nathan. They went down on the ground and I lost sight of them as everyone surged forward.

The women were left standing further up the bank as the men gathered round, shouting and cheering. Most of the voices were for George, but one or two female ones seemed to be for Nathan. He was obviously popular with some of the local girls. I saw a couple of them laughing and giggling as though they thought it was all great fun. Feeling disgusted, I turned away.

Then I saw Vera standing with a group of youths. She was fooling around – and she was the only girl. I forgot the fight as I saw red. Just what did she think she was doing?

I marched over to her, grabbing her coat sleeve and pulling her away from them. My sudden attack took them all by surprise and they went silent, except for Zac Jarrold who grinned as if he found it amusing.

'Big Betty to the rescue,' he said jeeringly.

'Mind your own business,' I said, then, glaring at Vera, 'What are you doing here?'

She looked a bit scared. 'Mum said I could come. I'm not doing any harm.'

'I'll bet Mum doesn't know you're the only girl with a gang of boys. Don't you know what could happen? I warned you. If Dad knew, he'd take his belt to you.'

'That's what you think. You don't know what he's like these days.' She looked at me sulkily. 'It's all right for you with your posh friends. Dad doesn't care what I do – nor does Mum.'

I was too angry to listen. 'Well, if no one else cares, I do. I'm taking you home now.'

'No!' she cried, pulling away from me. 'I won't be dragged home by you. I'm going myself.'

She ran off. I was about to go after her, then I heard a great roar behind me and I turned back to the fight. From where I was standing I could see through a gap in the crowd. It looked to me as if Nathan was getting a good hiding and I shuddered as I watched him stagger back and fall to his knees. He stayed there for a moment, shaking his head and the crowd thought he was finished. I felt the satisfaction all around me and suddenly I was angry.

'Get up!' I yelled at the top of my voice. 'Go on, Nathan. Show them all!'

His head went up. I didn't know whether he'd heard me or not, but all at once he was on his feet. He went at George and they were at it again, slogging it out punch for punch. I watched breathlessly. I didn't give a damn who was right and who was wrong in those last moments. I just wanted Nathan to win. I was so wrapped up in the fight that I didn't see Joe until he called to me.

'I'm taking you and Polly away out of this,' he said. 'The men can get themselves home.'

I went to him reluctantly, wanting to see the finish of the fight.

'It's such a shame,' I said as I walked to the wagon. 'It was fun, why did Nathan have to spoil things?'

'It wasn't really his fault.' Joe frowned. 'The ice had begun to melt. Nathan had to swerve to avoid a patch of slush. He thought he had enough speed to cut across without causing trouble for George, but it didn't work out. He tried to explain but George wouldn't listen.'

'No, I don't suppose he would.' I suspected that George Baxter had his own reasons for pressing the fight. 'I'm glad Nathan didn't cheat on purpose.'

'He should've kept his line even if the ice was bad,' Polly said as she joined us. 'I hope George thrashes him. He deserves it!'

'Come on now,' Joe chided her. 'It wasn't that bad.'

'He did it on purpose – the way he pushed his own cousin in the dyke and killed him when they were kids.'

A cold chill went through me in the sudden silence. Polly bit her lip as she saw the shock in my eyes. 'Forget I said that, Betty. It just slipped out.'

Just slipped out? I was turned to stone by the awful revelation she had so carelessly thrown at me.

'You had no right to say it.' Joe looked stern. 'That was an accident. Edward and Nathan were playing. Nathan pushed him and he slipped. They never should have been allowed to play on the edge of a dyke that was filled with water. It was Eben's fault as much as anyone's. He should have made them come away from it.'

'Nathan killed his own cousin? He killed Eben's son?' The horror of it made me feel faint, and for a moment Joe's face went fuzzy. I'd suspected something, but never anything as awful as this. It explained so much: the atmosphere I'd noticed between Mary Crawley and her nephew, that strange brooding look in Nathan's eyes, and the odd things he said about himself.

'No wonder he looks haunted sometimes,' I cried. 'It must be always on his mind.'

'It was an accident, Betty,' Joe insisted. 'I was a lad of fourteen at the time, but I was there and I saw it happen. Nathan shouted for help but it was too late when we got there. He was only five and Edward was seven. They were always fighting and quarrelling. It was because Edward slipped on the mud that he fell, and the water was nearly up to the top. It could just as easily have been Nathan who was drowned.'

Even if it had been an accident it was nonetheless terrible. It explained the friction between him and Eben. I could imagine how a man who wanted a son as badly as Eben did would feel about the man who had accidentally killed his first son. He must think of Nathan as a murderer. And it was clear to me that that was how Nathan thought of himself. He'd been so young when it happened; he must have seen the horror in people's eyes and heard them reviling him for his wickedness. He had grown up under the shadow of a crime he had not meant to commit, knowing that people were blaming him, hating him. Now that he was a man he must know that it was an accident, but the scars in his mind were too deep to heal. I had no need to look further for the shadow that hung over The Willows.

I was still trying to control my whirling thoughts when I became aware of the sudden hush that had fallen over the crowd. Turning my head to look, I saw that one man lay still on the ground while the other stood over him, reeling slightly, but victorious nonetheless. I felt a fierce, blinding surge of joy as I saw that the man on his feet was Nathan Crawley. I was glad that he had won!

Polly's mouth twisted with annoyance. 'He always has to win,' she said in a tone of disgust. 'It wouldn't have hurt him to lose for once.'

I stared at her, puzzled. Couldn't she see why Nathan had to win? Or was she like all the others who saw only the mask he showed to the world, the mask that hid the torture in his mind.

I didn't look at Polly as I climbed into the wagon. My joy had dimmed as swiftly as it had flared. I was silent as we drove back to the farm, lost in the confusion of my own thoughts. Now I knew what was behind the bleak look in Nathan's eyes sometimes. He blamed himself for Edward's death, of that much there was no doubt. Joe had said it was an accident, but only Nathan could know what had been in his own mind that fatal day . . .

Nathan was apparently none the worse for his fight, apart from a few bruises on his face. He spent the evening celebrating his win in the pub, arriving home roaring drunk in the early hours of the morning. Eben must have been waiting for him, because the quarrel between them was loud enough to wake the household. The shouting and yelling went on for nearly half an hour before a slamming door signalled the end of it. Polly thought it served Nathan right, but Frances was scared her cousin would go off in a huff. Surprisingly, it seemed to clear the air. Nathan accepted that he was at fault, and buckled down to work with a new determination.

Polly's brother had a black eye that gradually turned a

gorgeous purple, but otherwise he was unharmed. He was cheerful about the whole affair, and Polly got very indignant when she discovered that he'd spent the night drinking with Nathan and the others and that they were now the best of friends.

'Men!' she said furiously. 'You can't trust any of them. They're all the same when they get into that old pals act.'

Since George had also been a Navy man, and they must have had quite a bit in common, I didn't really think Polly could complain, but I kept quiet, turning the conversation to a new film magazine she'd just bought.

'I'd love to see Ingrid Bergman in *Gaslight*, wouldn't you, Polly?'

'I've seen it,' she replied, but it turned the conversation. 'I bought a box of Snowfire face-powder the other day, Betty, but I don't like it as much as my Panstick. You can have it if you like.'

I thanked her. She was so generous! I'd noticed that she took her time cleaning Nathan's room these days, and I suspected that she was piqued because he seemed to have lost interest in her. He no longer bothered to trap her in quiet corners and he would pass her in the hall with no more than a nod of the head.

I think I saw more of him than she did. He popped into his cousin's room almost every day now, sitting on the bed when she was taking her afternoon rest, talking and laughing. He came into the back parlour when we were there in the mornings, too, picking up Frances's drawings and my knitting to make unflattering comments about our work, and entertaining us with his Humphrey Bogart impressions. He tried John Wayne as well, but he wasn't as good at that. The slightly sinister, gangster image that Bogart exuded fitted Nathan very well. Sometimes he brought us new records: Glenn Miller, Vera Lynn or Bing Crosby, and he would ask me what I thought of the new songs, his eyes glittering with amusement as I tried to answer him seriously while keeping my distance. It wasn't easy not to be drawn into his net. He had a considerable amount of charm when he chose to turn it on, and that was happening more and more often. He seemed to take a real interest in me, asking questions about my family and the baby Mum was expecting.

'What are you hoping for?' he asked with a smile as he saw the little coats and bootees I was knitting. 'A brother or a sister?'

'It doesn't matter as long as my mother's all right.'

'Yes, of course,' he said, extracting from his silver case one of the expensive Passing Clouds cigarettes he always smoked. They were oval instead of round and I thought it was just like him to be different.

And so the days passed swiftly and I settled into my own little niche at the farm. Frances made her demands just as brusquely, but now I often anticipated her wishes. Despite her moods and her sulks, I liked her. It pleased me when she was happy, and I was sure her health was improving. She was eating more and she had put on some weight. She seemed more relaxed and she didn't have as many headaches.

I believed much of her illness had been due to her loneliness. Her headaches had been cries for attention. Now that I knew the tragedy that lay behind the atmosphere of the house, I thought I understood why Eben Crawley took no notice of his daughter. I understood, but that didn't make it right.

Frances felt that she was a disappointment to her father and she resented it. She hated being always in the shadow of her dead brother, but now with both Nathan and I to amuse her, she had no need to sulk.

Often now I teased Frances out of her black moods the way Nathan did. I told her about my life before I came to The Willows, and I was surprised that she seemed to envy me.

'You're so lucky, Betty,' she said. 'I wish I'd had lots of brothers and sisters to play with when I was little.'

'You had Nathan.'

'But he was away all the time,' she said and sighed. 'I

wish it was summer so that we could go for walks. I get so tired of being cooped up in the house.'

Glancing out of the window, I saw that the snow had melted. What was left looked dirty and unwholesome. The droves were soggy, making it almost impossible to get up or down, except by tractor.

'You wouldn't want to be out there now. It will soon be spring. Then we can go for walks together. We could make a study of wild flowers. Your mother would approve of that.'

A look passed between us. 'I'm stronger now. No one could object to my going out if I wrap up well. We might even get Joe to take us into Ely. We could go to the pictures one afternoon.'

'Sometimes in February it's so warm you would think it was spring.'

'Oh, Betty,' she cried, 'I'm so glad you're here. Before you came I used to get so miserable. You won't ever leave me, will you?'

'Not if you want me. Not while your mother is satisfied with my work.'

'She'll be satisfied if I'm happy.'

'You shan't be unhappy if I can help it.'

It was a pact between us. I couldn't have guessed then how binding it would be, nor what it would mean. All I knew that day was that I wanted to help her.

I stood for a moment to watch the heavy horses as they pulled the ploughs. Although there were two tractors on the farm, the horses were still used extensively for this kind of work to save fuel. There were two of them working independently on the long strip of rich, black land, each managed by one man with his hand lightly on the whipline, and followed by flocks of gulls who swooped on the fresh furrows with gleeful cries. How proud and strong the horses looked, I thought, their white silken manes tossing as they toiled in harness. It was a pleasure to see them and to feel the warmth of the sun again. At times during the long winter I'd wondered if it would ever break through the clouds. It was as yet only a pale weak thing, but I felt it was the herald of spring. I had come to bring Joe his docky, since he was too busy to return to the house for his midday meal. Now that the work of ploughing, cultivating and sowing had begun, we should see less of him in the kitchen. As I stood by the dyke, he turned and noticed me, waving his hand.

At work on the land, Joe was in his natural element. He strode confidently across the newly turned, fine, black earth, his easy, loping gait that of a countryman born and bred. As usual he was wearing his khaki trousers and a checked shirt, a flat cap covering his head. Although perhaps not handsome, he was a fine figure of a man.

'Ah, there you are, lass,' he said, taking the basket from me. 'I was ready for this.'

'Mrs Jackson has sent you a thermos of hot broth.'

'She's a thoughtful woman. Say thank you for me.'

'I will. It might cheer her up. She's been complaining about her chilblains all morning.'

I wished I could linger for a while. Now that winter was on the wane, it was pleasantly peaceful in the fens. I should have liked to wander along the riverbank and watch the moorhens and water rats. Soon the farmers and small-holders would be hiring the washes as spring feed for their bullocks. The dairy herd was kept closer to home so that the cows could be fetched up for the milking, but the beef cattle wandered at will by the riverbanks, and twice a day one of the men would walk or cycle the twelve miles there and back to count them.

'I'll be getting back then,' I said reluctantly. 'I've kept Frances waiting now and she has a chill. She'll be wanting a drink of honey and lemon.'

'The poor lass,' Joe said. 'It can't be much fun for her shut up in the house all the time.'

'She hates it. As soon as the weather is warmer, we're going to get out as much as we can.' I looked at him thoughtfully. 'There's a film matinee on Thursday afternoons in Ely; it's not so crowded as the Saturday show. Would you take us in one week and then bring us back, Joseph? Frances couldn't go on the buses; they're much too crowded, but we could go if you'd take us.'

Joe looked doubtful. 'I'll take you, Betty. I could do the shopping and hang around until you were ready – but will Mrs Crawley allow it?'

'She never refuses Frances anything – will you do it if she says yes?'

He smiled and nodded. 'You know I will – but make sure the mistress agrees first.'

'I will. I must go now.'

As I entered the yard at the back of the house, Polly was leaving one of the barns. Her hair was straggling down her neck and I watched her stop to brush the wisps of straw from her skirt. She walked quickly towards the house, and I ran to catch up with her, calling her name. She turned, frowning as she saw me.

'What are you doing here?'

'I've been to take Joseph his docky,' I said. 'I like him, don't you? He's kind and gentle. I think he would make a good husband.'

A look of amusement came into her eyes. 'Are you thinking of marrying him then, Betty?'

'Don't be silly. I'm too young to marry.' I tried to keep my expression innocent as I looked at her. 'He likes you a lot, Polly.'

She laughed and shook her head. 'Joe's a decent man, but he'll never be more than he is now. I want a man who can give me a better life. I shan't always be a servant.'

'Is money better than kindness? Joe would give his wife something more than rubies and diamonds.'

Her gaze sharpened. 'What's that supposed to mean? Have you been spying on me?'

'I wouldn't do that – not on purpose. You ought to be more careful, Polly.'

She caught hold of my arm, her fingers digging into me as she swung me round. 'Just what are you getting at?'

'Nothing – I didn't mean to upset you. It's only that I like Joe and I like you. I thought . . .'

'You mind your own business.' She shook me, her expression one of suspicion. 'You know something. I can see it in your eyes. Tell me, what do you think you know?'

'Nothing! Honestly. I didn't mean any harm. You're my friend, Polly. I wouldn't hurt you for anything.'

Her eyes glittered. 'I don't like spies. You keep your nose out of my affairs, Betty.'

'I didn't mean to spy on you.'

'Then just keep your mouth shut.'

'I haven't told and I won't.'

Temper flared in her eyes and she looked as if she meant to strike me, but the kitchen door opened and Mrs Jackson came out.

'Now what are you two arguing about?' she demanded. 'As if there wasn't enough trouble without the pair of you falling out. You've work to do, Polly – and Betty is needed at home.'

For a moment I stared at her, not understanding, then my heart began to jerk. I started towards her in a hurry. 'What's wrong? Is it Mum? Has she lost the baby?'

'Slow down, girl.' Mrs Jackson glared at me. 'The vicar drove over himself to bring us the news. Your mother lost the baby last night. She's alive but she's poorly and asking for you. You're to go home and stay for a few days; it's all arranged. Now get your coat and I'll give you some food. You can eat as you walk. It's a warm day so you'll not hurt.'

'Shall I tell Frances before I go?'

'She was sleeping a few minutes ago. Don't disturb her. The rest will do her good. Mary will tell her when she wakes up.'

I fetched my coat, my mind whirling in confusion. I knew Frances would be upset if I just rushed off, but I was in a hurry to get home. All I could think about was Mum. Mrs Jackson pushed a small paper bag into my hands.

'There's enough there for your supper as well. I'll send

Joe over with some calves' jelly for your mother tonight. You make it into a warm broth for her. It will do her the world of good.'

I nodded, my throat too tight for words. I was close to tears, and I felt guilty as I remembered the day Mum had told me about the baby. I'd been harsh with her at first, resenting the baby. Now it was dead before it had even drawn breath and I felt it was my fault. I should have been more understanding. It was two months since I'd visited. Even after the snow cleared, I'd simply sent my wages and the knitted coats with Joe. I'd abandoned Mum and now she was ill. She might be dying.

That thought kept hammering at my brain as I walked and ran in turn. The droves had never seemed so lonely, or so endless! It seemed as if I must run for ever and never reach my home. Tears began to course down my cheeks and I was sobbing noisily in my fear.

At first I was too immersed in my grief to hear the roar of the tractor's engine. Not until it was almost upon me did I turn my head. At that moment Nathan braked sharply and jumped down. Why I ran from him, I have no idea. I must have thought he meant to ravish me in the grass or something equally silly. He caught me before I got very far, grabbing my arm.

'Stop panicking, Betty. I haven't come to rape or murder you. Get on the tractor with me and I'll take you home.' He saw the tears on my cheeks and his tone softened. 'You silly little fool. Come on, let me help you. They should never have sent you off alone.'

He led me back to the tractor, giving me his hand to help me up. I had to perch on a little platform beside the seat, my legs pressing against his knee as he put it into gear once more. He grinned at me, and somehow I felt a little better. It was the first time I'd ridden on a tractor like this and it wasn't very comfortable, but I felt safe with Nathan, and I relaxed as I felt the pressure of his leg against mine. The journey still seemed to take forever, but my panic had receded. I was calmer inside, and grateful that he had bothered to come after me. When we reached the cottage, Nathan stopped the engine and got down to lift me to the ground. As his arms went round me, I had a curious desire to cling to him. He set me down and stood looking at me, his face serious.

'Do you want me to come in with you?'

'Best not. I expect it's in a mess.'

'That wouldn't matter.' He frowned as he saw I was uncomfortable. 'If you need anything, Betty, you know who to ask. Anything at all.'

'Thank you. It was very kind of you to . . .'

He walked away, shaking his head. I paused at the door to catch my breath and wipe my face with my handkerchief. I mustn't let Mum see I'd been crying.

The first thing I saw as I went in was Dad. He was sitting by the fire with his head bent, his face covered by his hands. The sight of him like that sent terror sweeping through me.

'Is she dead?'

He raised his head slowly, his face ravaged with grief.

'Not quite – though God knows how she lived through it. It was the worst, Betty.' He drew a long, shuddering breath. 'It was me. It was my doing. She said something and I hit her. I hit her several times. I was drunk and I didn't know what I was doing. When she screamed in pain and started bleeding, I . . .'

The sickness rose in my throat as I looked at him. He was asking me for sympathy. She was lying in the other room close to death and he was feeling sorry for himself! His guilt was too much for him. He wanted me to excuse his crimes. I could see the pleading in his eyes and I felt the anger surging in me.

'Did you have to do that?' I asked bitterly. 'Haven't you harmed her enough already?'

His mouth went slack with shock. I would never have dared to speak to him like that before I went to The Willows. As he stared at me in stunned silence, I went past him into their bedroom. I could hardly bear to look at him.

Mum had been ill before, but never like this. I could scarcely recognize the woman lying so still and pale against the stained pillows. The stench of vomit was so strong that it caught at my stomach, but no one had bothered to change the sheets. I felt angry again, angry that my mother should have to live in this. Moving cautiously towards the bed, I bent over her, fearing to disturb her. She looked so ill that my chest was tight with pain. Then she opened her eyes and looked up at me.

'You came quickly, Betty. I'm sorry they sent for you. We could've managed.'

She wouldn't admit she needed me even now. The knife twisted inside me, but I swallowed the hurt and smiled at her. 'You could do with some help, Mum. I'll stay for a few days, just until you're better.'

She nodded weakly. 'Perhaps it's best. Vera can't cope the way you do. She's taken Joe to a neighbour's for a while.'

It was the nearest she could get to an admission that she was glad to see me.

'Don't worry, Mum. I'm here now. I'll see to everything.' Emotion was stinging my eyes. 'I'm sorry. I'm sorry I was hard on you, and I'm sorry you've lost the baby.'

Her head moved on the pillow. 'You were right, Betty. I know I shouldn't have more babies, but I'm weak. I can't deny him. If only I'd been more like you – you're strong, like your grandfather. I was always weak . . .'

'Don't talk now.' I touched her hand. 'I'm going to look after you. Everything will be fine.'

'I think I'm dying, Betty.'

'No!' I choked back the scream building inside me. 'No. You'll get well. You're still a young woman. I'll make you a nourishing broth. You'll eat it and you'll get well. You can't die. I won't let you.'

'Always so practical. You think you can make the body well, but what about the spirit, Betty?' A little smile touched her lips. 'But you'll force me to live whether I want to or not, won't you? You're still my Betty. My reliable Betty . . .'

She was so weary. She didn't know what she was saying. Her eyes closed and I left her to sleep. In the kitchen Dad was still sitting by the fire, his eyes brooding as he stared into the flames. He didn't say a word as I started dicing vegetables and tossing them into a pot.

'Is there any meat in the house?'

He looked up then. 'There's a rabbit I caught yesterday before . . . I hid it when the doctor came.' He got up and went outside, returning with a small rabbit. 'Do you want me to skin it for you?'

'I can manage.'

He tossed it on the table in front of me. 'Don't bother cooking for me. I'm not hungry.'

'It's for her – and the children.' I wouldn't look at him. 'She needs something warming inside her. Do you want her to die?'

'I didn't mean to do it. For God's sake, Betty! I love your mother,' he cried, leaning on his hands on the table to stare into my face. 'I'm not a murderer.'

'That remains to be seen.' I was too angry to care what I said. 'Did you ever love her, Dad? Was there ever a time when you really cared?'

He looked at me, his face creased with pain. 'She was the loveliest thing I'd ever seen,' he said slowly. 'She'd come to the church garden fête with her mother, and she looked so pretty in that dress of white cotton and lace. I couldn't take my eyes off her. I kept following her all the afternoon.'

I was struck by the expression in his eyes. 'So that's how you met,' I said softly, not wanting to break his mood. 'What happened then?'

'I managed to get her away from her mother for a few minutes. She was nervous but her eyes were so bright – like the stars. I told her there was to be a dance in a marquee that evening, but she said her father wouldn't let her come. I kept persuading her and she kept saying no –

but she came at about nine o'clock. Her parents thought she was in bed. She'd slipped out of the bedroom window, and climbed down a tree just to meet me. I kissed her that night, and after that we met every night. I couldn't keep my hands off her; I never meant it to happen . . .' He looked at me then as if realising what he was saying. 'I never meant to bring her down to this, Betty. I loved her. It was all her father's fault.'

'It wouldn't be yours, would it, Dad? Like it wasn't your fault that you hit her last night. Don't you ever consider her?'

His eyes glinted with temper, and my hand tightened round the handle of my knife as we glared at each other. He noticed the slight movement of my fingers, and his mouth curled in a sneer.

'So you'd go for me, Betty? You're not like her. You take after her father.' He shrugged away to stand by the fire, looking at me resentfully. 'He was a hard, mean man, and you're like him.'

'If I'm hard, you've had a hand in it, Dad. You've helped to make me what I am.'

For a moment our eyes clashed, and his fell first. I went on dicing the rabbit meat into small pieces as he stood watching me indecisively. Then he made a growling sound in his throat, grabbed his coat and slammed out of the house. I closed my eyes for a moment, squeezing back the tears of self-pity. My father's cruel words had stabbed me to the heart. I wasn't like the hard man who had turned my mother out of his house without a penny when she told him she was carrying a soldier's child. I was fourteen, a child who had been forced to grow up too fast.

If Dad was sober when he came home that night it was only because he hadn't enough money to get drunk. The stew I'd made had all been eaten. I'd cooked it slowly so that the juices ran and it made a tasty broth, and I'd forced Mum to swallow spoonful after spoonful until I was satisfied. I hadn't had to persuade the others to eat their share: my mother hadn't been doing much cooking of late. I set a piece of two-day-old bread and a corner of cheese in front of my father.

'That's all there is until Joe comes.'

He made no reply but I noticed he ate the food. Not another word passed between us until Joe arrived with several sacks of food. He asked Dad to give him a hand with the unloading; he did so grudgingly, showing no sign of gratitude. There was a sack of potatoes, one of carrots and turnips, eggs, a side of bacon and some sugar.

'Is there anything else you want, Betty?' Joe asked. 'I'm off to the market tomorrow.'

I took ten shillings from my wages and gave him the rest. 'Spend this on food and coal, Joe. You know what to buy – things that will last for a while. Whatever you can get.'

'Are you sure, lass?' Joe glanced from me to Dad. 'I'll do the best I can, you know that.'

When the door had closed behind him, I gave my father the ten shillings I'd kept. 'From now on Joseph will buy the food to last you the month. There'll be ten shillings for you every month . . .'

'Damn you!' Dad looked at the coins in his hand. 'I'll not be told how to spend my money by my own daughter in my own house.'

'It's a church cottage,' I said calmly, though I was trembling inside. 'You live here for next to nothing because Mum does some sewing for the vicar's wife – and the money is mine. I earned it and you've no right . . .'

I stopped abruptly as he threw the coins in my face. 'Keep your money. You're no child of mine. I'll come back when you've gone.' He pushed past me roughly and went out.

I put my fingers to my cheek and felt the trickle of blood where the coins had cut me. It was only a scratch and didn't hurt much. I wiped the blood away with a damp cloth, then I picked up the coins and put them on the mantelpiece. I had almost stopped shaking now. I was lucky Dad hadn't been drunk. A scratch on the cheek was a small price to pay for what I'd achieved. If Mum hadn't the strength to deny her husband, I would have to do it for her. If the money was spent on food he could not drink it away. To buy drink he would have to work, and that meant he would have less time to spend in the pub.

Once I had stopped feeling sick, I was pleased with myself. I'd stood up to my father and won. It was a small achievement but one I could feel proud of. I was smiling as I spooned some of Mrs Jackson's special calves' jelly into a bowl and took it into the bedroom.

Mum was wide awake now. She looked at me with anxious eyes. 'Did I hear you quarrelling with your father, Betty?'

'It was nothing, Mum.'

She saw the mark on my cheek. 'Did he hit you? Why were you arguing? Tell me, Betty. I want to know.' I explained reluctantly and she frowned. 'You shouldn't have done that. A man needs his pride. You shouldn't have shamed him like that.'

'How can you say that – after what he did to you?'

'It was my fault. I made him angry.'

'And that excuses what he did?'

'He had the right.' She sighed as she saw the disgust in my face. 'You don't understand the way it is between a man and a woman, Betty. Whatever your Dad is, whatever he's done, I love him – and he loves me.'

'He has a fine way of showing it. He could have killed you.'

There was pride and anger in her face then. 'You're a stubborn child, Betty. Don't interfere in what you don't understand. You think you know so much but you don't. Only when you've loved a man will you know what I mean. Oh, I don't care about the money; it's best spent on food, though I'll want two pounds besides the ten shillings for your Dad – and don't argue for I shan't walk out like your father did.'

111

'I wasn't going to argue. You can have it all if you want. I was only trying to protect you and the children. Take it all, I don't care.'

'No. Give me what I've asked for and let Joe spend the rest. He'll make a better job of it than I can.' She held out her hand for the bowl of calves' jelly. 'Give me that and get some rest. You'll need your strength to walk back to the farm in the morning. Don't look at me like that, Betty. I know you did what you thought was best, but you were wrong.'

She had hurt me so much that I wanted to walk out of the cottage and never return, but if I did that there would be no one to look after her and she might die.

'I'm not going until you're better,' I said stubbornly. 'If I go you'll be out of bed before you're ready.'

She saw the firm set of my mouth and sighed. 'I'm too tired to argue. We'll talk in the morning.'

I left her then but my mind was made up. I did not leave the next morning, nor for five days after that. Dad stayed out one night, but he was back by breakfast time with three plump hares and a pheasant.

'Hang these in the larder, Betty,' he said. 'They should last us for a while.'

I wasn't sure if it was meant as a peace offering or merely a salve to his pride, but it was the end of hostilities between us for the time being. He was careful not to mention our quarrel and later that day I saw the coins had gone from the shelf.

Vera helped me when she came home from school in the evenings. She seemed very subdued, but when I tried to talk to her, she mumbled something about things not going right at school. I sensed that she was hiding something, but I was too worried about Mum to insist on an explanation. I supposed she was just sulking because I'd threatened to tell on her.

On the morning of the sixth day, Mum got out of bed and dressed herself. It was time for me to leave. I'd scrubbed the cottage from top to bottom; there were clean sheets on the beds and clean clothes for everyone. The larder shelves had more food packed on them than I'd ever seen there before. I was no longer needed.

'I'm not sure when I can come again,' I said. 'I may have to make up the time I've lost, but Joseph will bring your supplies on his way home from market.'

'And the money.'

'Yes, Mum.'

I felt as if a load had slipped from my shoulders as I left the cottage. As I walked briskly through the village, I was singing to myself. I waved to the people I saw: Mrs Goodjohn hanging her washing on the line, the Papworth children playing in the street, and old man Feast sitting on the wall in front of his garden, enjoying the sunshine. I knew them all, but I was no longer one of them. I was glad to be on my way back to the farm. I was going home. The Willows and the family who lived there had become more to me than my own.

Frances was cool towards me for a few days, reverting to the way she had been when I first arrived. Her eyes had an icy, distant look and she hardly spoke to me, refusing to listen when I tried to explain.

'You were asleep and I knew you were feeling ill. I didn't want to disturb you.'

'You rushed off, knowing I was ill. You don't care about me at all.'

'I do care. I didn't have much choice. My mother was very ill. I thought she might die.'

My explanations made little difference. Her feelings had been hurt and she sulked for nearly a week. Then one morning when I went into her room she suddenly smiled at me. It was as if the clouds had been torn from the sun. She caught my hand as I took her clothes to her.

'I've been mean to you, Betty. Will you forgive me?'

'There's nothing to forgive. I know I should have told you I was going, but I was so worried I didn't know what I was doing. It wasn't fair to you, though.'

Her eyes were bright as she looked at me. 'Next time, please tell me. I thought Mother was lying to me. I thought you'd been sent away – and that I would be alone again.'

'I hope there won't be a next time. I'm not taking my day off for a while, to make up for the time I lost. I'll stay with you instead.' I smiled at her a little shyly. 'I'd really rather be here with you anyway.'

She laughed then. 'And you will forgive me?'

'Yes. I like it best when we're friends.'

She considered this for a moment, then nodded. 'Yes, we are friends. I hadn't thought of it like that. I've never had a real friend before, you see.'

'Nor have I – not like you.'

Spring came and then summer. Frances was so much better that we spent part of every day walking in the droves, collecting wild flowers for our studies. Mrs Crawley was pleased with our industry. So pleased that she finally agreed to let us go to the pictures in Ely. It was the first time Frances had been to a cinema, and the first time she'd ever visited the little cathedral town.

As we left Sutton in the station wagon, Joe told her to look out for the ship of the fens.

'The ship of the fens?' she asked, puzzled. 'What's that?'

He chuckled. 'Why it's the cathedral, lass. Haven't you heard the saying before? You can see it for miles around; it's a landmark.'

I'd seen the magnificent cathedral that dominated the skyline of the busy market town, of course, but I hadn't known of its nickname. I saw what he meant as we got nearer. Its imposing towers dominated the landscape long before we reached the town itself, and there were moments when it did look like a great ship floating in the sky.

'It looks so big,' Frances said. 'I hadn't realized. Did they really build it all those years ago?'

Joe turned his head, giving us an indulgent look. 'It was built in the eleventh century they say, though the monastery was there long before that. I'm not much of a one for history. Why don't you take a look inside for yourselves?'

'Not today,' she said. 'We're going to see *Meet Me In Saint Louis* — I've never been to the pictures before.'

'I've only been a few times,' I said, sharing her excitement. 'I can't wait.' I looked at Joe. 'Why don't you come too?'

He shook his head and grinned. 'I've got things to do and people to see. Don't you worry about me. I'll be busy enough.'

He parked the car right outside the picture house, ignoring the muddle of traders' vans, horses and buses, leaning over to open the car door for us. Then, as we scrambled out, he produced a bag of chocolates from under the dashboard.

'Just to make it a proper treat,' he said. 'I'll be waiting for you when you come out so don't worry.'

As Joe drove away, I looked at Frances. 'Joe's a marvel, isn't he? The way he always manages to find what we need.'

'He trades on the black market,' Frances said. 'I should think he's making a fortune.'

'That's a bit unkind,' I said. 'I like Joe.'

'Oh, don't let's quarrel over him,' Frances said. 'I can't wait to get in.'

There was a queue for the cheap seats, but if you bought the dearer ones at half a crown you could get in straight away. Mary had given her daughter the money and Frances paid the five shillings. The usherette showed us into the very best seats in the circle upstairs.

'I've only ever been in the front row,' I whispered to Frances. 'That makes your eyes go a bit funny. It's much better up here.'

'Shush,' she hissed. 'The film is about to start — and give me the chocolates.'

The film was a musical about a family in St Louis during the 1904 St Louis World Fair, and it had some wonderful songs that set my toes tapping. I kept wanting to join in when Judy Garland sang the Trolley Song, and Frances kicked my ankle.

'Be quiet,' she hissed. 'Can't you behave yourself?'

I didn't care what Frances said. I was enjoying myself too much as I watched Judy Garland dancing with a little girl to the tune of 'Under The Bamboo Tree'. They had straw hats and canes, and Judy's dress was all ruffles and lace. My mind was filled with the excitement and glamour of it all. I was transported to another world: a world of handsome men and exciting women, where everything seemed possible. It showed me a world that I had not known existed and I wanted it to go on and on forever.

Frances was also entranced by the magical scenes up there on the big screen. She didn't open her mouth once, unless it was to reprimand me or stuff another chocolate inside. They were delicious and we had finished them when we went out into the mildness of a late spring afternoon.

'Wasn't it wonderful?' I cried as I blinked in the sunlight. 'Did you like the bit when she was going to leave the trolley and then she started to sing . . .' I burst into song, echoing the words I had just heard for the first time and catching Frances to swing her round in the street.

'I liked it when she sang about the boy next door best,' Frances said, her eyes sparkling. 'And the Christmas song – what was it called?'

'Have Yourself A Merry Little Christmas,' I said, and promptly began to sing it at the top of my voice.

'Betty, do behave yourself,' Frances said, but she giggled and began to sing as well, causing several people to turn and look at us because she sang out of tune.

Perhaps it was just as well that Joe drew up to the pavement then. He grinned as he saw us laughing together, leaning across to open the rear doors for us. The back of the car seemed to be piled up with mysterious parcels, and I caught a hint of whisky on his breath as he made room for us.

'I can see you enjoyed yourselves,' he said, winking at me as Frances got into the car first.

'It was wonderful, Joe,' I said. 'I hope we haven't kept you waiting too long?'

'No.' He climbed in the car and started the engine. 'I found something to do with the time.'

'I want to come again,' Frances said. 'They're showing a Bing Crosby film next week.'

'Well, we'll have to see,' Joe said easily. 'We're not too busy on the farm at the moment, but the petrol is needed for farm business. Once the harvest starts, I shan't have the time anyway.'

Frances looked sulky. I understood how she felt. She had spent so much time shut away in her room, and now that she'd had a glimpse of what life could be like, she naturally wanted more. She didn't complain though; I think even she realised that the farm had to come first. We were lucky that Joe had agreed to bring us this time. I too wished we could explore the fantasy world we had entered so briefly, but I knew I must console her.

'The pictures are fun as a treat,' I said. 'But if we came all the time it wouldn't be the same – we can find lots more to do, Frances.'

I could usually coax her out of her moods now. As time passed I became more sure of my position in the house. Even Mr Crawley inclined his head when our paths crossed. Life at the farm was slow and easy as summer deepened and the sunshine opened our world far beyond the confines of the house. We saw Nathan frequently as he rode his horse through the droves, a black dog loping at his heels. Sometimes we would hear the roar of the tractor and I would be reminded of the day he had come after me to take me home. Nathan always stopped to chat for a few minutes no matter how busy he was. He was good company and he made us laugh. He seemed to indulge in fewer drinking bouts and there were fewer quarrels in the house. Joe told Mrs Jackson that he thought he might settle after all.

I was fifteen in June. Frances gave me a tin of talcum powder and some Yardley soap, and Mrs Jackson made me a cake, which I shared with everyone. The others all gave me something, though there was nothing from my family, not even a card from the children. I hadn't expected a present from Nathan but, late in the evening, he walked into Frances's room and handed me a small parcel. Inside was a book of Robert Browning's poems, the flyleaf inscribed, 'With love from Nathan'. I blushed as I thanked him.

Since he'd chased after me to take me home when my mother was ill, there had been a new understanding between us. I was not quite as prickly, and he didn't torment me as much. Yet we were still wary of each other, as if we were afraid to like each other too much. Or perhaps it was only I who was afraid. Nathan was charming and handsome; it would have been natural for me to fall in love with him, but he reminded me too strongly of my father.

My family were all well. I visited now and then. Mum was almost back to her old self. Vera was growing up fast and her sulkiness vanished when I gave her presents of beads, scarves and a silk blouse that Frances had long outgrown. Little Joe soon wouldn't be little any more. He was doing well at school and full of himself. It might be a time of austerity for the country as a whole, but the Cantrel family was prospering as never before. It seemed that hardly a month passed without a gift from Frances or Mary; gifts of clothing or shoes that were no longer wanted, food, books or occasionally money. The war was still discussed often enough to remind everyone of the horrors we had lived through as a nation, but in my little world life seemed good.

It was a strange summer. There were freak storms that flattened the corn and threatened the harvest, but then came a settled period. The days were warm and sunny, ripening the corn to a rich, dark gold. Although I heard rumblings of bad prices, food shortages and the bumbling of the Labour government, I was cushioned against most of the rigours of post-war Britain. I had known such hardship in the cottage that rationing meant little to me. Besides, we were fortunate that we had Joe Morris as foreman at The Willows. His dabbling in the black market economy was probably illegal, but he wasn't the only one, and we all benefited from his scheming.

Nathan was working hard at the harvesting, and Frances and I watched as he and the other men scythed a swathe round the perimeter of the fields. The corn was left to lie for a few days, then the binders moved in, gathering the stalks into tight sheaves for the women and children to shock at intervals through the field. The shocks were then left to dry before the wagons were sent in to collect and stack them ready for the threshing. I was seeing harvesting as it had been done in the old days; the limitation on petrol had temporarily curtailed the use of more advanced machinery.

Sometimes I joined in with the shocking for an hour or so, for an extra pair of hands was always welcome. Frances would sit on a blanket and watch, but I was never allowed to work too long, for she would call to me and I would run back to her. We would wait until the men stopped for their docky, sharing the picnic we had brought with Nathan.

It suited Nathan to work in the sunshine. His skin turned a pale gold and his hair glinted with blue fire like the tip of a raven's wing. He was always cheerful these days, teasing us both as if we were of equal importance in his eyes. It was becoming harder and harder to keep him at a distance, and I was not sure that I really wanted to. I was beginning to relax, to lose some of the suspicion and distrust I'd had in men. They did not all have to be like Dad. Joe was gentle and kind, and Nathan was fun.

Frances adored him so it was impossible for me to dislike him. Besides, he set out to win me round.

He was going away for a while to visit friends after the harvest, and Frances was concerned that he might decide not to return. He delighted in teasing her. 'Will you miss me when I go?' he would ask her, laughing as she flung her arms around him and implored him to stay. When he had had enough of that sport, he would look at me, his eyes sparkling with devilment. 'And you, Betty, will you miss me?'

'No, sir,' I said, for I would not give him his own way even now. 'Not at all.'

'You're cruel to me, Betty,' he cried. 'She's cruel to me, Frances. A cruel, wicked girl.'

'I'm not cruel, sir.'

'Tell me you'll miss me – or I shan't come back at all.'

'Tell him, Betty.' Frances shrieked. 'Tell him!'

'He's teasing you, Frances. He wouldn't stay away on my account. Take no notice of him.'

'No, no, he means it,' she cried. 'You've got to tell him or I shall hate you for ever.'

And so I had to say I would miss him. Then they were laughing, the pair of them, rolling about and clutching each other in their mirth while my cheeks burned like fire. It was not the first or the last time they joined forces to taunt and tease me, but I did not mind. It was good-natured fun and I did not find it threatening. I liked being with them, a part of their lives. It made me happy to see the true affection between them and to share their pleasure. It was second nature to me now to obey Frances. Whenever I could, I anticipated her wishes. I think I would have done almost anything to please her. I was her servant, her slave, her friend and companion. It was a wonderful summer. How I wished it could go on for ever.

But harvesting was over at last and Nathan prepared to leave. The day before he went, he stopped me as I was coming back from the dairy with my apron full of eggs.

'Wait a minute, Betty,' he said. 'I want to talk to you.'

'Mrs Jackson is in a hurry for these, sir.'

'It won't take a moment.' He smiled at me, but without his usual mockery. 'I just want to say thank you.'

'For what, sir?'

'For my cousin's happiness. You've worked wonders. She's a different girl now. I used to worry about her when I was away, but I shan't in future.'

'Will you be away long, then?' My cheeks flushed as he raised his brow. 'I was thinking of Frances: she will miss you.'

'And I'll miss her. I'm very fond of her, Betty. In fact she's the one person I've truly loved.' His eyes clouded. 'My parents were killed in a train accident when I was a baby. I never really knew them. Mary and Eben took me in but I was always aware that I didn't belong . . . Well, Frances is the only one who cares whether I live or die – so take care of her, kiddo!'

He had lapsed back into his usual manner, but I was strangely honoured that he had confided in me and I glowed.

'I'll take care of her, I promise.'

'And who will look after you?'

'I can look after myself.'

He chuckled, amused. The glint of mockery was back in his eyes. 'I wonder if you can? Are you sure you're only fourteen, Betty?'

'I'm fifteen now.'

'Fifteen is it? Are you sure you're not sixteen? I don't think you always tell me the truth.'

'It is the truth. I wouldn't lie to you.'

'Oh, wouldn't you?' he cried. 'Kid, you'd swear black was white if it suited you. You can't hide from me, you know. I can see right into your mind. One day we'll put an end to all this nonsense.' His eyes went over me assessingly. 'You've lost weight, Betty. You've got a waist now.'

I felt the colour burn my cheeks. 'You shouldn't make fun of me. You say I'm cruel, but you're the cruel one.'

'Cruel – when I've just paid you a compliment? You're growing up, kid, and you're going to be something pretty soon now!'

I ducked my head down and ran past him, my cheeks flaming. He was wicked to tease me so! I should never be pretty. Polly was pretty, and I could never be like her. She was so smart when she was dressed up on her day off in her red dress and shoes, her beads and scarves. I thought she must make all the men in Ely turn their heads to look at her. Polly was pretty, I thought wistfully. I was too dull and dark to be like her.

Yet as I looked at myself long and hard in the mirror before I went to bed that night, I saw that Nathan was right about my waist. I hadn't noticed because my clothes were looser on me now, but when I pulled my apron strings tight, I could see that I did have a rather nice slim waist. I wasn't beautiful, though. My mouth was too big, my nose too long and my skin too dark. Nathan was simply making fun of me the way he always did.

Perhaps because Frances and I often spoke of Nathan, wondering what he was doing in London, my thoughts often turned to the world outside the farm. We hadn't been able to persuade Joe to take us into Ely again, but I hadn't forgotten that brief glimpse of a magical life where people sang and danced and wore beautiful clothes. I thought it must be wonderful to be a star of the silver screen, and sometimes when I sang one of the songs from *Meet Me In St Louis*, I secretly believed that my voice was in its own way as attractive as Judy Garland's. It was probably sheer vanity, but it made my heart beat faster as I dreamed of following in her footsteps. Why shouldn't I be a singer one day?

Foolishly, I mentioned my idea to Frances. She stared at me in silence, then her mouth curved in a sneer.

'Your voice isn't bad,' she said. 'But to sing like Judy Garland, you have to have real talent.'

'How do you know I haven't?'

122

'She's a famous American film star – you're only a village girl.' Frances frowned. 'Besides, you have to stay here with me. You promised.'

She resented the idea that I might have a life of my own. It was almost as though she wanted to own me body and soul.

'You might not want me when you get married,' I said.

'I don't suppose I ever shall.' She looked miserable. 'How am I ever going to meet anyone stuck in this house. You're mean to even think of leaving me.'

'I don't want to leave you – at least not yet.'

'You're so selfish!' she cried. 'You'll be just like Nathan, you'll go and leave me all alone. I'll have to stay here for ever and ever.'

There was no reasoning with her when she was in this mood.

'It was only a dream,' I said. 'I didn't mean to upset you.'

'Well, you have,' she said. 'Oh, go away and leave me to sleep.'

I left her lying with her eyes closed. I didn't blame her for being miserable. Anyone would get fed up with staying in so much, but there was more to it than that. She seemed to resent the idea that I might have any life apart from her.

As I went downstairs, I heard the sound of the wireless in the back parlour. Seeing both Joe and Mrs Jackson coming into the hall, I wondered what had been so important that they had gone into the parlour together to listen to the news.

'There isn't going to be another war, is there?' I asked as I saw their grave faces. 'You look as if you've heard bad news.'

'They've hanged that dreadful man,' Mrs Jackson said. 'I've been following the case in the papers – he committed two brutal murders, and him a military man, too.'

'He was cashiered three times,' Joe said. 'If what they said on the wireless was true, he must have been a cold-blooded killer.'

'Why? What did he say?' I asked curiously.

'Something about being hanged being no different to going on another mission – one that he knew he wouldn't be coming back from,' Joe replied. 'He was a cocky one right enough.'

'Well, he's got his comeuppance now,' Mrs Jackson said. 'I feel sorry for those poor women he murdered – and their families.' She looked at me. 'Sometimes I wonder what the world's coming to. Young women just aren't safe by themselves these days.'

Joe smiled and shook his head. 'That's a bit strong, Mrs Jackson. It couldn't happen in a place like Sutton. Don't go putting the fear into Betty now. She's safe enough here at the farm.'

'What was his name?' I asked. 'The man they hanged?'

'George Neville Heath,' Mrs Jackson said. 'Why?'

'I just wanted to know.' I shrugged. 'I heard a story about a woman they had to carry to the scaffold once – I just wondered what it would feel like to be hanged. Do you think it's very painful?'

'That's something I don't intend to find out,' Joe said with a grin. 'Don't you go worrying your head about it either, Betty. That man deserved to die for what he'd done. You put it right out of your head – and don't have nightmares over it.'

'I won't,' I said. 'I was just curious.'

I laughed and went into the kitchen. But that night I did dream about George Neville Heath. I'd never seen him, of course, but in my dreams he was a handsome man with large whiskers, dressed in the uniform of an RAF pilot. He was standing in front of the hangman, and he was laughing. He had a drink in his hand and he lifted it in salute.

'It's just like flying a mission, Betty,' he said. 'Why don't you try it? It's easy . . . easy . . .'

I woke with a start, feeling the cold sweat of fear on my body. Polly lit the lamp and turned to look at me sleepily.

'What's the matter, Betty?' she asked, half annoyed that I'd woken her. 'Did you have a nightmare?'

'Yes,' I said, shivering. 'It was horrible.'

'That will teach you to eat pickled onions and cheese for your supper,' she said. 'Try to sleep now. It will soon be morning.'

'Sorry,' I muttered. 'Can I cuddle up to you?'

'All right,' she said. 'Turn over and I'll put my arm round you.'

'Thanks, Polly,' I said. 'I don't know why it scared me so much. It was just a dream . . .'

Chapter Five

I'd been shopping with Joe in Ely. It was close to Christmas again and the weather was very cold. I'd enjoyed myself buying gifts for all the family, but I was glad to get back to the warmth of the house. It had taken longer than I'd expected and I was worried about Frances. Would she be sulking because I'd left her alone all this time? Dumping my parcels on my bed, I hurried along the passage to Frances's room, eager to share my experiences with her. I'd bought some new magazines that I knew she would want to see: *Woman, Picture Post* and *Radio Pictorial* – and I'd bought us a tuppenny Mars bar each. I went straight in without knocking, halting in surprise as I saw she had visitors.

One of them was Nathan – so he was home then! – but the other two were strangers to me. I stared rudely, taken by surprise. There was a girl of about seventeen, very pretty with pale fair hair and sea-green eyes, and a man. My attention was drawn to him immediately for he was the most attractive man I'd ever seen. Perhaps it was because most men I knew had dark hair that I was so stunned by his appearance. His hair was a shining silver-blond that set off his startlingly blue eyes. I thought he looked rather like a photograph of Leslie Howard I'd seen in one of my film magazines. It had been taken during the filming of *Gone With The Wind*, when he'd been playing Ashley Wilkes. In fact this stranger was just like I imagined a Southern gentleman to be. I stared and then he smiled at me and my knees trembled.

'And who have we here?' he asked in a soft, husky

126

voice that brought the colour flaming to my cheeks. 'Is this another of your delightful cousins, Nathan?'

'What do you want, Betty?' Frances asked before Nathan could reply.

Her look and the tone of her voice told me that I was intruding. She was annoyed with me for bursting in unannounced and I knew that I should have knocked. I stood dumbly on the threshold, feeling foolish and awkward as I heard Nathan tell them I was both maid and companion to his cousin. A look of disdain came into the girl's eyes and she deliberately turned her head away from me.

'I beg your pardon, Frances,' I managed at last. 'I – I didn't know you had company. I came to see if you needed me.'

There was a hint of malicious amusement in her eyes. 'Not for the moment. You may come back in half an hour and help me dress for dinner.'

'Yes, miss,' I said meekly.

I was dismissed and I left, fighting my jealousy and my anger. I had no right to be hurt, but I couldn't help myself. How often I had thought it wrong for Frances to be so much alone. It wasn't fair that she should be a prisoner of the house, seldom seeing anyone but the vicar or a few of her mother's friends. She was sixteen, almost a young woman. She needed the company of others.

I told myself all these things as I changed into my drab skirt and blouse, but it didn't help much. I felt it most when I looked at my reflection in the mirror. I'd been wearing my Sunday dress for the trip to Ely, and I hadn't looked too bad, but now my skin looked sallow. I thought about the strangers in Frances's room, and the way the man had smiled at me. For a moment there had been a flicker of interest in his eyes, but he would not be interested in me now. He was accustomed to girls who wore pretty clothes like his companion. She had been wearing a dress of deep royal blue with a velvet collar. There had been an air of confidence about her, and I'd seen contempt in her eyes as she looked at me. I didn't even know her name but I hated her instantly. I sensed that because of her, Frances would have no time for me this Christmas.

I had my feelings under control when I went back to help Frances dress. As I'd expected, she was full of her new friends.

'Isn't she pretty,' she cried excitedly. 'Her name is Christabel Blair, and her brother's name is James. Nathan met them in London. James was a fighter pilot in the war, and when his plane was shot down over Germany, he managed to get himself and his wounded gunner right through the enemy lines to safety in Switzerland.' Frances's eyes sparkled.

'How on earth did he manage that?' I asked, but I was impressed. It was just like Leslie Howard in *Pimpernel Smith*!

'He won't talk about it much, but Christabel says he did all sorts of daring things.'

'Like what?'

'Well, he once stole a German lorry and some uniforms and drove right through a check-point without stopping. The Germans were so surprised that they didn't start firing until he was almost out of range.'

'Sounds as if the Germans were half asleep to me.'

'Don't be so critical,' Frances said crossly. 'I'm telling you it's all perfectly true.'

I nodded, refusing to say more on the subject. I was a little annoyed to discover that James Blair didn't just look like a hero, he was one.

'Did you see Christabel's dress?' Frances didn't seem to notice my lack of enthusiasm. 'She bought it from Hardy Amies' new couture department. She's so beautiful. Nathan likes her a lot. I could tell.'

I was surprised that she wasn't jealous, but perhaps she was too excited to think what it might mean if Nathan were to fall in love with someone.

'Her dress was very smart,' I agreed in a flat tone. 'What do you want to wear tonight?'

'Oh, my blue velvet I think.' She nodded as I took it from the wardrobe. 'Christabel has said I must stay with her at her home in London next summer.'

'That will be nice for you.'

Something in my voice caught her attention. 'I don't suppose Father will let me go. Did you have a good day, Betty?'

'Yes.' I'd wanted to tell her all about it but now it seemed unimportant. 'I enjoyed shopping.'

Her eyes were wistful. 'I wish I could have come with you.'

Immediately, I was ashamed. I'd no right to grudge her her friends when I was free to come and go as I pleased.

'I've finished your hair,' I said. 'I expect they're waiting for you downstairs.'

I tried not to feel jealous as she laughed and ran from the room. I had to learn that there would be other people in her life. Other people and other experiences that I couldn't share, because she was a daughter of the house and I was not. Again I felt the resentment against Fate. If my mother had married someone . . . someone like James Blair . . . then I should have had all the things that Frances had.

I heard laughter and music coming from the front parlour that evening. It went on long after I'd gone up to bed, and I could hear the faint echo through my open window. I sat hunched up in bed, shivering in the chill night air, hugging my knees as I fought my misery. Polly shut the window as soon as she came in.

'Not asleep, Betty?' she said. 'They've been having a good time downstairs tonight, I can tell you. That Mr Blair is a real gentleman. He opened the door for me when I had my hands full with a loaded tray.'

I turned on my side, shutting my eyes. I didn't want to hear her singing the visitors' praises.

In the morning when I went to help Frances dress, I expected to be told that I wouldn't be needed for the rest of the day. I was surprised when she said that I was to join her as usual in the back parlour.

'You can bring a book to read or your knitting,' she said carelessly. 'I expect we shall play Monopoly or something – but you can keep me company when the others go out for a walk before lunch.'

It was too cold for Frances to go with them. I understood now why I was being invited to join them, but I didn't mind. I was just so happy that I would be there, listening to their talk and laughter, though I had no illusions about Christabel's probable reaction.

I looked at my dull grey skirt. 'May I change into my Sunday dress if I'm quick?'

Frances nodded, her eyes slightly malicious. 'Hurry up then. I shan't wait more than ten minutes.'

Christabel and James Blair were already in the back parlour when we got there. He was reading a copy of *The Times*, his long legs stretched out in front of the fire. Christabel was sitting looking out of the window, a rather bored expression on her face. She had a glossy American fashion magazine on her lap, and she was speaking as we entered.

'How long do you think it will be before Nathan . . .' Her words trailed away as she saw us and she jumped up. 'Your cousin had to supervise the loading of some cattle for the market. I didn't realise he actually had to work on the farm.'

It was obvious she disliked being left to amuse herself. Her idea of a few days in the country was horse riding and lively house-guests. I felt an unworthy surge of satisfaction at her dissatisfaction.

'Nathan works most of the time,' Frances said. 'He doesn't have to, of course. When he takes control of his trust fund he'll be rich. Until then he only has the income. While he lives here, my father expects him to work.'

'And why not?' James smiled lazily as he laid down his

newspaper. 'I've been telling my sister that not everyone is as idle as we are.'

'You're not idle,' Frances cried. 'You were an RAF pilot in the war.'

'Forced on me by circumstances beyond my control.' James's smile was so charming that you could not tell whether or not he was joking. 'Now that the war is over, I shall take up my normal life again: travel and the pursuit of pleasure.'

'James!' Christabel pulled a face at him. 'You'll have Frances thinking that you're a useless good-for-nothing. You help Father run the estate.'

'I cast an eye over things now and then,' he agreed. 'But Father really doesn't need help.' James's gaze came to rest on me and I blushed as he smiled. 'What are you reading, Betty?'

'We're reading *Westward Ho!* by Charles Kingsley, and an Agatha Christie,' I said. 'Depending on what sort of a mood Frances is in.'

'Ah, I see.' James looked very amused. 'Do you like books?'

'I have shelves full of them,' Frances said without waiting for me to answer. 'I let Betty share them with me. Before she came here all she read was romantic novels.'

I turned away, biting my lip. I knew better than to put myself forward. Frances had let me share her friends for a while, but I was meant to sit and listen in the background. I retired to a chair near the long window that looked out at the barns. It was a damp, dismal day and the mist had settled over the fens. Even if her visitors decided to take their walk, Frances could certainly not go with them.

She had suggested a game of whist. A fourth person was needed. All eyes turned towards me. I was about to be summoned to the table, then the door opened and Nathan entered. I felt relieved as I settled down to my book. I was sure I would have had to be Christabel's partner, and I knew I could never have played well enough to please her. Listening to her chiding Nathan for

131

playing a spade when it should have been a club, I was glad I had not been asked to take part.

I half expected him to be angry, but then I saw that he looked amused. He seemed to enjoy Christabel's imperious ways, pitting his wits against hers, and flirting with her outrageously. I wondered if Frances was right about him liking Christabel a lot.

And so I lived a strange life those next few days. In the mornings I was allowed a glimpse of what went on between the Crawleys and their guests, but at night all I could do was listen to their laughter from a distance. While Eben was the head of the household, I was not likely to be invited to sit at his dinner-table.

Sometimes I felt vaguely resentful, but I knew that I was lucky Frances let me share as much as she did. She told me everything that had been said or done when I was not there, and she did not neglect to give me a very special Christmas gift.

'I hope it fits,' she said as she handed me a large parcel. 'I asked Nathan to get it so you can blame him if it's not right.'

I could see she was excited about giving me the present, and my fingers trembled as I struggled with the knots in the fine string. Inside was a dress made of the softest wool I'd ever touched. It had long sleeves with tight cuffs and black buttons, and it was a deep emerald in colour, with a little stand-up collar of satin. The skirt had panels at the back and front.

'It's far too good for me,' I cried. 'It's so beautiful.'

'You can wear it to the servants' party. It's from Nathan as well as me.'

My cheeks were pink as I looked at her. 'Will you thank him for me?'

'You can thank him yourself – at the party if you like,' she said. 'We're all coming to your party; Nathan, Christabel, James and me – but don't tell the others yet. It's supposed to be a secret.'

I laughed with her. I liked to be included in her secrets.

132

Not that I needed to tell the others. I think Mrs Crawley had a word in Mrs Jackson's ear. Perhaps she wanted to make sure that everyone was on their best behaviour when her guests popped in for a quick visit.

It certainly placed some restraint on the farm labourers and their families. They didn't drink or talk as freely as the previous year, though the fiddler had just begun to play as the 'surprise' guests arrived.

'Oh, were you going to dance?' Frances cried, her eyes bright with excitement. 'Nathan, you must ask Polly to dance with you!'

The only dance possible to the fiddler's tune was a polka. Neither Polly nor Nathan were very good at it, but they entered into the spirit of the music with a good will. Frances laughed and insisted that Joe Morris should dance with her, though he protested that he was too clumsy and would tread on her toes. In actual fact, he managed very well, taking great care of his delicate partner.

'Perhaps you would care to dance, Betty?'

I had been watching the others and I jumped as James Blair spoke. I turned to face him, my heart suddenly racing. 'I – I'm not sure I know how, sir.'

The smile he gave me turned my knees to water. 'Nor can Nathan or Frances claim to know how to dance. It doesn't seem to have bothered them. I think we could do as well, don't you?'

There was something about his gentle manner that appealed to me. I'd never met anyone quite like him before, and I felt that he was a true gentleman. He had breeding and quality. He was the kind of man my mother should have married. Feeling a little nervous, I placed my hand in his and let him lead me on to the floor. He smiled at me again, and explained what he was about to do.

'Now if I put my arm about your waist, like this,' he said, 'and you take my hand like that. Now all we have to do is count. One two three, and one two three – do you see how it goes?'

'I hope I don't step on your toes, sir.'

'I'm far more likely to step on yours.'

I knew as soon as we began to dance that he wasn't at all likely to step on my toes. He was a wonderful dancer, light on his feet and graceful as he pirouetted me around the floor. All I had to do was to follow him. He made it so easy for me. I laughed up at him, beginning to enjoy myself.

'This is fun, sir.'

'I knew you would enjoy it,' he said with another smile. 'And you dance very well. I think you must have polka-ed before.'

'No, I haven't. I'm just following you.'

'Well, let's see if you can follow me. Your turn to dance with Polly, James.'

I was startled to see Nathan standing just behind James, and I felt a little spurt of annoyance. Why did he have to interrupt just as I was beginning to get the hang of it? A flicker of annoyance passed across James's face, but he was too polite to make a fuss. He gave me a rueful look and relinquished my hand to Nathan, who seized it and pulled me away into the middle of the floor, his arm going round my waist possessively. I could feel his hand in the small of my back, compelling me to do what he wanted and my confidence wavered. I tried to wrench away from him, but he held me firmly in position as he began to whirl me round and round.

'Oh, not too fast,' I pleaded. 'I can't keep up with you.'

'You were doing well enough with James.' There was a harsh note in his voice and his mouth was slanted in a cruel smile. I sensed that he was angry, but I did not know why.

The fiddler was playing faster and faster, as if caught up in some kind of madness. From the corner of my eye, I saw that Joe and Frances had abandoned their attempt to keep up with him. James and Polly were floundering, but Nathan refused to be beaten. He whirled me faster, laughing as the music became wilder and the room began to whirl madly around me as I gasped, begging him to stop as everything dissolved into a dizzy blurr. All I could see was his face and his glittering, angry eyes. Eyes that seemed to burn with a strange green fire. I was afraid of him, afraid of his wildness and the strange mood that had him in its grip.

'Stop. Stop!' I cried. 'I can't breathe.'

'We can't let him beat us, kid.'

Why did he always have to win? It was sheer obstinacy that was keeping him going. I was vaguely aware that we were alone on the floor and that everyone was watching us. I wanted to stop but the music went on and on, and Nathan would not give in. He was laughing as he forced me to follow his flashing feet round and round. My chest was beginning to hurt and I felt I should die. If I didn't stop soon my chest would burst. I gave a cry of despair and I saw the mockery in his eyes. He would not give up, while the fiddler played, if it killed both of us! Then, quite suddenly, the music ceased. As Nathan stopped abruptly, I swayed, almost falling. His arms went round me, catching me against him, and then he was kissing me: kissing me with the same intensity as he had had when he whirled me around the room, kissing me full on the lips in front of everyone. My head was spinning so madly that I could do nothing but lean against him. It must have looked as if I were eager for his kiss, as though I welcomed his attentions.

'That will be quite enough, Betty.' Mrs Jackson had appeared from nowhere. She took hold of my arm, dragging me away from my support. I nearly fell and I had to cling on to her arm. 'I beg your pardon, Nathan. She must have had too much cider. You know what these young girls are like.' I dimly perceived that I was being blamed for the incident, but I was still too dazed to refute it. I stumbled as she pushed me in front of her, away from Nathan. 'Behave yourself, girl!'

'It wasn't my fault.'

'Be quiet and do as I tell you. You can help bring in some more food.'

I was hustled from the barn, my cheeks flaming. Mrs Jackson pushed me in front of her as we crossed the yard, and I shivered in the bitter cold. When we reached the kitchen, I turned on her angrily. 'It was his fault, Mrs Jackson. He wouldn't let me stop.'

'I'm well aware of what happened,' she said. 'You'd still have been dancing if Mr Blair hadn't made the fiddler stop. There never was such an obstinate man as Nathan Crawley – but you brought it on yourself by dancing with him. And there was no need to cling to him like that when he kissed you.'

'I was dizzy. I could hardly stand.' I glared right back at her. 'You can't imagine I wanted him to kiss me? Besides, I'm only fifteen.'

'What's that got to do with it? In that dress you could pass for seventeen at least. Plenty of girls younger than you . . .' She stopped herself in time. 'A girl with your background has to be careful, Betty. I'm telling you for your own good, so don't look at me like that. You're a Cantrel and folks round here are only waiting for you to make a mistake to pounce on you. If you do something foolish, they'll never let you forget it.'

'I shan't do anything.'

'Just you watch out for Nathan then. You've been warned about him before.'

'Nathan isn't interested in me, it's . . .' I broke off. I'd been about to say he was interested in Polly but I couldn't betray my friend.

'You just take my word for it.' Mrs Jackson sniffed. 'I saw the look in his eyes when you were dancing with Mr Blair. What do you think that was all about, eh? He was trying to show Mr Blair that you were his. Like two dogs fighting over a bone it was, the way they looked at each other.'

'Nathan was jealous over me?' It was so ridiculous that I laughed.

'You can laugh, my girl, but if you don't watch what you're doing, he'll use you for his own amusement and then walk right over you when he's had his fun.'

'Isn't that what most men do?'

Her eyes narrowed. 'Some are worse than others, Betty, believe me. He wouldn't marry you, you must know that.'

'Of course I do.' I stared at her soberly. 'I do know it and I shall be careful, honestly, I shall. But it wasn't my fault. Please believe me.'

'I'll take your word for it, but there's a good many as won't. Now pick that plate up and come back to the hall, and if anyone asks you to dance say no.'

I nodded, picking up the dish of pies and following her meekly. When we got back to the hall, the family had gone. I wasn't sure whether to be glad or sorry. I hadn't enjoyed being made a fool of by Nathan, but I'd very much enjoyed the short time I'd spent with James. I wished we hadn't been interrupted. James was so pleasant to be with: I could have danced with him forever. Perhaps it was best that they had gone. It would be all too easy to fall in love with a man like that.

Nathan and I came face to face the next morning as I was fetching some butter from the dairy. I saw him walking towards me and I waited, burning with indignation. He'd made a fool of me and he wasn't going to get away with it! There was a wary expression on his face, and I realised that he expected me to be angry. A hesitant smile flickered on his lips as he met my stormy gaze.

'I know what you're going to say, and you're right. It was a stupid thing to do. I didn't think how it would affect you. I'm sorry you were blamed, Betty. Will you forgive me? Please?'

I felt like a pricked balloon as the anger drained out of me. Suddenly, I saw the funny side of it and I laughed. 'She was so cross. I've been warned to be careful of you. She thinks you've got wicked plans for me.'

'And she's quite right. You looked so lovely last night, Betty. I lost my head.'

'Now don't start. I know you're only teasing. It was an impulse last night. So I'm prepared to forgive you this once.'

'You're very generous.'

'Don't mock me.' I shook my head at him. There was no knowing why he did the things he did, and I was no mind reader. 'You've apologised so we'll forget it – and thank you for my dress . . .'

He laughed as I blushed. 'Frances left the choice to me, and I was right. That colour suits you. You should always wear jewel colours. Bold and bright like your eyes.'

'I don't think Mrs Crawley would approve – and I'm sure Mrs Jackson wouldn't. She'd say they were the colours of a harlot!'

'Many of the most exciting women in history have been concubines or courtesans – harlots in Aunt Hilda's book. Wouldn't you rather be Bathsheba or Jezebel than a kitchen drudge? Read your bible, Betty.'

'I have, and they all came to a bad end.'

'Oh, Betty, Betty, you do amuse me!' His eyes gleamed. 'One day you're going to get such a surprise – and I want to be there when it happens. I intend to be there!'

The tone of his voice surprised me. I didn't like the way he was looking at me, and I began to back away. I felt odd and I thought I might faint. I didn't want him to look at me like that. I knew exactly what it meant and it scared me. Suddenly, I turned and ran towards the kitchen.

'Betty! Betty, come back here. I didn't mean to frighten you.'

He might not have meant to but he had. I heard him calling to me but I didn't stop to look back. I was really afraid this time. For one moment I'd felt drawn to him; he'd awakened something in me that had lain dormant until I looked into his eyes. I'd felt the beginning of passion and I didn't want to feel anything for Nathan Crawley. He was too much like my father!

I'd been for a walk in the drove when I met James later that day. I saw him coming towards me, and I stopped, feeling conscious of my old clothes and my windblown hair. As he drew level, I blushed and looked at him shyly.

'Have you been far?' he asked, and I shook my head. 'It's a lovely day, isn't it?'

'The wind's cold,' I replied, hardly knowing how to answer.

'Yes.' He nodded, looking thoughtful. 'Too cold for my sister or Frances – but not too cold for you, Betty.'

'No, sir. I like a bit of fresh air.'

'I enjoyed our dance last night. I'm sorry it all turned out so badly for you. I hope you didn't get scolded too much?'

The concern in his eyes touched me. I thought how kind he was. So gentle and pleasant mannered, not a bit like Nathan.

'Mrs Jackson told me off, but I don't mind that,' I said. 'I was sorry you'd gone when I got back.'

'I was sorry, too. I should've liked to dance with you again. Something slower – perhaps a waltz.'

Something in his eyes at that moment made my heart skip a beat. I thought he liked me, and I knew I was very attracted to him. He was the man I had pictured so often in my dreams, only then I'd seen him as my father, the man my mother should have married. He was intelligent, cultured, patient and understanding – but now I was seeing him as a man I could love.

'W-when are you leaving?' I stammered, my cheeks growing warm under his gaze.

'We must leave the day after tomorrow.'

'Frances will be sorry to see you go,' I said. I couldn't say that I too would miss him, but it was there in my eyes.

'And I shall be sorry to go,' he replied softly. 'Very sorry indeed, Betty.'

The look he gave me made my heart sing. I believed that he was saying he would be sorry to leave me, and for a moment I was wildly happy. Then I suddenly remembered who and what I was. Men like James Blair didn't marry girls like me. It would be foolish to fall in love with him.

'I must go, sir,' I said, and walked on quickly, refusing to turn my head when he called my name.

Frances was tired after the visit. She stayed in bed for three days and went into one of her sulks because Christabel hadn't made a definite arrangement for the summer.

'I don't suppose she'll ask me,' Frances said fretfully. 'Just because it was too cold for me to go out. She'll think I'm an invalid.'

'Don't be silly,' Nathan said. 'You couldn't help the weather. Besides, Christabel liked you, she told me so. She would've liked to stay longer but her family had guests coming for the New Year holiday.'

'James said he was very sorry to be leaving,' I blurted out without thinking, and then bit my lip as they both stared at me.

'Did he say anything else?' she asked, an odd wistful note in her voice. 'Anything about me?'

As I looked at her, I realized that she too had fallen under his spell. It wasn't really surprising. James was exactly the type to appeal to her, with his gentle ways, sweet smile and kind manner. Frances was almost seventeen. She was a young woman. None of us had realised it because she was delicate and we looked on her as a semi-invalid, but it was true. If I had succumbed to James's charm in the short time I had spent alone with him, how much more likely was it that she should fall in love with him?

I heard an odd rumble of annoyance from Nathan's throat, and I turned to glance at him. From the angry glint in his eyes it was obvious that he was thinking along similar lines and was not best pleased by it.

'Of course James said he was sorry to leave,' he

muttered. 'He'd hardly say he couldn't wait to get away, would he?'

'He wouldn't say he was sorry if he didn't mean it.' I looked at Frances. 'Why don't you write to Christabel?'

Her face lit up. 'Yes, I will.'

'You'll be wasting your time,' Nathan said, glaring at me. 'He's going to America. It might be months before he gets back.'

As her face fell, I returned Nathan's glare. 'You'll be writing to Christabel, won't you? And James is sure to hear from her.'

'You're right.' Frances laughed, sensing the conflict between Nathan and me. 'I'll do as you say, Betty.'

'It's time I fetched your lunch,' I said, feeling flushed with triumph. For once Nathan had been beaten!

My triumph came to an abrupt end. He came after me as I left the room, catching me as I opened the door to the back stairs. I thought he would let me go when I stepped inside, but he followed me and closed the door, trapping me on the bend of the stairs. His eyes were dark with anger and his lips had thinned to a tight line. I was surprised at the fury I'd aroused with my little game. Surely he could accept defeat for once?

'And just what do you think you're playing at?' he asked, breathing hard.

'I was only trying to make Frances happy,' I said defiantly. 'She's set her heart on that visit to London.'

'I suppose you think she'll take you with her?' Nathan had somehow backed me into a corner. 'Don't think I haven't noticed your little tricks, Betty.'

'What are you talking about?'

'I saw the way you flirted with James at every opportunity. And now I know that you were sneaking away to meet him like the little slut you are!'

'No!' I stared at him in dismay. He'd never used such hard words to me before. He'd mocked me often enough, but this was different. 'We met by accident.'

141

'Don't lie to me! I can stand anything, but not lies from you.'

Before I realised what he intended, he pinned me against the wall, and then he began to kiss me. The kiss he'd given me at the party had taken my breath away, but that had been in fun. This was meant to hurt and humiliate me. I sensed the difference at once. His hand tangled in the hair at the back of my head, forcing it back as he took possession of my mouth, and it was a possession. There was no gentleness or tenderness in him as his teeth ground against mine and I tasted blood. It was a painful, bitter experience and it gave me no pleasure. I was panting and frightened as I struggled to push him away. When at last he had had enough of his sport, he stood back, still holding me trapped with his arm across the corner of the stairwell, a strange, gloating look in his eyes.

'Why did you do that?' I asked, scrubbing my hand across my bleeding lips. 'I'm not Polly, you know.'

'If you were, you could fornicate with who you liked for all I care!'

It was odd to hear such a biblical word on his lips. Could this be the same man who had laughingly attempted to get Polly into his bed? The same man who had been thrown out of his school for hanging the headmaster's wife's drawers on the flagpole? Morality and Nathan were strange bedfellows! Why should he care what I did and with whom? I lifted my chin proudly.

'I haven't been fornicating with anyone. I've got more sense than to lift my skirts for the first man who smiles at me.'

For a moment there was no change in his expression, then I saw a hint of laughter in his eyes. 'I'm inclined to believe you, kid.'

'I should think so!'

'So you were just getting your own back. You're a clever little cat, Betty.'

'And you're a vicious brute!'

'Vicious brute, am I?' For a moment his eyes glinted. 'I'm tempted to show you just how much of a brute I can be . . .'

As I gave a cry of protest, his mouth twisted in disgust.

'Go and get Frances's lunch before I lose my temper again.'

I fled down the stairs, glancing back to see him still standing there staring after me angrily. I would have to be stupid not to realise what all his hints meant, though until now I'd thought he was just playing games. Now I knew he was in earnest. He intended to have me, and have me he would, in his bed, or the barn, or in some lonely drove. He'd made up his mind to it and Nathan always had to win.

Chapter Six

The weather was bitterly cold. The snow had lain on the fields for weeks on end, and the newspapers were calling this winter of 1947 the coldest for fifty years or more. On the hill farms sheep and cattle were dying for lack of fodder. Many of them had had to be slaughtered because they were in a pitiful condition, their flesh cracked and torn by the biting cold. Some villages had been cut off for weeks, and no milk or post could get through.

'We're lucky here,' Joe said when I complained about the long weeks of snow and ice. 'At least while the ground's hard we can get about. You wait until the thaw comes – that's when the trouble will start.'

'I think I'd rather have the mud,' I said. 'If only it wasn't so cold. Poor Frances is shivering all day despite the fire in her room. She says she feels like screaming every time she looks out of the window.'

'Ay, it must be hard for her, poor lass,' Joe said sympathetically.

'It's bad for everyone,' Mrs Jackson said. 'Run and see if there're any eggs in the dairy – and if there aren't go to the hen house. I haven't an egg left in the kitchen.'

'Wrap up well then, Betty,' Joe advised. 'And take care not to slip on the ice. The snow has gone but the ice is dangerous.'

'I'll take care,' I said, pulling on my coat and a scarf. 'I'll do my best, Mrs Jackson, but you know the hens haven't been laying well recently – they hate the cold as well.'

'Well, do the best you can then.'

I went outside. The wind was bitter and it made my eyes sting. I tucked my head down, heading for the dairy. I hoped I should be lucky and not have to go all the way to the hen house, but the bowl used to store eggs collected by the men was empty. I slapped my arms, shivering as I went back out of the dairy and across the yard. Joe was right: it was very slippery! I thought the thaw might be on the way after all, although it still felt very cold.

The hen house was at the far end of the yard, beyond the cow byres. The stock were bleating pitifully as they huddled together in their stalls. I felt sorry for them, though they had plenty of fodder and nice, fresh straw to keep them warm. Luckily, there were several eggs in the nest boxes. I collected enough to fill my basket and started back. As I came round the back of the byres, I saw Nathan standing by the pump in the middle of the yard. I halted, staring at him in surprise. He had thrown down a shovel and was washing his hands and boots with cold water – washing the blood from his hands. He had blood all over him. On his hands, his face and his shirt.

I stared at him in a kind of fascinated horror as all sorts of explanations went through my mind, I would have thought that perhaps the men had been slaughtering a pig or a bullock, except that I knew it was always done at the slaughter house and never on the farm itself. Mrs Jackson refused to cook meat unless it was properly hung and butchered into recognisable joints. So how had Nathan got himself covered in blood?

Since our quarrel on the stairs, I had avoided him as much as possible. If I saw him coming when I was crossing the yard, I hid until he had gone. I couldn't avoid him all the time, and I had to be polite to him when he visited Frances, but I never allowed my eyes to meet his. Sometimes I thought my efforts only served to amuse him. It was as if he were biding his time, just waiting for the right moment to strike. As I stood there in the chill of that winter day, my mind conjuring up the most horrible pictures, Nathan turned and saw me.

'What are you staring at?'

The look he gave me was fearful. I swallowed nervously, knowing that I had to go past him to reach the kitchen. 'Nothing. I have to take these for Mrs Jackson.' I moved tentatively forward as he suddenly stripped off his shirt and held his head under the pump. The water cascaded over him, making his skin glisten. He raised his head as I drew level with him, mopping at his face with his shirt tails.

'You'll catch your death of cold.'

'Perhaps that would please some people round here.'

'What do you mean?'

'You needn't look so terrified. I haven't murdered anyone.' He scowled at me. 'Murder was done but not by my hand.'

'Murder?' I felt a surge of alarm. 'Has someone been killed?'

'No one important. At least in my uncle's eyes.' He saw my expression and his eyes sparkled. 'Don't look so scared. It was only a dog.'

'A – a dog?'

'Yes, a dog.' Nathan looked grim now. 'My dear Uncle Eben likes dogs that fight, did you know that?' I shook my head and he nodded. 'He keeps them in a special shed away from the farm so that the sainted Mary doesn't find out his nasty little secret, and every now and then he matches them against dogs from other kennels. They usually fight to the death, but sometimes one is badly mauled and . . .'

'Don't! I don't want to hear it,' I cried. Suddenly I recalled the mournful howling I had heard at various times. The only dog I'd actually seen about the farm was the one that followed Nathan when he was out riding or on the tractor. 'Why do men have to be so cruel? How could you watch it?'

'As a matter of fact I didn't. I merely put the poor creature out of its misery.' His mouth tightened. 'Someone had to do it.' He pulled on his jacket as he spoke and I

146

saw dark stains where he had carried the bleeding dog in his arms.

I sensed that he was upset about what had happened and I moved towards him without thinking, laying my hand on his jacket sleeve. 'I'm sorry, Nathan, I shouldn't have jumped to conclusions.'

'No . . .' A wry smile twisted his mouth. 'It's not the first time, is it?'

'I don't understand.'

'I think you do.'

'You talk in riddles. I think you enjoy confusing me.'

'Then why have you been avoiding me?'

'I haven't.' I blushed as he raised his brows. 'Well, only a little. You say such odd things to me.'

'Do you want me to speak more plainly, Betty?' There was a hint of mischief in his eyes. 'Meet me in the barn after supper and I'll tell you exactly what I mean.'

The fire rushed into my cheeks. I shook my head, moving past him swiftly.

It was a mistake to run away, and it was a mistake to listen to what Joe and Mrs Jackson were saying over supper that evening. Frances was dining with her family and I was eating with the others in the kitchen. Joe began it by shaking his head and muttering to himself.

'Nothing the matter with that pie I hope?' Mrs Jackson asked huffily.

'The pie?' Joe looked up. 'Nay, I was thinking of something else. It were a real bad business today and no mistake. The master had no business to do it. The dog belonged to Mr Nathan and always had. He were right upset.'

'Be quiet, Joe.' Mrs Jackson frowned at him. 'I don't condone what Eben did, never have, but there's no need for the girls to know.'

'What's that then?' Polly asked curiously.

'Nothing that concerns you!' she said sharply.

Having been warned, Joe would say no more despite

Polly's probing, but he didn't need to as far as I was concerned. No wonder Nathan had looked so grim. Eben Crawley had taken a dog that belonged to his nephew and entered it into one of his beastly dogfights. I had no idea why he should do such a thing, unless it was to deliberately hurt or punish Nathan.

An odd shaft of pain went through me as I recalled the look of pain in Nathan's eyes. I had been too shocked by his revelations about the master's secret vice, of which I had previously not had the least idea, to put two and two together. Now I understood why he had acted so strangely. He had had to put down his own dog to save it from further suffering and then bury it. I knew that must have hurt him, and I was sorry for the suspicions I'd had as I watched him wash the blood away. I had practically accused him of being responsible for the dog's death. Nathan was always getting blamed for something he hadn't done. It was unjust, and I was as bad as everyone else. I was suddenly aware of a need to apologise. He had never done me any real harm, and now I wanted him to know I understood.

I told Mrs Jackson I was going to bed, then I slipped out of a side door and into the yard. Immediately, I noticed a difference in the air. Why, it was almost mild! The thaw had definitely set in. It would soon be spring now. I hurried across the yard to the hay barn. I suppose it was a foolish thing to do, but my sympathy had been aroused. Nathan had been right when he said we had something in common; I was looked down on because I was a Cantrel and he was still being punished because of something he had done as a child. I wasn't sure that Nathan would be in the barn; he had probably only been teasing me again when he suggested it and he would not expect me to meet him. Yet the door was unlocked, and as I opened it and slipped inside, I sensed that I was not alone.

'Nathan . . .' I called softly. 'Nathan, I must talk to you . . .' I moved cautiously into the interior. It was dark and a little creepy, but it smelt warm and there was a mustiness from the hay. 'Are you there?' I whispered.

I jumped as someone put their arms about me from behind. Then Nathan's lips were against my hair, moving feverishly to my earlobe and then my cheek as I tried to turn my face in protest. 'What are you . . .'

He swung me round in his arms, and I smelt the whisky on his breath just before he kissed me. 'Betty, I didn't think you would come,' he murmured thickly. 'My precious darling, how could you know how much I needed you tonight?'

'No, Nathan . . .' I tried to speak, but his kisses drowned the words.

He caught me behind the knees, sweeping me off my feet before I realised what was happening. I struggled but he only laughed as he carried me, his lips still on mine, to a soft pile of hay. I was easy for him to carry; those powerful shoulders of his were tremendously strong. I felt his strength as I pushed against him, trying to get up. Then he was in the hay with me, his lips covering mine again as I attempted to speak. His body was across mine, preventing me from rising. I pushed at his shoulders, making what mumbled protest I could, but it was useless even to try. He was too drunk to listen to reason. I kept calling his name as his lips moved over my face, touching briefly on my eyelids, my forehead, my throat, but always returning to my mouth before I could say more than his name. It was as if he were determined that I should not speak, as though while my protests were unspoken he could deny them to himself. Then his hands were at my breast, caressing me through the material of my blouse before wrenching at the buttons to slip inside. I gasped at the touch of his hands on my flesh, arching wildly beneath him in a desperate attempt to free myself.

'Don't be frightened,' he murmured against my ear. 'I love you, Betty. I'll be good to you.'

'No, Nathan!' I cried. 'I didn't come here for this. Let me go now or I'll hate you for ever.'

At last I had managed to speak. I felt his body tense. For a moment he continued to hold me pressed beneath him, then he groaned in frustration and rolled onto his back in the hay beside me. It was several seconds before he spoke.

'What did you come for then?'

I lay with my eyes closed, a single tear squeezing from beneath my lashes and rolling down my cheek.

'I came to say I was sorry about your dog. When you told me what happened, I didn't realise it was yours, I thought it was a shame so . . .'

There was no answer. At first I thought he was sulking, then I turned and lifted myself on one elbow to look down at him. His eyes were closed and his mouth was slightly open.

'Nathan?' I touched his shoulder cautiously. 'Nathan, did you hear me?'

A gentle snore was the only response I got. I stared at him, half suspecting that he was only pretending to be asleep. I shook him hard, annoyed that he should play games. He grunted, murmured something I couldn't catch and went on sleeping.

'Damn you, Nathan!' I said, angry that he could fall asleep so suddenly after doing his best to seduce me. Then I suddenly saw the funny side of it. I realised that even if I hadn't resisted his love-making he would probably have fallen asleep before he could complete my seduction. 'Oh, Nathan,' I laughed. 'You're going to be so angry with yourself in the morning.'

I got up and tidied my clothes, brushing the straw from my skirt and hair. There was an old blanket on a hook. I took it down, shook it and covered Nathan. There was no point in trying to rouse him, he was sleeping too soundly. He would be all right in the barn. I had to think about getting myself back into the house without being seen. If anyone saw me sneaking back in and discovered that I'd been with Nathan in the barn there would be hell to pay.

I looked out of the barn. No one was about and the

windows of the house were dark. With any luck I would be able to sneak in without being seen.

Relief flooded through me as I reached my bedroom and found it empty. At least I wouldn't have to explain where I'd been to Polly.

'The river is rising fast,' Joe said as he came in. 'It's all the water coming down from Bedford. I shouldn't be surprised if we're in for some flooding.'

Mrs Jackson looked at him, shaking her head. 'As if things weren't bad enough after the winter. All that snow . . .'

'It's the melting snow as is causing the problem. We'll need to keep an eye on things. I've told Eben that the beef cattle ought to be fetched up from the washes, and he says he'll send a batch to market. Sensible, if you ask me. If the fens are flooded there'll be no spring grass.'

'It won't be so bad, will it?' Mrs Jackson asked anxiously.

'Perhaps not.' Joe's face was grim. 'We'll just have to hope for the best.'

The back door opened and Polly came in, her cheeks flushed from the fresh air. 'Mud, nothing but mud,' she complained. 'Sometimes I wonder why I ever came to this place. It's so dirty.'

'Wipe your shoes,' Mrs Jackson said, scowling at her. 'Or you'll be scrubbing this floor again.'

Polly tossed her head. 'Anyone would think you were the mistress here.'

'Don't squabble,' Joe said. 'We'll have enough to worry about before many days have passed.'

As he went out, Polly looked at Mrs Jackson. 'What's that all about then?'

'Joe says the river is too high. He's worried about the stock on the banks.'

'Oh.' Polly immediately lost interest. 'Is that all?' She looked at me. 'If you're making a drink, Betty, make me one, will you? I think I've got a bit of a cold coming on.'

'That's all we need,' Mrs Jackson grumbled.

'Of course I'll make you one,' I said. 'Would you like an aspirin?'

'Yes please.' Polly went to sit by the fire. 'I hate colds, they make me miserable.'

I gave her a mug of Ovaltine and picked up my tray. Frances was feeling down in the dumps too. I hoped she hadn't caught Polly's cold.

'The roads at Earith and Welney are completely impassable,' Joe said as he came in for his breakfast on the morning of the thirteenth of March, having been up all night patrolling the river banks with other local men. He grinned as Mrs Jackson loaded a plate with bacon, eggs and fried potatoes. 'I could do with that. I'm fair famished, but the ones I feel sorry for are the German prisoners they've brought in to help with the sandbagging. The poor beggars look half starved.'

Mrs Jackson sniffed. 'They don't deserve your sympathy. After all the misery that Hitler caused . . .'

'It's not their fault,' Joe said. 'They're just normal men like me and the others round here. Besides, the war's over now.'

She sniffed but said nothing. I finished my breakfast and went out to fetch a jug of milk.

Nathan had just driven in on the tractor. I turned to go, but he called to me. Reluctantly, I stood and waited for him.

'I wanted to talk to you,' he said. 'About the other night.'

'There's nothing to say,' I glared at him. 'You were drunk.'

'I know . . .' He frowned. 'I seem to remember something happened between us, but I can't recall exactly what . . .' He stared at me awkwardly. 'Did I – did we . . .'

'If you want to know the truth,' I said crossly, 'you tried to rape me but you were too drunk.'

'Tried to rape you?' He wrinkled his brow. 'I can't believe that, Betty. I might have tried it on, but I wouldn't hurt you – surely you know that?'

'I don't know anything,' I said. 'You're just like my father. It's what you want that matters.'

'Like your father?' He stared at me incredulously. 'You can't really think that, Betty?'

'Can't I?' I said. 'You did your best to prove it the other night.'

I glared at him again, turned and went in.

Mary Crawley was with Frances when I took in her tray. Frances was clearly excited. 'We're going to Ely,' she cried as she saw me. 'Father is afraid the banks may give way and he wants us to leave now. We're going to stay with Uncle Henry.'

'You'll enjoy that,' I said, my eyes flicking to Mrs Crawley. 'What am I to do, ma'am?'

'We can't take you with us. My husband's brother has only so many spare rooms – and we must leave a bed for Hilda. I suggest that you go home. Eben doesn't think the floods will reach the village even if the worst happens.'

'When are you leaving?'

'Later today. I want you to pack some clothes for Frances, and make sure she has plenty of warm things for the journey. We don't want her catching cold again.'

'Oh, Mother,' Frances cried. 'Sometimes you make so much fuss.'

'I haven't forgotten what happened at Christmas.' Mary looked annoyed as she went out, and I realised she was reluctant to leave.

'I wish you could come, Betty,' Frances said. 'We could have so much fun together. I tried to persuade Mother, but she wouldn't budge this time.'

'You'll have a good time with your uncle,' I said. 'You know how much you enjoy his visits. Is your father coming with you?'

'Oh, no,' she said. 'He wouldn't stay with Uncle

Henry. Besides, he'll remain at the farm until the last moment. The men are going to start transporting the stock and feedstuffs to a barn on high ground at Sutton as soon as it looks necessary.'

'I shall miss you,' I said. 'But perhaps it will be over soon. The road at Earith often floods; it doesn't mean the river banks will go at Sutton or Haddenham.'

'I should think it's all a fuss about nothing,' Frances said with a careless laugh. 'But I'm not going to miss a chance to stay with Uncle Henry.'

It took me a while to pack Frances's things because she kept changing her mind about what she wanted. In the end Joe had to carry two trunks full of her possessions down to the shooting brake.

'Well,' she said as we finished at last. 'You never know how long I'll be there – and if the floods do come, everything could be ruined.'

'They'll never rise this high,' I said, disbelievingly. 'It will be just some flooding on the fields.'

'Take care of yourself, Betty.' Frances kissed me before she left. 'I shall miss you.'

'I shall miss you,' I said. 'Have a good time at your uncle's.'

Eben Crawley was driving them to Ely himself. I watched as the car went out of the yard, mud flying everywhere, then I returned to the kitchen. Mrs Jackson was packing a box with stores from the larder.

'Aren't you going to Ely then?' I asked.

'I'll go when I'm ready,' she replied with a frown. 'I'm blowed if I'll leave all my preserves to be washed away in the floods. And then there's all the furniture – that's got to be taken up to the top floor. We'll put as much in the attics as we can.'

'Is it going to be really bad then?'

'I just don't know, Betty.' She looked more worried than I'd ever seen her before. 'I know Eben's worried, and so is Joe. They've already begun to move some of the livestock.' She looked at me as I joined her at the table, beginning to pack some of the jars and pots into one of the boxes. 'What are you doing? Mary said you could get off home as soon as you liked.'

'I'll go when you go, Mrs Jackson,' I said. 'There's a lot of work to do. We're safe enough for the moment. Joe will tell us if there's danger.'

She looked at me hard for a moment, then she smiled. 'Joe was right about you, Betty. I'll not say no to some help.'

For the next few days we worked ceaselessly, packing food stores and some of the more valuable items from the house to be taken to Ely. All the best furniture was carted upstairs, to be packed tightly into the attics or the bedrooms. Polly, Mrs Jackson and I had to manage it between us, because the men were too busy to help. The barns were full of valuable feedstuffs, corn and hay. They were trying to move as much as they could just in case the worst happened, and it was becoming increasingly likely that it would. Every day we heard new reports of flooding in the neighbouring towns and villages.

The waters in the rivers were approaching the top of the flood banks, which were nearly twenty feet above the level of the fens in some places. By the fourteenth of March, the river at Ely had overflowed and was lapping at the doors of the boat-yard. By the next day houses and an inn in the area were flooded. Fortunately, Frances's uncle lived in St Mary's Street, well away from the river. We heard rumours of flooding across the main Ely to Cambridge Road. The next evening things became critical. Terrible winds swept across the district, whipping the water to great waves that flowed over the banks, making the men working on them retreat in haste. In other places men reinforcing the banks could scarcely stand on their feet in the force of the hurricane winds. Telephone lines were blown down, and trees were felled, blocking roads and cutting off the lines of communication. Hundreds of men; troops, German prisoners of war, and local men, were working round the clock to try and save the fens from flooding.

It was in the early hours of Monday, the seventeenth of March, that something woke me. Polly was still sleeping, worn out by all the extra work we'd had to do. I lay for a moment, wondering what had woken me. I'd thought it was a door banging. Making my decision suddenly, I got up and pulled my clothes on over my nightdress, which dangled untidily beneath my skirt, then I crept out of the room, not wanting to disturb Polly. It was probably nothing.

Approaching the kitchen, I saw that the light was on, and there were voices coming from inside. I pushed open the door and went in, stopping in surprise as I saw several men there. Joe and Nathan were getting food from the pantry, and the kettle was on the range. I stared at the strangers, puzzled by the clothes they wore. Then I realized they were wearing the uniform of German soldiers.

'It's a wicked night out there,' Joe said. 'These poor beggars were wet through and hungry. Nathan suggested bringing them back for a hot drink and some food.'

I looked at the exhausted faces of the men clustered round the fire, and my sympathy was aroused. They were the enemy, but they were also human beings.

'I'll get some soup and bread for them if you like,' I said.

I busied myself about the kitchen, heating a good nourishing broth in the big soup kettle over the fire, and fetching meat and bread from the pantry. Nathan and Joe served the men, and I saw their faces light up as the bowls of hot soup were put before them.

'Men need food inside them when they're doing the kind of work these poor devils have been doing,' Nathan said. 'Our local MP has been down to take a look and he's promised to see that everyone concerned with the flood prevention work gets more rations, but there's nothing like a bit of practical help.'

The food soon vanished. Then, just as the Germans were about to leave, one of them came up to me with a little bow.

156

'We wish to thank you for your hospitality, Fraulein Betty,' he said. 'You have been very kind and we shall not forget.'

I blushed, so surprised at his perfect English that I didn't know what to say. He smiled slightly, bowed again and then followed the others to the door.

Nathan grinned at me. 'You've got an admirer,' he said, then went out and closed the door.

I scowled at the kitchen door. Trust him to make something out of it!

Polly had to shake me hard to wake me in the morning. She was already dressed and she looked at me sympathetically, a little smile on her lips.

'Time to get up, Betty. I know how you feel – I was that tired last night – but it's all over for us. We're to pack the last of our things in the shooting brake and Joe will take us to Sutton.'

'Will you go home?'

'I shall stay with my brother and his wife for a while. I'll get Joe to drop me at the toll and I can walk the rest of the way. You'll stay with your Mum I expect?'

'Yes. Mrs Jackson has given me a box of provisions so I shan't be a burden to them. I heard that some families are being evacuated to the Mepal aerodrome?'

'Yes, that's right,' Polly said, thrusting a handful of her things into a big bag. 'Well, that's all I'm bothered about. What about you?'

'My things are all ready,' I said, picking up my suitcase. 'Is Joseph waiting for us now?'

'He had something to do first. We'll have time for breakfast.'

The kitchen was the only room downstairs that still had furniture in it. Joe had promised Mrs Jackson that he would see to it as soon as we'd gone. We all had a breakfast of eggs and bacon, and then the last boxes and bags were loaded into the back of the shooting brake and we were off.

I glanced back at the house, wondering what would become of it. If the floods reached this far, would it stand up to water damage? Would I ever return? I felt a tingle of apprehension as I looked back.

'Where are Mr Crawley and Nathan?' I asked Joe. 'Are you leaving soon?'

'There's still work to be done,' he replied with a frown. 'We want to save as much as we can.'

As we drove into the village, we passed others who were being evacuated from their homes: a farmer's wife pushing a cart with bed linen and pieces of furniture, cars loaded with personal treasures, and men driving cows before them, away from the danger that threatened us all.

I felt sad to be parted from my friends under such circumstances, though I was still hopeful that it would not be for long. Despite all the stories of riverbanks giving way, I could still hardly believe that the whole of the fens would flood. I was close to tears when Joe dropped me outside the cottage.

'You got out just in time,' Dad said when he saw me come in. 'They're fighting a losing battle at Over Fen. The water's higher than in the Old West River. The Willows will be flooded within a day or two.'

He sounded almost gleeful. I knew he disliked Eben Crawley, but I was disgusted that he could gloat over people's misfortunes.

'Well, they've managed to clear most of the barns, and the stock are safe,' I said. 'It's only the house. We'll have to see what happens.'

'Maybe it won't be too bad, Betty,' Mum said. 'It was good of Mrs Jackson to send us these provisions.'

'She didn't want anything to be wasted,' I replied with a smile. 'She's like that.'

Mum nodded. 'She was always careful as a girl. Not that I knew her well. Her family lived in Ely – in the house Henry Crawley still lives in, I think. But she courted a Chatteris boy for a while.'

'Was he Mr Jackson?'

158

My mother shook her head. 'No. I never knew him. Hilda was older than me. I only met her a few times, that's all.'

'She never mentions her husband – is he dead?'

'Yes. It was a long time ago, Betty.' Mum frowned. 'So you're home for a while then?'

'It seems like it.'

'You won't know what to do with yourself.'

'I'll find something to do. I can help you.' I looked at her anxiously. 'I hope the floods won't reach this far.'

'I hope not,' she said.

By half-past twelve that day the waters were rushing through a fifty-yard gap into Over Fen, sweeping on and over the bank into Hillrow Fen. All the hard work had been in vain; it was useless to continue and soon thousands of acres of valuable farmland would be under water. The men were withdrawn as the trickle became a flood. Looking out of the cottage window, I saw a stream of lorries, tractors, horses and wagons and cars going through the village.

Everyone was talking about how dangerous the situation was. There was both excitement and apprehension. Some people had taken in relatives who'd been forced to leave their homes.

'It's like the war all over again,' a neighbour said when she came round. 'Terrible it is. Terrible.'

No one could have guessed how terrible the next few days would prove to be. The flood advanced inexorably, covering the rich, fertile fields with a sheet of dirty grey water. Houses, barns and haystacks were surrounded by the merciless tide, marooned like little islands in a desolate sea. Some of the haystacks were swept away to end up on someone else's farm.

As the days passed the water kept rising. The flood extended to Haddenham North Fen, joining up with the Earith water at the back of Sutton, only a short distance from our cottage. We could stand at the top of the hill and

159

look across the fen; it was completely submerged, only the tops of trees, telegraph poles and the roofs of houses were visible.

'They say some houses have been totally destroyed,' my father said when he came in one afternoon a few days later. 'It's up to ten or twelve feet in some places.'

'That's dreadful,' Mum said. 'It will ruin all that lovely wallpaper at The Willows, and the carpets.'

'The carpets are in the attics,' I said. 'Some of the best ones were taken away. Mr Crawley started moving stuff early. He won't lose too much because of the flood.'

'He's more careful of his goods than he was of his life then – and his nephew's.'

'What do you mean?' I felt a start of fear as I looked at Dad. 'What's happened?'

He frowned, his eyes narrowed as he looked at me. 'I don't know all of it, Betty, but there's some queer tales going around.'

'What sort of tales?'

'They say Eben and Nathan Crawley were caught by the flood. Something about rescuing dogs. I only heard a bit of it, and you know what people are.'

'But are they safe?' I cried, my heart hammering in my chest. 'They're not drowned?'

'They say Nathan was almost drowned.' My father frowned as he looked at me. 'Why so much interest, Betty?'

'Mr Crawley is my employer, Dad.' I stared at him in exasperation. 'Can't you tell me what happened?'

'Well . . .' he said slowly. 'What I heard was that this boat was out looking for people who'd been trapped in their houses. They picked up a couple of German prisoners who'd been helping on the banks, then they saw two men on top of a shed that was almost submerged . . .' Dad paused, looking at me oddly.

'Go on,' I said. 'You can't stop now.'

'The way I heard it, they were struggling with each other, then one pushed the other one into the water and

160

he was swept away. It looked as if he'd had a bang on the head and was unconscious.'

'Oh no!' I gasped. 'Who fell in the water?'

'Nathan . . .' Dad saw the look in my eyes and frowned. 'You're mighty interested in this Nathan Crawley, Betty. I hope you haven't been doing anything silly?'

'Of course not,' I lied brazenly. 'What happened then? Is he dead?'

'No, not as far as I know. That's the strange part. One of the Jerrys dived in and fished him out. Quite a hero he was.' Father frowned again. 'I mean, why should a German prisoner risk his own life for a man he didn't know?'

'Because of a kindness done in secret,' I might have said, but I held my tongue. There would be enough speculation over the incident without me making things worse.

'He's all right then?' I said. 'Nathan Crawley?'

'As far as I know. He was alive when they fished him out. They'll have taken him to hospital I should think.'

'And the German prisoner?'

'Oh, he's fine. He was a strong swimmer.'

'They ought to give him a medal.'

'I'd shoot all the buggers if I had my way.'

'Mind your tongue, Rob,' my mother said sharply. 'Don't swear in front of the children.'

He glared at her. 'Betty isn't a child. She's heard worse than that I dare say.'

'Joe doesn't swear,' I said. 'At least, not in the house.' I looked at my father. 'You haven't heard how Joe Morris is I suppose? Do you know if he got away all right?'

'No idea.' Dad yawned and scratched his head. 'I could do with a cup of tea, Lizzie.'

As Mum filled the kettle, I took my coat from a hook behind the door. My father looked at me sharply.

'You just wait a minute. Where do you think you're going?'

161

'Up the street. I'm going to the vicar's house to ask if they've heard about Joseph – and Nathan Crawley.'

'Then you can take that coat off. I'm not having my daughter run after the Crawleys.'

'Oh, leave her alone,' my mother said. 'It's only natural that she should be anxious for news. She's lived with them for a while now.'

'That's just it.' Dad glared at me. 'You'd better not get yourself talked about, my girl, or I'll take my belt to you.'

'I won't be long,' I said, and went out quickly before he made good his threat.

From the top of the hill I could see the desolation of the floods. It had caused untold damage to the crops and farm buildings. I'd heard of one man who'd gone back to his bungalow in a boat and rowed right through the holes in the walls; another man waded back into the water to rescue his building society passbook. There were so many stories circulating, and it was difficult to know which were true.

I was lost in my own thoughts as I walked up the street, then I heard someone calling to me. I turned round in anticipation, giving a cry of delight as I saw Joe Morris.

'I was just coming to see you,' he said as I ran to him. He caught me up and swung me off my feet. 'It's good to see you, Betty.'

I hugged him, laughing with relief. 'I was so worried about you, Joseph – especially when I heard about Mr Crawley and . . .'

Joe's face creased with worry. 'You mustn't believe all folks say, Betty. Eben was trying to hold Nathan, to stop him slipping into the water. When he fell, he struck his head on a piece of debris.'

'Are you sure, Joseph? You know how Mr Crawley feels about Nathan.'

'Eben's no murderer.'

'If it was an accident, I'm glad.' I breathed a sigh of frustration. 'Why do things always have to be so horrible? Why do people hurt each other?'

Joe shook his head. 'I'm blessed if I know, lass.'

'Everything seems so bleak.'

'You mustn't let it get you down, Betty.' Joe seemed to hesitate, then, 'There's a dance at the church hall on Saturday. The vicar wondered if he should cancel it in the circumstances, but then someone suggested a raffle to help some of the worst hit.'

'Oh, that's a wonderful idea, Joseph,' I cried. 'I've never been to a dance before – not a real dance. Come and ask Mum if I can go with you.'

'Were you on your way somewhere?'

'I was going to ask about you – and Mr Nathan – up at the vicar's.'

'Nathan is in hospital, but only for observation. He'll be fine, Betty.'

'Then I've no need to go. Come on, let's ask Mum.'

I was wearing the dress Frances and Nathan had given me when Joe called for me that Saturday. He brought me a red carnation on a pin to wear on my dress and he drove me up the street in the shooting brake. I felt very grand and grown-up. Dad hadn't taken too kindly to the idea, but my mother was all for it.

'Betty is almost sixteen,' she'd said. 'Be glad it's a sensible man that's asked her, and not some I could mention.'

Vera was green with jealousy when she saw me getting ready. 'Why does Betty have all the luck?' she asked sullenly. 'Why can't I go to the dance as well?'

'Because you're too young – and because Joe asked her,' Mum said. 'Your turn will come.'

Vera flounced off in a temper, going out and slamming the door behind her. I looked at Mum thoughtfully. 'Maybe Joseph would take Vera too if I asked him.'

'No, Betty.' She shook her head and sighed. 'She's in too much of a hurry. She's got to learn she can't have it all her own way.'

So I went to the dance with Joe and Vera was left

behind. I felt a bit mean at first, but then, as I saw the lights and heard the music, I forgot my sister's tantrums. My fingers clung to Joe's arm as we walked in, and I was trembling inside. It was so exciting!

Several heads turned as we entered, and Joe was greeted by one or two of the men. I looked at him curiously.

'Have you been to a dance here before?'

'I used to come, before the war. I was courting then.'

'Oh . . .' I digested this in silence. Somehow I'd never thought of Joe courting a girl.

Joe laughed and shook his head. 'It's a long story, Betty. She married someone else.'

I wanted to ask him if that had upset him, but I couldn't pry into his private affairs. Especially in a public place like this. 'This is a waltz,' Joe said. 'We'll watch for a while so you can see how it goes. It's easy really. All you have to do is follow me.'

My feet tapped to the music. I had always loved music. Singing was something I did naturally. I could pick up a tune I'd heard only a couple of times, and it was the same with dancing. I seemed to feel the rhythm inside me. Besides, Joe was a good dancer and all I had to do was to follow his lead. It was wonderful. I liked the dancing, the music, the lights and the laughter of people all around me. I'd never had so much fun.

'Oh, I do like this,' I said, smiling up at Joe. 'It was so good of you to bring me.'

'I'm glad you're enjoying yourself.'

The music ended and we walked to the end of the room.

'Would you like a glass of orange juice, Betty?'

'Yes please.'

'I won't be a moment. I'm thirsty myself.'

The musicians had begun to play again. I watched the dancers, absorbed in learning the steps of the military two-step.

'Do you want to try it, Betty?'

164

I jumped as I heard the familiar voice. Spinning round, I stared at Nathan, feeling flustered.

'I thought you were in hospital?'

'I was, but I'm not now.'

'So I see. Are you better?'

'Well, I'm not dead yet. Dance with me, Betty.' He frowned as I hesitated. 'I'll behave. I promise.'

'Just for a while then. Joe's getting me a drink.'

As Nathan took my hand, the music changed again, a tango this time. It was easy to follow him; he held me correctly, not too tightly, and I breathed a sigh of relief.

'Relax, kid. I'm hardly likely to ravish you in the middle of a dance floor.'

'Don't make a joke of it!'

'Why are you angry? Because I tried – or because I didn't manage it?'

'If you say things like that, I'll walk away and leave you.'

'I just wondered.' He grinned at me. 'I certainly made a mess of it, didn't I?'

'Yes.' I saw a dark bruise on his temple. 'Was that where you fell?'

'I didn't fall. I was pushed. Eben tried to kill me.'

His words shocked me so much that I stumbled and trod on his foot. 'I'm sorry,' I muttered. 'I – I want to sit down.'

'We'll go outside for a moment. You've gone as white as a sheet.'

He had a tight hold on my arm. Short of making a scene, I could do nothing but acquiesce as he strode from the room, taking me with him. I caught sight of Joe with my drink, but he didn't see me. Once we were outside in the cool air, I voiced my protest.

'Don't you ever ask, Nathan? Do you always do just what you want?'

'I was afraid you might faint.'

'Is it surprising after what you said?'

'I'm sorry. It was stupid, springing it on you like that.'

165

'Joe said the stories weren't true. He said Eben was trying to hold you on the roof.'

'Joe wasn't there. He believes my uncle's story. Believe me, Betty. Eben wanted to kill me.'

'But why? Was it because — because of Edward?'

'Partly. Deep down it was probably an urge for revenge, but there was more . . .' Nathan paused, his face grim. I waited, instinctively holding my tongue.

'I'd remembered the dogs,' Nathan said, the words forming slowly. 'In the rush we'd forgotten them. I knew the fens were flooding but I thought I had time. I had to try. I couldn't just let them drown. But when I got there I saw Eben was before me . . .'

Nathan's eyes glittered in the moonlight and a chill ran through me. I could hardly breathe as I waited for him to go on.

'He had a rifle in his hand. He had shot them all. Every last one of them.'

'Oh no!' I cried involuntarily. 'Why? Why would he do that?'

'They were bred to fight. He wanted to keep his secret. If he'd brought them up to the village . . .'

'Everyone would have known.' I stared at Nathan. 'That's vile!'

'Yes.' His mouth thinned. 'I just went for him, Betty. I wanted to thrash him. I've put up with his insults for years — well, I owed him something, but not any more. That's over.'

'But the flood — I don't understand?'

'We were so angry, fighting so bitterly, we didn't see it coming. Besides, it was so sudden. There was a terrific roaring and then the water came towards us like a great wall. We scrambled up on the roof of the shed and hung on. When the water hit, I thought the whole building would collapse. I don't know how it stood up to the force . . .'

'I've heard that houses crumbled when struck by the full force of the water.'

166

'Maybe we were just lucky. Anyway, we clung on all that day and through the night. In the morning the boat came.'

'But what happened then?'

'I think Eben panicked. He was afraid that I would tell Mary what he'd done.'

'And will you?'

'You don't think much of me, do you, Betty?'

'I'm sorry. What will you do now?'

'I can't stay here. I'll never live at The Willows again – even if it's still standing.'

'It's still intact at the moment. Joe's been back to look.'

'Well, I'm not going back. I won't accuse Eben in public, but I've finished with him.'

'What about Frances?'

'I'll see her before I leave.'

'She's going to be upset.'

'I know.' He hesitated, then, 'Will you come with me, Betty?'

'Come with you?' I looked up at him.

'You can trust me. I give you my word.'

Inside the hall they were playing Glenn Miller's 'String of Pearls'. Joe would be looking for me. I hesitated a moment longer, then I nodded. 'Yes, I'll come, but now I'm going back inside. Joe brought me to this dance and he'll take me home.'

Nathan smiled oddly. 'I'm going anyway. I only came because your mother said you were here.'

'You went to the cottage?' As he walked away, I called after him. 'Why? Why, Nathan?'

He turned and glanced back, that smile still on his lips. 'I had to make sure you were all right,' he said.

I shook my head, disbelieving, and he walked on. Shivering, suddenly aware of a cold breeze, I turned and went inside.

Chapter Seven

Nathan was wearing a dark blue blazer, grey flannels and an open-necked white shirt with a yellow silk cravat when he came to fetch me the next day, and his skin smelt of Palmolive shaving soap. He waited outside for me, leaning across to open the car door without saying anything. His expression was grim as he drove to Ely, and I thought he must be concerned about telling Frances he was leaving.

'She'll understand,' I said. 'She'll be upset, but she'll understand.'

'Perhaps.' He frowned. 'As long as she doesn't get to hear about the fight with Eben.'

'She won't hear of it from me.'

Nathan nodded. 'She feels her father hates her, Betty. If she knew it was because of him that I . . .'

'Yes, I know. I shan't tell her, and I'm sure Mrs Crawley won't.'

'I just don't want her to mope,' he said. 'She's had a rotten life one way and another. Mary almost died having her, and Eben has never forgiven her for not being a son. I've tried to make up for . . . Well, she has you now.'

'Yes, she has me.' I smiled at him. 'Don't worry.'

Nathan stopped the car outside a house in St Mary's Street and I got out. As he was locking the door, Frances rushed out to hug us both on the pavement, her eyes glowing with excitement.

'I saw you arrive,' she said. 'I'm so pleased you've come, Nathan – and you, Betty. Uncle Henry says there's a room in the attic you can have. I was going to write to you, but there's no need now. You can fetch your things when Nathan takes you home and come back tomorrow.'

'Slow down, Frances,' Nathan said. 'Give Betty time to think. She might not be able to join you at a moment's notice.'

'Just give me the chance,' I said as Frances drew us inside the narrow hallway. 'I've been envying you being in Ely, Frances. Have you been going to the cinema?'

'Yes, twice,' she said, laughing. 'I saw *Till The Clouds Roll By* and *The Fleet's In* – Dorothy Lamour was in that. I'll tell you all about it later.'

I was trying to listen to Frances and take in my surroundings at the same time. The front door of Henry Crawley's house was painted black with two panels of stained glass either side of the central wooden strut. The light that came through had a yellowish tinge which made the blue striped wallpaper look as though it had green patches. There was a carved hardwood stand to one side of the hall, with a well for walking sticks and umbrellas, hooks for coats and a square mirror in the middle. I caught sight of our faces as we passed it. Frances looked flushed with excitement; I was the same as usual, but Nathan looked stern.

The sitting-room into which Frances led us was a surprise. I'd expected the same dull over-stuffed furniture as at The Willows, but the chairs had bright, chintz, loose covers that matched the curtains and the carpet was pale green. It gave the house a modern look that was both welcoming and comfortable.

'Mother and Uncle Henry are out,' Frances said. 'I had a headache or I would have gone with Mother. I'm glad I didn't now.'

'You mean you're on your own?' Nathan asked, frowning.

'Apart from Mrs Maggs, yes.' Frances laughed as his brows went up. 'Mrs Maggs is a cat. Don't look so shocked. I can look after myself.'

'Doesn't your uncle have any servants?'

Frances looked at me. 'A woman comes in twice a week and cleans. Uncle Henry does all his own cooking, Betty. He says he can manage and he's very good at it.' She laughed again, sounding so much brighter than her normal self that I was surprised. 'Mother tried to help out in the kitchen but he chased her out, and said that if she wasn't satisfied with his cooking, he would take us out to eat.'

Nathan sat down in one of the easy chairs by the fireplace, and Frances perched on the arm; I chose a hard chair by a writing table near the window. I could see the main road and the church, also the half-timbered house where Oliver Cromwell had once lived. Beyond the green was the cathedral.

'Have you been into the cathedral yet?' I asked Frances.

'Yes, for a few minutes,' she said. 'Uncle Henry bought me a bicycle; I've been down to the river and in the park behind where the monastery used to be.'

'And what does Mary say to all this?' Nathan asked.

'She was frightened I might fall off,' Frances replied carelessly, 'but Uncle Henry convinced her that I was perfectly safe. He took me into the Palace Green and taught me to ride.'

Somehow I was sure that Nathan didn't just mean the bicycle. Mary had always wrapped her daughter in cotton wool, she must be finding it difficult to adjust. Frances had suddenly been given a freedom she had never known before, and I thought it had worked a tiny miracle. She looked so well and so much happier. As she chattered on and on, Nathan seemed to relax. He sat quietly, listening to us but not saying much. We must have been talking for nearly an hour when he cleared his throat and stood up. He leaned against the mantelpiece.

'I'm glad you're having such a good time, Frances,' he said. 'You won't miss me, brat.'

'Are you going away?' She stared at him, her smile

fading. 'I know you can't do much on the farm until the flood goes down – but you are coming back?'

'No,' he said quietly. 'Not to the farm anyway. Eben and I talked it over. He's letting me go.'

Her eyes were bright with tears. 'You mean you had a quarrel,' she cried bitterly. 'Why does everyone treat me as if I were a child? I heard Mother and Uncle Henry talking. I know what happened, Nathan.'

Nathan was silent for a moment. 'Then you know I can't go back, even for you . . .'

Frances clenched her hands into tight fists. She looked as if she was about to burst into tears, then the door of the sitting-room opened and Henry Crawley walked in.

'Well, isn't this nice? I thought it might be you, Nathan – and you've brought Betty to see us.' He crossed the room to embrace Frances, giving her a warm hug. 'How's my favourite girl then? That nasty headache all gone?'

Frances gave a little shudder and blinked. A single tear trickled down her cheek. 'Nathan's going away, Uncle Henry. I shan't see him any more.'

'Of course you will,' Henry Crawley said, chucking her under the chin. 'He can stay with me sometimes and you can come too, puss.' Turning to Nathan he nodded his approval. 'It's about time you made the break, my boy. In my opinion you should never have gone back there after the war. If you need money to tide you over, you can rely on me.'

'I have enough for the moment.' Nathan smiled gratefully. 'Eben has refused to release my father's trust, but he'll have to give me an allowance. Anyway, a friend of mine offered me a job when I was last in London.'

'Father's so cruel,' Frances said suddenly, her eyes very bright. 'It's all his fault. I hate him!'

'That's enough of that, my girl,' Henry said. 'Eben's quarrel is with Nathan, and nothing to do with you.'

'Uncle Henry is right,' Nathan said, opening his arms to her. 'Come and give me a kiss and tell me you still love me.'

'You know I do!'

Frances ran to him and he embraced her, growling and pretending to bite chunks out of her neck. The moment of danger had passed. She was laughing and pouting up at him.

'You will write to me? You promise faithfully?'

'Cross my heart and hope to die.'

'I don't want you to die. Oh, Nathan, when shall I see you again?' The tears were very close once more as she gazed up at him.

'Perhaps you could meet your cousin if you visit Christabel Blair in the summer,' I said, and then blushed as they all looked at me.

'That's a wonderful idea,' Frances cried. 'Father wouldn't even have to know about it.'

'Eben's not stupid enough to try to prevent you seeing your own cousin,' Henry said. 'Will you stay to tea, Nathan?'

'Well, I should be getting Betty back.' Nathan glanced at me.

'Betty wants to stay.' Frances looked at me pleadingly. 'I want to show her my room – and the room she'll be using.'

'That's a splendid idea,' Uncle Henry replied. 'I'd like a few minutes alone with Nathan – why don't you take your friend upstairs, sweetheart? We'll have tea when you come down.'

Nathan was quiet and thoughtful as he drove back to Sutton that evening. When he stopped the car outside the cottage, I attempted to get out but he caught my arm. I turned to look at him.

'What do you want? I have to go in. Dad will wonder where I've got to.'

'Stay a few minutes, Betty. Please? I shan't see you for months.'

'Are you off tomorrow then?'

'Yes.' He ran his fingers through his thick hair. I

thought he looked tired. 'Frances seemed well, didn't she? It's doing her good being with Uncle Henry.'

'Yes. She was full of it when we went upstairs. He spoils her and she loves it.'

'Who wouldn't after the life she's had?' He frowned as I looked at him. 'Henry's a good man. She'll be all right with him. It's when she has to go back to the farm that I'm worried about.'

'I'll look after her.'

'I know.' He laughed ruefully. 'She's a spoilt brat and I'm worrying for nothing – but she means a lot to me.'

'Yes, I know.'

He looked at me seriously. 'Are you still angry about that night in the barn?'

'No – nothing happened. Besides, you were drunk.'

'Yes.' His mouth quirked. 'Too drunk as it turned out. I've regretted that, Betty.'

I felt hot as I saw the look in his eyes. 'I'd better go.'

'Perhaps you had.' He leant towards me, brushing his lips softly over mine. 'Next time I won't be too drunk, kid. I promise you that.'

That wicked glint was back. I got out of the car hastily, my heart thumping. Nathan was laughing as he drove away.

I caught the early bus into Ely the next day. Frances was waiting for me, watching from the upstairs window. She looked flushed as if she had a slight fever.

'I've been coughing all night,' she said. 'Mother says I've got to stay indoors for a few days in case I'm catching a chill. She got quite cross with Uncle Henry and they had a tiff.'

'Well, you've been rushing around on that bike, haven't you?'

'It's so much fun. It makes me feel alive and – and normal. Shut up in my room at The Willows I used to imagine horrible things.'

'Like what?'

173

'Oh, I don't know.' She shrugged. 'Sometimes I thought that I should have to stay there for the rest of my life. I – I thought . . .' she faltered.

'Go on,' I said. 'Tell me.'

'I thought it was a punishment,' she said slowly. 'I thought my parents were angry with me because I was alive and Edward was dead.'

'That's awful! Oh, Frances, how frightened you must have been.'

She stared at me, and I could see fear in her eyes, then it vanished. 'Well, it's all different now.' She was laughing again. 'Uncle Henry's going to lend you his bike so that we can go out together as soon as I'm better. What do you think of that?'

Frances's fever vanished overnight and she was full of energy, eager to make the most of her time in Ely. Whenever anyone said that the flood waters were beginning to go down, she pulled a face.

'I wish we never had to go back to the farm,' she said to me over and over again. 'I wish I could run away to London like Nathan.'

'Perhaps you will one day. Anyway, we can't go back yet. Even when the flood goes down, they'll have to make sure the house foundations are safe, and then there'll be endless clearing up to do. People say most of the houses are overrun with rats. It's a good thing your father moved so much stuff. It will be weeks yet, Frances. Your mother won't take you back until it's all done.'

'I don't care if we have to stay here forever!' Frances cried. 'Come on, Betty, let's cycle down to the river and watch the boats. I'd love to go out in a punt, wouldn't you?'

'No,' I said quickly. 'I'd be afraid of falling in. I can't swim and nor can you. We can take some bread for the swans, though. I wonder if the cygnets have grown since last week?'

'Let's go and see,' she said. 'The sun's shining and it's really warm out.'

174

I awoke sweating with fear. I'd been dreaming – a terrible dream that haunted me even though I was now awake. I'd been locked in a little room with no windows and a thick steel door. I kept beating at the door, crying and begging to be let out, but no one would answer me. All around me I could hear people crying and screaming and I knew I was in prison.

'But I didn't do it,' I whispered. 'I didn't kill Edward. Let me out . . . Please let me out . . .'

I switched on the bedside lamp to be certain that I was in Henry Crawley's little attic room, feeling relieved as I saw the familiar things. It must have been the cheese I'd had for supper.

But I knew why I had dreamed like that. I'd been remembering what Frances had told me. How awful it must have been for her, thinking that she was being punished because she was alive and her brother was dead. It didn't surprise me that she felt so much resentment against her father.

The days went by too quickly for us. We took our bikes out almost every fine day, peddling up and down Forehill as we headed for the quayside. On market days the roads were busy with traffic, but at other times the little lanes that led to and from the river were so quiet that you could hear the droning of bees. My memories of that halcyon period would always be of sunlit afternoons spent lazing by the river, walks up Lover's Lane in search of scented purple violets and the deep yellow of buttercups that we made into chains to hang around our necks. But the most vivid memory was of Frances laughing. She was transformed from the sulky, sullen girl I had first known into one of the sweetest friends anyone could ever have.

There were also the trips to the cinema on wet days. We sat side by side munching sweets or broken biscuits that we purchased from a shop on the hill, drinking in the magical scenes that came to life for us on the big silver

175

screen. We saw *Gone With The Wind* at the Rex Cinema, both of us weeping buckets as Scarlett lifted her beautiful face to the camera and said, 'I'll go back to Tara . . . I'll think of a way to get him back . . .' And we saw Larry Parks as Al Jolson in *The Jolson Story*, singing to his Mammy . . .

It was a wonderful, happy time for us both, but I had always known that eventually it must end.

'I don't want to go.' Frances stared at her mother sullenly. 'Why can't I stay here? I hate it at the farm.'

Mary Crawley frowned. 'The farm is your home, Frances. You should be pleased to be going home. Besides, we've imposed on your Uncle Henry for far too long already.'

'Uncle Henry doesn't want me to go.' Frances turned imploring eyes on him. 'Tell her you want me to stay here! Please tell her!'

Henry Crawley looked unhappy. 'You shouldn't speak to your mother like that,' he said chidingly. 'It's not that I want you to go, puss. You can come again . . .'

'When?' she demanded, her eyes bright. 'When can I come back?'

'When your mother — and father — say you can.'

'If Father has any say in it that will be never.'

Frances looked sulky. Henry Crawley was obviously uncomfortable. He was a kindly man who had opened his house to his brother's wife and child, but he was also a bachelor and his life must have been turned upside down for the past month or two. He was probably longing for a little peace.

'It's May now,' I said to Frances. 'You won't have to stay in the house. We can ride your bike in the droves — and in a couple of months you'll be going to London to visit Christabel.'

She stared at me and the glitter faded from her eyes. 'Yes, I shall,' she said. 'Maybe it won't be so bad . . .'

*

176

Frances was depressed and fretful after we moved back to the farm. Mary had had her room freshly decorated, though much of the rest of the house was still bearing signs of the water from the floods.

'We're lucky it's as good as it is,' Mrs Jackson said to me when I remarked on the stains I saw on rugs, carpets and chair legs. 'Some folk lost everything. What the water didn't destroy, the rats did.'

'At least the best stuff was saved,' I said. 'It's a good thing Mr Crawley moved it all out.'

'Aye, it is that.' She frowned at me. 'So what have you two been up to in Ely without me to keep an eye on you?'

Mrs Jackson had stayed only a few days with her brother Henry, deciding to visit a woman friend in Cornwall she hadn't seen for years. On her return to Cambridgeshire, she had gone straight back to the farm to help with the cleaning up. I laughed as she looked at me suspiciously.

'Nothing that you wouldn't approve of,' I said. 'Mr Henry was very kind to us; he lent me his bike and he paid for Frances and I to go to the pictures twice every week.'

'Henry always was a soft fool,' she said. 'I love the man dearly, but it would drive me mad to live with him for long. Henry's an old woman in the kitchen.'

She gave me a broad wink that set me giggling. 'Oh, you shouldn't,' I said, clutching my sides. 'Mrs Jackson, I think you've been getting in bad ways in Cornwall. What have you been up to?'

She frowned at me. 'Less of your cheek, Betty Cantrel. If you've time on your hands, you get into the parlour and polish the furniture. It's all dull from standing in the barns in Sutton. Give it a good rub, will you?'

I took the tin of Mansion polish and two dusters from the cupboard and went into the dining-room. Every effort had been made to set the room to rights, and there was new paper on the walls, but I could still smell a faint, musty odour of damp. I thought it would be months before it went altogether, even though we opened the windows every day to let the air blow through.

Mrs Jackson was right about the furniture. It was dull from lack of care. I rubbed hard at several chair backs, then I got down on my hands and knees to polish the claw feet of the breakfast table. I was crouched beneath the embroidered cloth that covered the table when I heard raised voices nearby. It was the master and mistress, and they were having a quarrel. I was thrown into a panic – what should I do? Should I let them know I was there or hope that they would go away? I hesitated, and then it was too late. The argument had begun in earnest. If I tried to leave, I should bring their wrath down upon my own head. I stayed perfectly still, hidden, not daring to move.

'This is ridiculous, Eben. You can't refuse to let Nathan have an allowance. The money belongs to him. You have no right to withhold it.'

'As the sole trustee of his father's estate, I have the right to do as I please.'

'No, Eben, that's not so. Besides, if he goes to a solicitor it could mean trouble for you. Supposing someone discovered what you did all those years ago? It would be such a terrible scandal.'

'It was too long ago. No one knows but you, Mary. I've covered my tracks, and I paid the money back. It was merely a loan.' Eben Crawley sounded oddly defensive. 'I was in trouble at the time, I needed that money – and your father refused to lend me a penny.'

'I know you repaid Nathan's money,' Mary said. 'But you had no right to take it. Morally, this farm belongs to Nathan. Without his money you would have been bankrupted like so many others.'

'Nathan wouldn't want the farm if I offered it to him. He hates the fens – and me. He's made that quite clear. Besides, no one will ever know. I bought and sold investments on my nephew's behalf, that's all.'

'You were always good at forging signatures.'

'And you've felt the benefit of it, Mary. No, don't look

178

at me like that. When your father lost most of his money through bad investments, we'd all have been in trouble if it wasn't for me and my little talent. So don't you look down your nose at me.'

'I know you did what you thought was best at the time,' Mary said. 'But you should be grateful that Nathan's money was there. If Henry knew what you'd done . . .'

'Well, he doesn't.'

'You can't hold Edward's death against Nathan for ever. God knows I've grieved enough over it, but it wasn't Nathan's fault. I don't blame him for hating this place. You've made him suffer for Edward's accident over and over again – hanging would have been kinder.'

'I'd hang him if I could. He robbed me of my boy.'

'Edward's gone. You have a daughter. Why don't you show her a little affection sometimes? You've never cared for her the way you did Edward.'

'And why's that?' There was a harsh note in his voice. 'He was born out of love, but you'd turned against me by the time Frances was born. You could hardly bear me near you.'

Crouched beneath the table, I was getting a crick in my neck. I wanted to block my ears or cry out to them to stop, but I was afraid. I'd heard far too much!

'That's not true,' Mary said. 'I almost died when Edward was born. I should never have had Frances. Look how delicate she's always been . . .'

'Don't worry.' His voice was heavy with sarcasm. 'I'm not asking you to share my bed again. I've done with begging. There are other women who don't find it distasteful to give me what you can't – or won't.'

'Do you think I don't know about you and your sluts? And all your other little vices? You needn't have killed those poor dogs. I was always aware of them.' There was the sound of her hand connecting with his cheek and then silence. He was breathing hard and I was terrified of what might happen next.

179

'You've asked for this, Mary,' he said, and his voice was curiously flat. 'I've put up with your coldness for years, but now I've had enough. Yes, there have been other women – and one of them is going to give me a son to inherit the farm.'

'You can't do that – what about Frances?'

'I don't give a damn about Frances. Leave her the money you inherited from your parents.'

'But she should have it all!'

'I paid back the money I borrowed from Nathan's trust and I built up this farm with my own blood and sweat. I'll do what I damn well please with it!'

How much I was learning. Everyone in the village had always taken it for granted that Eben Crawley's money had come through his wife! In reality he'd stolen it from his own brother's son, forging signatures to cover his tracks. I trembled as I realised what it all meant.

'Bring a bastard into this house and I'll leave you.'

'My dear Mary, I couldn't give a tinker's curse what you do.'

'You – you bastard! You'll be sorry for this.'

'I've been sorry for years. Sorry I married you. It was a hell of a price to pay for a roll in the hay.'

'Do you have to be so coarse? But then you always were. You say you paid a price, but I've paid too. I sometimes wonder why I bothered to marry you. It might have been better to have had my child adopted.'

'What are you talking about?'

She laughed bitterly. It was a cruel sound and it made me shiver. I put my hands over my ears, wishing desperately that I had escaped while there was still time. I didn't want to hear all this bitterness.

'You thought Edward was conceived in love – well, he was, Eben, but not with you. Why do you think I suddenly gave in to you when I'd hardly bothered to speak to you before? You came to my father's house, looking at me with your sheep's eyes, begging me for a kind word or a look that you could go home and dream

180

about. Oh, how I despised you for your weakness. I smiled at you that day for one reason and one reason only. I knew I was pregnant, and I knew you wanted a rich wife. It was so easy to fool you – you didn't even know I wasn't a virgin, did you? But I'd made sure that you were just drunk enough . . .'

A queer strangled sound came from his throat. 'You're lying. You bitch! You're lying – you have to be. Edward was mine.'

She laughed again, triumphantly. 'Perhaps, perhaps not. You will never be quite sure, will you? Even if I tell you it was a lie, you'll never be really certain again.'

'I could kill you.'

'Go on then, kill me. You were always a clumsy, coarse brute. You never once made love to me. It was always mauling that I had to endure until you were satisfied. But did you ever stop to wonder if I felt anything? Well, I'll tell you – I hated every second . . .'

I heard a muffled curse, then a crashing sound as he picked up something from the table and threw it across the room. Judging by the noise it made it was a heavy crystal decanter and it splintered into hundreds of pieces.

'Damn you,' he muttered. 'May your soul rot in Hell!'

His heavy footsteps shook the floor and the door slammed after him, then there was silence. I scarcely dared to breathe and I wished the ground would open up beneath me. I could hardly believe I'd heard Mary Crawley say such terrible things. She had always seemed such a calm, good person.

'You can come out now, Betty.'

She knew I was there! She must have known it all the time. Yet she had said all those cruel and bitter things to her husband, knowing that I would hear them. Perhaps it had given her a feeling of security to know that I was there, in case he had attacked her. I felt sick with fright as I crawled out from under the table, my cheeks flushed. I was too scared to look at her as I mumbled an excuse.

'I was polishing, ma'am. I didn't know what to do.'

'Look at me.' Her voice sharpened as I hesitated. 'I said, look at me.'

I raised my eyes to hers. 'I'm sorry, ma'am.'

'Do you make a habit of listening to other people's conversations?'

'No, ma'am. I'm sorry, ma'am.' I stared at the floor, sure that I was about to be dismissed.

'You're an intelligent girl, Betty. You know I can dismiss you without a reference, don't you? You know that would make it difficult for you to find similar work elsewhere?'

'Yes, ma'am.'

'So now you know my secret, Betty.' She looked at me hard. 'Or had your mother already told you what I was once foolish enough to tell her?'

'No, ma'am. She didn't tell me anything – except that you would be a good mistress if I obeyed you.'

Mary nodded, her eyes thoughtful. 'She kept her word then, that's something. Well, Eben knows now so there's no real reason for me to keep you here, is there?'

I stared at her, my eyes wide with fear. 'Are – are you going to send me away?'

She frowned, then shook her head. 'I was angry when Lizzie threatened me, but you've been good for Frances. If I let you stay here, will you swear to be loyal to me? You won't say a word about what Eben did?'

'I swear it, ma'am. I won't tell a soul.'

'And you will tell me what other people say?' She reached out and gripped my wrist, hurting me. 'What have you heard or seen in this house that I should know?'

Her eyes were piercing me. 'I – I don't know what you mean,' I said, but I did. Oh, I did! She wanted me to tell her about her husband and Polly.

'So you refuse to tell me?'

'No, ma'am. I haven't seen anything. On my honour.' Her eyes narrowed. She wasn't sure whether I was lying or not. 'I'm usually with Miss Frances, ma'am, but if I do see anything, I'll come and tell you.'

'Are you giving me your word?'

'Yes, ma'am. I – I've never liked the master much – and Miss Frances is upset because Mr Nathan has gone away.'

A little smile touched her mouth. 'Yes, I know how devoted you are to Frances. Well, Betty, I'll give you the benefit of the doubt this time. I know I don't have to warn you not to repeat a word of what you've heard. If I discover that you have, I shall dismiss you.'

'You won't have to do that, ma'am.'

'You could be useful to me . . . Yes, it could be useful to have a spy in the house. A spy who was on my side. I intend to make Eben pay for his cheating, Betty. A mistress I could tolerate, but a bastard child I shall not. If he tries to bring a bastard into this house it will cost him dearly.'

'Would you really leave him, ma'am?'

She smiled strangely. 'Only if I have to. He owes me and I intend he shall pay.'

A cold chill went through me as I looked at her. At that moment I pitied Eben Crawley.

The breach between the master and mistress was causing friction in the kitchen. Mrs Jackson had had a quarrel with her brother and she was firmly on Mary's side.

'I don't know what the row was about,' she said. 'But I do know Mary's had enough to put up with all these years. When my brother first married her I thought he was a fool. I didn't like her at the start; I thought there was something odd about the way she suddenly took up with him. She'd been courting a gent from London on the sly until . . .' Mrs Jackson became aware of me at the sink. 'Well, the least said about that the better. If you've finished that, Betty, you'd best get back upstairs.'

'I'll be done in a minute,' I said, not wanting to be shut out of the discussion.

'This gent from London,' Joe said. 'Wasn't he married? I remember someone saying something like that once.'

Mrs Jackson nodded significantly. 'Mary was real taken with him. I can't recall his name now.'

'She was always a cold one,' Polly said. 'Don't you tell me she had a lover – she hasn't got it in her.'

'And how would you know, miss?' Mrs Jackson glared at her.

'I just know, that's all. She makes the master miserable, I know that.'

'Do you indeed! You just be careful, my girl. You'll find yourself in trouble if you don't watch out.'

I had known for some time that she had suspected what was going on between Polly and her brother, though it was only through a look I'd intercepted or a smothered curse.

'You don't know anything,' replied Polly, a smile on her lips. 'Things are going to be very different one day soon. You'll sing another tune then.'

'If you mean what I think you mean, I shall walk out of that door pretty quick. Henry might be an old fusspot, but I'd sooner live with him than a serpent.'

'Suit yourself. There's plenty ready to take your place.'

'Not with a slut as mistress of the house.'

It was the first time that Mrs Jackson had spoken out so plainly. Polly gasped, her cheeks going bright red. She got up from the table, picked up a tin of wax polish and rushed from the room.

'You shouldn't have said that,' Joe protested. 'Polly's a good girl. She's had her head turned with promises, that's all.'

'Oh, you men are all the same! Show you a pretty face, and you split your breeches getting it out. You can't wait to . . .'

'Mrs Jackson, Remember Betty is listening.'

'She knows what I mean. With a father like hers she'd have to be a fool not to know – and that's one thing she's not.' Mrs Jackson banged a pot on the stove, chipping the enamel. 'Mary is too good for Eben and that's a fact.'

'Maybe she was too good for any man. Some women were never meant for marriage – if you get my meaning.'

Mrs Jackson sniffed. 'You might be right at that, but she's entitled to some respect in her own house.'

'I'm not condoning what's been going on,' Joe said unhappily. 'But don't be too hard on Polly.'

If they were discussing it so openly, how long would it be before Mrs Crawley found out?

I paid a flying visit to my mother, choosing a time when Frances had gone to bed with one of her headaches. Vera was lying on the sofa when I arrived, eating an apple and listening to 'Have a Go Joe' on the wireless. It was a quiz show with Wilfred Pickles and Mabel at the piano, and Vera was evidently enjoying it. She frowned as I entered, as if I were intruding.

'Shouldn't you be at school?' I asked.

'I've got a cold,' she said, pulling a face at me. 'Besides, I've been helping Mum.'

'It looks like it,' I said, glancing round the cottage. 'Can't you do a bit more, Vera? The windows are filthy and the floor hasn't been scrubbed for ages.'

'Vera has a lot of school work to catch up on,' my mother said. 'She's been away such a lot this last year. Anyway, she's feeling poorly at the moment.'

'Oh well, if you don't care.' I shrugged, annoyed that my mother should defend her. 'Here, Vera, take our Joe up the street and buy him some sweets. A quarter of Dobson's raspberry drops or some fruit gums – and get something for yourself. I want to talk to Mum.'

She went reluctantly, glaring at me. 'You want to talk to Mum so everyone else has to do what you say. Who do you think you are, Lady Muck?'

'Stop quarrelling,' Mum said. 'Do as Betty says, Vera. I'm going to make a cup of tea.'

She filled the kettle and put it on the range. Vera slammed out, causing the windows to rattle in their rotten frames.

'You should make her do more, Mum.'

'I know.' My mother sighed. 'I just can't cope, Betty.

185

Vera isn't like you. She's got a sullen streak in her. And just lately I don't know what's the matter with her. Something seems to be eating at her.' She paused and looked at me. 'So what did you want then?'

'You blackmailed Mary Crawley into giving me that job, didn't you?'

Her cheeks flushed. 'Did she tell you?'

I nodded. 'Blackmail's against the law you know.'

'Has she given you the sack?' My mother looked worried.

'No. She's keeping me on, because I look after Frances so well.'

'Thank goodness for that.' She stared at me. 'I had to do it, Betty. She said no at first – and I couldn't let you go on the land, could I?'

'No,' I said slowly. 'You shouldn't have done it, and I didn't like it at first – but now I'm glad.'

I could sense the storm clouds gathering and the atmosphere was thick with tension. It touched everyone, even Joe. Frances noticed, though she didn't say much. Mr Crawley still ate his meals in the dining-room, but the mistress had all hers carried upstairs to her sitting-room. It made more work for us all, and Mrs Jackson never stopped grumbling.

'Much more of this and I go,' she said. 'Eben never has a civil word to say, and Mary keeps to herself. I'd be better off working as a housekeeper for wages!'

Once when she'd been threatening to leave, I asked Joe if she would really go. He shook his head and grinned. 'I doubt it. She's been here too long. Besides, we know her secrets.'

'What do you mean?'

He shook his head and wouldn't say any more. I was annoyed. It was provoking of him to hint at something and then refuse to tell.

We were peeling potatoes at the sink. Joe's remarks had

made me curious. Recalling the time Mrs Jackson had warned me to beware of gossips, I wondered if she had ever been the victim of cruel tongues, and forgetting to be cautious I asked her.

She looked at me oddly. 'What makes you ask, Betty?'

'I just wondered . . .' She didn't seem angry so I ventured further. 'I was wondering about Mr Jackson . . .'

'He's dead.' She sliced a potato into clean water. 'I'm a widow and have been for fifteen years. There's no mystery about it.'

'Oh, I'm sorry.'

'Forget it. It wasn't a love-match.'

She wasn't going to tell me any more, but perhaps that was best. It was sometimes uncomfortable to know too many secrets.

A month had passed since I heard the quarrel between Eben and Mary. I was making the bed in Mr Crawley's room when I noticed a handkerchief caught in the sheets. Picking it up, I saw the name clearly embroidered in one corner. It was the handkerchief I had made for Polly that first Christmas. She had been with him, here in the house – in his own bed! I stared at it in dismay, then tucked it into my apron pocket.

'What have you found, Betty?'

I jumped guiltily at the sound of Mary Crawley's voice. I'd never known her to come to the bedrooms while we were cleaning them before. Why had she come now? It could not have been at a worse moment.

'Just a handkerchief, ma'am. It's dirty. I was going to put it in the wash.'

'Show me.' She held out her hand. 'Give it to me.'

I felt sick as I looked at her. Her bright eyes were boring into me, and I knew there was no way I could deceive her. She would know if I tried to lie. If I gave her the handkerchief I should betray Polly, but if I disobeyed she would dismiss me instantly. I knew that I wanted to stay at The Willows, and I hated myself as I put my hand into my apron pocket.

'I was going to tell you,' I lied. She knew I was lying but she only nodded.

'Of course.' She glanced at the handkerchief and her mouth tightened. She didn't seem shocked or surprised. 'You will not speak of this to anyone, do you understand?'

'Yes, ma'am.'

'Very well, you may go.'

There was an ache in my chest as I left the room. I had betrayed Polly to save myself. I felt like Judas. The shame lodged in my chest like a hard lump. I could scarcely look at Polly when we met in the kitchen a few minutes later. She smiled at me and started to talk about my family, and I realised that she had been more friendly again recently.

'I saw your Vera in the village the other day,' she said. 'She's getting to be a fine girl. She was asking if there was a chance of a job here for her.'

'Vera thinks being at The Willows is second only to being in Heaven.' I sounded odd and Polly looked surprised. 'She can't wait to leave home and get a job. I think she's afraid there'll be more to do at home when Mum gets the new baby.'

'Another baby? Your mother nearly died the last time. I thought the doctor said there wasn't to be another?'

'He did – it's Dad's fault.'

'Maybe she'll be better this time. If she takes it easy.' Polly smiled again. 'You tell your Vera to look after her.'

I wished Polly wouldn't be so friendly, so concerned. I felt my guilt burning inside me every time I looked at her. She seemed so happy, as though something was making her just bubble over with joy. My nerves were on edge and I jumped every time the door opened, thinking that the summons for Polly must come at any moment.

When bedtime came and nothing had happened, I gave a sigh of relief. Maybe Mary wasn't going to dismiss her after all.

I woke with a start to see Polly standing in the doorway.

188

Her face looked pinched and sallow, and she seemed to be in a state of shock. I jumped out of bed and ran to her, taking her shaking hand to lead her to the bed. She sat down on the edge, her eyes dazed.

'She came to the room while we were . . .' A shudder ran through her. 'She knows . . . She has known for a long time . . .'

'What are you talking about Polly?'

'She even knows about the baby. I wasn't sure myself until the last couple of days so how . . .' Polly was babbling on as if talking to herself. 'She said she'll ruin him, and me, if I have the baby. She could do it, too.'

'How could she ruin him, Polly? It would cause a scandal, but he's not a man to care about that.'

'I don't rightly know.' Polly shook her head, trying to clear her thoughts. 'He did something bad once. Forged a signature on some documents. He could go to prison. She has kept some of the evidence . . .'

If Mary had kept documents that proved Eben had stolen from his nephew's estate, she had a powerful hold over him. Eben could not have known that she had anything which could prove his guilt.

'Surely she wouldn't,' I said. 'She couldn't do that to her own husband.'

'She will if he brings a bastard into the house.' Polly stared at me wildly. 'She swore it – and I believe her.'

I had heard Mary tell Eben that he would be sorry. She had only been waiting for proof – and I'd given it to her!

'Polly,' I said, 'I'm so sorry.'

She stared at me blindly. 'He promised me it would be all right,' she said in a tone of bewilderment. 'He said that he would look after me if I gave him a son. He said it wouldn't matter what folk said. She would leave him and I'd be as good as his wife.'

'What are you going to do?'

'I don't know. I can't go home, my father would kill me.' She stared at me, fear in her eyes. 'She said I'm to have my wages and go – or a thousand pounds if I get rid of the baby. I'm scared, Betty . . .'

'The master wouldn't let you get rid of his child. He'll stand by you.'

'You don't know the worst of it.' Polly caught back a sob. 'She says she'll give him a child if I . . . He still wants her, Betty.' Polly gripped my arm. 'He said that he hated her. He vowed nothing would make him go back to her bed – but he lied. He still loves her. I saw it in his face when she gave him her ultimatum. He still wants her . . .'

How could any man still want a woman who had done what Mary had? He had sworn he was done with begging, now it seemed he was prepared to begin again. He would stand by and see Polly driven from the house. Worse still, he would allow his child to be murdered in its mother's womb! I had thought of Mary Crawley as a saint, but now I was not sure who was the saint and who the sinner.

'You can't kill your own child, Polly.'

'I can't face being poor all my life. I'd rather die than live the way your Mum does.'

'Why don't you ask Joe for help? He likes you – he might marry you.'

'He'd have to leave his job. She wouldn't have me in the house. She hates me – and my child. She wants it dead.'

I felt the horror and sickness swirling in my mind. 'You mustn't give in to her, Polly. Let me talk to Joe.'

Her mouth hardened. 'I'm going to take her money. I don't want Eben's brat. I only agreed to please him.' Her eyes were dark with pain. 'Everyone thinks I'm a slut, but I loved him. I really loved him. I thought he loved me . . .'

Pity for her brought a lump to my throat. She had never really stood a chance against Mary Crawley. The mistress was clever and ruthless, while Polly was just a pretty, ordinary girl. She had behaved badly, but now she would pay for it, while the master – the master would get what he had wanted all the time.

I felt sick and wretched as I watched Polly pack her

190

bags. It was too much for me and I began to cry. Polly looked surprised, then she put her arm about my shoulders.

'I've never seen you cry, Betty. Not even when your Mum was bad. Bless you for caring, but don't take on so. I'll get over it. I'll take her money and I'll – I'll go to London. I've always wanted to get away from the fens and now's my chance.'

'Oh, Polly,' I cried. 'Polly, please don't do it.' I was overcome with grief and guilt. 'Why won't you tell Joe? I know he would help you.'

She laughed harshly. 'I'd almost rather be dead. No, Betty, in future I'm going to make men pay for what Eben Crawley did to me. Don't you worry, Betty. I'll make out. I'll be just fine . . .'

I watched until the car was out of sight, then I turned to go in. I'd reasoned with Polly up until the last minute, but she was set on going. She had the first half of what Mary had promised her, and she would get the rest from a lawyer in London when it was all over. I was afraid she would regret her decision, but she wouldn't listen to me.

'I'll write sometimes,' she'd promised. 'You take care of yourself now, Betty.'

Mrs Jackson was at the sink washing dishes when I went in. She was angry. 'How we're to manage I don't know. Going off like that without a word to anyone. She was always selfish!'

'It wasn't Polly's fault . . .' I broke off as the door opened and Mary Crawley came in.

'I want to talk to you, Betty. Please come to the sitting-room when you've taken Frances her breakfast.'

'And I want a word with you, Mary,' Mrs Jackson said. 'I can't manage this house alone, and that's the truth.'

'No, of course not, Hilda. I wouldn't expect you to. Betty will continue to help you – and perhaps the woman who came in at Christmas . . .'

'Sarah Robinson? She has three small children. She could only work part time.'

191

'That should be enough. I don't want anyone to live in in future. Except you and Betty.' She glanced at me. 'Don't forget I want to speak to you, Betty.'

She went out, leaving Mrs Jackson staring after her in annoyance. 'Well! Trust Mary to think Polly can be replaced by a woman who comes in for a few hours. That means more work for me and you, my girl.'

'I don't mind. If I get up an hour earlier I can finish the downstairs rooms before breakfast.'

'You'll have to. Even if Sarah comes in, it won't make up for Polly. Whatever else she was, she was a good worker. We're going to miss her.'

'Yes,' I said sadly. 'We're going to miss her.'

Frances was curious about Polly leaving so suddenly. 'What happened?' she asked, when I took in her tray. 'There's been a row, hasn't there?'

'How do you know?'

'I heard noises – a woman shouting and doors banging.'

'Then you heard more than me.'

'So you don't know what's going on then?'

'Polly has upset your mother. I don't know why.'

Her eyes narrowed. 'Don't lie to me. I always know when you're lying. Polly was Father's whore, wasn't she?'

'You shouldn't use words like that.'

'It's in the Bible. Anyway, I know it's true. Nathan told me when I asked him ages ago. He said Polly was a whore. He said she would lift her skirts for any man . . .'

I knew it was likely that Polly had let Nathan make love to her when he bought her the pendant, but that didn't give him the right to call her names.

'Polly told me she was in love with your father.'

'So you do know what's going on.' She smiled triumphantly. 'I'm right. I know I am so don't try and deny it.'

'I know she's been dismissed for carrying on with the master, but she's not a whore.'

192

'Isn't she?' Frances screwed up her nose. 'You seem as if you feel sorry for her. What about my mother?'

What could I say? I cared for Frances too much to fling the truth at her.

'Well, whatever she was, she's gone, and it's going to mean more work for me. I must go now. Your mother wants to talk to me.'

'You haven't done anything wrong, have you?'

'Not that I know of. Maybe I forgot to dust under the beds again.'

'Oh, Betty!' Frances laughed and I left before she could ask more questions.

I was nervous as I hurried to Mary's room. I'd made a joke of it to Frances, but I wasn't sure what to expect – she might be going to dismiss me, too!

'Come in, Betty.' Mary smiled as I hovered in the doorway. 'I shan't eat you. Shut the door behind you, please.'

'Yes, ma'am. Have I done something wrong?'

'I don't know – have you?' She shook her head. 'No, I won't tease you. How long have you been with us now?'

'Almost eighteen months.'

'That long? How time flies.' Her eyes went over me. 'You've been loyal to me and to my daughter. I want you to go on being loyal. Do you understand me?'

'Yes, ma'am. I haven't said anything about what I heard.'

'If you had, I should have dismissed you.' Her fingers strayed to the brooch at her throat. 'I'm increasing your wages to five pounds a week.'

I stared at her. I was due for a raise – but she was doubling the amount she'd first paid me. 'I – I'm very grateful.'

She smiled slightly. 'From what I've heard, you give most of your money to your mother. Keep some for yourself in future and buy some new clothes. You'll need to dress properly if you're to accompany Frances to London.'

She couldn't have promised me anything I wanted more. 'I – I should like that.'

'I thought you might.' She made a dismissive gesture. 'I'm sure you've lots to do.'

I felt dazed as I left. The increase in wages was far too much. I was being paid to keep her secrets – but more than that was the chance to go to London. It would be a wonderful adventure; a chance to see something of the world . . . As I walked downstairs, I realised there was something more. I should be staying in the Blairs' house. I should see James Blair again . . . James Blair . . . A little smile curved my lips and I knew that it was what I'd secretly hoped for.

Mary took her daughter to an expensive shop in Cambridge to buy her new clothes for the London visit. Frances came home with three pretty patterned Viyella dresses, a full circle white cotton skirt and a matching jacket with a nipped-in waist, and several rayon blouses. She was having some more dresses made up from the material her mother had been hoarding from before the war. She also had two pairs of fashionable Portland shoes with three-inch heels.

I spent all my own clothing coupons and Mum's and the whole of my extra money for the first month on two cotton and rayon frocks, a wool-mixture coat, cotton gloves and a pair of Barratt shoes. I bought the dresses from the market, and they looked cheap beside Frances's but I'd never felt so smart. I was very excited about it all and on tenterhooks lest Mary Crawley should change her mind.

Two days before we were due to leave for London, Mrs Crawley sent for me. My heart was pounding wildly as I hurried to her sitting-room. If she said I couldn't go now, I would just die!

She smiled at me as I went in. 'I just wanted to make sure that you have all you need for this trip to London, Betty.'

'Yes, thank you,' I said, sighing with relief. 'I think I have everything.'

'Gloves, shoes – and a hat?'

'Yes, ma'am.'

'Good.' She nodded approvingly. 'You will need money for your expenses. I think this should cover it.' She held out three five-pound notes.

As I took the money from her, the cuff of her sleeve fell back and I caught sight of a purple bruise on the soft underside of her wrist. She saw me staring and pulled the cuff down, an odd expression in her eyes.

'Did Mr Crawley do that?' I asked.

'Don't concern yourself,' she said. 'He hasn't really hurt me, nor will he. Say nothing of this to Frances – or Nathan, if you should see him.'

Her husband was taking his revenge on her for what she had done. 'No, ma'am,' I said. I hesitated, then, 'Why do you let him treat you like that? You could ruin him if you told Mr Nathan what he'd done.'

'And myself with him? I knew what was going on, but I did nothing about it.' She laughed harshly. 'Polly might have believed I would do it, but Eben never did. He has what he wants now, and so do I.'

'But you hate him – don't you?'

'I despise him. Hate is a strong emotion. To hate you must feel deeply. Eben has never touched the citadel within me.' She smiled slightly, as if at some secret triumph. 'He understands that, Betty, that's why he's sometimes driven to physical violence. He wants to break me – yet he would never dare to go too far.'

'If a man hit me, I should hit him back.'

A quiver of amusement went through her. 'Yes, I think you would. Woe betide the man who betrays you! Now then, we shall discuss this visit to the Blairs. Frances has never been away from her home without me before. I'm relying on you to take great care of her. Don't let her catch cold, and see that she doesn't overtire herself.'

'Yes, Mrs Crawley, I understand.'

As I went out, I was thinking about the way Eben Crawley ill-treated his wife. Nathan was in London. He'd promised to visit us at the Blairs' house and we were sure to see him. I wondered if I ought to tell him what was going on at the farm – but if I did he would want to know why, and I'd given my word that I wouldn't tell what I knew. After all, Eben had repaid the money, and it wasn't really any of my business . . .

Polly's brother George paid a surprise visit to the farm. I thought he'd come for a chat with Joe, but it was me he wanted to see. I asked him about his wife, who was expecting her first child, and then waited for him to tell me what was on his mind.

'It wasn't like Polly to go off without telling me,' he said. 'Do you know why she did it? I know you two got on well. I thought she might have confided in you?'

I shook my head. 'I think she just wanted a change,' I said, feeling wretched as I lied to him. Polly had warned me not to tell him the truth because of his temper. I think she thought he might have a go at Eben if he suspected what had been going on. 'I'm sure she'll write to you when she's settled down.'

'Perhaps.' He scratched his head. 'She didn't say anything about Nathan Crawley?'

'No.' I looked at him, happy to be truthful. 'I think he was annoying her once, but that was over ages ago.'

'Thanks, Betty.' He looked relieved. 'I'd best be off now.' He reached the kitchen door and then looked back. 'I saw your Vera with that Jarrold boy again. People are beginning to talk about her.' He looked sheepish. 'I just thought you should know.'

I nodded grimly. 'Thank you, George. I shall have to sort her out myself. My mother's not well enough – and you know what Dad is.'

He smiled awkwardly. 'You didn't mind me saying?'

'I'm grateful to you. Vera's going to get a shock when she comes out of school today!'

I borrowed Frances's bicycle and peddled furiously through the droves. I was very angry. Vera was still a child, far too young to be getting herself a reputation for going with boys. Especially that Zac Jarrold!

I was waiting outside the school gates when Vera came out with a crowd of her friends. She gave me a scared look, her face pale.

'What's the matter?' she asked. 'Is something wrong with Mum?'

'No more than usual,' I said coldly, taking hold of her arm. 'And she'd be better if you did your fair share of the chores. I want a word with you, young lady.'

'I've promised Jilly I'll go to her house,' Vera said resentfully. 'We're going to listen to the wireless.'

'You're coming home with me,' I said firmly. 'I'm going away for a while, and before I do I want you to promise me you won't have anything to do with that boy.'

'What boy?' she asked, her eyes sly. 'I don't know what you're talking about.'

I stared at my sister, feeling suddenly that I didn't really know her. I'd kept a picture in my mind of a rather skinny kid who sulked now and then but was decent and honest in her heart. Now I wasn't so sure.

'Don't lie to me, Vera,' I said. 'You've been seen with Zac Jarrold. He's bad news. You would be a fool to trust him.'

There was a flash of anger in her eyes. 'You're only jealous because he likes me better than you.'

'That's not true, and you know it. He asked me out once but I turned him down. He's probably using you to get back at me.'

'You would think that,' she said bitterly. 'You think the whole world revolves around you, don't you? Just because you are the eldest. You're going to London; you've got new clothes and money to spend on yourself – what about me? I have to stay here and watch Dad get drunk every night. Why shouldn't I have a little fun with

Zac? He's the only one who ever gives me any affection . . .'

'Vera, you haven't let him – you wouldn't do anything silly?'

She stared at me, tears in her eyes. 'You don't know anything,' she said. 'It was all right for you – you got away. You don't know what I . . .' She brushed the tears from her eyes defiantly. 'Don't preach to me, Betty. You're not one of us any more.'

I let go of her arm and she started to run after her friends, leaving me too shocked to stop her.

Joe drove us to the station in Ely. He bought our tickets, saw our luggage safely stowed and found us a carriage that was already occupied by a friendly matron who was going all the way to London to visit her daughter.

'You'll be all right now,' he said, smiling at us. 'Have a good time, both of you.'

Frances had already settled herself in the seat by the window. I stood on the platform with Joe, taking longer over my goodbyes.

'I'll send you a postcard, Joseph,' I said.

'You do that, lass.' His smile was warm but tinged with a hint of regret. 'Enjoy yourself – but don't forget us, will you?'

'Of course not,' I said. The guard was waving his flag and the station master had begun to close the carriage doors. 'I'd better go now, Joseph.'

'Do come on, Betty,' Frances commanded. 'Or the train will go without you.'

There was no fear of that, but I got in and Joe closed the door. I waved to him as the train began to move.

'Did you bring my pills?' Frances looked at me. 'We haven't forgotten anything, have we?'

'I checked everything,' I said. 'Don't worry, it's all packed.'

'Is this your first trip to London?' The friendly women smiled at us. 'I go up once a month to see my daughter. I'll

198

show you where to find a taxi or the buses when we get there if you like.'

'We're being met by friends,' Frances said grandly.

I thought she was a little rude, but it didn't seem to deter our companion. She continued to chatter throughout the journey.

That didn't stop either Frances or me enjoying the scenery, nor me from indulging in my day-dreams. I was excited and nervous about visiting London for the first time, but I was also concerned about my family, what with Mum so tired and Vera behaving badly. I couldn't tell my mother what I thought was going on, it would worry her too much, and I didn't want to risk her having yet another miscarriage. My father's remedy would be to take his belt to her, and I didn't want Vera to be hurt.

It was a problem, but for the moment I could do nothing about it. I decided to put it all out of my mind. This was my chance to learn something of life outside a small fen village, and I was looking forward to exploring the city. I hoped I would be able to see some of the musical shows that I'd heard about, and there were lots of new films that wouldn't come to Ely for months.

A surge of excitement went through me as I leaned forward to get a better view of the towns we passed. I was going to London!

PART TWO

Chapter Eight

Another day of waiting is nearly over . . . Laurence, my lawyer, has been to see me again today and tried, once more, to persuade me to appeal against my sentence.

As soon as he came in, I sensed his excitement. I sat down at the table facing him, resentful at being brought back to the present and reality.

'I've had a letter from a friend of yours,' he said, waving a white envelope at me. 'She says she has new evidence that will help you.'

'You've had a letter from Frances?' My head went up sharply.

He took out the letter and glanced at the signature. 'It's from a Mrs Kingston,' he said.

'I don't know anyone of that name – may I see it please?'

He gave me the letter. Glancing at the handwriting, a little flicker of surprise went through me. I knew who this was, but the name . . . I looked at the impressive printed heading: *Mrs Charles Kingston*. So, she has found happiness. I smiled as I realised whom she had married, but in an instant my smile vanished. She is happy now, but if her new name were linked with that of a convicted murderess, she could lose everything.

Swiftly, I tore the letter to shreds.

'What are you doing?' Laurence cried. 'I need that for the appeal.'

'I don't want you to appeal,' I cried. 'Just go away. Leave me alone! Leave me to my memories . . .'

In the warm summer that followed the worst winter on record for years, London was like an old warrior, scarred and bloodied, but not defeated. The determined spirit that had carried its people through the blitz was still alive despite the grip of austerity; they had taken everything that Hitler could throw at them and triumphed – a little bit of deprivation wasn't going to stop them now. There might be bread rationing, tighter controls and the threat of a poor harvest, but the will to fight back was there. It was there in the cheeky grins of the East End spivs in their zoot suits, fishtail ties and squashed-down trilby hats; it blared at you from juke-boxes and dance halls where the latest craze was the bop – the bop was loud and defiant, beating out into the heart of the city.

As I stepped down on to the platform of Liverpool Street Station with Frances that blazingly hot day in August 1947, I was not consciously aware of these things, but I caught the mood almost at once. Pigeons fluttered beneath gothic arches or scattered at the hurrying feet of the crowds swelling in and out from the streets. The station that had once been the finest and cleanest in London was grimy and noisy, but it pulsated with life. On the train I'd been excited, a little apprehensive of actually being in the city for the first time, but now I was suddenly eager to see for myself. I turned to Frances, clutching tightly onto the basket I had carried so carefully during our journey.

'Isn't this wonderful?'

She stared at me without comprehension, frowning. 'My head aches. Christabel was supposed to meet us – this place smells awful.'

'It's exciting, though, isn't it?'

I scanned the faces of the crowds, looking for one I could recognise. Then my gaze came to rest on a man, and my heart temporarily stopped beating before racing on. He was tall and well-dressed, his blond hair cut short and slicked down with brilliantine. I had a moment to note how handsome he looked, then his blue eyes met mine and he smiled.

'There's James Blair,' I said to Frances. 'He's seen us now.'

The look of sulkiness on her face vanished and she smiled in delight. She gave a cry of pleasure and began to walk quickly to meet him. I'd given her one of the new home perms a few days before and the curls clung attractively to her forehead and the nape of her neck. Her clothes were an adapted version of the new look that had come from Paris that spring, and excitement lent a sparkle to her eyes.

I saw the way James looked at her as he took both her hands in his, and I felt a little prick of jealousy. She was laughing up at him, transformed from the rather sullen picture she had presented a few seconds earlier.

'You must forgive Christabel,' he was saying. 'She mixed her dates and found she had an engagement this afternoon. Naturally, she was very upset and she begged me to meet you in her stead, which I was delighted to do.'

'I forgive her,' Frances cried. 'It's so good to be here, James. I was afraid I would be ill – or that my father would forbid me to come.'

He chuckled, tucking her arm through his before turning to me. 'Ah,' he murmured, 'the faithful Betty. I've spoken to a porter about your luggage. Perhaps you would care to make sure he has everything?'

I flushed as I turned away. Was he giving me a subtle reminder that I was a servant?

Threading my way through the throng of travellers, I arrived at the guard's van just as crates of live chickens were being unloaded. A porter was dealing with our luggage. I went up to him and he grinned at me.

'I'm Betty Cantrel,' I said. 'Mr Blair sent me to make sure you had all our luggage?'

'And have I?' He had a cockney accent and his manner was too familiar. He reminded me of Zac Jarrold, and that made me think of the quarrel with Vera. Vera worried me and I frowned as I made a quick count of the luggage.

'It seems to be correct,' I said. 'Do you know where to find Mr Blair's car?'

'Yes, miss.'

He set off at a smart pace that made it difficult for me to keep up with him. I knew he was doing it on purpose, but refusing to be beaten, I hung on to his wake.

Outside the station a shiny black Humber was drawn up at the kerb. James had opened the door for Frances and was helping her to settle inside. He turned and saw me. I climbed into the back of the car, still clutching my basket. James looked at me.

'Do you want to put that with the rest of the bags?'

'No. It's fragile. I'll keep it with me.'

James tipped the porter and got into the driving seat next to Frances. 'Father lent me his car,' he said, smiling. 'Petrol isn't too much of a problem for him; he qualifies for extra coupons because of his company – important industry.'

'What does he make?' I asked, curious because it was the first time James had mentioned his father's company in my hearing.

James glanced over his shoulder. 'Machine tools. Without Father's companies the rest of industry can't get going as fast as the government would like, so he's been given priority status. He's geared up to helping the export drive at the moment. We need to earn dollars.'

'He must be a very busy man,' I said.

James smiled oddly. 'Yes, he is.'

The car moved off, merging into the traffic. I looked eagerly out of the window as we drove through the streets, feasting my eyes on so much that was new and wonderful to me. It was like having the pictures on the cinema screen all around me, and my whole body tingled with excitement. I wanted to see everything at once. The car went too fast for me, whizzing past the brightly lit shop windows so that I could only catch a glimpse as we passed. Cars, buses, cycles, lorries and the occasional horse and cart jostled for position on the crowded roads, and the noise was tremendous. After the stillness of the fens, it was the noise and the fast pace of life that made the most vivid impression on me. Everyone seemed to be in a hurry, though I was also aware of the beauty of old buildings and green parks that appeared like an oasis in the general confusion. James mentioned the names of some of the buildings we passed; churches built by Wren, offices of great companies and the Bank of England in Threadneedle Street, which was so magnificent that it looked like a palace to me. But then, so many of the buildings could have been the dwelling-places of kings as far as I was concerned.

'It's beautiful,' I breathed. 'Oh, why did no one ever tell me it was like this?'

I didn't realise I'd spoken aloud until James laughed. 'Beautiful! London?' He glanced at me in his driving mirror. 'Some of the buildings perhaps. You haven't seen the slums yet. That's one of Mother's pet themes – wait until you meet her.'

I didn't answer immediately, but I knew that even on a wet, miserable day London would still hold its magic for me. I could see the dirty back-streets, the litter in the gutters and the wooden hoardings that fenced off derelict bomb sites. Vandals had scribbled on the advertising posters, mostly anti-government slogans demanding new housing, now! So many homes had been lost in the Blitz that it was impossible to replace them fast enough, despite the arrival of prefabricated buildings that looked like rows of little grey boxes. London might be dirty and noisy, but it was also beautiful, dignified and most of all, alive!

'It doesn't matter about the dirt,' I said at last. 'It's – oh, I can't describe it! It's the buzz I can feel – the magic of being a part of all this.'

'You never fail to surprise me, Betty. I never suspected you of being a romantic.'

As he glanced up at his mirror, I saw laughter in those startlingly blue eyes of his and I flushed with annoyance. He was making fun of me.

'Romantic! Betty?' Frances's laugh was sharp and spiteful. 'Really, James! You shouldn't tease her. She's just excited because she hasn't been to London before.'

Frances hadn't either, but she was angry with me for taking his attention away from her. I sat back in my seat, realising I had upset her. For the remainder of the drive I held my tongue, saying nothing even when we stopped outside a house in an elegant square. In the middle of the square was a garden with wrought iron railings and benches for the residents to sit amongst the trees and flowers. The sun was very hot and I could hear birds singing. We might have been back in the country again, except for the faint echo of the traffic.

James got out and opened the door for Frances and then for me. I hesitated as he led the way up two white steps to the front door, wondering if I ought to use the servants' entrance. There were steps leading down to the basement, but even as I moved tentatively towards them, James turned and beckoned to me.

'This way, Betty,' he said smiling.

The door was opened by a maid wearing a black Gor-Ray skirt and a white blouse. She smiled at us, taking James's driving gloves and laying them on the hall table.

'This is Maisie,' he said. 'She looks after us all so well that we should be lost without her. If you need anything while you're staying here, Maisie is the one to ask.'

She laughed and blushed. 'Go on with you, sir. Mrs Blair says will you take the ladies up to her straight away please?'

'Thank you, Maisie.' James moved towards the staircase. 'Mother's sitting-room is on the first floor. I know she's anxious to meet you both – but if you'd like to go to your rooms first?'

'I'm looking forward to meeting her,' Frances said.

I made no comment, simply following them up the stairs, still clutching my basket. The interior of the house was every bit as elegant as the outside suggested. Regency-striped wallpaper gave the hall and stairs a richness that was also very welcoming, and the furniture was all antique. I was no expert, but the style made me think of the grace of earlier centuries, possibly the eighteenth, I thought. It was far superior to anything I'd seen at The Willows.

We were shown into a cool sitting-room at the back of the house. It had long windows that overlooked a small garden and was shaded from the sun. I received an impression of a tasteful blend of greens and beiges, then a woman floated towards us in a cloud of perfume and pink chiffon.

'So here they are then,' she said, her voice tinkling and bright like the notes of a piano. 'Introduce us, darling.'

James smiled indulgently. 'Mother, this is Frances Crawley. And Betty Cantrel.'

'It's lovely to meet you, Mrs Blair.' Frances offered her hand.

'Thelma. You must call me Thelma.' Mrs Blair enveloped her in an effusive embrace. 'Christabel has told me all about you, Frances. I'm so glad you could come. I hope the journey hasn't tired you too much?' Not waiting for an answer, she turned to me. 'And you're Frances's little friend. You're very welcome here, my dear. I hope you will both enjoy your visit.'

'Thank you, Mrs Blair,' I said.

'Thelma. Everyone calls me Thelma. We're all friends in this house, Betty. I don't believe in titles. We were all created equal, were we not?'

'Mother is a free-thinker,' James said, a smile hovering. 'She believes that in an ideal society we would all live together eating with our fingers from communal bowls and wearing identical white robes.'

'James, darling!' His mother frowned at him. 'You will have our guests wondering what sort of a house they've come to.' She glanced at the basket I was still clutching to my breast. 'Isn't anyone seeing to your luggage?'

'This is a present for you,' I said, holding it out to her. 'Mrs Jackson thought they would come in handy.'

'What is it?' she asked doubtfully.

I drew back the gauze covering, revealing a brown stone jar and a dozen eggs packed carefully in straw. 'Just some eggs and butter.'

'*Just* some eggs and butter – real farm butter!' She gave a little shriek of delight. 'Did you hear that, James? You marvellous girl! You've no idea how difficult it is to buy fresh eggs in London these days. Come here and let me kiss you.'

'Aunt Hilda thought you might like them,' Frances said a little jealously. 'I hope Betty hasn't broken any.'

'I'm sure she hasn't.' Thelma Blair took the basket and set it down. She didn't try to kiss me. 'This wretched austerity business has made us all into scavengers. Simply everyone carries a string bag wherever they go – just in case a shop has something that isn't on ration. And the queues are impossible!'

'We aren't exactly starving, Mother.'

'Only because we can buy on the black market. Think of all those poor people who can't afford the prices.'

'You're not going to get on your hobby-horse just yet, I hope? Frances and Betty have come a long way.'

For a moment her eyes flashed with annoyance. She had pale blue eyes and hair the colour of ripe corn. 'You're perfectly right, James. We'll have some tea and then I'll take the girls up to their rooms. Ring the bell for Maisie, will you, darling?'

My room was next to Frances's. We shared a bathroom. When Mrs Blair showed us where we were to sleep, I was embarrassed. She was treating me as if I were exactly the same as Frances. I wanted to tell her that she'd made a mistake, but I felt awkward and tongue-tied. After she had gone, I looked round the luxurious room guiltily. She must think that I was a friend of Frances's, but surely Christabel or James had told her that I was part companion, part maid, to her guest? I stared at my suitcase, wondering whether I dare unpack. Someone might come at any moment and tell me I had to move. I heard a knock at my door and went to open it.

'I've come to help you unpack,' Maisie said. 'I've finished Miss Crawley's things. Is there anything I can do for you? Would you like me to press your dress for dinner this evening?'

'Dinner?' I felt hot and uncomfortable. 'You mean – in the kitchen with you?'

'Lord, no!' Maisie laughed. 'Whatever gave you that idea? We have ours at five o'clock, thank goodness. You'll be joining the family later. The dining-room is on the ground floor – to the left of the hall as you came in.'

I thanked her, my cheeks flushed. She was looking at me curiously and that made me feel even worse. My skin crawled with embarrassment. She must think I was a very strange guest. She would be certain of it when she saw how few clothes I'd brought with me; enough for the life below stairs I had expected to share, but inadequate for a proper visit with the Blairs.

Maisie was thin and she had big hands. I noticed that the skin between her fingers was cracked and sore. She seemed a very friendly girl, and she chatted about general things as she unpacked my clothes, hanging them carefully in the big wardrobe and asking me about the fens.

'Must have been terrible when them floods came,' she said. 'I'm from the country myself – a little village in Sussex – but I wouldn't go back there. Even the way things are now, it's better in town.'

I nodded, feeling miserable. Maisie was sympathetic. I ought to confide in her, but somehow I couldn't.

'Well, I'll be off now,' she said. 'If you want anything, you ring that bell next to the bed.' She smiled at me and went out.

I decided to visit Frances.

She frowned at me as I went in. I saw she was perched on the edge of the bed, looking rather lost and un-comfortable, and I realised that she was almost as nervous as I was.

'Mrs Blair is very kind, isn't she?' I said cautiously. 'Do you think she knows who I am?'

'Of course.' Frances rubbed at her forehead. 'She's very clever. Christabel told me she's a sculptress. She has lots of arty friends. I suppose that's why she talks like that. She's a sort of . . . I can't think of the word.'

'Bohemian?' Frances nodded and I sighed. 'Do you think any of her friends are invited for dinner? . . . Only I don't know what to wear.'

'Wear the green dress I bought you; it's better than any of your own. You did bring it?'

'Yes.' I felt relieved. 'Will that be all right?'

'It hardly makes any difference. No one is going to look at you.' She sounded irritable.

'What's the matter? Is your headache worse?'

'Yes. I've had it all the time. Did you bring those pills Mother got me from that doctor friend of hers?'

'Yes.' I looked at her doubtfully. 'Do you think you ought to take one now? They make you sleepy. Why not just have an aspirin?'

'Yes, perhaps I will.' She glanced at her wrist-watch. 'It will soon be time for dinner.'

'Not until later. They don't keep country hours here.'

'Well, of course I knew that. I'll take an aspirin and lie down for a while.'

'Are you going to have a bath?'

'Not yet – why?'

'Do you think I could?'

She laughed suddenly. 'I don't see why not. But don't use all the hot water, will you?'

I'd never dared to use the bath at The Willows, washing all over instead in the sink in my room. Scattering a few pink, scented crystals into the warm water, I climbed in. It was pure heaven! The soap was Grossmith's and smelt delicious; I thought Mrs Blair was very kind to provide us with such luxury. It occurred to me that it might have been bought on the black market, and it seemed odd that Thelma Blair should encourage such practices. Everyone who could afford to, did it, of course, but surely it was against her principles of equality for all?

Frances looked much better after her rest. The dress she wore that evening was one of her new ones. It had a peplum with a fringe. Fringes were in fashion now. The new look from Paris was longer and fuller, but it took more coupons. Women had soon discovered that one way to add length was to sew a frill to the hem, and the idea had caught on. The magazines were full of illustrations of how to update an old frock.

I was wearing my green dress. It seemed suddenly dated, though it suited me as well as it had at Christmas. I had draped a plaid shawl Frances had once given me over my shoulders and brushed my hair into a neat pleat at the back. I could still smell the scented soap on my skin. I felt very warm and the palms of my hands were damp. I gave Frances a nervous smile as we went down to Mrs Blair's sitting-room.

'You haven't given her the room next to . . .' Christabel stopped speaking as we entered. She flushed, a frown of annoyance on her face as she saw me. 'Frances,' she said, getting up from her chair. 'How wonderful to see you. I love your dress. This new look is so exciting, isn't it? Princess Margaret is wearing it and Princess Elizabeth has ordered it for her trousseau.'

'Will you be able to watch the wedding procession?' Frances asked. 'It's so romantic the way the royal family went off for that cruise to South Africa in February, and the engagement to Philip Mountbatten was announced so soon after they came back – don't you think so?'

Christabel smiled triumphantly. 'I probably shan't be in London for the royal wedding. I'm engaged myself. I had tea with Freddie's parents this afternoon, that's why I couldn't meet you.'

'You're engaged?' Frances looked surprised. 'Oh, I can see your ring. It's beautiful!'

Christabel held out her hand to show off the ring. It was a huge square-cut diamond, and her expression was smug. She was obviously very pleased with herself and I guessed that 'Freddie' must be rich. She had not spoken to me.

'That ring is positively vulgar,' Thelma Blair said. 'Stop showing off, darling. Betty, won't you come and sit next to me?' She smiled at me benevolently as I obeyed. 'You have an interesting face. Would you sit for me while you're here?'

'Sit for you? You mean you want to draw a picture of me?'

She went into a peal of musical laughter. 'Nothing so timid, my dear. I want to mould you in clay, to gouge out those angles in your cheeks and finger that marvellous hair. Why have you screwed it up like that? You should let it go free. Express yourself, Betty. Don't be afraid of . . .'

'Mother, stop bullying Betty.' James brought us both a drink. 'She's here to enjoy herself. She doesn't want to waste hours sitting in your studio.'

'I wouldn't mind,' I said and then blushed as Thelma gave a crow of delight.

'You see, James! I knew Betty was a kindred spirit the moment I saw her.' She turned her inquisitive gaze on me. 'What are you going to do with your life, my dear? You weren't born to waste your time in the country. You should become a photographic model. I can just see your face on the front cover of *Vogue*. You have the looks for it.'

The sherry was in crystal glasses so fragile that I was afraid the stem would break in my hand, but the sherry was sour and thin. I put down the glass.

'I – sometimes I think I should like to sing, but I don't suppose I'd be any good at it.'

'Nathan said you could sing.' James looked thoughtful. 'Would you like to see *Oklahoma* while you're here? It's on at the Theatre Royal, Drury Lane. I haven't seen it yet, but I hear it's good.'

'I've seen it,' Christabel said suddenly. 'Freddie has four tickets for *Bless the Bride* at the Adelphi – we could all go. You and Frances and . . .'

'I've heard Lizbeth Webb is superb in that. She used to be the vocalist for a dance band, but they say this show will make her. I'll see if I can get extra tickets, then we can go as a party.' Thelma gave a slight shake of her head as her daughter pulled a face. 'I'll speak to Freddie about it.'

'Is Father going to be in for dinner?' asked James as there was a pregnant silence. 'I wrote to de Havilland's and they've given me an interview for next week.'

'As a test pilot, I suppose?' His mother frowned at him. 'You know what your father thinks of that idea, James. You *are* his only son; he wants you to follow him into the business – or at least look after Hurstleigh.'

'The estate runs itself,' James said. 'I can still keep an eye on things. It would be different if Father would agree to open the park to the public. That would give me something to get my teeth into.'

'Your father will never agree to it, not while he can afford to keep Hurstleigh as it is.'

'Then it will have to be de Havilland's. Now if Father was in something like that, I might be interested in working for him.'

'But why a test pilot?' she asked. 'It's so dangerous, my darling. If you must fly, why can't you get a job in a civilian airline?'

'Have you any idea how many ex-RAF pilots are in line for the few jobs around?'

Thelma Blair frowned. 'You're so restless, James. There's so much you could do.'

'What?'

'Well, there's your books. You could spend more time cataloguing them – and you're so good at sport. Why can't you take up something like that?'

James grinned at her. 'Like motor racing?'

'You're impossible tonight. I can't be bothered with you.' She got to her feet. 'Shall we go into dinner everyone?'

'What a good idea, Mother.' James bowed and offered her his arm. 'Allow me.'

I was glad that there were only the five of us at the table that first evening. Even though it was a family dinner, the long table was set with a bewildering array of cutlery and fine glass. I felt nervous as the first course was served, afraid that my manners might not be good enough for the company I was in, and I blessed Mrs Jackson for all her scolding. At least I knew the proper way to eat soup!

The soup was thin and watery. I swallowed it with difficulty, thinking that it would never have been served at The Willows. It was followed by a piece of tasteless fish in a lumpy white sauce. I managed to eat mine, but Frances had only a mouthful or two. The main course was something dark and oily that I suspected was whale meat. Mrs Jackson had tried it once and refused to have it in her kitchen again.

James frowned as he saw Frances push the food unhappily around her plate. 'This is almost inedible,' he said. 'They do it better at a Lyons Corner House. You must speak to Mrs Good, Mother.'

'We've had three cooks in a year,' she replied. 'If you looked at the columns of help-wanted adverts in *The Times*, James, you might appreciate my problem. Girls don't want to be servants these days, and who can blame them? We're so lucky to have Maisie – Mrs Good is her aunt.' She looked at my plate. 'Besides, Betty has eaten everything. It wasn't so bad, was it, my dear?'

'It was very nice,' I lied staunchly. 'Frances never eats very much.'

'No, I don't,' Frances agreed, relieved. 'It was lovely, thank you.'

'There, you see.' Thelma smiled at me. 'You are so fussy, James. Even as a child you would never eat your food.'

'Yes, Mother.' He looked at me. 'I always knew you had courage, Betty.'

I blushed and drank some water.

'So, what are your plans for tomorrow?' Thelma looked at her daughter.

'Freddie's parents have asked Frances and me for lunch.'

'What about Betty?'

Christabel pulled a face and said nothing. I felt myself getting hot with embarrassment.

'I should like to explore London,' I said. 'I could catch a bus into the centre and go window shopping.'

'I'll take you to the Tower and the Waxworks if you like,' James offered. 'Is there anything else you particularly want to see?'

'All of it!' I looked at him, my heart racing.

'Betty will see all those things with us,' Christabel said, annoyed that her plan had backfired. 'I thought you would drive us to Richmond.'

'You can get a taxi,' James said. 'Or go on the bus.'

Frances was looking daggers at me. 'Please drive your sister to Richmond,' I said. 'I can manage quite well on the bus. In fact, I'm looking forward to it.'

'I was hoping to persuade Betty to sit for me,' Thelma said. 'I'm sure she would rather visit the sights with Frances. You can all go another day. There's plenty of time.'

'I'd love to sit for you, Mrs Blair,' I said, swallowing my disappointment. How I should have loved to go exploring with James!

'Thelma, my dear.' She smiled at me from across the table. 'Well, that's all settled then.'

I spent the morning in Oxford Street, wandering in and out of the shops. Selfridges, Peter Robinson and Marks and Spencer were amongst my favourites. I could wander round looking at everything without anyone asking me what I wanted. I had decided to buy some more clothes with the money Mary Crawley had given me for expenses. I was lucky because some of the shops had a few special bargains on sale. With the last of my coupons

I bought myself a floral cotton skirt and three rayon blouses, all for thirty-five shillings; they would help eke out my slender wardrobe.

I loved looking in the windows. Even though the shops were short of some goods, there was still plenty to see. I could have spent all day wandering the busy streets, but I'd promised Mrs Blair that I would be back at one o'clock. Purchasing a big bag of fruit from a cheeky barrow boy, I caught a bus that would take me most of the way to the Blair's house. If Frances couldn't eat her meals, she could survive on an apple and some pears.

I changed into my new blouse and skirt and went to Thelma's sitting-room. She invited me to enter, and I found her writing a letter on lilac notepaper. She sealed the envelope and smiled at me.

'What a pretty skirt. I've finished now – shall we go to my studio?'

'Yes. I'm looking forward to it. Where do you work?'

'I have part of a converted stable in a little mews not far from here. They used to keep the horses and carriages there until a few years ago. I think you'll like it, Betty.'

Her studio was charming. She had kept the exposed beams, staining them black to contrast with whitewashed walls. The main room was upstairs, long and light, and rather cluttered with the tools she used for her trade; there was a workbench, a kiln for firing the smaller models in clay and various chisels for her stonework. Several busts of people she had modelled stood about on shelves or pedestals, and I recognised the faces of her son and daughter.

'These are very good,' I said, touching the bust of James. 'This looks exactly like him.'

'I'm glad you approve.' Her eyes sparkled with amusement. 'What do you think of this?' She whisked a cloth from a statuette of a naked man. 'It's not life-size of course, but I modelled it on James.'

The statuette was about three feet high and magnificently done. Every muscle rippled with strength, every line was carefully drawn, every detail accurate. I stared at it in fascination, my cheeks hot.

'I – it's wonderful,' I muttered, embarrassed because it was so obviously James.

'You mustn't be shy, Betty,' she said. 'There's nothing wrong with looking at the human body. A man's body in the prime of his youth is beautiful.' Her eyes ran over me assessingly. 'You too have a beautiful body.' She smiled as I blushed. 'Now I've embarrassed you. I won't ask you to undress today. We'll just do a head and shoulders for now, but I should like to do something like this for you.'

'I . . .' I swallowed nervously. 'You wouldn't show it to anyone, would you?'

'You mean anyone who knows you?' She laughed. 'I shan't press you, Betty. Think about it. I've plenty of time if you have the patience.'

'I – I'll think about it.'

'Good.' Her eyes gleamed. 'Remember what I've said. Never be ashamed to express yourself. Now, sit down and we'll begin.'

Over a period of several days, James, Frances, Christabel and I toured the places of interest, visiting the jewel room at the Tower, the waxworks museum – including, at Frances's insistence, the Chamber of Horrors – the outside of Buckingham Palace, the Mall, Kew Gardens, and the Houses of Parliament. On the third afternoon everyone was exhausted and we all went to the Savoy Hotel for tea.

'I can't imagine why you wanted to see the Chamber of Horrors,' Christabel said, sipping her tea. 'That awful Christie with his sink – and Burke and Hare.'

'They were the ones who used to murder people and sell their bodies for medical research, weren't they?' Frances smiled oddly. 'Didn't you wonder what was in their minds when they killed?'

'I prefer not to think about it. Hanging is too good for such evil creatures!' Christabel cried.

'It must be terrible to hang,' I said. 'At least Burke's and Hare's victims didn't know they were going to die; they didn't have to sit in a condemned cell wondering about it before they died.'

'So you're in favour of abolishing hanging then, Betty?' James looked at me, a challenge in his eyes. 'What would you do if someone killed your young brother right in front of your eyes?'

'I'd kill him!' I said fiercely, then realised I'd fallen into his trap. 'Well, I'd be angry then, and I'd strike in hot blood. Hanging is cold-blooded and – and I'm not sure how I'd feel by the time it actually came to it.'

'I'd want him to hang,' Frances said, her eyes glittering. 'If he'd killed someone I loved, I'd never forgive.'

'Oh, for goodness sake let's change the subject,' Christabel said with a shudder. 'It's time we went home. We have to be at the theatre at seven-thirty.'

I sat enthralled, entranced, mesmerised by the sheer power of the music. I had thought nothing could be better than the musical films I'd seen at the cinema, but now I knew nothing could compare with a live show, the way the music seemed to swell all around you, sweeping you along with it to the heights of ecstasy. When I heard the show-stopping songs, 'This Is My Lovely Day', and 'Ma Belle Marguerite', I wanted to jump to my feet and join in. It was wonderful, exciting, young. I was fired with ambition – this was what I wanted to do with my life!

I applauded wildly, just as everyone else did. People rose to their feet, cheering. I was caught up in the excitement of it. It might be me on that stage one day. Why shouldn't I be as successful as Lizbeth Webb? Only a short while ago she had been a vocalist with a dance band, now she was a West End star. There was no reason why I shouldn't find myself a job like that. Thelma Blair had told me to express myself; if I asked her she might help me to get started. Why shouldn't I pursue my dreams?

*

'Christabel says Freddie's parents are on holiday in Paris, but they'll be back at the weekend and they're giving a big dance,' Frances said as she began to undress. 'I'm glad Mother had that evening dress made for me. She'd been saving the material for something special.'

'You'll look lovely in that,' I said. 'Peach is your colour.'

'Yes.' She giggled suddenly. 'Didn't we have a marvellous time tonight? I just love champagne, don't you?'

'I didn't have any.'

Freddie had taken us all out to supper after the show. We had gone to a nightclub, succeeding in getting in even though in my cotton skirt and blouse I was hardly dressed for it. Freddy knew the man on the door and I'd seen a wad of notes change hands. They gave us a table tucked away in a corner.

'You're too young to be here, Betty,' Freddie said. 'Don't drink anything but orange juice and we'll get away with it – providing the flatfeet don't decide to raid us.' He winked at me.

I liked Freddie. His father had made a fortune manufacturing boots for the army during the war, and now Freddie was branching out into ladies' fashion shoes. He was constantly short of materials, and swore about the 'bloody incompetence' of the government, but he was confident that the business would expand rapidly, and with his parents' fortune behind him, he could afford to wait for the boom that would surely come in the next few years. He'd met Christabel when his parents bought a house in Richmond, where they'd decided to retire, handing over the business to their son.

The nightclub had been smoky and hot. I drank several glasses of orange juice. Frances had been drinking champagne. She hiccuped several times and giggled again, swaying a little unsteadily as she headed for the bed. I looked at her suspiciously.

'You're drunk,' I said. 'Just how many glasses of champagne did you have?'

'Oh, only five or six,' she said. 'Mind your own bloody business, Betty. I don't have to account for my actions to you.'

She'd heard Freddie swearing; he did it quite often without realising what he'd said. From him it didn't sound too bad, but coming from Frances it was coarse and unpleasant. Mary Crawley would have a fit if she'd heard her!

'Don't swear like that,' I said. 'James doesn't swear in front of you – I don't think he would like it.'

She turned on me, suddenly vicious, her eyes glittering. 'Don't you dare to tell me what James likes or doesn't like!' She grabbed my arm, digging her nails into my flesh. 'And you can keep your bloody claws out of him – do you hear? I'm warning you, Betty. If you make up to James, I'll make you pay for it!'

I was shocked by the jealous spite I saw in her eyes. It was almost as though at that moment she actually hated me. I'd sometimes been aware of a faint resentment in her towards me, but nothing like this. It was the drink talking of course.

'Frances, I'm sorry,' I began, gasping as she suddenly struck out at me, her fingers curling into talons as she went for my eyes.

I was startled into action. Clenching my fist like a boxer, I hit her hard on the chin. To my amazement, she gave a little sigh and fell back on the bed. For a moment I was terrified that I'd killed her, then she moaned softly.

'Frances?' I said anxiously. Her lashes fluttered but she didn't open her eyes. 'I'm sorry, Frances. I just hope you won't remember this in the morning.'

I tucked her up in bed. I was feeling upset as I left the room. She must have had more to drink than I'd realised, and it had brought out the worst in her. I should have to be very careful in future. If she ever suspected that I was attracted to James . . .

Frances had one of her headaches the next day. She asked for her pills and I gave her one, removing the others to my own room. Mary had warned me that too many could be dangerous, and I always made a point of counting them.

When I went downstairs, I found Christabel and her mother discussing Frances in the sitting-room.

'Should we send for a doctor?' Thelma Blair asked. 'Is Frances ill?'

'It's just one of her headaches. She has them now and then. I've given her a pill. She'll sleep for a while now, and then she should be better.'

'Pills aren't the answer,' Thelma said. 'I've noticed that Frances is very highly strung. Has her mother thought of seeking special help?'

'I don't understand.'

'In my experience these migraines aren't always physical. Frances is obviously a sensitive girl. She might benefit from a talk with a psychiatrist.'

'Mother!' Christabel cried. 'Frances isn't crazy.'

'I wasn't for a moment suggesting that she was,' Thelma said, frowning. 'No, nothing like that. It's just that she seems . . . well, perhaps I'm wrong.'

I wondered what might have happened if Frances had made a scene the previous evening. Mrs Blair wouldn't have approved of her young guest getting drunk, of that I was sure. My right hook had left a small bruise on Frances's chin, but thankfully, she didn't remember anything about it – and I'd no intention of reminding her!

'I hope you don't mind giving me so much of your time?' Thelma asked as we walked to her studio. 'Would you rather have gone with Christabel and Frances?'

'I can't play tennis,' I said, knowing that I hadn't been invited to the party. 'Besides, it's too hot – and I wanted to ask you something.'

'Frances can't play either,' she said, unlocking the door. 'She's only going to watch.'

'I know, but Christabel didn't want me to go with them.'

'My daughter is often selfish. I apologise for her.' She took off the large Spanish shawl she was wearing and slipped on an overall. 'What did you want to ask me?'

'If I decided to try for work as a singer, could you help me?'

She looked surprised, then pleased. 'I can't promise anything, but I know some people. It's a pity Noel isn't in England at the moment or I'd ask him to tea and introduce you. He knows simply everyone.'

'Do you mean Noel Coward?' I asked, impressed.

She smiled as if amused. 'Yes, my dear. Poor Noel is feeling a little sorry for himself; he's had some bad reviews so he's taken himself off to America – Tallulah Bankhead is playing in *Private Lives* over there. He told me he was half dreading it, but felt he must see her. Are you thinking of staying on?'

'I thought I might come back next year, when I'm seventeen.'

'Come and see me then.' She raised her brows. 'Have you thought about what I asked you?'

I nodded shyly. 'I – I'd like to do it, if you think it's all right?'

'Of course it's all right. I shall look at you with an artist's eye. You will be exactly the same to me as a piece of rock or a flower.'

'Then – then I'll do it.'

She nodded thoughtfully. 'I shall want you to lie down on the floor – on that black rug. Go behind the screen and take your clothes off, Betty.'

I obeyed, feeling nervous. No one but my mother had ever seen me naked. When Polly was around, I'd always slipped my nightdress on over my underclothes and wriggled out of them afterwards. I felt a little sinful but also rather modern and adult. I knew Thelma was pleased with my decision and I desperately wanted her approval. I had the feeling that she liked me more than she liked Frances, and I wanted her to like me. I had started to dream about a new life in which Thelma and her son would play major roles.

I came out from behind the screen, my head down, half afraid of meeting her eyes.

'Put your head up, Betty. Stand proud.' Her gaze went over me assessingly. 'You are every bit as beautiful as I'd imagined. You certainly have no need to be shy.' Her manner was clinical, rather like a doctor, and my shyness eased.

'Thank you,' I said. 'Shall I lie down?'

'Yes. I want you on your side, leaning on your elbow with your hair falling over your breasts.'

I lay down, trying to remember exactly what she'd said. 'Is this right?'

'Perfect. You are a natural model, Betty. I'm sure you could find work in that field if not as a singer.'

I didn't reply. Thelma liked me to hold my pose for as long as possible. She worked swiftly, her fingers strong and confident as she moulded the clay. Half an hour passed without either of us speaking. She was so intent that when the phone rang in the downstairs hall, she was startled.

'Damn!' she said. 'I was just getting there. Take a rest, Betty, while I answer it.'

She went out and I rolled over onto my back. It was very warm. The sun was shining directly on the studio window. I closed my eyes, relaxing in the delicious warmth. It felt so good. I imagined that I was floating in the shallow waters of a South Sea island. I could almost smell the scent of exotic blooms wafting from inland and feel the kiss of a soft breeze on my skin. I stretched lazily, experiencing an odd sensation that I'd never felt before . . . a feeling of wanting something to complete the mood I was in, but I didn't know what I wanted. I ran my hands over my body, enjoying the silky texture of my skin as it luxuriated in the heat. It was almost like being in the bath . . .

A little sound made me open my eyes. For a moment I blinked in the strong sunlight, then I saw *him* standing there, looking down at me. He was staring intently, as though he couldn't take his eyes off me. I was shocked, embarrassed and then angry.

'Go away, Nathan!' I screamed, scrambling to my feet and looking urgently for something to cover myself. I couldn't see anything so I made a dash for the screen. 'Go away!' I yelled again. 'You rotten beast! How could you?'

'Thelma said to come up,' he said, and I heard him moving towards the screen.

'Stay where you are, Nathan. Don't you dare to come near me.' I began to pull on my clothes, my fingers shaking as I attempted to button my blouse.

'I've stopped. I'm sorry, Betty. I didn't know you would be . . .'

'You could have turned your back.'

'I was just surprised.' He chuckled. 'You looked as if you were enjoying yourself. I couldn't help watching.'

'Go away. I hate you!'

'I'm sorry, Betty. I didn't mean to upset you. I came to ask if you would like to go out to tea with me? Maisie told me Frances and Christabel were at a tennis party so I thought . . .'

I came round the edge of the screen fully dressed. 'No thank you. I would rather not.'

'Just because I saw you without your clothes on? There're clubs in London where I can see naked women anytime I like.'

'You were watching me,' I said crossly, 'spying on me!'

'Don't be an idiot.' He looked annoyed now. 'Why do you always think the worst of me? You obviously didn't mind posing for Thelma.'

'That's different.'

'Why? You don't imagine she's going to hide her work in a cupboard, do you? She'll probably sell it for a lot of money.'

'Liar! She wouldn't do that.'

He didn't get a chance to answer, because the door opened and Thelma came in. She smiled at us both, unaware of any tension between us.

'I'm glad you dressed, Betty. I shan't be able to continue today...' She suddenly laughed. 'I hope Nathan didn't startle you? He often pops in to see me here and I just sent him up as usual.'

Nathan was a family friend. Thelma hadn't meant to embarrass me. I just smiled and shook my head.

'So what are you going to do now, Betty?' she asked.

'I'm taking her out to tea,' Nathan said before I could answer.

'That's good,' she replied, smiling. 'Now don't forget you're coming to dinner with us soon.'

'I'll look forward to it.' He smiled with the ease of friendship.

We were shooed out of the studio so that Thelma could lock up. She waved at us and walked off, leaving me with Nathan.

'You're stuck with me so you might as well enjoy it,' he said, grinning. 'Come on, Betty. It's a lovely afternoon – why not make the most of it. We'll have tea somewhere and...'

'Will you take me to Hyde Park?' I asked. 'I'd like to go in a boat on the Serpentine.'

Nathan's eyes were brimming with laughter. 'Ice creams and lemonade instead of tea, Betty? Why not? It's ages since I had that kind of fun. We'll take the Underground to Kensington High Street, walk through the gardens and cross over Rotten Row. That's where Edward VII rode with Lillie Langtry, you know.'

I saw the mischief in his eyes and scowled. 'I'm only going out with you because I've nothing else to do – so don't get ideas!'

'I wouldn't dream of it,' he said, but that devil was in his eyes. He grabbed my hand, starting to run and pulling me with him. 'Let's go, Betty. If I've only got a few hours, I want to use every second!'

'You went on the Serpentine with Nathan?' Frances looked at me and I could see the jealousy in her eyes. 'I wish I'd been here when he called. Christabel's friends are snobs. You were lucky you didn't have to sit there and listen to them. I would much rather have been with you.'

She looked sulky and I realised she resented the fact that I'd been enjoying myself, while she'd been made to feel like a little country girl.

'Never mind,' I said. 'Thelma has invited Nathan for dinner tomorrow. You'll see him then.'

She cheered up a little, but she was still slightly annoyed that I'd seen him first.

'It wouldn't have been so bad if James had come to that wretched party,' she said as I began to brush her hair. 'He always seems so busy.'

So then I knew her bad mood was really because she wasn't seeing as much of James as she'd hoped. I'd noticed that she laughed a lot when he was around, hanging on his every word and looking up at him in adoration. I was afraid that she was showing her feelings too plainly, wearing her heart on her sleeve. I knew James liked her, but he was several years older and he must know lots of attractive women. I hoped Frances wasn't in for a big disappointment.

'So,' she said suddenly, looking at me in the mirror. 'How did you get on at Thelma's studio?'

'Oh, she had to go out. We didn't get much done really.'

Frances smiled smugly. 'She probably decided you weren't worth the bother, that's why she said she had to leave.'

That jealous look was in her eyes again. She really did resent the fact that I was having a good time!

Frances decided to spend the morning in bed. She was sulking because Christabel was going somewhere with Freddie and she wasn't invited. Thelma was busy too, so I wasn't needed at the studio. I thought about going out, but I was afraid to leave the house just in case Frances's headache was a real one this time. I wandered down to the first landing, deciding to take a look in James's library.

I'd heard Thelma mention her son's books once or twice. He collected rare editions, and apparently he had some valuable books. As I went into the room, I saw Maisie kneeling on the floor. She was making an odd, choking noise and I realised she was crying.

'What's wrong?' I asked.

She nearly jumped out of her skin, getting to her feet and wiping her hand across her wet cheeks as she saw me. 'Lor, you did startle me,' she said. 'I thought it was Mr James.'

'Why should that worry you?'

'I dropped some of his books.'

'That's not such a terrible crime is it?'

'You don't understand. I was dusting and I've muddled them all up. He's been cataloguing them for ages and he keeps them in a certain order. He'll be furious with me for ruining all his work.'

'But can't you put them back the way they were? Are they in alphabetical order or by subject matter?'

She looked at me blankly. 'I don't know. I've never been very good at reading – that's why I went into service instead of a shop. You won't tell Mrs Blair, will you?'

'No, I won't tell her.' I smiled at Maisie. 'Shall I have a look and see what I can do?'

Her face lit up. 'Would you? He's so particular about his books. I'm afraid of getting the push.'

'He wouldn't be so cruel,' I said. 'But I'll help you put things right if I can.'

I saw that she had taken the books from three shelves and put them all together on the table. Looking at one or two of them, I understood why James was so fussy about his books. They were all beautifully bound and some of them were quite old. When I moved one large volume a sheet of paper covered in neat handwriting fell out. A quick perusal told me that it was a list of the books and that they were arranged by title and subject matter.

'You carry on dusting, Maisie,' I said. 'I'll see to these.'

'I've done in here. I'll start on Mrs Blair's sitting-room, if you're sure?'

'I think I know how to do them. Don't worry, Maisie.'

She smiled and went out and I began to sort through the piles of leather-bound books, checking them against the list I'd found. The shelves were graded in size, and once I'd discovered the key, it was a simple matter to replace the books. I had almost finished when the door opened behind me.

'It's nearly done, Maisie. He'll never know you . . .' I said as I turned, and then stopped as I saw it was James. 'Oh, I thought it was someone else.'

James frowned as he came towards me, looking annoyed. 'Has Maisie been at my books again? I've told her not to touch them.'

'She was only dusting them. No harm has been done.'

His blue eyes flashed impatiently. I was surprised as I saw his mouth tighten with temper. This was a side of James I hadn't seen before. 'I suppose they're in a muddle again?' He ran his finger along a shelf and then looked at me. 'Did you put these back?'

'Yes. I hope they're as you like them? I used your own list.'

His frown cleared. 'As a matter of fact they're in better order than they were.' He smiled suddenly. 'Are you interested in books, Betty?'

'Yes. I'm not very well read, I'm afraid. We did the classics at school of course, but I've fallen behind since then. Frances chooses the books she likes.'

'What do you like?'

I blushed faintly. 'Well, I like Agatha Christie murders, and romantic novels – but I also like poetry.'

He took a book from the top shelf, stroking the faded leather binding reverently. 'This is a first edition of Lord

Byron's *Childe Harold's Pilgrimage*. Have you read any of his work?'

'A little. At school.'

He held the book out. 'You may borrow it if you wish.'

'It must be valuable. I should be afraid of damaging it.'

He laughed. 'Books are meant to be read. Take it and read it. Tell me what you think – and take this as well.' He stopped to take a book from the cupboard below.

I looked at it curiously. '*Forever Amber* by Kathleen Winsor – I think I've heard something about this.'

James nodded, his eyes bright. 'It was banned in Boston in America when it was published, and last year it was blacklisted in the rest of Massachusetts. It's a rather racy story of a woman who becomes the mistress of a man she loves and then pursues him when he deserts her, having lots of rather wicked adventures on the way.' He laughed as I stared at him. 'I collect all kinds of books, Betty, not just valuable ones. The fact that this was banned makes it of interest to me. Mother has read it and she adores it.'

'Oh, well, that's all right then. If Thelma has read it, I can.'

James frowned slightly. 'You mustn't let my mother influence you too much.'

'What do you mean?' I stared at him, bewildered.

'Nothing really. I just don't want you to get hurt.' He smiled again. 'Now you must excuse me. I have an appointment at my club.'

I watched as he went out. I couldn't understand James. Sometimes he was so kind to me. He'd lent me one of his precious books, but then he'd suddenly withdrawn, as if he were afraid of something. I was sure he liked me, but it seemed as if there was a barrier between us; a barrier he either would not, or did not want to break down.

Chapter Nine

James's father was not often at home for dinner. He was usually at a business meeting or dining at his club with a government official or an important client. He was, however, there on the evening Nathan dined with us; a quiet, unassuming man with greying hair and rather tired eyes. Most of the time he talked about cricket, then became involved in an argument about politics with his wife.

'I don't care what you say, John,' she said. 'It's time things were better. All through the war we were promised it would be all right afterwards. Now it looks as if we're going to be taxed out of existence.'

'There's an acute sterling crisis, my dear. Cripps has no choice. If we don't get our exports up things will get worse.'

'You mean everything we manufacture has to go abroad, so we all have to go without?'

'Not quite everything.' He smiled at her patiently. 'Don't worry, Thelma, production will rise. We'll get through. What about something to cheer us all up? Let's have a drink, shall we? Christabel, why don't you play the piano? Something lively.'

She smiled at him sweetly. 'All right, Daddy. Perhaps Betty will sing for us.' Her gaze turned on me. 'You can sing, can't you?'

'Yes.' I felt a little hot but I wasn't going to run away from her challenge. 'Have you got the music from that show we saw?'

'You mean *Bless The Bride?*'

'Yes. I'll sing "This Is My Lovely Day",' I smiled innocently at her. 'If you can play it?'

'Of course I can. As a matter of fact, Freddie bought me the sheet music.' She looked triumphant, as if she thought she'd called my bluff.

'I bought the record,' I said, 'and a song sheet. It's the first time I've sung it, so you'll have to make allowances if I don't get it quite right.'

The words and music were in my head. I'd played the record on the gramophone in the downstairs sitting-room several times when they were all out, and I was sure I knew it well enough to go right through. As Christabel tried out the notes, I waited until she was ready, then nodded.

'That sounds about right for me, play it like that.'

She began to play. I knew at once that she was good. I might not understand about the different keys, but I had a natural ear. I sang the words I had memorised. In my mind I had a clear picture of Lizbeth Webb as she sang on stage. I was the girl who was about to be married, the girl who would always remember her lovely day. The music floated out of me. I sang from the heart with all the longing and hope that was in me. I was untrained, a country girl with the barest of educations, ignorant of the world, untested and untried, but I put all my own feelings and desires into that song, and when I'd finished my cheeks were wet with tears.

There was silence as the last notes died away. I felt tense, still caught up in the joy and the underlying sadness of the song. Then suddenly James started to clap.

'That was wonderful, Betty,' he said, 'absolutely wonderful.'

'You were as good as Lizbeth Webb,' Thelma said. 'Magnificent, my dear.'

'Christabel played it well,' I said, blushing.

Christabel, Frances and Nathan had said nothing as the others enthused over my voice. I suspected that Frances was annoyed that I'd become the centre of

233

attention. Christabel had obviously hoped to make me look foolish, yet she could hardly ignore my compliment.

'You sing very well,' she said coldly. 'Perhaps you should go on the stage.'

'I could find her a job tomorrow,' Nathan put in suddenly. 'But I doubt if she'll take me up on it.'

'Why not?' Thelma cried. 'You shouldn't ignore your talent, Betty.'

Frances's eyes glittered and I realised she was jealous of all the fuss I was getting. I shook my head. 'I'm too young to think about it yet,' I said quickly.

Christabel turned to Frances. 'What are you wearing to Freddie's dance on Saturday?' She had succeeded in changing the subject and Frances smiled at her.

'I've a peach satin dress. I'll show it to you tomorrow.'

'What will you wear, Betty?' Thelma looked at me. 'Freddie's sent you an invitation, you know.'

'I – I didn't know.' I stared at her, acutely embarrassed. 'I – I can't go. I don't have anything suitable.'

She frowned, then waved her hand dismissively. 'Don't worry about clothes. We'll find you something. You can't miss the dance. We're all going.'

'You must certainly go,' Mr Blair said kindly. 'We can't leave you here alone.'

'I suppose you think you're clever showing off like that?' Frances asked spitefully as I helped her get ready for bed. 'If you think James is interested in you just because you can sing a bit, you're wrong.'

'I don't think it,' I said. 'Don't be like this with me. I'm sorry if I upset you because I sang tonight.'

'Oh, leave me alone,' she cried, her face sulky. 'I'm angry with you. Just don't show off when we go to this dance, that's all.'

I wondered what was wrong with her. She didn't seem to be enjoying herself as much as she'd expected. I'd thought she would be happy, as she had been when we stayed with her Uncle Henry. Instead she was sulky and resentful, particularly of me.

Thinking about the things she'd said, I realised that this visit might be even more difficult for her than it was for me. I'd spent time with Thelma at her studio and gone exploring London on my own. Frances had accompanied Christabel almost everywhere, and some of Christabel's friends were very snooty. Frances must have felt that they looked down on her. She might have rich parents, but she was still only a country girl. Like me, she didn't quite know how to behave in society, though I got on well with Thelma — but perhaps that made it worse.

'You'll look prettier than any of them on Saturday,' I said as she got into bed. 'I'll wash and curl your hair if you like?'

'Thanks, Betty.' She smiled oddly. 'I don't really hate you. You're my only real friend.'

'I know,' I said. 'Sleep well.'

Freddie had taken Christabel and Frances to see his new shoe designs. He'd promised them both they could pick out a pair for themselves.

'I'll bring you a pair if I can,' Frances promised. 'Something to wear for the dance. It will make up for my being so awful to you lately.'

'I could do with some shoes.' I smiled at her.

After Frances had gone, I wondered what to do. I could either go exploring again or pose for Thelma. I decided to ask her what she thought. As I went down to her sitting-room, I was feeling happy, excited at the prospect of going to a society dance. It was sure to be a grand affair. Freddie's parents liked to entertain, and despite the difficult times, there was certain to be lots of delicious food. I'd heard they were bringing in strawberries from France and all kinds of exotic things I'd never heard of, let alone tasted.

Busy with my own thoughts, I'd reached Thelma's room without realising it. The door was open and I could hear voices. James was arguing with his mother. I was about to turn away when I realised they were quarrelling over me.

'You're so damned thoughtless,' James said angrily. 'Filling that poor girl's head with impossible dreams. You know what kind of a home she comes from. A mother who couldn't care less what happens to her, and a father who's drunk half the time!'

'All the more reason to encourage her to break away. Really, James, you're such a snob.'

'You're the snob, Mother. You pretend to believe in equality, but all you really believe in is yourself. If you want to make Betty happy, let her decide for herself.'

'I've done my best to make her welcome.'

'What about this wretched dance then? She hasn't a thing to wear. You're not blind – you've seen her clothes.'

'She can borrow something of Christabel's . . .'

'You'd send her to a dance like that in one of Christabel's old dresses? Don't you know what those cats my sister goes around with would do to her? Even if she were dressed decently, she wouldn't know how to behave.'

'I was only trying to . . .'

I'd heard enough! My cheeks were flaming and I could feel the tears stinging behind my eyes. How could they discuss me like that? How could James say such cruel things? I'd thought he liked me. I'd thought they both liked me. Now I saw that they were only being kind to me because they pitied me.

Whirling round, I rushed down the stairs. I had to get out. I couldn't bear to be in the house! I wasn't sure I could face either of them again. I was breathing hard, shaking with anger as the shame swept over me. I felt humiliated and betrayed. I had trusted Thelma. I dared not examine my feelings for James.

I catapulted out of the front door straight into Nathan's arms. He had been about to knock at the door. I tried to push past him, but he caught me, holding me firmly as I struggled wildly.

'Calm down, Betty,' he commanded. 'What's the matter?'

'They despise me,' I said, choking on a sob. 'I thought Thelma was so kind, but it was only pity.' I was trembling and sobbing bitterly as all that I'd heard came pouring out. 'I can't stay here. I won't!'

Nathan's mouth was tight. 'I told you not to put too much faith in any of the Blairs,' he said grimly. His fingers curled around my wrist and he pulled me towards an open-topped sports car at the kerb. 'Come on, Betty. You need time to think.'

I hung back but my resistance was only token. Getting into the front seat, I wiped the tears from my cheeks as he drove away. 'Where are we going?'

He glanced at me and smiled. 'Where would you like to go? Shall I take you to the seaside?'

'Have you got enough petrol?'

'Let me worry about that – there're ways and means if you know what you're doing. Don't worry, I shan't get locked up for using priority petrol for pleasure.'

'You sound like Joe,' I said, looking at him curiously. 'What do you do for a living, Nathan?'

He shot an amused glance at me. 'Curiosity killed the cat, that's what they say. A bit of this and that – I buy derelict property and renovate it, amongst other things.' His brows went up. 'Shall we go then?'

'All right.' I stuck my chin in the air. 'I don't care.'

'That's my girl,' he said and laughed.

The wind whipped into our faces, blowing my hair into tangles. I was beginning to enjoy the drive. Nathan gave me a look of satisfaction.

'Feeling better now?'

'Yes. I'm sorry I made such a fuss.'

'I'm not.' I raised my brows and he laughed. 'You wouldn't have come with me if you hadn't been in a state.'

'That's true.' I laughed. 'Now I have, I might as well enjoy myself.'

I was gripped by a reckless mood. I'd run away without a word to anyone, and there might be trouble when I got back, but at that moment I didn't care.

Nathan took me to Southend. The tide was a long way out, but it was the first time I'd ever been to the seaside and I was determined to dip my toes in the water. I took off my shoes and stockings; Nathan rolled up his trousers to the knees and took my hand. We walked across the rather muddy-looking sand, our bare feet squelching in the little pools left by the tide.

Reaching the water at last, I gave a little scream and ran into it. Nathan laughed and dropped his shoes on the sand. We spent the next twenty minutes or so behaving like children let off school. I'm not sure who splashed who first, but once started neither of us was going to give in. By the time we'd finished both of us were soaked to the skin, and my hair was hanging in wet strips about my face.

'You look like a drowned rat,' I said to Nathan.

'And you look like a mermaid.'

The expression on his face made me shiver.

'Are you turning cold?'

I shook my head. 'I'll soon dry in the sun. What shall we do now?'

'What the butler saw?' His brows went up. 'We'll get a pot of tea on the pier. There's a towel in the boot of the car. We can at least dry your hair.'

We ran back across the sand. Once started, it was a contest again. With Nathan it would always be that way. I was determined to beat him and I ran as fast as I could. The blood was drumming in my head and I had a pain in my chest, but I pushed myself to bursting point. For a while I managed to keep ahead, then he caught me as we reached the dry sand, bringing me down with a rugby tackle. I lay laughing, exhausted and panting as I gazed up at him.

'Betty,' he said, his eyes suddenly blazing. 'Betty . . .'

I rolled away as he bent over me. 'Come on, I want my tea – and I want to see what the butler saw!'

We dried ourselves as best we could and combed our hair. Neither of us looked particularly respectable, but no one seemed to care. It was summer and we were at the seaside. We had tea and cakes on the pier.

'Enjoying yourself?'

'Yes. I wish . . .'

Nathan looked at me. 'What do you wish?'

'That life could always be like this.'

'Perhaps it could if . . .'

I jumped to my feet, suddenly nervous. 'Come on, I want some pennies for the slot machines.'

The pier still had some of the old machines that you looked into and wound a handle at the side to watch a naughty lady in her knickers, but there were also many newer ones that shot steel balls round and round and paid out sixpence, fourpence or tuppence if you got them in the right hole. Nathan seemed to have the knack of it, but as he kept giving his winnings to me and I was hopeless, we soon ran through our pennies.

It was beginning to get chilly as we left the pier. I shivered and looked up at the sky, holding out my hand as a few spots of rain began to fall.

'It's going to rain.'

'Come on, hurry.'

Nathan grabbed my hand. We ran for the car, and he pulled the hood up before the rain had managed to do more than dampen the seats. The clouds had come over suddenly, and it looked as though there might be a thunderstorm.

'Put this around your shoulders, kid.' Nathan gave me his jacket, which had been lying on the back seat. 'You look pale. What's wrong?'

'I don't like storms.' I held his jacket round me. 'What about you?'

'I'm not cold.' He smiled at me. 'I'd better get you back before they send out a search party.'

I nodded. 'Yes, I suppose so.'

Nathan's eyes were sharper than steel. 'Go in with your

head up, kiddo. You're going to that dance tomorrow if I have to drag you there.'

'Am I?' I looked at him doubtfully. 'What shall I wear?'

He grinned and the devil was back. 'Cinderella needs a fairy godmother, does she? Well, just don't leave a glass slipper behind for the prince – it will go back on Monday.'

'I don't understand,' I said.

'You don't have to.' He started the engine. 'Just trust me, kid. Just trust me.'

At that moment there was a terrific crack of thunder and I saw lightning over the sea.

'You don't deserve these,' Frances said crossly the following morning as she handed me a brown paper parcel. 'I fainted at Freddie's factory and I needed you when I came home. Everyone was worried about you. Why did you go off like that?'

'Nathan took me to the seaside. It was on the spur of the moment. I'm sorry, Frances. Are you feeling better now?'

'Yes.' She frowned at me. 'I'm going to stay in bed until tea-time so that I feel rested for the dance this evening.'

I looked at her anxiously. 'You have been rushing around a lot. Do you want me to call a doctor?'

'No, of course not. I wouldn't be able to go to the dance then.'

There was a resentful look in her eyes. 'Are you sure you want to? We could say you aren't well if you'd rather not go.'

'I want to dance with James.' Frances bit her lip. 'I – I think I'm in love with him. I don't particularly want to mix with Christabel's friends, but I can't let James think I'm an invalid.'

'You really do care about him, don't you?' She nodded, her face tight and desperate. 'Then we'll go to the dance. If I'm there, they'll leave you alone. Christabel likes you; she doesn't like me. Her friends

240

will be too busy turning up their noses at me to worry about you.'

Frances laughed and sat up. 'Poor Betty. What are you going to wear?'

'Nathan said he would hire something for me. Don't you worry about it. I'll give those stuck-up cats something to talk about!'

I left Frances in bed and took a flying trip to Petticoat Lane to buy some presents for my brother and sister. When I got back, Thelma asked if I could spare her an hour or so at the studio.

'I can finish from memory if you'd rather not,' she said.

'Why not?' I asked, unsmiling. 'As long as I'm back in time to help Frances get ready.'

'Oh, you'll have plenty of time. I have a hand-held dryer you can borrow if you like.' Thelma looked at me awkwardly. 'Did you have a nice day yesterday?'

'Wonderful. Nathan took me to the sea.'

'That was nice.' She frowned, still obviously uncomfortable. 'About your clothes for this evening, my dear. Christabel has looked out several dresses for you to choose from.'

'That's all been taken care of,' I said airily. 'Don't worry, Mrs Blair. I shan't disgrace you.' She stared at me, her cheeks faintly flushed as she heard the note of contempt in my voice. I smiled then. 'Let's go to the studio, shall we? I'm looking forward to being immortalised in clay.'

When I got back to my room, I found a huge cardboard box on the bed. I opened the lid, smiled as I saw what was inside and shut it again. On the table beside the bed was a small box and one of Nathan's calling cards. He had written a short message on the back.

'This doesn't turn into a pumpkin at midnight. I'll be waiting for you. So don't let me down.'

Opening the box, I took out the gold locket and chain. It was small and delicate and I liked it.

'I won't let you down, Nathan,' I said. 'That's a promise.'

Looking in the mirror, I saw that my eyes had the brilliance of diamonds.

'Oh, no. I won't let you down!'

Two of Frances's special pills were missing. I always counted them so that I wouldn't give her too many by mistake. I went through them three times to make certain; there were twenty and there should have been twenty-two. I couldn't think what had happened. Frances couldn't have taken them, because I would have known. They always made her so sleepy. Two would be guaranteed to knock anyone out for several hours. Besides, I always kept them hidden.

'You can't count, that's your trouble,' I said, putting them carefully back in their hiding place. 'You must have been in a dream.'

Frances's hair was finger-waved and finished in bouncing curls. She was ready except for her gown.

'I can manage now,' she said. 'You'd better get dressed yourself.'

'Go down when you're ready. I shan't be long.'

'All right.' She smiled at me, obviously excited. 'What colour is your dress?'

'Red,' I replied. 'You'll be surprised when you see it.'

'Red . . .' She would have said more but there was a knock at the door. 'Who is it?'

'It's Maisie, miss. I have something for you.'

'Come in.' Frances looked at me in surprise, then gave a cry of pleasure as she saw what Maisie was carrying. 'How beautiful! Is it for me?'

'From Mr James, miss.' Maisie smiled as she handed her a spray of creamy orchids. 'To pin on your dress.'

'From James – they're gorgeous. Look, Betty, look how beautiful they are.'

'Lovely,' I agreed. 'I must hurry or I'll be late.'

I saw Maisie look at me but she didn't say anything. I wasn't surprised when I saw the spray of white rosebuds in my room. I inhaled their perfume then laid them down. Roses were not for me that evening.

It took me twenty minutes to dress – I'd bathed while Frances's hair was drying – and when I looked in the mirror I was well satisfied with the effect. My dress was a dark crimson velvet with a boned bodice, a sweetheart neckline and long tight sleeves, the skirt clinging seductively to my hips and swirling at the hem. There was a wide band of sequinned embroidery round the shaped neckline, which allowed a glimpse of my breasts, and a satin cummerbund. With my hair swept up on top of my head and the lipstick I had bought that morning, I looked at least eighteen. I wore Nathan's locket but not James's roses. The shoes Frances had bought me were black satin and they fitted me better than the patent ones Nathan had provided.

With a last glance in the mirror, I went downstairs, prepared for battle.

Frances was already there, wearing her peach satin dress and the orchids. She looked younger than her years, sweet and pretty. They were all enjoying a drink, laughing. Then they suddenly noticed me. Christabel went quite pale. Frances blinked in disbelief, everyone else just stared. Then James came towards me.

'You look beautiful, Betty,' he said. 'Stunning, in fact,'

'Thank you. Is Nathan here yet?' I turned away from him coolly. 'I like your dress, Christabel.'

She was wearing white silk. Very expensive. Well cut and dull. I wouldn't have changed places with her for a thousand pounds!

'Nathan is going to meet us there,' Thelma said. 'You look nice, my dear. You'll ride with John and me. Freddie's car only has room for four and you girls don't want to crush your dresses, do you?'

'That's fine,' I said, smiling as the two couples went out. It suited me exactly. If Christabel got there first, she'd have time to warn her friends. They'd all be waiting for me to walk in – and I wanted to make an entrance!

Mr Blair had to take a last-minute phone call. I drank two glasses of sherry while we were waiting. It still tasted awful, but it helped to calm my nerves. We were at least half an hour behind the others. Plenty of time for Christabel to circulate. And she had. I was aware of heads turning as I followed Thelma and her husband into the ballroom. I heard a loud whisper as I passed a group of girls. I recognised one of them as a girl called Miranda, who was a particular friend of Christabel – and James! If the way she was making eyes at him meant anything.

'Well, of all the nerve!'

'She looks like a tart.'

I turned to face the girls who had spoken and smiled.

'Here you are then.' Freddie came up to me. 'I'd begun to think you'd got lost. The first dance is mine, you know. I'm going to get in before the rush starts.'

'Is there going to be a rush?' I asked, smiling up at him innocently.

'You bloody well know there is,' he said. 'You're a dark horse, my girl, if ever there was one.'

'Am I?' I fluttered my eyelashes provocatively. 'I don't know what you mean.'

'By George you're a teaser,' he said. 'If I wasn't engaged to . . .'

'But you are, aren't you?' I murmured, running the tip of my tongue over my lips. 'All tied up hand and foot. Such a shame. Now if you were free . . .'

'You little . . .' He gave me a hot, lustful look. 'I might just show you how free I am later on.'

I gurgled with laughter, flirting with him outrageously. 'I might just take you up on that, Freddie.'

He growled in his throat and caught me tight against him. From across the room, I saw Christabel's face. She was furious! I looked up at Freddie again and smiled.

'You dance so well.'

'You know what you do well, don't you?'

'No – what?'

Before Freddie could reply the music ended. As we walked from the floor, three men in their middle-twenties converged on us. They all had clean, bright faces and slicked-down hair, and they were all grinning like sharks.

'Trust Freddie to grab the best for himself. Come on, old man, introduce us.'

Freddie laughed and obliged goodnaturedly. 'Harry Clarke. George Harris. Philip Freeman – now don't fight over her, lads. Betty is more than willing to dance with all of you.' He winked at me and walked off.

'I haven't seen you around,' Harry Clarke said. 'You don't want anything to do with this shower. I'm your man, Betty.'

'I'm thirsty,' I said. 'Did I see a waiter with champagne?'

'I'll get it,' Philip Freeman offered.

'Then I'll dance with you after Harry,' I said. 'And whoever fetches me the next one . . .'

They all laughed. Harry took my arm and guided me into a waltz. 'Who are you?' he asked. 'You obviously know Freddie well.'

'Do I?' I glanced up at him wickedly. 'Haven't you ever heard of Cinderella?'

'Of course! Why didn't I guess? You're the one those cats were on about.'

I lifted my chin. 'So what are you going to do about it?'

'What would you like me to do?'

'Help me have a good time.'

'I'll do that,' he said. 'Serves that lot right. I'll keep their men coming – a glass of champagne for a dance, that's what you said.'

I giggled. 'That's what I said . . .'

The men and the champagne kept coming. I took a sip from each glass – I wasn't about to fall flat on my face and make a fool of myself – and I flirted with the men. All of them. I was enjoying myself. I'd never had this much fun in my life. Especially when I saw the expressions on the faces of Christabel and her friends. I could imagine what they were saying about me, and I couldn't care less!

Frances was dancing with James. She looked happy. He was smiling down at her, holding her very carefully, as if she were made of delicate china. I was pleased for her, but I couldn't help feeling a little spurt of jealousy. He hadn't asked me to dance once. I suddenly felt lost and lonely – and Nathan still hadn't arrived!

'This place is suffocating,' Harry Clarke said. 'I'm warm. Aren't you, Betty?'

'Yes, a bit,' I admitted, looking wistfully across the room at James and Frances. I was beginning to feel lightheaded. The champagne was catching up with me.

'Shall we go outside for a few minutes?'

I looked at him suspiciously. 'Why?'

'Just to get cool.'

'All right then. For a couple of minutes.' No one was going to miss me. I'd hardly spoken to James or Frances all night!

It was cooler in the garden. There were fairy lights in the trees.

'Let's go to the summerhouse and look at the stars,' Harry said. 'We can be alone for a while.'

'I'd prefer to stay here.'

His eyes slanted. 'You've changed your tune all of a sudden, haven't you? You've been coming on strong all night, now you freeze up on me – why?'

'It was a game,' I said, feeling awkward. 'I wanted to give Christabel's friends something to talk about.'

'So that's it then?' He was angry now. 'You're a prick teaser, Betty. A bloody prick teaser – and I thought you were the real thing.'

My cheeks burned. 'Don't talk dirty,' I mumbled. 'I never promised you anything.'

'Not in so many words.'

'Not in any way.' I turned to go in and he caught my wrist. 'You're hurting me. Let go.'

'Girls like you deserve all they get,' he snarled. 'You don't play games with . . .'

Someone came out on to the veranda. His shadow loomed large across the fancy paving.

'I suggest you let her go,' Nathan said. 'Betty, we're leaving.'

'And who the hell are you?' Harry demanded.

'The one who bought the dress she's wearing.' Nathan smiled, his teeth white and gleaming in the half-light. 'Any more questions?'

For a moment their eyes clashed and then Harry's fell; he walked off without another word.

'What did you tell him that for?' I cried angrily. 'You made me sound like a slut.'

'That's the way you've been behaving by all accounts.'

'Beast!' I went to slap his face but he caught my hand. 'You chose the dress, so it's your fault if they all thought I was a tart.'

'I meant you to look like a courtesan, not a tuppenny whore.'

'What's the difference?' I yelled. 'And why weren't you here?'

'I was delayed. Don't blame me, Betty. I didn't tell you to throw yourself at every man here.'

'I didn't.' I glared at him. 'Oh, I do hate you, Nathan Crawley!'

'Tell me something new.' His grip tightened on my arm. 'Did you have a coat?' I shook my head. 'We'll leave by the back way then. Come on.'

'I want to dance some more.'

'We're leaving.'

'What about Frances and . . .'

'They've gone.'

'Without me?' I stared in disbelief. 'They wouldn't!'

'I told Thelma I'd bring you home. Her husband is ill. They've taken him to the hospital.'

'To – what's wrong?'

'They think it could be a heart-attack.'

247

'No!' I swayed slightly. 'That's awful. We must go. James will be so upset. Do you know which hospital?'

'You can't go, Betty. They won't want you there.'

I felt as if he'd slapped me. 'No, I suppose not.'

'I'll take you home.'

'Where's that?' I asked bitterly, meaning that I had no real home.

He smiled slightly. 'You'll see.'

I knew he hadn't understood. Suddenly, I felt deflated, my head was spinning and I just wanted to sit down. I went with him quietly, getting into the car and closing my eyes as he drove off.

I must have slept, for when Nathan stopped the car I wasn't aware of my surroundings. I moved reluctantly, not wanting to get out. He took my hands, pulling me to my feet. My knees felt shaky and I swayed towards him.

'I'm tired,' I said. 'I want to go to bed.'

'Just how much champagne did you have?' he asked.

'Just a few sips,' I replied, then giggled and swayed against him. 'It was fun, Nathan. I liked dancing with them all. You should have seen the girls' faces.'

He smiled wryly. 'I wish I had been there. Come on, kiddo. I'm going to give you some black coffee before I take you back.'

'Where are we?' I looked round, surprised to discover that we weren't in the square. The street was dimly lit and we seemed to be outside a tobacconist's shop.

'This is where I live,' Nathan said. 'We'll get you sobered up, then I'll drive you home.'

'Don't want to go home.' I smiled at him. 'Dance with me, Nathan. Don't you want to dance with me?'

He put his arm around me and I leaned against his shoulder. He smelt nice, nicer than any of the men I'd danced with. I told him so and he laughed. Once the door was open, we were in a dark passage at the side of the shop. He switched on the light, making me blink.

'It's too bright,' I complained.

'We'll soon be upstairs,' he said. 'Coffee, that's what you need, my girl.'

Nathan supported me up the stairs. I couldn't understand why he seemed so serious. Now that I'd woken up, I could feel the bubbles in my head again. I felt like laughing. I wasn't quite sure where I was, or how I'd got there, but I was enjoying myself. Nathan put the bright light out.

'That's better,' I said. 'This is nice.'

The room had subdued lighting that didn't hurt my eyes, squashy leather furniture and soft cushions. I kicked my shoes off and wriggled my toes in a fluffy white rug.

'Coffee,' said Nathan. 'Don't go to sleep, Betty.'

'I want to dance,' I said. 'Haven't you got any champagne? I like the bubbles.'

'Betty.' He looked at me oddly. 'I'm trying to do the decent thing. Don't tempt me.'

I closed my eyes, swaying to the music in my head. For a moment I danced alone, and then Nathan's arms were around me. He held me close, closer than any of the others had earlier. We moved in time to the music but went nowhere. His lips were on my throat, warm and soft and sweet, easing the hurt inside me.

'Betty,' he whispered. 'Darling, I want to make love to you.'

The Blairs had gone home and left me. Frances was in love with James, and he'd danced with her all evening. My outrageous behaviour at the dance hadn't made him jealous. He pitied me – but Nathan liked me as I was. Nathan wanted me.

I pressed against him, turning my face to his for his kiss. He groaned, his breath harsh as he bent down to catch me behind the knees, carrying me through into a bedroom. The lights were soft and gentle. I was dreaming, only half aware of what was going on. I felt happy, relaxed. I smiled at Nathan as he laid me down.

'You're not too drunk, are you, Betty? You know what you're doing?'

'Of course I know,' I said crossly. 'I'm not stupid. You do think I'm beautiful, don't you, Nathan? You do care about me?'

'More than you think.' He smiled and bent to brush his lips over mine. 'You fought me in the barn. Are you going to fight me now?'

'Unzip me.' I rolled over on to my stomach. 'Go on then.' I felt his hand at my neck, then the zip went down. I lay back, waving my arms at him. 'Pull the sleeves, they're tight.'

He pulled and the dress slid off me; I wriggled up the bed and tugged it over my hips. Underneath I was wearing nothing but a pair of silk panties that Frances had given me. I slipped them off and then lay still.

'Your turn now.' I made a face. 'You're staring again.'

'Only because you're so lovely,' he said. 'That's why I couldn't take my eyes off you the other day. You're gorgeous, darling, do you know that?'

'Be quick,' I said. 'I'm getting cold.'

He grinned. 'Impatient, Betty. I'll soon warm you up.'

I gave him a nervous smile. When Nathan's arms were around me, I wasn't frightened, but now I had begun to think. I closed my eyes as he undressed, my fingers clawed the sheets. What was I doing?

Then he was beside me on the bed. I jumped as his warm flesh touched mine.

'Nathan, I'm frightened,' I whispered, suddenly turning to press myself against him. 'Hold me, love me . . .'

'Betty, I love you,' he murmured. 'I want you so much . . . so much.'

'Nathan . . .'

I needed to be held and comforted. His body was warm and hard. I clung to him, smelling the freshness of his skin. He began to stroke my back: long, firm strokes that made me relax. It felt good. The tension was easing out of me. I was enjoying the sensation it gave me. It was like the way I'd felt lying naked in the sunshine, only this time I knew what I wanted. I lifted my face for his kiss. His mouth was soft and tender as he possessed mine. A little shudder went through me. I moaned and pressed even closer. I could feel the heat of him, and the throbbing urgency of his passion. I lay on my back, dreaming of my South Sea island as he began to kiss my breasts, my navel and the sensitive skin between my thighs.

I was starting to pant, my body jerking with little spasms. His tongue flicked and teased my breasts until the nipples hardened and he took them gently into his mouth, sucking like a greedy babe. A feeling of such intense pleasure shot through me at that moment that I arched towards him, crying his name.

'Nathan . . . Nathan . . .'

'That's it,' he murmured. 'That's right, my sweet Betty. I knew you would love it. I knew it from the first moment I saw you.'

My hands clawed at his shoulders. I was no longer dreaming of the island. I was achingly aware of him and I wanted him to ease the frustrated longing within me.

'Oh, Nathan, I want . . .'

His hand moved down to caress and open me, and then he thrust that hard, throbbing male organ deep inside me. I jerked and cried out in pain. Oh, how he hurt me in those first few seconds, but the searing pain did not last long, and as I relaxed, I began to feel that breathy excitement again. Our bodies moved in a slow, sensual rhythm, making me cry out with pleasure over and over again. My nails scored his back as I writhed beneath him, reaching for some dark, distant place within me. Then it was suddenly all over, my goal unreached. Nathan gave a sharp cry, shuddering several times as he emptied himself inside me and then lay still.

I lay in the darkness, feeling the disappointment steal over me. There was a strange emptiness inside me. I had been swept along on a false tide of passion, but now it was all over and that bright promise had fizzled out, leaving me with nothing. I had suddenly realised what I had done. In my hurt and loneliness, I had clung to a warm body, but it was the wrong man. How could I have let Nathan make love to me, when it was James I wanted?

'Don't cry,' Nathan whispered, touching my cheek. 'I'm sorry if I was too impatient. It will be better next time, I promise. I've wanted you for such a long time.'

'I'm not crying.'

'Yes, you are, but it doesn't matter. You're entitled to, the first time.' He smoothed a tear from my cheek, then leant over to kiss me. I turned my face away. 'What's the matter? Are you angry because I rushed it? I've said I'm sorry. I'll make sure you enjoy it the next time.'

'There isn't going to be a next time.'

'What do you mean?' He thrust me back into the pillows as I tried to rise. 'Where do you think you're going?'

'Where I should have gone an hour ago.'

'You said you wanted it.' He looked at me, bewilderment and hurt in his eyes. 'It wasn't that bad. Not many girls get an orgasm the first time. It will get better – you liked most of it anyway.'

'I know. It wasn't your fault. Please let me go, Nathan.'

'No – not until you tell me what's wrong.' He leant over me, looking into my face. 'It's him, isn't it? You wanted it to be James. Damn you, Betty! Damn you! Why didn't you stop me? Why did you let me go all the way if you . . .'

He jumped out of bed and went through a door. I heard water running, splashing into a basin. It sounded as if he were taking a shower. It was a long time before he came back and I was almost asleep. When I looked at him, he was fully dressed.

'I've made some coffee,' he said. 'Do you want a shower before you go?'

'Please,' I said, hardly daring to look at him. 'Can I have the coffee first?'

'Of course.' His eyes were angry. 'I'm not a barbarian. I shan't throw you out.'

He handed me a mug of black coffee with no sugar. It tasted awful, but I drank most of it. When he disappeared into the living-room, I jumped up and ran for the shower. It made me feel fresher, but it couldn't take away the misery inside me. I still couldn't believe what I'd done.

He was waiting in the living-room. He glanced at me coldly as I came in fully dressed.

'Are you ready?'

'Yes.' My limbs were stiff. I was frightened of this man with the angry eyes and tight lips. It wasn't the Nathan I had known and liked. I admitted it now, I had liked him, even though we'd had this need to fight all the time. 'I'm sorry Nathan.'

'So am I.' He didn't smile. 'I'll take you back. With any luck the family will still be at the hospital. If not, you can tell them you stayed on at the dance.'

Nathan drove me home. As we passed the ABC cinema, I saw a Robert Mitchum film was showing. There was an advert for coupon-free white nylon from parachutes to make into clothing in a shop window, and a girl with beautiful hair, extolling the virtues of Drene shampoo, smiled down at me from a hoarding at the side of the road. Life went on as usual, but not for me. I felt that nothing would ever be the same again.

Maisie let me in. Her eyes were red from crying. I asked her if there was any news and she shook her head.

'Everyone is at the hospital. It must be bad or they would've come back by now.'

'Maybe they're just waiting for some news.'

'Yes.' She blew into her handkerchief. 'Mr Blair is a good man. It's a terrible shame.'

'We must hope for the best, Maisie. Goodnight.'

Upstairs in my room, I stared at myself in the mirror. Did I look any different? Would anyone know? Supposing I were pregnant? How could I have been such a fool? I must have been out of my mind! I must have drunk too much champagne . . .

None of the excuses helped. I'd let Nathan make love

253

to me and there was no going back. Whatever happened now, I should just have to take the consequences.

It was more than an hour before Frances came back. She looked exhausted.

'James is staying on at the hospital,' she said. 'He made the rest of us leave. I didn't want to leave him, but I'm so tired.'

I helped her get ready for bed. 'Will you want one of your pills?' I asked.

A little smile flickered over her lips. 'No, I don't think so, not tonight. I'm so sleepy. I'll drop off as soon as you've gone.'

'Goodnight then,' I said.

She looked at me suddenly. 'You certainly upset some of Christabel's friends tonight, Betty. I'm glad you did it. They deserve whatever they got – especially that bitch Miranda.' A secret smile flickered on her lips. 'Goodnight, Betty.'

I went out and shut the door.

Maisie brought me a cup of tea. I had slept badly and I felt heavy-eyed. I asked if she had heard any news.

'Mr James is home,' she said. 'He came in an hour ago. I think Mr Blair survived the night, but I don't know the details.'

'If he's still alive, that's something. Have you seen Mrs Blair?'

'She's sleeping.'

After Maisie left, I drank my tea and tried to think clearly. I felt very guilty. I knew just what had happened was as much my fault as Nathan's, perhaps in a way I was more to blame than him. I'd behaved badly at the dance; I'd drunk too much champagne, and then I'd enticed Nathan to dance with me. Shame washed over me. Nice girls just didn't do things like that. They allowed a few kisses and maybe some petting, but they didn't get themselves seduced. But then, perhaps I wasn't a nice girl.

254

I was a Cantrel. I had bad blood. I realised now that it was probably in my nature to do what I had done, and I didn't like myself very much. I'd scolded Vera, and now I'd done the very thing I'd warned her not to. The tragedy of it was, I was in love with James.

'Don't be a fool!' I said the words aloud. 'He doesn't want you – so what does it matter?'

Somehow it did matter to me, very much. I felt that I'd let myself down.

I washed and dressed before peeping in at Frances. She was still asleep. Fetching the two books James had let me borrow, I decided to return them to the library. We would be going home soon – besides, I didn't feel as if I were entitled to them now. I wasn't the same girl I had been the day he lent them to me.

I slipped downstairs. The house was so quiet. You could feel the tension and fear.

Laying the books on the table in the library, I turned to leave. Just as I reached the door it opened. James stood there looking at me, white and drawn, his eyes dark from lack of sleep.

'Oh, I'm sorry. I've just returned your books.'

'I hope you enjoyed them?'

He looked so vulnerable that I wanted to put my arms around him and hold him. 'Yes, thank you. Is there any news?'

'They think he will recover, but this was a warning. He'll need to take things more easily in future.'

'At least there's hope for him, James.'

'Yes.' He smiled oddly. 'He'll get his dearest wish at last. I shall have to join the firm. If I don't he'll kill himself by working too hard.'

'Surely he has managers . . .'

'My father doesn't trust anyone but himself. Perhaps not even me.'

'But if you – what about your job with de Havilland's? Did you get it?'

A wry smile twisted his lips. 'They've offered it to me. I shall turn it down, of course.'

I could hear a faint note of resentment in his voice, and I guessed it would cost him dearly to abandon his own plans for a job that he would hate. 'Oh, James. I'm so sorry.'

'Are you, Betty?' He looked at me. 'I thought you were angry with me. You heard the quarrel with Mother, didn't you? That's why you went off like that.'

I flushed as his eyes reproached me. 'I was angry and – and humiliated. I don't like being pitied, James. Especially by you.'

'You thought that?' He frowned. 'But I don't pity you. Surely you know how much I admire you? You have so much spirit, such courage. I was angry with my mother for suggesting you should wear Christabel's old clothes. She could have bought you a new dress.'

'But you said I wouldn't know how to behave. I thought you were ashamed to take me there.'

'I was merely pointing out to Mother that you would not be familiar with society manners. Some people would use your ignorance to patronise or make fun of you. I didn't want you to be hurt. It does not mean that I think any the less of you because you come from a different background.'

A single tear slid down my cheek. 'Don't,' I whispered. 'I've been such a fool . . .'

James laughed. 'Don't cry, Betty. I knew what you were doing at the dance. Frances told me it was to protect her. Oh, my dear, it was so amusing. I wanted to applaud you, but I was waiting until the end. It was my intention to ask you for the last dance. To show them all that I approved . . .'

The tears were flowing now. James took out his handkerchief and gently wiped my face. I stared at him, the pain twisting inside me. He was so kind and good, and I was almost sure that he did care for me, but it was too late. He would despise me if he knew what I had done.

'Excuse me,' I said. 'I must see if Frances is awake.'

I walked past him and went out of the room.

'I'm sorry to have to ask you to leave,' Thelma said. 'But I can't spare the time to entertain you – and it was only another day or two.'

'We understand,' Frances said. 'We both want to thank you for your hospitality – and we hope Mr Blair will soon be home.'

Thelma smiled coolly. I was sure she had never really liked Frances. 'We all hope for that. Goodbye, Betty.'

'Thank you,' I said. 'You have been very kind.'

Neither Frances nor I had been invited to return at a later date. I had the feeling that she was relieved we were going, that she did not particularly want her children to become too involved with the Crawleys.

James did his best to make up for his mother's coolness. He drove us to the station, bought us both flowers, fruit, and packets of milk chocolates; there were no boxes these days. He gave Frances a romantic novel by Angela Thirkell and me a copy of *For Whom The Bell Tolls* by Hemingway.

'I think it is his greatest novel,' James said. 'I hope it will encourage you to go on with your reading, Betty.'

'I'll write to Christabel,' Frances said. 'You and Christabel must come and stay with us before Christmas. Please say you will!' She gave him an imploring look.

His smile caressed her. 'Christabel will write to you soon. I expect to be busy for a while – but as soon as my father is a little better . . .' James turned to me. 'Take care of her for me, Betty.'

'Of course,' I said, not meeting his eyes.

I could not wait for him to leave us. It hurt too much when he looked at me with those clear blue eyes.

Frances was miserable after he'd gone. She sat picking the petals from the flowers he had given her, her face strained.

'He was going to ask me to marry him that night,' she

257

said. 'I know he was.' Her eyes blazed suddenly. 'Why did his father have to be ill?'

'I don't suppose he did it deliberately, Frances. Besides, your father wouldn't approve of an engagement just yet. Perhaps at Christmas – or next spring.'

She sighed and stopped pulling at the flowers. 'I know you're right. I'm sure James will ask me soon.'

'Are you sure you want to marry him?'

'Yes.' She looked at me. 'I'm in love with him.'

'I know. I – I think he loves you.'

'Do you?' She was suddenly eager. 'I'm not just imagining it?'

'He seems very fond of you.'

She smiled and nodded. 'Yes, he is, isn't he?'

I looked out of the window. I had always known that James was not for me, but that didn't stop it hurting.

Frances was laughing. I looked at her, wondering what she was thinking.

'Did you hear about Miranda, Betty?'

'No – what about her?'

'She passed out after we left the dance. She was so drunk that she slept for thirty-six hours.'

'Miranda was drunk?' I frowned as I saw her gloating expression and I remembered that Miranda had been making eyes at James at the dance. 'Drunk, Frances – or drugged? Did you put one of your pills in her champagne?'

'As if I would, Betty.'

Frances put on a hurt look, but I wondered. She'd tried to attack me when she thought I'd been taking too much of James's attention away from her – and Miranda had been a friend of the family for much longer than either of us. I thought that Frances might just be capable of such an act if she were really jealous.

'That could have been dangerous,' I said. 'Don't you know that?'

'I've no idea what you're on about,' Frances said sulkily. 'I'm going to read my book.'

I stared at her, suspecting that she was lying, but then I put it out of my mind. No real harm had been done, and I couldn't be sure . . .

Chapter Ten

Getting up early to finish the chores before breakfast came hard after the life of luxury I'd been living in London. On the first morning I was late and I had to rush around to get it all done. I was yawning as I went into the kitchen. Mrs Jackson looked at me and frowned.

'A fat lot of good it did you going to London, miss. I suppose you think you're too good for us now?'

I glanced at her resentfully. 'I'm sorry I overslept. I was tired.'

'By the look of you, you've been burning the candle at both ends. You've got shadows under your eyes.' Her eyes narrowed in suspicion. 'Just what have you been up to?'

I flushed and turned away from her probing gaze. 'I don't know what you mean. I'm just a bit tired, that's all.'

'That's all, is it?' She gave a snort of disbelief. 'You can't fool me, my girl. There's something different about you. I just hope you won't live to regret it, whatever it was.'

I was saved from replying by Joe's arrival. He smiled at me and offered a bunch of roses.

'I picked these from my garden,' he said. 'Welcome home, Betty.'

Emotion stung my throat. Impulsively, I kissed his cheek. 'Thank you, Joe. I'm glad to be back.'

Colour surged up his neck into his face. 'Me and Mrs Jackson thought you'd want to be off to the big city once you'd had a taste of it?'

'It was fun,' I admitted. 'I did think I might like to go

back in a year or so. I'm not sure yet!' I felt Mrs Jackson's eyes on me. 'Mrs Blair said I could find work as a model, but I'd like to sing.'

'You've had your head stuffed with nonsense,' she grumbled. 'Just remember Polly. She had big ideas, too.'

'Leave her alone,' Joe said. 'She's only just come home. Your scolding will be what drives her away.'

'No, it won't,' I said and laughed. 'You're my friends. You can say what you like. Anyway, I want to stay here for the moment.'

Three days later my period started. It was a heavy one and I felt sick and dizzy with it, but I'd never been so happy to feel that pain in my back and stomach. Mrs Jackson made me sit by the fire for a while. She gave me an aspirin and a cup of tea.

'I know what it's like,' she said, more sympathetic than I'd ever known her before. 'When I was your age I suffered with terrible cramps in the stomach. My mother made me carry on as if nothing was wrong, but then, she didn't like me much.'

I looked at her curiously. 'Weren't you happy at home?'

She laughed harshly. 'I had three brothers and I was the eldest. Mother adored her boys, but she couldn't stand the sight of me. That's why . . .' She sighed and shook her head. 'Well, that's water under the bridge now. I paid for my mistakes.'

'Do you think anyone is ever happy?'

She looked at me thoughtfully. 'Who knows? I suppose happiness comes to us all now and then, the trick is in knowing when you're happy.'

I watched her as she went back to her cooking. Mrs Jackson didn't frighten me any more. I'd discovered that her bark was worse than her bite, and I'd come to like and trust her. If ever I were in trouble, she was the one I'd go to for help – but I'd been lucky. I'd got away with it this time.

*

Vera was reading a girls' magazine called *Schoolfriend* when I went in. She looked up, her eyes wary. I knew she was remembering our quarrel and expected another lecture.

'Thanks for the postcard,' she said, attempting to be friendly. 'Did you have a good time?'

'Yes – mostly. I enjoyed looking round London. Perhaps one day we could go up on the train together. When I've saved some money. Would you like that?'

Her eyes lit up. 'You know I would!'

'Well, it won't be just yet, but as soon as I can afford it, we'll go. You'd like to see Madame Tussaud's and the Tower – oh, there's lots of things you'd like.'

'I want to go, too,' Little Joe said, looking at me shyly. 'Can I come, Betty?'

'I'll take you one day,' I promised, then I looked at Mum. 'How are you?'

Her body was heavy and swollen, but she smiled and said she was well. 'Do you want a cup of tea, Betty?'

'I'd love one, Mum.' I handed her a small parcel. 'This is for you, Joe, these are yours – Vera, I hope you like what I chose for you.'

'Presents, Betty?' Mother frowned. 'I'd rather have the money.'

'I've got three pounds left. You can have that – you've had your share of my wages from Joe Morris as usual?'

She nodded, smiling as I gave her the money. 'You're a good girl, Betty. You've done well for yourself at The Willows.'

'Yes, Mum.' I laughed. 'That's what you wanted, isn't it?'

'Oh thanks, Betty,' Vera cried as she opened her presents. 'Perfume – no one has perfume these days. Wherever did you get it?' She opened one of the tiny blue bottles. 'It smells lovely.'

'I think the skirt will fit. It's a Gor-Ray, Vera, and those shoes are the latest fashion. Just mind you don't twist your ankle, the wedges are quite high.'

'They're wonderful,' she cried. 'You are good to me, Betty.' She blushed, then, 'I'm sorry for what I said to you before you went away.'

'It doesn't matter. Perhaps I was a bit hard on you.' I smiled at her. 'How are things at school now?'

'Vera's in the play they're putting on for the royal wedding,' Mum said.

'We're doing all sorts of things,' Vera said. 'Will you come and watch me, Betty?'

'Yes, if I can.' I stood up, feeling relieved. 'I'd better get back now. Frances is in a bit of a mood. She's missing her friends. It's so different in London; I suppose she feels like a prisoner again now. Especially with the prospect of winter coming on.'

'And how do you feel, Betty?' Mum looked at me.

'Oh, I don't mind.' I shrugged. 'Maybe I'll go back one day – but don't worry, it won't be just yet.'

Mum had the baby a week later. It was another girl. I went to see them as soon as I could. Dorothy Ann Cantrel was a tiny scrap of a thing but very contented.

'She's beautiful, Mum,' I said.

'Yes.' She smiled as she looked into the cradle. 'And such a good baby.'

So my mother was well, the baby was thriving, and I no longer had the shadow of an unwanted pregnancy hanging over me. Sometimes I found myself thinking how dull it was in the fens, but at least it was safe, away from temptation.

I thought about Nathan whenever I looked at the locket he'd given me. It reminded me of my guilt, so I kept it in a drawer. It was too confusing and painful to think about either Nathan or James. Instead, I concentrated on keeping Frances cheerful, and that wasn't easy.

She'd had a taste of freedom and she found life at The Willows too confining. She talked endlessly of the Blairs' visit.

I wanted to warn her not to set her mind on it, but that

would only have made her more miserable, so I kept my doubts to myself.

Vera was very good in her school play. It was Sheridan's *School for Scandal* and she took the part of Maria. It was part of a pageant to celebrate the marriage of Princess Elizabeth to Philip Mountbatten on the twentieth of November.

The newspapers were full of pictures of the wedding and stories about the princess's dress. It was said that she was entitled to a hundred clothing coupons, and her bridesmaids twenty-three each. The Queen wore oyster-white satin to a reception at the palace, and the jewels were described as magnificent.

Vera glowed with triumph when I greeted her after the play. 'I was good, wasn't I?' she asked. 'Everyone says so.'

'You were wonderful,' I agreed, pleased to see her happy for once.

'That's what I'm going to be when I leave school,' she said. 'I'm going to be an actress. I want to be rich and famous so I can have beautiful clothes like Princess Elizabeth.'

I laughed then. 'You'll have to be very rich, Vera. Just one of those couture dresses can cost as much as two hundred and fifty pounds.'

Vera's eyes glittered. 'You'll see,' she said. 'You can laugh – but one day I'll surprise you.'

'I wasn't laughing at you, Vera,' I said. 'But it's not as easy as that.'

Vera wasn't listening. I didn't say any more. When the time came for her to leave school and take a job, she'd settle for reality, not dreams. I had my dreams, too, but I realised it was unlikely that they would ever come true. Sometimes I thought about being on stage in a theatre in London, and I sang the songs I heard on the wireless, but in my heart I knew that if I left The Willows and went to London, I should probably end up working in

Woolworths. Before I could even think of it, I had to save some money – and with a new baby sister needing clothes and a pram, that wasn't going to be easy. For the time being I must be grateful for my job, and to Mary Crawley for a generous wage.

Mary was seated at her desk when I went in. She had been writing in a slim notebook bound in white leather, but she closed it and slipped it into her desk as I approached. I'd seen her with similar books before, and I wondered what she found to write in it. She seldom went out any more, and we had few visitors at the farm.

'You sent for me, ma'am?'

'Yes. I've received an odd letter from Nathan.'

'I don't understand you.'

'A few months ago you overheard a private conversation . . .'

'I've said nothing of that to anyone.'

'I wanted to be certain.' Her hands moved restlessly.

'Has he not said what he wants?'

'Just that he wishes to discuss something very important with me. I'm worried that he might do something rash if he ever discovered . . .'

'He will not discover it from me.'

'You are very loyal. Wait a moment, I have a gift for . . .' She stood up, but as she took the first step, she swayed and had to sit down again. 'I am a little dizzy. Please fetch my jewellery box.'

I hesitated, concerned. 'Are you ill?'

She closed her eyes for a moment, then unbuttoned the high neck of her blouse. I gasped as I saw the bruises round her throat. 'Eben has been more violent of late . . .'

'Why do you put up with it? Why don't you take Frances and leave?'

'I think he might kill me if I tried.'

'Perhaps you should tell Nathan.'

'No! Neither he nor Frances must ever know. Swear to me that you will not tell them!'

'You know I won't.'

'Yes. Yes, of course.' She smiled at me. 'Now, fetch my box. I want to give you a present.'

I didn't want a present, but I knew I mustn't offend her. She selected a silver brooch with garnets and pearls. Her hand was shaking, and I realised that she was a frightened woman, no longer in command.

She dismissed me and I left, but I thought about Mary a lot in the following days. Eben Crawley was a beast and I wondered why she didn't just leave him. It seemed to me that she would have been far better off living alone – but then, women often stayed with men who mistreated them . . .

I'd received a letter from Polly. She said that the abortion was all over and she'd had the money from the solicitors. It was a bright, cheerful letter, with no hint of remorse for what she'd done. She gave me her address, asking if I'd write to her and saying that if I was ever in town I should go and see her. I wished it had come before the visit to the Blairs so that I could have called on her. Since Christabel was getting married in the spring, I didn't imagine that I would be asked to stay again. It was unlikely that Frances would either.

She asked her friends to stay at The Willows in December, and it was a while before they answered. When the letter finally arrived, Frances was jubilant.

'I'm going to ask Father to agree to our engagement,' she told me, her eyes glowing as she read and reread her letter.

'But James hasn't asked you yet,' I pointed out. 'Don't you think you should let him speak to your father?'

'I'm going to talk to him first. I don't want him to be taken by surprise and say no.'

I tried to reason with her but she just got cross with me and told me I was jealous because James liked her better than me. She cornered her father when he came in to lunch, which was unfortunate because he was in a bad mood. He told her bluntly not to be a fool and she was crying when I saw her afterwards.

'He said I was too young to even think of getting married,' she sobbed bitterly. 'He said it might be better if I never got married because of my health.'

'He doesn't mean it,' I said, trying to soothe her. 'Besides, once you're twenty-one he can't stop you.'

'But that's years away,' she cried.

'But you are young . . .'

'I hate him,' she cried, and her eyes glittered with resentment. 'He made Nathan go away and now . . .' she glared at me. 'Don't you dare to agree with him!'

'I wasn't,' I said. 'But in a year or . . .'

'Father wants to keep me a prisoner,' she said bitterly. 'He hates me because I'm not Edward – but I won't stay here. I hate this house. I'll never be well while I stay here. I have to get away.' She looked at me. 'I have to!'

'Why don't you ask your mother to take you abroad this winter? You'd feel better in a warmer climate – and you might even see James . . .'

She looked at me then, her eyes bright. 'You are clever,' she said. 'I don't know what I'd do without you.'

The sun has broken through the clouds and is shining through the bars of my cell window. It warms me as it touches my face, lifting my spirits. I have always loved the sunshine. In that, Frances and I are alike.

Frances, my friend. Frances, my tormentor. Frances, the chief influence of my early life . . . I wonder how different both our lives might have been if we had never met.

But then I would never have met Nathan or James . . . I would never have earned fame and fortune as a singer . . . I would not now be sitting in the condemned cell convicted of murder.

If I could change it all. If I could go back now to the day I first went to The Willows, would I? I'm not sure.

I'm not sure even now where it all went wrong. Why was I so blind? Why didn't I see . . .

Sighing, I lie back on my hard bunk and close my eyes, letting the memories drift into my mind. A smile touches my lips. I'm back at the farm, and the stench of the prison seems to fade away.

I went to see my mother and Vera. Mum looked tired but she was happy and cheerful, seeming very wrapped up in the new baby. I'd knitted her some clothes and she was very pleased with them.

Vera seemed sulky again. I tried talking to her, but I couldn't get more than a few words out of her.

'I'll be glad when I can leave school,' was all she would say. 'I'll be glad to get away from here.'

'What's wrong, Vera?' I asked. 'Can't you tell me?'

She looked close to tears and I thought she was going to tell me something important, but then she shook her head.

'It's nothing. Nothing I can tell you,' she muttered.

I was worried as I walked back to The Willows. Something was very wrong with my sister but how could I help her if she wouldn't talk to me?

It was the tenth of December. I'd been helping Mrs Jackson to make the puddings. I suppose I was dreaming, for she suddenly snatched the bowl from my hands, making a sound of exasperation in her throat.

'Puddings need a good stir,' she said. 'I'll do it myself. I've run out of eggs. See if the men have collected any, will you, Betty?'

'I'm sorry,' I said, as I slipped on my coat. 'I was thinking about my sister.'

'You're always in a dream.' She stared at me. 'If you've something on your mind, you'd best out with it.'

'I'm worried about Vera. She acts so strangely these days. I know something is wrong, but she won't tell me.

It's almost as if she's afraid to say anything, and she can't wait to get away from home.'

Mrs Jackson frowned. 'You get her on her own, Betty. See if you can't persuade her to tell you. If that doesn't work, bring her to visit me. I'll see if I can get to the bottom of it.'

'Thank you.' I smiled at her.

'Now run and get me those eggs – and put your coat on. I don't want you down with a cold, I've far too much to do.'

She would never change. At least that was one thing I could rely on.

I smiled as I went out into the yard. It was slippery with mud after all the rain, though the wind had begun to dry it. I hadn't realised how strong the wind was now, and bitterly cold as it swept across from the fens. We could have done with some thick hedges to shelter the yard. It felt cold enough for snow and there was some mist floating in patches across the fen. Freezing fog. It was going to be a wretched night. Already the light was beginning to fade.

My attention was caught by the barn door banging. Someone had left it open again. I was reminded of another winter's day when I heard Polly laughing with Eben Crawley. I hesitated, looking at the door. Someone should shut it . . .

My feet seemed to have a will of their own as they carried me across the yard. I didn't really want to shut that door, but it was as if something was making me do it. It wasn't just curiosity, though that was my besetting sin, but a strange feeling that something was about to happen. I should have learned my lesson the first time. I should have turned and gone in search of Mrs Jackson's eggs, but wild horses could not have prevented me from going inside that barn. I had a prickling sensation at the nape of my neck and a premonition that something terrible had happened.

A man was kneeling on the ground with his back to me.

Even though I could not see his face, I knew immediately that it was Nathan. He was bending over the curiously still body of his uncle. Eben Crawley lay on his back on the ground, his arms and legs grotesquely sprawled as though he had fallen from the platform above. His head was turned at an angle and his face was a queer white colour, his eyes open and staring blindly up at me. He was dead.

'Nathan!' I cried. 'My God, what have you done?'

Nathan turned to look at me, his expression a mixture of guilt, fear and something else I could not fathom. At that moment a sickening thought struck me – Eben had not fallen, he had been pushed! It was murder.

'Why did you come?' Nathan asked, angry now. 'Why do you always have to be where you're not wanted?'

He had not denied my accusation. I stared at him in horror as he rose to his feet, a scream of hysteria building inside.

'You killed him,' I whispered. 'You – you murderer!'

I opened my mouth to scream, but Nathan sprang at me, grabbing me and covering my mouth with his hand. I bit him, fighting wildly. I was terrified that he would kill me too, and I kicked and struggled with all my strength.

'Stop it, you little fool,' Nathan hissed. 'I'm not going to hurt you, and I didn't kill him. I just found him here like this.'

I shook my head, my eyes wild. His fingers dug into my flesh as he held me firmly. I saw the cold anger in his face and shivered, suddenly going limp. If he wanted to kill me, he could break my neck with his bare hands. It was useless to fight.

'I'm not going to hurt you,' he said again. 'I want you to promise me you won't scream. I'll let you go if you give me your word.'

I nodded dumbly. The panic was receding now. I felt calmer.

'That's better,' Nathan said, and let me go. 'Now, answer my question, why did you come here?'

270

'The door was banging . . .' I shivered. 'Why did you do it, Nathan? I know you hated him but . . .'

'I didn't kill him.' Nathan's eyes were like granite. 'I know it looks that way, but I give you my word that I didn't do anything. I just came in here and found him like this. You have to believe me, Betty.'

'Do I?' I looked up into his eyes, seeing the desperate appeal, and suddenly I wasn't so sure. Nathan was many things, but could he actually murder in cold blood? 'You could have been arguing,' I said slowly. 'He might have fallen – or maybe it was an accident . . .'

'I didn't push him, Betty. It might have been an accident, but I wasn't here. I didn't see him fall. Please, you must believe me.'

I'm not sure why but suddenly I knew that he was innocent. As I looked into his eyes, I had a feeling that he was telling me the truth.

'Why is it important that I should believe you, Nathan?'

He looked at me, and then he smiled. 'If I told you that you wouldn't believe me. But don't you see, if you don't believe me, no one will. They'll say I murdered him in revenge for what he did to me. They'll hang me, Betty . . .'

A little silence hung between us.

'Hang you . . .' I whispered. My hand crept to my throat. I could feel it closing. I could feel the breath being squeezed slowly from my body, my life ebbing away. 'Nathan . . .'

Nathan caught me as I swayed towards him, holding me as the dizziness swept over me. He stroked my hair, his face against it as I shuddered and wept in his arms.

'I'm sorry,' he said softly. 'It was a terrible shock for you. I didn't mean to upset you. I seem to be good at that, don't I?'

I stopped feeling ill and drew away from him. 'Don't blame yourself, Nathan. I've forgiven you. I know it was as much my fault as yours.'

'No,' he said, and smiled. 'But thank you for being generous.'

'So,' I said as I felt calmer. 'What are we going to do?'

His eyes glittered as he looked at me.

'Do, Betty? That's rather up to you, isn't it?'

'What do you mean?'

'What are *you* going to do?'

'I – I don't know.' I gazed into his eyes. 'What must I do, Nathan? Tell me what to do.'

'If you tell anyone what you've seen, they'll think the same as you did. They'll say I murdered my uncle.'

'I'll swear it was an accident,' I cried, looking at him eagerly. 'I'll say I was with you and we both saw him fall.'

'They might not believe you. Think, Betty. They'll want to know why I came back.'

'Why did you?'

'I wanted to ask Mary something . . .' Nathan frowned. 'Also I intended to speak to Eben, to ask him to release the trust.'

I stared at him as the doubts began to creep in again. Had he quarrelled with his uncle, and had that quarrel led to Eben's death? I could not know for certain, though my instincts told me to believe him. I knew that the evidence was against him. If I had doubts, it was almost certain that others would be convinced of his guilt. As I stood there in the gloom of that barn I knew one thing very clearly: I would not do anything that might lead to Nathan being convicted of murder. The thought that he might hang terrified me.

'I'll swear I was with you all the time,' I said. 'I'll swear it on the Bible.'

'You would do that for me?'

'For Frances, for Mary – and you.' I glanced away from the brightness of his eyes. 'A scandal like this could ruin your family.'

'I always knew you would swear black was white if it suited you,' he said and grinned. 'Believe me, Betty. I didn't kill him.'

'I believe you.'

'Do you? You should, because it's true.' He wrinkled his brow. 'We must think about this. It might still seem odd if we said we were together. It would be better if I'd never been here. No one saw me come. It was misty as I drove through the village. It's nearly dark now . . .'

'What are you asking me to do?'

I waited, my nerves tingling.

His eyes seemed to hold mine, dominating me with his willpower.

'Let me get away, then start screaming and run into the yard. You found him. No one else was here. You haven't seen me. He fell and you found him.'

A chill ran down my spine as I looked into those unfathomable eyes. His suggestion frightened me, but I knew he was right. If I said we were together they would all want to know why; the only reason we could be going into the barn together was to make love. By saving Nathan's skin that way, I should be labelled a whore. Nathan's way was best.

'Can you get away without being seen?'

'I left my car in the drove. I'll have to risk it.'

Why had he left his car in the drove? A warning bell sounded in my head, but it was too late to change my mind. I was committed.

'Go on then. I'll count to one hundred. Will that be long enough?'

'Yes.' He grabbed me and kissed me hard on the mouth. 'Bless you, Betty. One day I'll make this up to you. I promise.'

He slipped out of the door. I stood very still, my heart beating like a wild thing. I couldn't bear to look at the body of the man on the ground. A feeling of unease crept over me in the damp chill of that barn. What had I done? What had I agreed to? I began to count slowly. My mouth was dry. Had I been a terrible fool? Supposing someone had seen me enter the barn earlier? Or Nathan leaving?

there were so many things that could go wrong. Supposing Nathan had deliberately murdered his uncle?

I went cold all over. I dug my nails into the palms of my hands. I had to keep calm. I had to believe it was an accident . . . No, no, it would seem strange if I were too calm. I had reached a count of ninety-nine. I couldn't stand it any longer. I put my hands over my ears, opened my mouth and screamed. How easy it was to keep on once I had started. All the horror of it came rushing over me. I ran out into the yard, screaming hysterically. The kitchen door was flung open and both Joe and Mrs Jackson came running out.

'Lord have mercy! What's wrong with the girl?' she cried.

I couldn't answer her. I was shaking all over and the screams just kept on and on coming. Then she slapped my face hard. I sagged and would have fallen if Joe hadn't caught me. Shivering, I leant against his chest and wept.

'The master . . .' I choked. 'I think he's dead. I—I found him in the barn. I think he fell . . .'

'My God!' Joe pushed me towards Mrs Jackson. 'Look after her. I'd better see for myself.'

Mrs Jackson caught my arm as he strode off, giving me a little shake. 'Pull yourself together, Betty. Tell me exactly what happened.'

A deep shudder went through me. 'I don't know. I think he must have fallen, but I didn't see anything. I found him lying there when I went in.'

'Why did you go to the barn? I sent you for eggs.'

There was sharp suspicion in her eyes. I was frightened now. I had found the body. Supposing I was suspected of murdering Eben!

'The door was banging in the wind. I went to fasten it. I— I heard something . . .' Even to my own ears the excuse sounded lame.

'Did you hear him fall?'

'Perhaps. It was a thud—yes, it might have been that.'

Why was she staring at me like that? She thought I'd killed him! My heart contracted with fright.

'Did you see anyone else?'

'What do you mean?'

'Did you see anyone in the barn?'

'Just Mr Crawley. Lying there . . .'

'And then what did you do?'

What had I done? I'd talked to Nathan. Schemed to cover up his presence in the barn. I couldn't say that. I had to think of something fast.

'Nothing. For a while I couldn't move. I was too shocked. Then I knelt down and looked at his face. I – I spoke to him but he didn't answer. When I realised he was dead I lost my head. I started screaming and ran into the yard.' Shivering, I tugged at her sleeve. 'Can we go in? I feel sick.'

'I'll make some tea.' She glanced at my face. 'A little brandy wouldn't go amiss by the look of you.'

'I can't seem to stop shaking.'

'I'm not surprised. It isn't every day you find a dead body.'

We went into the kitchen. She filled the kettle while I sat in a chair by the fire. I felt her eyes on me and looked up. 'What's the matter?'

'Here's your brandy. I've put some sugar in it. Drink it all. It's good for shock.'

It burnt my throat as it went down. I choked and gave her the glass.

'It's a shock but no great loss,' she said. 'He was ill-treating Mary. I've not liked the way he's been looking at you lately either.'

I wasn't sure whether I was more shocked at her casual attitude to her brother's death or the implication in her last words. Though I'd always known there wasn't much love lost between Eben and Mrs Jackson.

'The way he . . .'

'You're a young woman now, Betty. He'd have noticed that.' She frowned as she saw the look on my face. 'Don't

275

be shocked. There was never much affection between Eben and me – I needed a home and he gave me one. I've repaid him for it a dozen times over.'

'You – you don't think . . .' A chill of fear ran down my back. 'I didn't push him over the edge, I swear it.'

'Of course you didn't,' she said. 'Why, you hadn't been gone more than a minute or two. Joe and I will both swear to that.'

'Joe wasn't here when . . . You do think I killed him, don't you? You think he had a go at me and . . . It's not true!'

Mrs Jackson's eyes slid away. She turned to pick up the kettle. 'Now whatever gave you that idea? You found him. I believe you. Joe will believe you. There's no need to worry, Betty.'

She brought me a mug of steaming hot tea. I could tell by her manner that she thought I was lying. She believed Eben had tried to rape me and that in the struggle I had pushed him to his death. Yet she was prepared to stand by me – that's why she'd told me her brother meant little to her.

There was no point in swearing my innocence again. She had made up her mind. A spasm of fear went through me. I might be questioned by the police, they might think I was guilty, too. What had I let myself in for? Yet it was too late to change my mind. I had to stick to my story now.

Joe came in as I was finishing my tea. He shook his head as he came to warm his hands at the fire.

'This is a bad business and no mistake. It might have been avoided if only Eben had listened to me.'

'What do you mean?' Mrs Jackson looked at him curiously.

'There's some loose boards in the loft. I told him about them weeks back but he said it wasn't important. I've been up to have a look, and I can see where one of them has given way.'

'So you think it was an accident then?'

276

'Oh, no doubt of it,' Joe said. 'The board is rotten and has pulled away from the edge. He must have stepped on it without realising.'

'Thank God for that!' Mrs Jackson coloured as Joe stared at her. 'I was thinking of Betty. We don't want trouble . . .'

'No, of course not.' He smiled at me. 'Are you feeling better now, lass?'

'Yes, thank you. It was just the shock.'

'Very unpleasant.' He nodded. 'I've had two of the men take him up to his room and I've sent for the doctor, though it's plain what happened.'

Looking at Joe, I had the feeling he was covering up for me too. Seeing the nod Mrs Jackson gave him, I realised they both suspected there was more to the incident than I'd said, but they were prepared to stand by me.

'What about Mrs Crawley?' I asked. 'Has she been told?'

'Not yet.' Joe frowned. 'Will you speak to her, Mrs Jackson?'

'No,' I said quickly. 'I think it should be me.'

They looked at each other. 'Do you feel up to it?'

'Yes.' I stood up. 'I want to do it.'

'If you're sure . . .' Joe was doubtful but Mrs Jackson nodded.

'Let her go,' she said.

The wind was getting up. It howled about the chimneys. How I hated the wind! It sounded evil. I wondered about Nathan, had he got away?

Breathing deeply to calm myself, I knocked at Mary's door. I must be careful. She had a shrewd mind and would know if I showed any hesitation. There was silence for a moment and I thought I heard the chink of glass against glass.

'Who is it?'

'It's Betty, ma'am. May I come in please? I have to speak to you.'

'Very well.'

As I opened the door the scent of lavender water caught my nostrils. Mary was by the fireplace, her back towards me. She seemed to straighten her shoulders as if gathering her courage before turning to face me.

'What do you want?' There was a strange glitter in her eyes and her cheeks were flushed.

'You must prepare yourself for a shock, ma'am.'

She gripped the mantelpiece. 'Something has happened – is it my husband?'

How could she have guessed? What had she seen? To have seen anyone leaving the barn she would have had to be standing in one of the servants' rooms ... or at Frances's window ...

'He was in the hayloft. There were some rotten boards. They gave way beneath him and he fell.'

She looked surprised, relieved. 'You're sure he fell because of the boards?'

She must have seen Nathan!

'It looks that way, ma'am. Joe warned him about them weeks ago. Besides, what else could it have been?'

'I thought he might have – turned dizzy. He had complained of feeling unwell recently.'

She was lying. Why?

'It was the rotten boards.'

'I see. He is dead, I suppose?'

It was the question most wives would have asked first, but after the way Eben had treated her I couldn't blame her. She must be relieved that her brutal husband was gone. I remembered how calmly Mrs Jackson had taken the news, and I thought that she too must have suspected what was going on. It was probably the only reason she stayed in the house, to give Mary a little support. Eben was a beast and I doubted that any of his family would really miss him.

'Joe had the master carried to his room,' I said. 'He sent for the doctor, though there's no hope. His neck is broken.'

The tension seemed to ease out of her. 'Yes, that was right. Thank you. I shall take charge now.' The old confidence was back in her voice. 'I can manage now.'

'Shall I tell Frances, ma'am?'

She hesitated for a moment, then nodded. 'Yes, perhaps that would be best,' she said. 'You will be gentle with her, Betty? You know how fond she was of her father.'

Frances had been nothing of the sort, but it was the way people always talked when someone had died. Eben would no doubt become a saint now that he'd passed on.

'Yes, ma'am,' I said carefully. 'I'll explain to her.'

'Good.' She nodded. 'You can go now . . .' As I turned to leave, she called after me. 'Who found him?'

'I did.'

Her dark eyes looked almost black. 'Of course,' she said in that disturbing, soft voice of hers. 'Thank you, Betty. You may leave everything to me now.'

Frances was sleeping when I went into her room. I shook her gently and she woke with a start, yawning and rubbing her eyes.

'What's wrong?' she asked grumpily. 'Why did you wake me up?'

'I have to tell you, Frances,' I said. 'You mustn't be too upset because he couldn't have suffered much.'

Something flickered in her eyes. 'Don't talk in riddles, Betty! Tell me what you mean.'

'It's your father – he's had an accident. He fell from the hayloft and broke his neck.'

'Is – is he dead?' Her bottom lip trembled.

'I'm sorry. Yes, he is.'

Frances threw herself down and hid her face, her shoulders shaking. 'Go away,' she mumbled into her pillow. 'Leave me alone.'

I touched her hand but she shook me off, telling me to go. For a moment I hesitated, but then I went. Perhaps I'd been wrong. Frances must have cared more than I'd thought . . .

Nathan returned for his uncle's funeral. The service was well attended by local people. Eben might not have been popular but he was respected and the church was full. Mary looked pale but calm. Frances had red eyes. She wept all through the service. People looked at her sympathetically and shook their heads.

Mary received everyone's condolences with an air of sad resignation. There was a great deal of feeling for her. A brief inquiry into the incident had been made by the local constable, but no one doubted that it had been caused by Eben's own negligence.

Several people came back to the house after the service. I was busy helping Mrs Jackson and had no opportunity to talk to Nathan, but I understood he was to stay overnight and leave in the morning.

I awoke with a start as someone shook my shoulder. The light was on and my cry was stifled as I saw who it was. I sat up warily, holding the sheets protectively against me.

'What do you want?'

Nathan's hand moved lingeringly down my bare arm. 'What I want is to lie beside you and kiss every bit of your body . . .' He laughed as I jerked away from him. 'Don't worry, Betty, I didn't come here for that – though if you were to invite me . . .'

'Well, I won't – so what did you come for?'

'I wanted to thank you.' He sat on the edge of the bed, but made no attempt to touch me. 'You saved me and my family from an unpleasant scandal . . . I may even owe you my life.'

'I did it for Frances's sake. If it had all come out her hopes of marrying James Blair would be over.'

'Is that true?' His eyes probed mine and I nodded. He sighed. 'We all do things for Frances, don't we? Whatever your reasons, I'm grateful. I'd like to give you a present.'

'I don't want anything. Besides, you gave me that locket . . .' I faltered as his eyes gleamed.

'Do you ever think of that night, Betty?'

'No.' I drew back. 'Go away, Nathan.'

'Give me another chance,' he whispered. 'Let me love you, Betty. I won't do anything you don't want. I just want to please you, to show you how much pleasure we could have together. You must like me a little or you wouldn't have lied for me.' I shook my head, a tear trickling from the corner of my eye. He wiped it away with the tips of his fingers and I trembled. 'One day you'll understand,' he said. 'I can't force you.' He kissed my cheek gently. 'Take care of yourself.'

I kept my eyes shut as I heard the door close. Then I turned my face to the pillow with a groan. He would never know how close I'd been to capitulation.

It wasn't that I loved him, it was just that I sometimes felt lonely. I wanted someone to love me. More accurately, I wanted James Blair to love me, but that was just a wild dream. James was a gentleman, far beyond me. But it didn't stop me thinking about him as I drifted into sleep. I wondered if the Blairs would still come for Christmas, and if I should see James again.

Frances was miserable because her friends had cancelled their visit. Mary had written to them, and she had also cancelled the traditional dinner on Christmas Eve.

'Why can't James and Christabel come?' Frances asked her mother sulkily.

'Because it wouldn't be right with your father just in his grave.'

'Why should I have to suffer because he's dead? No one cares about me. I have to stay in the house because of this wretched weather. If you loved me, you'd take me away somewhere where it's warmer.'

'It won't be for ever, Frances,' her mother said. 'I intend to make changes, but you must be patient for a while.'

281

Frances demanded to know what she meant, but she only shook her head. After Mary had gone, she asked me what I thought her mother had meant.

'I don't know, Frances. She'll tell you when she's ready.'

'But I want to know now. I hate it when people keep secrets from me.'

What she hated most was the fact that she would not be seeing James, but she cheered up a little when cards and presents arrived from the Blairs. James had sent her a pretty necklace. I knew she'd been hoping for a ring, but he had signed his card, 'With love from James', and that brought a smile to her face.

'At least I'll have you for Christmas,' she said. 'You will stay with me, Betty?'

I'd hoped to have the day with my family but I could not refuse her. 'Of course I will,' I said.

Joe took me on a quick visit to my home. I gave the presents to my mother and she promised to hide them. Vera followed me outside. She looked pale and she was very thin.

'Do you think Mrs Crawley would take me on at The Willows?' she said. 'I leave school next term.'

'I thought you wanted to be an actress?'

She kicked at the ground awkwardly. 'I'd need money, wouldn't I? If I could earn a bit first . . .'

'I don't think she'd take you on,' I said. 'Why don't you get a job in Ely for a start?'

She pulled a miserable face. 'I want to get away, Betty. I can't stand it here.'

I glanced at Joe. 'Look, I haven't time to talk now. I'll be over as soon as I can and we'll talk again.'

'I won't be trapped here for ever,' she said. 'I'm warning you, Betty. I can't take much more of it. You don't know what it's like.'

'We'll talk soon,' I promised. 'Give Mum a hand as much as you can, Vera. She looks tired.'

'It's all right for you,' she said sullenly.

'I hope you like your present,' I said. 'I must go. Joe has a lot to do.'

I was thoughtful as Joe drove back to the farm. I wondered if Mary would give Vera a chance. We could do with an extra pair of hands, but could I trust her not to let me down? She was lazy and quarrelsome, and she would probably resent working in the kitchen while I spent my time with Frances. Perhaps it would be better not to say anything.

The holiday came and went quietly at the farm. Nathan sent cards and presents, but did not visit. Even the servants' party was a muted affair. I left early and went to sit with Frances in the back parlour. We played cards and ate sweets, but it was all a farce. An atmosphere of gloom had settled over the house.

The weather didn't help. Throughout the following months the days were dull and dark, almost as though the sun had chosen to desert us. The yard was thick with mud. Even the stock looked miserable in their byres.

When the change came it was sudden. One day it was raining, the next we awoke to a bright spring morning. It was dry for a whole week. Birds began their courtship ritual, and Mary Crawley drove herself into Ely. It was nearly dusk when she returned. She spent some time alone with her daugher, and that evening they dined together in the parlour for the first time in months. When I went in to Frances the next morning, I saw a new sparkle in her eyes.

'I know a secret,' she said.

'Whatever it is, it's obviously pleased you. I haven't seen you this bright in weeks.'

'Aren't you going to ask me what it is?'

'If you tell me it won't be a secret any more.'

'Oh, Betty!' she cried, pouting. 'Mother said I can tell you.'

'Go on then, what are you so excited about?'

'Mother is selling the farm.'

283

'Selling . . .' A prickling sensation started at the nape of my neck. 'What about the house?'

'All of it.' She looked triumphant. 'We're going to travel for a year or two – France and Italy for a start.'

The prickling sensation was spreading through me. 'When will you be leaving?'

'Next week.' She could scarcely contain her delight. 'It's all arranged. Mother has to sign some papers, then we'll be off. Think of it, Betty. No more rain and fog. I shan't have to stay indoors all the time.'

'I'm glad for you. I – I shall miss you.'

She went into a peal of malicious laughter. 'Oh, poor Betty! Your face! I couldn't resist – but of course you're coming with us. You didn't really think I'd go without you?'

'I'm coming with you?' I caught my breath. 'Oh, Frances, I don't know what to say.'

She ran to embrace me. 'You don't have to say anything. I couldn't manage without you. I told Mother you had to come.'

The tears streamed down my face. I was too happy for words.

Frances was tugging at her nightdress. 'I want to get dressed. It's a lovely day. I want to go for a walk.'

'You'll have to wrap up well,' I said. 'The wind is cold. We don't want you catching a chill now . . .'

The walk seemed to do her good. She had a fresh colour in her cheeks when we got back, and she had hardly stopped talking. 'We'll go everywhere,' she said. 'All those places we've seen in pictures and dreamed of visiting.'

'Venice – shall we go to Venice?'

'Everywhere. I want to see it all. I'm so tired of being cooped up in this hateful house.'

When we got back to the yard, I noticed the vicar's car. 'I wonder what he's doing here,' I remarked.

'Mother probably asked him to call. She wants to tell him that we're going away.'

We parted company at the front door and I went round to the back.

There was no one in the kitchen. I took some bread from the pantry and began to slice it thinly, the way Frances liked it. I'd almost finished the trays when Mrs Jackson entered. Her face was very pale.

'You're wanted in the parlour, Betty.'

I sensed that something was wrong. 'Why?'

'You'll know soon enough.'

What had I done to upset her? She seemed as though she couldn't look at me. My feet were leaden as I made my way to the parlour. Had someone discovered that I'd lied about the night Eben Crawley died?

Chapter Eleven

All eyes turned on me as I entered the parlour. My stomach churned. Something was definitely wrong. Frances looked upset and Mary Crawley was concerned.

'Betty . . .' It was the vicar who spoke, his voice hushed and dramatic. 'I'm afraid I have bad news for you.'

'Bad news?' I blinked at him stupidly. What could he mean?

'Your mother . . .' He seemed to wilt under his burden. 'Your mother died suddenly last night. They think it was her heart . . .'

I gasped as if he had punched me in the stomach, staring at him in disbelief. 'Mum dead? She can't be. She's still a young woman . . .'

'She'd had a hard life.' He looked at me sadly. 'I'm sorry, Betty. It does happen sometimes.'

I shook my head, refusing to accept what he was saying. Mum couldn't be dead. Not my mother. She'd been ill often enough, but she'd seemed much better lately. The last time I'd seen her she'd been happier than usual. I just couldn't believe she'd gone so suddenly.

'No . . .' I whispered. 'Not Mum. Please not my mother.' There was a terrible tightness in my chest. Something was beating in my head. A drum. Bang . . . bang . . . bang. It went on and on until I thought I should scream. Mum couldn't be dead. I loved her. I needed her. I wanted to tell her how much I loved her. I'd never been able to say it and now it was too late. 'Oh, Mum,' I cried, staring at the vicar's anxious face. 'It's not fair. It's not right!'

'Life often seems unfair.' His voice was droning on somewhere beyond me. I couldn't see his face for the mist. 'I'm terribly sorry, my child, but you'll be needed at home. There's no alternative. No acceptable alternative . . .'

'Betty can't go home. I need her.' That was Frances's anguished cry. 'Tell him, Betty! Tell him you want to stay with me.'

I stared at her. She looked upset, a little petulant, as if she thought it had all happened to spite her.

'Isn't there another girl?' Mary Crawley asked. 'Couldn't she look after the family?'

'You mean Vera?' the vicar said. 'Apparently she went off a few days ago. The father is incapable of caring for two children. The only alternative is a home . . .'

'No! They're not to be taken into care,' I cried. 'I won't let that happen.'

'You can't do it,' Frances cried. 'Why should you? Tell them you want to come with me.'

Of course I wanted to go with her. I should have had to be mad to want to reject all she was offering me in favour of the life that awaited me at the cottage. The prospect of taking my mother's place appalled me, but I couldn't desert my family now, when they needed me most.

'I can't,' I said stiffly. 'I have to take care of them; they're my family.'

'I thought I was more important to you?' Frances's eyes were bright with angry tears. 'I thought you really cared about me, Betty.'

'I do. You know I do.'

'If you did you wouldn't desert me.'

I stared at her, torn in two by conflicting emotions. I wanted to be with Frances but my duty was to my family. 'You have to understand. I don't want to do this. I have to.'

'Perhaps Betty could join you at a later date?' the vicar suggested. 'We might be able to find families for the children in time.'

'No! If she leaves now I don't want to see her again.' Her look was icy. 'Make your choice now, Betty.'

'Frances,' I said pleadingly. 'Please try to understand.'

'No. If you leave me I'll never forgive you.'

It was an ultimatum. I must either desert my family when they needed me or she would cut me out of her life. It was a painful choice, but how could I put my own pleasure before the needs of the family I loved? And I did love them. My mother's death had shown me that.

'I have to go back. They need me . . .'

'I needed you, but you've made your choice.' She looked at me as if she hated me, then turned and walked from the room.

'Frances . . .'

'I'm sorry.' Mary was speaking now. 'I'm sure she doesn't mean it. She'll be sorry when she calms down.'

'She meant it,' I said. 'Besides, it doesn't make any difference. I have to stay and look after the children. It's my duty – and I want to do it. I can't let them be put in a home.'

'I understand perfectly, and I believe you've made the right choice. Frances is much healthier now. She will get over her disappointment. You'd better pack your things. Joe will run you home.'

'Thank you, Mrs Crawley. 'I'm sorry to leave you like this.'

'And I'm sorry to see you go. You've been very loyal to us, Betty.' She got up and went over to a desk, taking out a cheque book and writing in it. 'I'm giving you your wages for the month, Betty, and an extra fifty pounds to help you manage until you're settled.'

'Thank you,' I said. 'You've been very kind to me.'

The vicar was beaming at her, thinking how generous she'd been, but there was something in Mary's manner that made me feel she was relieved to see me go. She'd kept me on because I was good for Frances, and perhaps because I knew what Eben had done with Nathan's estate all those years ago, but now Eben was dead and she was free. Neither she nor Frances really needed me now. It was the end of an episode and fifty pounds was a small enough price to pay to finish it.

'That was most generous of you,' the vicar was saying as I went out. 'We're all going to miss you . . .'

'I could do no less,' Mary said. 'It is a terrible shame. Betty has come on so well since she's been with us.'

I went upstairs feeling shaken. I was still stunned, unable to take in what had happened to me. I'd believed myself secure at The Willows. I was needed here – but that was no longer true. I'd served my purpose. Frances was much stronger. She would make new friends on her travels. Very soon she would forget me. I was the one who would miss her.

I wanted to say goodbye. I couldn't bear it that we should part as enemies when we had been so much to each other. I went slowly down the hall. Her door was locked. I could hear the sound of muffled weeping. It stopped as I knocked and called her name.

'I've come to say goodbye, Frances.'

'Go away. I have nothing to say to you.'

'Please, Frances. Let me in. You know I don't want to leave you. You know I have to do this.'

'I'm not interested. You're ungrateful and selfish. I don't want to see you ever again.'

'Don't hate me,' I said, my heart heavy. How quickly she had changed towards me. One moment we were planning a bright future, now that dream had gone. 'I do care for you, Frances, and I always shall. I'm very grateful for all you've given me. We could still write to each other. We could still be friends.'

'No!' she cried angrily. 'You've let me down. Go away, Betty.'

I turned away, my eyes smarting with tears, but I wouldn't let myself cry. I'd done all I could and she'd rejected me. It was her own fault if she was unhappy.

I packed my possessions into a battered suitcase. I would take the dress that Frances had given me, but not the uniforms; they were not mine. Besides, I had several decent dresses of my own now. They would have to last me a long time.

Suddenly the realisation of what it all meant hit me. I sat down on the edge of the bed as the tears began to roll silently down my face. My mother was dead. I should never see her again. I was going back to look after two children and a drunken father, to take my mother's place and I was not yet seventeen. I was trapped, and despair washed over me. Only hours before the world had seemed a wondrous place, now it had shrunk to one tiny cottage.

Joe and Mrs Jackson were sharing a pot of tea in the kitchen. There was sympathy in their eyes as they looked at me.

'You should have let me fetch that bag,' Joe said.

'It's not heavy.'

'Have a cup of tea with us, Betty. There's no hurry. Dorothy Ann is with a neighbour.'

'Thank you.' I took the cup from her and sat down. It was one of the best cups. A rare honour. 'I shall miss you both.'

'I'm leaving at the end of the week. I could have stayed on as a housekeeper for the new owners, but Henry wants me to live with him in Ely.' She pulled a face. 'I'll try it for a while, but Eben left me a small legacy and I've a mind to set up in a small boarding house in Cornwall with that friend I visited after the floods. While I'm in Ely, I'd like it if you were to visit me, Betty.'

'I will if I can. It might be difficult with the baby.'

'You can bring the little lamb with you,' she said. 'You don't want to let yourself be a prisoner.'

'Then I'd like to come sometimes.'

'I'll take you when I go to the market,' Joe said. 'I'm staying on here for the moment. Until I see how I get on with the new master.'

'You'll be fine. You're a good foreman, Joe.' I smiled at him.

'We'll see.' He finished his tea. 'I've been thinking of buying a few acres of my own. Maybe get my own place – and a wife.'

'You're a good man, Joseph. You deserve to be happy.'

'I was fond of your mum,' he said, surprising me. 'By rights it should have been your father. If ever a man has tried to drink himself to death, it's him.'

'It should have been Dad,' I said angrily. 'It's him that killed her. She was worn out with worry and pain.'

'Betty!' Mrs Jackson exclaimed. 'You shouldn't say such things about your own father.'

'Why? You've always despised him.'

'Betty . . .' Her voice was softly chiding. 'Don't be bitter, girl. I know how you feel.'

'How can you? You don't know what it's like to have a drunken father.'

She gave me a rueful smile. 'My Pa was a weakling, ruled by my mother all his life. When we were kids we used to wait for him to fall asleep then dangle a bit of cheese in front of his nose. He hated cheese and it made him snort and sneeze.'

'Well, there you are then.'

'My pa was all right – but Mr Jackson was a drunkard. He started beating me a week after we were married. It went on for six months, then he fell into a water-logged ditch and drowned on his way home from the pub, leaving me to pay his debts. I had to sell everything and find work as a waitress. That's when I went to London. I couldn't face all the talk. It made me bitter for a while, but I got over it.'

I stared at her, hardly crediting that she was telling me her life story. At least I understood now why she had warned me about the gossips – and men.

'People wondered why I married him. I wanted a home of my own. My mother and I never got on. She said I was too plain to get myself a man. I suppose that's why I jumped at the chance when Alf asked me to marry him. I paid for my mistake. I married in haste and repented at leisure all right.'

'You were just unlucky,' Joe said. 'Not all men are like that.'

Mrs Jackson had always seemed so hard, but now I saw that she had acquired her crusty shell out of necessity. She had wanted a home of her own, but she had been forced to live in other people's for most of her life.

'Mum never blamed Dad . . .' I sighed. 'I suppose it isn't for me to judge. It was her life.'

'Just don't let him dominate yours,' she said with a smile. 'Remember I'll be around if you need help.'

'Thank you.' I hesitated and then kissed her cheek. 'Goodbye, Mrs Jackson. You've been a good friend to me.'

I caught the suspicion of tears in her eyes before she turned away to clear the table, clattering the best cups into the sink. It would be a wonder if one of them wasn't chipped.

'Get on with you, girl,' she said huskily. 'My name's Hilda. You can write to me at my brother's if you like.'

'I shall.' I grinned at Joe as we went out into the yard. 'Did you hear that? She told me to call her Hilda.'

'Ay.' He smiled in that slow, gentle way of his. 'I've never dared meself. But she's not a bad sort when you get to know her.'

'No . . . I shall miss her.'

He started the engine and the car moved into the drove. I didn't turn my head to look back. Regrets wouldn't help me now. Glancing at Joe, I knew that I had to tell him something. I should see him now and then, but it wouldn't be the same.

'I didn't push Eben Crawley over the edge,' I said. 'I know you've always wondered.'

He looked at me, nodding thoughtfully. 'I thought at first you might have been defending yourself – but then I found a button from Nathan's coat.'

'What do you mean?' I stared at him, a chill at the base of my spine.

'There had been a struggle up in the hayloft. I could see that by the state of things. There was nothing to see by the time the constable came, though.'

'So – you think Nathan and his uncle had a fight?'

'It looked that way to me.'

'But he swore to me . . .' I broke off. 'Forget that, Joe.'

'Me and Mrs Jackson talked it over. We reckoned you were protecting someone.'

'It could have ruined the family, even if Nathan were innocent. Mud always sticks.'

'Ay, there would've been a fine scandal.' Joe frowned. 'The Crawley's owe you a lot one way and another.'

'And you, Joe.'

'I did it for you, lass, not them.' He stared straight ahead. 'Just you remember that. If you ever need me, I'll be here.'

The kitchen was filthy. It couldn't have been swept or cleaned in weeks. For a moment as I stared at it despair washed over me. How could I stand living here now? I wanted to turn round and walk back out again. Then I realised there was no point in indulging in self-pity. It would take me a while to get the place clean, but I would make a start tomorrow – and I'd invest some of my fifty pounds in a bit of lino for the floor. Joe would get it for me in Ely next time he went, and it would make the floor easier to scrub.

My brother Joe was investigating a parcel of cakes Mrs Jackson had sent. There were three boxes of provisions waiting to be unpacked. Mrs Jackson had refused to leave her preserves behind for the new owners.

'They'll do you more good than strangers, Betty,' she'd said. At least we should eat well for a while.

Dorothy Ann was sleeping peacefully in her cot. She was an exceptionally good baby, I thought, pausing to look at her serene face. She hadn't grown much since I'd last seen her.

I went into my mother's bedroom. She was lying in her coffin, wearing the new nightdress I'd bought her for her birthday. Seeing her like that made my mouth go dry and I felt peculiar for a second, then I chided myself.

'You never raised your hand to me but the once,' I said, kissing her cold cheek. 'And I deserved that. I loved you, Mum. I hope you can hear me wherever you are. If there's any justice you'll be in Heaven. You deserve that. You never had much in this world. I pray you'll find something better in the next.'

As I went back into the kitchen I saw Dad had come in. He was drinking Mrs Jackson's home-made elderberry wine straight from the stone jar, and he swayed unsteadily on his feet as he turned to look at me. He was unshaven and dirty, his shirt stained with sweat, blood and beer, but it was the expression in his eyes that struck me. A terrible lost, pain-crazed look that told me he was a man in torment. He had loved her! He had needed Mum. Without her he was like a fish out of water, floundering helplessly. Why, oh why had he not done more to show his love when she was alive?

'Be careful with that wine, Dad. It's very strong.'

'I need it, Betty. Don't begrudge it me.'

'I don't. Just try to be sober for the funeral.'

The moment the words were out I wished them unsaid. His mouth went slack and he dropped the jug. Slumping down in a chair, he covered his face with his hands and began to weep, his body jerking with the force of his grief. Little Joe shrank away from him, fear in his eyes. He obviously thought he was drunk again, but I knew it would take gallons of wine to wash away his pain.

Moved to pity, I knelt at his side. 'It wasn't your fault, Dad,' I said. It might not be true, but I couldn't see him suffer like that.

He looked at me and his eyes were so old that I was shocked. I sensed it was a grief that ran deep. Mum's death was only a part of it. His eyes were bloodshot and his nose was running. He looked like a strange, mis-shapen child.

'I loved her, Betty. I always loved her. She was so lovely in her white dress.'

'Yes, I suppose you did love her then,' I said. 'I loved her too.'

'I didn't mean to drag her down. At the start I wanted to give her everything. It was the drinking. I've tried to stop it, but it gets hold of me. I can't fight it. I need it, girl.'

For a moment longer we looked into each other's eyes, then he turned away, reaching for the wine jug. I knew that nothing I could do would help him.

I got to my feet and went to Dorothy Ann's cot. When I picked her up, I could feel she was soaked. Yet she hadn't cried. As I changed her clothes, I noticed her bottom was covered in a rash.

'That must hurt her,' I said. 'It's odd she didn't cry when she wet herself.'

'She's odd altogether,' Dad muttered. 'Never cries much. Won't eat unless you force her to swallow. I reckon there's something wrong with her.'

I frowned as I looked at my sister's lovely face. 'What does the doctor say?'

'Your mother wouldn't have him. She said there was nothing wrong with the brat – but I reckon she's a bit touched in the head.'

'Dad! You've no call to say that. She might just be slow.'

'You're as soft as your mother if you think that. If it was left to me, I'd have smothered her long ago.'

Holding the child protectively, I glared at him. 'You'll not touch her while I'm here. I'll do my bit, Dad, but if you harm Dottie, I'm off. Joe could stay with the vicar until a family was found for him.'

'Still threatening me, eh, Betty?' His face was sullen as he looked at me. 'I shan't touch her. Did they give you any money when you left?'

'I took most of it in food,' I lied. Most of my money was safe in Joe's pocket. I knew better than to bring it into this house! I laid ten shillings on the table. 'That's all I can spare. You'll have to work for your beer money in the future.'

There was suspicion in his face. He thought I had money but he didn't dare push it too far in case I walked out. He resented me and he hated having to rely on me, but he needed me as a support. For the moment at least he wouldn't dare to upset me too much. We were going to have to try and live together.

'Take the money, Dad. I'll get some more from somewhere. Maybe I can take in washing or scrub floors.'

He looked at me oddly. 'You're a good-looking girl. You could get money without working too hard if you tried.'

It was a moment before I understood what he meant. I felt sick as I saw the smirk on his face. Getting up from my seat, I laid Dorothy Ann in her cot. She smiled up at me, the smile of an innocent. I spoke very carefully, without turning round.

'I shall forget you said that – because if I didn't, I couldn't stay in this house a moment longer. I'd rather starve than become a whore.'

'You've got me wrong, Betty. I wasn't suggesting you . . .'

I felt the touch of his hand on my shoulder and swung round, my eyes blazing. 'Get away from me! Don't you ever touch me, Dad. I'm not my mother and I won't be a substitute for her. Nor shall I go whoring to keep you in drink.'

The expression in his eyes changed rapidly: shame, frustration, and then sullen anger. 'You always were a mean little bitch.'

'Go to the pub, Dad,' I said quietly. 'Stay there until your money's gone – but when you come back you can sleep in the shed. I'll put a blanket out for you. While I'm in this house you don't come in unless you're sober.'

He glared at me, and the fury was so intense in his eyes that I thought he would hit me. Then my brother crept out of his corner and put his hand in mine.

'I'm hungry,' he said in a small voice. 'Where's Mum, Betty? Why doesn't she get out of that box?'

Dad's face creased with pain. He swung away from us and slammed out of the door.

I took a deep breath and looked down at my brother. 'Mum's gone to Heaven, Joe,' I said. 'You know that, don't you?'

He nodded solemnly, his eyes wide and dark. He looked like a tiny edition of Dad, but his smile had all Mum's sweetness. I smiled at him, feeling a rush of fierce, protective love. He was my brother and I was quite sure he'd known what he was risking when he'd come to stand beside me, even though he wasn't quite seven years old.

'I'm here now, Joe,' I said. 'It will be all right, I promise. I'll get your supper in a minute. Will you help me put all this food away in the larder?'

He nodded, his eyes still dark with emotion. 'Have you come back for good, Betty?'

'I'll stay as long as I can, Joe,' I said. 'It depends on Dad – but, whatever happens, I'll see you and Dottie are safe. I won't leave you alone with Dad. I give you my word.'

He nodded without smiling. 'Vera said you didn't care about us.'

'Of course I care. I'm your sister.'

'Vera's my sister. She just upped and left us.'

'Do you know where she went?'

'She said she was going to find a job. She talked about working in a hotel until she went on the stage.'

'She's far too young to find herself a job. Did Dad look for her?'

'I don't think so, I don't know, Betty.' He looked worried.

'It doesn't matter,' I said. 'Perhaps she'll come back soon.'

I was worried about Vera. She had no idea of how hard

it would be to survive on her own. The dangers facing my sister horrified me, but I must not let Joe see that. He was too young to have such a burden on his shoulders.

'Don't worry, Joe,' I said. 'I'll take care of you and Dorothy. We'll manage.'

He gave me a wobbly smile. As I began to peel and chop the vegetables for our meal, I felt my own mood lighten a little. I'd given up a life I'd enjoyed to come home, but Joe had never had a chance to enjoy his short life. Somehow I was going to change that. Somehow I was going to put the joy back into life for him and Dorothy Ann.

In the months that followed I was slowly but inexorably sucked back into the life of the village. Neighbours came to offer advice and help, staying to gossip over a cup of tea. I discovered that there was a great deal of kindness in the folk of Sutton. They brought me sympathy, support, small gifts of vegetables and eggs.

At first it was hard to adjust. I'd lived in a strange, enclosed environment for more than two years, with leisure to walk, read and learn. Now there were scarcely enough hours in the day. The cottage itself was not difficult to keep clean once I had scrubbed it through, but I was determined to begin as I meant to go on. We would grow as much of our own food as possible so that I could conserve my small store of money. I had saved ten pounds before I left the farm but I'd spent five of it on paint and things for the cottage, so I had fifty-five left. It wouldn't last for ever. There was a large garden at the back of the cottage, which had been allowed to grow up with weeds. I talked to Joe Morris about it and he was full of enthusiasm.

'With the right management you could have fresh vegetables for most of the year,' he said. 'I'll help you as much as I can.'

'Once it's cleared, I can keep the weeds down. Maybe Dad will help with the digging – but I'd be grateful if you could make me a wire run for the chickens.'

'I'll do that first,' he promised.

Joe was as good as his word, arriving the following Sunday with all the materials we needed. It took him the best part of the day, but he stuck at it until it was finished.

It was only fair that I should ask him to join us for our evening meal. He sat at the table with the children, looking relaxed and happy to be there.

'It's nice to be with a real family now and then,' he said. 'You're a good cook, Betty.'

'Not as good as Mrs Jackson, but the children don't complain.' I smiled at him across the table. 'Now all I want is some hens.'

'You leave it to me,' he said. 'I'll see what I can do at the market this Thursday.'

I wasn't sure what he intended but that Thursday afternoon his car pulled up outside the cottage and little Joe went running out to meet him. He came back grinning from ear to ear, carrying a covered box. Setting it down carefully on the kitchen floor, he took the lid off to reveal a dozen or more fluffy yellow chicks.

'I bought them for a shilling,' Joe Morris said as he came in. 'It was the end of the market and the farmer wanted to get rid of them. You'll need to keep them in the kitchen for a while. They won't all survive but you should rear several of them. In the meantime I've brought you three hens, all guaranteed to be good layers, and a cockerel.'

'Oh, Joseph,' I cried, laughing. 'You're a marvel. I don't know what I'd do without you.'

His homely face lit up with pleasure. 'I like doing things for you and the children. I thought I'd make a start on the garden this weekend.'

'I didn't mean you to do all the work, Joseph. Dad should do his bit.'

'It will get done all the sooner with two of us, unless I'd be in the way?'

'Don't you ever say such a daft thing again, Joe Morris! We all love having you here.'

'Well, just until the hard work is done then.'

The 1948 Olympic Games were the first to be held in Britain for forty years. We all listened excitedly to the radio, cheering every time Britain won a medal – there were four silver medals for our athletes and a horse named Foxhunter helped to win a bronze for the show-jumping team. It was quite an achievement for a country and a people who had suffered as we had.

'It just shows things are getting better,' Joe said. 'It won't be long before all this rationing is over – not that it's done me any harm.'

Joe had slipped into the habit of spending his Sunday afternoons and evenings with us. Every time he came he brought something for me or the children. Comics or sweets for my brother, a rattle or a fluffy toy for Dorothy Ann. He'd bought the Crawley's gramophone and the records before they went, and he gave them to me.

'I know you like music, Betty,' he said. 'And I've got you a bike as well; it will make it easier for you to get up the street.'

'You spoil me,' I said. 'You shouldn't spend your money on us, Joe.'

He winked at me. 'I'm not short of a bob or two, lass.'

At first I'd hoped for a letter from Frances but as the weeks and months slipped by, I knew she would not write. I wondered where she was and what she was doing, and sometimes when I was tired I found myself resenting what had happened. I was seventeen and tied to a ready-made family for at least the next ten years. There were times when I yearned to be free, when I thought of my stay in London with longing, remembering the ambition I'd had to be a singer. A dream that could now never come true.

I wondered about Vera, too. I'd had one postcard from Brighton, saying that she was well, but that was all. It didn't stop me being anxious, but I couldn't go and look for her, though Joe did offer to take me.

I shook my head. 'She might have gone there just for the day,' I said. 'If she wanted to come home, she would.'

My father was making an effort. I think the sight of Joe digging for hours had shamed him into looking for work. He found an odd job now and then, and he had periods when he stayed sober, but it never lasted for long. When he was drunk he was difficult to manage and we often ended by shouting at each other, but he never laid a hand on me. I think he was frightened of what Joe might do if he did.

Sometimes he sneered at me because Joe Morris was always at the cottage on Sundays. 'A fine admirer you've got,' he said when I told him Joe was taking us to the seaside. 'A looker like you could do better.'

'Joe Morris is a friend. He comes because he enjoys being with the children. He's fond of Joey.'

'No doubt he wishes I was out of the way so that he could move in and take over.'

'Don't talk daft. He's nearly old enough to be my father.'

'Some men like 'em young. You just watch yourself, Betty. Folk have started talking.'

'Let them talk then!' I glared at him. 'Joe Morris has been good to us. Without him we should be back where we were when I first went to the farm. I've nothing to be ashamed of. If people want to make up filthy tales, then let them. Besides, I don't believe they are gossiping. It's just in your mind.'

He shrugged his shoulders. 'Have it your own way then — but don't say I didn't warn you.'

I watched as he slammed out of the door, feeling furious. Was he so jealous of Joe Morris that he had to put sordid doubts in my mind? Not once in all the time I'd known him had Joe said or done anything that might make me think . . . It was ridiculous! Joe had no designs on my body. He was just a good friend. If folk wanted to read more into it than that, it was their own fault.

*

It was early in October that first year when I was given a sharp reminder of the family from the farm. I was working in my garden, weeding some of the winter greens, when a shadow fell across me and I looked up to see Nathan Crawley standing there. For a moment my heart jerked with surprise and I found that I was breathing hard. What on earth was he doing here? He hated the fens.

'Has something happened to Frances?'

'Your first thought would be for her,' he said, a wry smile on his lips. 'As far as I know, she's in the South of France having a wonderful time.'

'You haven't heard from her recently then?'

'Not from Frances. Mary writes every now and then, mostly about business.'

'Why have you come to Sutton?'

'I had to see a lawyer about my trust.'

'It had to be that. Nothing else would drag you back to this place.'

'Are you sure of that, Betty?'

A little shiver went through me. 'What other reason could you have?'

'I wanted to see how you were getting on.'

I laughed harshly. 'You must be joking! You didn't even ask me if . . .'

'If you were having a child?' He smiled oddly. 'In the barn you said you had forgiven me. If you'd been pregnant I think you'd have told me, don't you?'

'Maybe.' I frowned at him. 'So why did you come?'

'I wanted to see if you were managing. You were not treated well by my family. Mary could have given you more – and Frances behaved abominally.'

'She was upset. I don't blame her.'

'Why are you so understanding with everyone but me?'

'Don't start, Nathan.'

His eyes glittered with anger as he stood over me, and for a moment I thought he was going to hit me. My chin went up and I glared back at him, daring him to try it.

'Why did you come?'

'I wondered if you were happy, Betty. It's as simple as that. I'm in a position to help you now. I know you wanted to sing. I could find you a job in a nightclub. They want a singer. Someone young and unknown. I thought it might appeal to you?'

I stared at him for a moment, my heart beating fast. A job singing in a nightclub! It sounded so exciting – but I couldn't go. I couldn't leave my brother and sister. I shook my head, pretending I wasn't interested.

'I don't want to sing in a nightclub,' I said. 'If I ever get the chance, I want to be in a musical – like *Kiss Me Kate*.'

He nodded, his eyes thoughtful. 'Have it your own way, Betty. I thought it would be a start for you – in my opinion it would suit you better.' He sighed as he looked at me. 'At least let me give you some money.'

'I don't want your money.'

'How long do you think you're going to live on what Mary gave you?'

'I'll manage. When did you suddenly come into money anyway?'

Nathan grinned. 'Suspicious, Betty? Mary persuaded the lawyers that I was capable of handling my own trust. I'm doing okay one way and another. I told you I buy property – and I have other interests. I can afford to help you.'

'I've told you, I don't need your help.'

'Always so stubborn.' He shook his head. 'The offer stands for as long as I'm around. Don't let your pride ruin your life, Betty. I'm going to give you my card. You can always reach me at this address. You don't need me now, but one day you may change your mind.' He thrust a small white card into my hand. 'I may have done you a great wrong in your mind, but give me some credit for decency. I'm just trying to help.'

'No strings attached?' I gazed up at him. 'I'm sorry, Nathan, I don't believe you.'

His eyes glittered and then he turned and strode off

303

towards the front of the cottage. I hesitated momentarily, then I ran after him, catching him as he was about to get into his car.

'I didn't mean that,' I said breathlessly. 'I'm sorry. You're right. I'm too proud. I can manage for the moment, but I'll remember if I need help.'

He smiled at me. 'That's my kid,' he said softly and got into his car.

I stared after him as he drove away. He was no longer running the small Alfa Romeo he'd had when he took me to the seaside. Now he had a sleek black Daimler saloon that looked very expensive. Obviously Nathan was doing very well for himself . . .

Chapter Twelve

It was 1949 and things had at last begun to improve. Sir Stafford Cripps had imposed potato rationing in 1947 but in 1948 Mr Harold Wilson, President of the Board of Trade, removed it. The school-leaving age had been raised to fifteen, a National Insurance scheme had been introduced to provide for family allowances, sickness and unemployment benefit, and retirement pensions, and the mood of austerity that had gripped the country was gradually lifting. It was now possible to go abroad on a Thomas Cook package holiday, and reports of flying saucers had appeared in the newspapers. Danny Kaye had charmed London audiences by sitting on the edge of the stage and making them sing silly songs, and the campaign for nuclear disarmament had begun with a march from Aldermaston. People were beginning to recover from the war and learn to live again. There were always stories in the newspapers about Princess Margaret going to nightclubs and arriving home with the milk.

Joe and I had begun to dig the garden for the new spring plantings. We laughed and joked with each other as we dug and raked, little Joe clearing the rubbish to make a compost heap. Dorothy Ann sat watching us from the high chair Joe had bought her. She was eighteen months old now and she could crawl on all fours, but she still couldn't walk unaided. Her only words were Betty and Joe, and she was still in nappies, but we all adored the beautiful, backward child. Except Dad, of course.

That summer I was eighteen. Joe bought me a new

dress and a string of seed pearls. I stared at them as I opened the box, feeling stunned. It was a wildly extravagant gift and it worried me. He should not have spent so much on me.

'Oh, Joseph,' I whispered. 'They're beautiful – but much too expensive. You shouldn't have done it.'

'Why not?' he asked, his cheeks flushed. 'You deserve them, lass. You work all hours and you never think of yourself. You're a beautiful young woman, Betty. By rights you should be enjoying your own life, not caring for a young family.'

'I'm happy enough,' I said, and it was true. I no longer hankered over what might have been.

'I know that.' He smiled at me in an odd, shy way. 'Don't deny me the pleasure, lass. I've no one of my own. You and the children are my family.'

What could I do but smile and put on my new dress and necklace for everyone to admire?

It was feast day in Sutton. Every year the annual fair was held in the field behind the pub next to the church. Its coming created a mild excitement in the village and almost everyone put in an appearance.

I gave my brother a few shillings to spend, and he ran ahead of me as we set out. The sun was shining brightly, adding to the pleasure of the occasion. I pushed Dorothy Ann's pram, listening to the sound of the music. Flags were fluttering in the breeze and the atmosphere was one of fun and laughter.

'Going to the feast then, Betty?'

'Yes. I couldn't let the children miss it.'

'That would be a shame . . .' The woman's eyes were curious as they took note of my smart dress and pearl necklace. 'Joe Morris not with you then?'

'He'll be along later if he can manage it. He's not finished with the harvest yet.'

'Well, you'd know. Regular visitor, isn't he?'

'Yes, Mrs Jarrold he is. The children adore him. He plays with them for hours.'

I pushed the pram onwards, determined not to let her sly hints bother me. I had nothing to hide, why should I mind a little gossip?

The fair was in full swing. There were stalls with striped awnings, roundabouts and swings. All kinds of games and competitions. The vicar's wife was running a cake stall and she had a glass jar full of beans with a large notice inviting us all to guess how many it contained.

I bought some gingerbread for Dorothy Ann, breaking off a small piece for her. She munched contentedly. Crumbs went everywhere and she dribbled on her clean bib, but I was used to that.

Little Joe was haring round like a mad thing. I stood watching him, enjoying the sound of his laughter and the sunshine. It was several minutes before I became aware of voices behind me, deliberately raised for me to hear.

'I reckon there'll be two in that pram before long.'

This was followed by spiteful laughter and giggling. I glanced over my shoulder, recognising the girls. They were both of a similar age and worked on the land together. I sometimes saw them as they walked home at night, but they never spoke to me.

'Bound to be sooner or later. My Mum says he's there till past seven at night. Winter and summer. Stands to reason something's going on . . .'

I called to my brother and moved on, past the dodgems and the roundabouts, not wanting to listen to their spiteful talk. I was intent on enjoying myself and I wasn't going to let them spoil my day. I stopped to watch a group of young men on the rifle range. One of them came over to me.

'Having a good time then?' he asked cheekily. 'How about coming for a drink with me?'

It was Zac Jarrold, the youth Vera had been seen hanging around with. Except that he was a man now. Instead of going back to London with the other evacuees after the war, he'd found a job on the land and settled in Sutton.

'No thank you,' I said, disliking the look in his eyes. 'I can't leave Dorothy Ann.'

'Can't you find someone to look after the kid? If you don't want a drink we can find something more interesting to do.'

'Like what?' I asked, glaring at him as I saw the suggestive look in his eyes.

He winked. 'You know what I mean. Why don't you try doing it with someone your own age for a change? Old Joe Morris is past it. 'Sides, he can't be much good or you'd be in the pudding club by now.'

'Wash your mouth out with salt, Zac Jarrold! You've no call to say such filthy things to me.'

'Why not?' He eyed me with derision. 'It's what everyone says. If Joe ain't getting it, why's he there all the time? Stand to reason he wouldn't work his guts out for nothing. Anyway, you're the same as your sister Vera, I reckon – and she loved it!'

I was so angry I just exploded. How dare he talk about Vera like that? Abandoning my grip on the pram, I lunged at Zac, slapping him hard across the face three times.

'You've got a filthy mind!' I yelled. 'Joe Morris is my friend, that's all. He helps me and I give him a cooked dinner, nothing more. He's a decent man, not a filthy little toad like you.'

Zac's mouth fell open. He stared at me, too stunned to say anything or attempt to hit me back. It was just as well, because at that moment I could have cheerfully killed him. His mates were whispering and laughing in the background, and everyone was staring at us.

'You'll be sorry for this,' he muttered, then swung round and strode off in the direction of the pub.

I glared at his friends and they stopped laughing, turning away in embarrassment. I could see a couple of women whispering to each other, and I knew what they were saying. That Cantrel girl had made a show of herself. Well, it was only to be expected. She had bad blood in her, didn't she?

I pushed Dorothy Ann's pram to where my brother was paying for a lucky dip in the bran bucket. I was very angry, and resolved not to let the gossips drive me away. I had as much right to be here as anyone else. I'd done nothing wrong, and I seethed inwardly at the unfairness of it.

Joe Morris was making his way towards me. He was wearing his Sunday suit and grinning like a kid let out of school. I knew he must have worked like hell to get away in time to join me, and I smiled at him in welcome. I wasn't going to let a lot of busybodies spoil our day!

'So here you are then,' he said, beaming. 'I thought I'd never get away. The tractor broke down first thing and put us behind.'

'You must have been up at the crack of dawn.'

'Earlier,' he agreed cheerfully. 'It was worth it. Now we can enjoy ourselves.'

Joe put his hand in his pocket as my brother ran to him, giving him a handful of change. 'Come back when you run out,' he said. 'I'm going to have a go at the hoop-la.'

'You spoil him, Joseph,' I said.

'Well, it's only once a year.'

'But you're always giving him something.'

'I'd do a lot more for him and you, if you'd let me. You're my family now. Surely you know that?'

There was something in his look at that moment that told me he was aware of what had been going on. I felt a funny fluttering in my stomach, and I knew what he was asking me.

'I – I don't know,' I said, looking at him anxiously.

'You don't have to say anything now,' he reassured me. 'This is neither the time nor the place. We're going to have a little fun – and they can all think what they like!'

Someone *had* told him about the quarrel with Zac. That's why he had spoken so openly. Seeing the hard glitter in his eyes, I knew that Joe was ready to defend me with his fists or his tongue. It was so unlike him to be this agressive that I suddenly felt like laughing.

'Why not?' I asked with a smile. 'Black can't get any blacker, can it?'

Joe Morris asked me to marry him that evening. He'd spent the whole of the afternoon at the feast with us, bundling Dorothy Ann's pram and two tired but contented youngsters into the back of his car when it was over. He came in with us, staying to supper and lingering until the children were in bed.

'You'll have a cup of tea before you go?' I asked. 'It was a wonderful afternoon, Joe. I can't thank you enough.'

He took the kettle from my hands and made me sit down. 'Stop fussing, Betty. You're like a cat on live coals. I've something to say and we'd best get it over.'

'You heard what Zac said to me, didn't you? Someone told you.'

He nodded grimly. 'It made me mad enough to spit, but I blame myself. I should have known what they'd say.'

'It was the way Zac looked at me. I suppose I shouldn't have hit him.'

'It was better that you hit him than me. I might have killed the bugger if I'd got my hands on him.'

'Joseph!' I stared in surprise. 'That's the first time I've heard you swear.'

'Sorry.' He laughed ruefully. 'I'm that angry over it, Betty. He won't get away with it. He'll apologise and mean it, or I'll know the reason why.'

'How fierce you are,' I said, laughing. 'I don't think I've ever seen you really angry before.'

'I've not had cause to be. I won't have anyone upsetting you.'

'Oh, Joe . . .' I was surprised at the look in his eyes.

He stopped me with a shake of his head. 'Let me finish, lass. You know what I am. I'm a worker. I'll work for you and the children until I drop. You'll have everything I can

310

provide. A decent home, pretty clothes, security.' A faint flush came into his cheeks. 'I know I'm not much of a catch for a pretty lass like you – but I'm right fond of you. Always have been.'

'I thought you had a soft spot for Polly?'

'I was taken with her. I'd have wed her if she'd have had me, but I knew she would never have stayed faithful to me. She wasn't a bad girl, but she wasn't like you, Betty.'

'What do you mean?'

He smiled gently. 'You're loyal, honest and unselfish. Not many would have done what you did – coming back here when you could . . .'

'Don't make me a martyr,' I said sharply. 'Don't think I didn't resent having to give up my chance of going with Frances. I had no choice. My family needed me.'

'You made the best of it. You're not bitter now, are you?'

'No,' I sighed. 'Sometimes – just sometimes I think of what might have been. I wonder where Frances is and what she's doing.'

'That's only natural.' Joe frowned. 'I thought you might have heard from one of them before now. That's why I haven't spoken until now. You had thoughts of being a singer – I don't want to tie you down, Betty.'

'Impossible dreams.' I shook my head. 'I've stopped thinking about it, Joe. I'd have liked to remain friends with Frances, but I don't blame her for what happened. I did break my promise to her – and she was used to having her own way.'

'She was an ungrateful little madam.'

'Don't say that, Joe. She was my friend. I still care for her. She came into my life at a time when I needed her, and she gave me quite a lot despite the way it finished.'

'Then I'll say no more on it, lass.'

'Thank you.' I looked at him. 'I've so much to thank *you* for. I'm not sure how to answer you just yet.'

'I didn't expect an answer tonight. I wouldn't have

spoken just yet if it hadn't been for the way folk talk – but I won't have them upsetting you.'

'I'm not really upset now.' I laughed harshly. 'I should have expected it. I'm a Cantrel, Joseph.'

'You're yourself and no one else. You can't help what your pa is. Besides, he's not such a bad man. I know he likes a drink and he's lazy . . .'

'And he beat my mother insensible and drove her into an early grave,' I said bitterly. 'I know he's my father but sometimes I hate him. That frightens me. It isn't right to feel like that about your own father.'

'He hasn't been giving you any trouble, has he?'

'No. He wouldn't dare, not while you're my friend. I think he knows what you would do if he laid a finger on me.' I looked at Joe anxiously. 'I wouldn't want to lose your friendship.'

'You won't,' he replied, smiling gently. 'I'd be only too happy to see you courted by a man who was really worthy of you – like that James Blair who was Nathan's friend. A real gentleman he was.'

'What makes you say that?' I stared at him in surprise. How could he know that James had always been special to me?

'Oh, it was just something about the way he looked at you. Made me think he was taken with you.'

'James would never marry a girl like me. Besides, it was Frances he was fond of. I think they may marry one day.'

'Is that so?' Joe shook his head. 'Well, that just shows how wrong you can be. I thought it was you he wanted.'

'That's different. Wanting and loving aren't always the same thing.'

'You're right there.' Joe got to his feet. 'I'd best be going. It's getting late and the tongues will be wagging.'

'You'll come on Sunday as usual?'

'I'll be here.' He smiled at me. 'Don't let them keep you awake, lass. They can hurt you, but in the end it's only talk.'

'I know. I'll think about marrying you, Joe. I really will.'

I sat by the fire after he'd left. I wanted to think carefully about the future, about what I wanted to do with my life. Joe would be a good father to the children and a considerate husband. He was several years older than me, but that didn't matter so much. I liked him and we got on well together, that was more than many husbands and wives could say. It wouldn't be a love match but a marriage of convenience, for Joe as well as me. He was fond of me, but I didn't think he was in love with me. I had no doubt that he was lonely and he missed the old way of life, when we were all together in the kitchen.

I thought about James Blair, too. It was odd that Joe should mention him. I hadn't thought anyone knew how I felt – except perhaps Nathan.

I wondered how James was getting on working for his father. I had an idea that he would hate it; he must feel almost as trapped as I had at times. But perhaps he had accepted his new life. Perhaps he was already married – maybe even to Frances.

I wasn't sure whether that made me feel jealous or not. I had scarcely known James, perhaps my feelings for him were merely infatuation. Yet I could still remember the gentleness of his smile, and I knew that I would always think of him as the perfect man.

I smiled to myself as I gazed into the fire, knowing that my thoughts were foolish. James had always been way out of my reach.

Marriage with Joe would give me security. There would be few surprises and little excitement, but I couldn't expect it. If I'd wanted to live dangerously, I should have accepted Nathan's offer of a job in London.

Thinking about Nathan's last visit made me wonder just what he did for a living. He talked vaguely about dealing in property – but what were his other interests? I had a feeling that Nathan might do anything, whether it was legal or not. How did he come to know there was an opening for a singer at that nightclub, and how could he be sure that the owner would be willing to take me on? Unless he was the owner himself . . . That wouldn't surprise me. Nathan was the kind of man who would enjoy that sort of life, a life full of excitement and perhaps danger . . .

Sighing, I got to my feet and went through to my brother's bedroom. He opened his eyes as I looked at him.

'What's wrong, Betty?'

'Nothing's wrong.' I stroked the hair back from his forehead. 'Did you have a good time today?'

'It was great. Especially after Joe came. I do love him, Betty.'

'Do you? Would you like it if we all went to live with him?'

He sat up eagerly. 'Leave here and live on the farm with Joe always?'

'Yes. He's the manager now. We would live in the big house. You'd have to get up very early to bike to school in the mornings, though.'

'I wouldn't mind that.' His eyes were bright with excitement. Are you going to marry him, Betty?'

'I might – how do you feel about that?'

'I'd like it, if you would?'

'Well, I haven't made up my mind yet, but I think I might say yes.'

'That would be great,' my brother said. 'I've always wanted to live on a farm.'

'We'll see,' I said, bending down to kiss his cheek. 'Go to sleep now.'

It's night but they always keep a light burning in my cell. I lie with my eyes closed, trying to ignore it. How long have I been here now? The days and nights seem to merge as one, confusing me. Sometimes I long for it all to be over, then I wouldn't have to remember any more. The memories are becoming painful, and I try to shut them out, but they crowd in on me, forcing me back to that terrible time.

How could I have guessed that night as I sat on the edge of my brother's bed, talking happily of the future – how could I have known what Fate had in store for us?

A cry of grief escapes me, bringing a wardress to my side. She bends to peer at my face, asking if I'm ill, but I turn my face to the wall. No one can help me. There is no escape for me. The memories are there, clamouring to be let back into my mind . . .

I told Joe I would marry him when he came on Sunday. He looked surprised, as if he'd been expecting me to turn him down, and then he grinned.

'That's the best news I've had in years,' he said. 'I'm damned if I know what to say.'

'Well, you could say you were pleased,' I teased. 'And you could kiss me.'

'Are you sure, Betty?' He looked awkward.

'We're to be married, Joe. So we'd best start as we mean to go on. You're so good with children; I know you'd like a son of your own. And I want to be a proper wife to you.'

'I wasn't sure how you'd feel about that,' he said, moving to put his arms around me. 'I'm so much older than you.'

'Come here, you big softie,' I said. I took his hands and placed them around my waist, then I reached up and put my arms around his neck. 'Kiss me, Joe.'

I lifted my face imperiously and he chuckled deep in his throat. 'I might have known it would be all or nothing with you.' His voice cracked. 'Betty. Betty, love, I'll be good to you. I swear I will. You'll never regret this if I can help it.'

He kissed me and it was a true man's kiss, warm and sweet with a hint of passion. It felt good to be in his arms, and I knew then that it would not be too much of a sacrifice to be Joe's wife.

Joe met my father at the gate. I had some idea of what they were saying, and I watched anxiously as they seemed to argue for a while, then they reached an agreement and shook hands. Pa even managed a smile when he came in.

'So you're wanting my blessing then? Joe's a good man, Betty. I'll not stand in your way.'

He had been drinking just enough to put him in a good mood. It might be different another day, when he'd had time to think.

'Will you come to the vicarage with us and give your permission this afternoon?'

'While I'm sober, Betty? Yes, perhaps you're right.' His tone was mocking. 'Put the dinner on the table then, girl.'

He joked with Joe as we ate. I saw my brother looking at him in surprise. It was a long time since we'd seen him in such a good mood.

It continued as we all trooped through the village. He kept patting Joe on the back and winking at me. He even gave his son a piggy-back ride. I wondered how Joe had managed to get him in such a happy frame of mind.

The vicar welcomed our news. He invited us all into his house and spent several minutes talking about the arrangements; then he turned to my father.

'And what about you, Mr Cantrel?' he asked. 'How will you manage when your daughter leaves home?'

'I'm going with her.' Dad's eyes glinted with a malicious humour as he looked at me. 'I'm going to have Joe's old cottage when he moves into the house.'

I looked at Joe in alarm. Surely he hadn't been that foolish? It took me all my time to control my tongue, but I managed to hold my temper until we left the vicarage.

'What's this about Dad coming with us?' I demanded as we started home.

Joe looked at me sheepishly. 'He can't manage alone. He'll have his own place but he can eat with us and I'll find him some jobs . . .'

316

'No!' I could have screamed in frustration. 'I don't want him with us. Oh, Joe, why did you do it?'

'Joe's got a kinder heart than you, Betty.' Dad grinned at me. 'He knew I couldn't bear to be parted from my loved ones.'

'Your loved ones?' I echoed incredulously. 'You don't give a damn about anyone but yourself.'

'Betty, don't talk to your father like that.'

I stared at Joe angrily. Then I started to push the pram faster, wanting to run.

'Betty!' Joe called. 'Betty, wait for me.'

I refused to slow down. I'd thought I was getting away from Dad. It was one of the reasons I'd agreed to the marriage.

Joe caught up with me at the cottage gate. I turned on him with accusing eyes.

'How could you do it, Joe?'

'He made it a condition, Betty. Besides, how could I refuse?' Joe frowned. 'Your Dad's sick. He can't live much longer – a year or two at best. It's his liver – from the drinking.'

'What do you mean? He isn't ill.'

'He hasn't told you but he's in constant pain. The doctor warned him to stop drinking years ago, but he says it's the only relief he gets.'

'I don't believe it. He only said it to make you feel sorry for him.'

'No, Betty. I've known for a while now.'

'He's not lying?'

'No. We can't desert him.'

There was such a look of appeal in Joe's eyes that I felt myself wavering. It wasn't fair. Why should I have to look after Dad? His illness was his own fault. I knew what it would mean. I should have to cook and clean for him, clearing up whenever he vomited all over the place as he often did when he'd been drinking . . . Was that a sign of his illness? When I thought about it, I realised it was a recent thing.

317

Trapped! Trapped! Trapped! The words echoed in my head.

It wasn't right. It wasn't fair. I owed my father nothing. Yet I knew I couldn't turn my back on him now.

'No,' I said dully. 'I suppose we can't desert him now.'

Joe accompanied me to church on the Sunday morning. It was October now and a chill had crept into the air. It was still bright and dry but the summer was over and the leaves had begun to fall.

There were whispers and giggles when the banns were read, but also smiles of approval. Some still believed that I had erred, but they were willing to forgive now that Joe had done the right thing by me.

'Well, that's that,' Joe said with satisfaction as we came out. 'You'll get no more trouble now.'

I nodded and smiled. I'd seen Zac Jarrold scowling at me as we came out of church and I knew he would never forgive me for making a fool of him at the fair, but with Joe around there was nothing he could do to harm me.

I wondered about our Vera a lot. Was it true that she'd been with Zac? And what made her go off the way she had? I reproached myself for not taking more notice at the time. If only I'd taken her on that day trip to London I'd promised her. I'd always meant to, but somehow there hadn't been time.

Joe had his arm tucked through mine. We walked along the street, turning up our coat collars as the wind began to rise. I looked out over the sweeping fenland and a shiver went through me. The fields were bare of their summer green, the earth black and freshly turned. The scene seemed stark and bleak to me that day, and I had a feeling of being chained to this place for ever. I knew exactly how a bird must feel looking out from behind the bars of a cage. I wanted to spread my wings and fly away.

I was listening to a new record Joe had bought me. It was Edith Piaf, a French singer I admired enormously. Her

318

voice had a special quality, a magic that made a lump come to my throat every time I heard her. I loved her songs and I sang them to myself as I worked. I was going to bake some cakes for tea. As I glanced out of the window, I saw my father at the gate. He was talking to the postman. I wondered if there was a letter for me. Sometimes Polly scribbled a few lines, and I still half hoped that Frances would write to me one day.

I looked at Dad as he came in, his hand in his pocket. 'Is there anything for me?'

He looked at me oddly, seeming to hesitate, then he shook his head. 'No, Betty,' he said. 'Were you expecting a letter?'

'No, not really,' I said. 'I saw the postman and wondered, that's all.'

'He was just showing me a picture of his kids,' he said. 'There was nothing for you.'

His manner seemed a bit odd, but I was only half listening to him. My mind was wrapped up in the music of Piaf, singing 'La Vie En Rose'.

'Never mind,' I said. 'I expect Hilda will write as soon as she hears my news. Now, I'd better get on or I'll never get these cakes done.'

Dad frowned as he watched me. 'One thing I heard today. Our Joe's been playing with some gipsy kids. You tell him to stay away from them, Betty.'

'Why?' I looked at him in surprise. 'What's wrong with that?'

'Don't like gipsies,' he said. 'Dirty beggars, I always think. He might catch something.'

'Like fleas, you mean?' I laughed and shook my head. 'You're prejudiced, Dad. But I'll give him a good scrub when he gets home, don't worry.'

Joe called to see me the next morning. He was on his way to the railway station with a load of sugar beet. I hadn't expected to see him and I was up to my elbows in washing suds.

'A letter came for you from Polly,' he said. 'It was

319

delivered to the farm by mistake. I thought I'd pop it in – and I wanted to give you this.' He laid a brown envelope on the table.

'What's that, Joe?'

'It's to buy your wedding dress. You'll need clothes for the children and your pa, too.'

I opened the envelope reluctantly. There was a hundred pounds inside. I stared at it awkwardly. 'It's far too much, Joe.'

'I've told you before. I'm not short of a few quid. I want you to have the best. Take it and buy what you want. You'll need clothes for the honeymoon. If you get someone to look after Dorothy Ann we can go into Cambridge one day next week; you'll get a better choice there. Thanks to Harold Wilson, you won't need clothing coupons any more. You can buy what you like, Betty.'

'It was great him tearing up his ration card like that. It's the first time I've ever been able to choose just what I want, Joe.'

'That's why I've given you the money. I thought we'd have a small reception at the church hall. We'll ask George Baxter and his wife, Mrs Jackson and a few more – if you'd like that?'

'It sounds lovely. We'll go into Cambridge next Monday, if that suits you?'

'Fine.' He smiled. 'I'll see you on Sunday then.'

After Joe had gone I put the money in a safe place. Dad wouldn't touch it if he was sober, but there was no telling what he might do if the drink was in him. I left the washing to soak for a while and read my letter from Polly. It was funny that I'd asked Dad only the day before if there was a letter for me. I must have been psychic.

Polly's letter was cheerful and brief, telling me she was well and that she had moved. I had written after her first letter to ask if I could tell George where she was, but she had never mentioned her brother. It was up to her. I'd promised not to tell and that was that.

I wondered what she would say when I wrote that I was going to marry Joe.

I went back to my washing. Dorothy Ann had been quieter than usual all day. When I tried to feed her, she pushed my hand away and refused to eat. It wasn't like her; though she never ate much, I could usually persuade her to take something. She seemed a little flushed and her skin felt hot. I thought she might be getting a chill. When I thought about it, I realised she'd been acting strangely for a couple of days now. It was always so difficult to tell when Dottie was ill. Instead of screaming, she simply curled up in her cot and sucked her thumb.

When the washing was out on the line, I took her on my knee and nursed her, singing a nursery rhyme to her: 'Rock-a-bye baby on the treetops. When the wind blows, the cradle will rock . . .' She always loved that; it was her favourite.

She was sleeping when little Joe came home from school. His face was glowing and he was excited. He'd been playing football and he was full of it.

'I'm going to be in the school team for the match on Saturday,' he told me proudly.

'That's good, Joe,' I said. 'I'll get tea now. I've baked your favourite cake. You can eat it while you listen to Dick Barton on the radio.'

I woke up that night to hear a strange sound. For a moment I didn't realise what the odd, choking cry was. Then I realised that Dorothy Ann was crying. I was out of bed in a flash. My little sister hardly ever cried. Something must be really wrong with her.

I found Joey standing by her cot. He looked at me anxiously. 'What's wrong with her, Betty? She seems as if she's choking.'

'I don't know,' I said. 'She was a little flushed earlier but she went to sleep after I cuddled her. I'll have her on my lap in front of the fire.'

Joe followed me into the kitchen looking worried. 'Shall I make a cup of tea, Betty?'

I smiled at my brother. 'Yes, that would be nice, Joe.'

Dottie had begun to make those odd sounds again. 'Something's in her throat,' I said. I pulled her mouth open and stuck my finger in, feeling a sticky mucus at the back of her throat. It was a kind of membrane and it was affecting her breathing. I cleared it as best I could and she seemed easier. 'That's better.'

Joe still looked anxious. 'What is it, Betty?'

'I don't know – she still feels hot.'

I sat rocking Dorothy Ann in my arms. Joe made a cup of tea and we both drank it. I told him to go to bed, but then the choking began again. I put my finger in the baby's mouth and found more of the mucus.

A shiver of horror went through me as I realised what it might be. Why hadn't I thought of it before? Diphtheria! I remembered Mum telling me about an outbreak years before I was old enough to remember it. I tried to remember what she'd said; it was an infectious throat disease that particularly affected children. It was serious in adults but a killer in children.

I looked at my brother. 'I think you'd better get dressed, Joe. We should have the doctor.'

He nodded, his face grave. 'Is it diphtheria, Betty? Only – only those gipsy children that Dad said I shouldn't play with, they say some of them have gone down with it. I heard a teacher talking about it at school today.'

'Oh, Joe . . .' I stared at him. 'Let's hope you haven't got it as well.'

'I feel all right,' he said. 'I'll get dressed . . . Betty, did I give it to her?'

He looked as if he were about to cry. 'It's not your fault,' I said. 'Any of us could have picked it up. Besides, you said you feel all right. Hurry up, will you, love?'

Dottie was crying bitterly. It was terrible to watch her suffer. She had always been so contented, now her breath was tortured and rasping. I was frightened. I had no idea what to do.

I heard rather than saw my brother fly through the

kitchen. I wished now that I'd sent for the doctor that afternoon, but I hadn't realised it was serious. I prayed that our Joe hadn't picked up the terrible disease. Let it be just a chill or something similar.

It seemed a long time before the doctor arrived. I could see he had dressed in a hurry, because his waistcoat was buttoned wrongly. He looked worried and my stomach began to tie itself in knots.

'Joe said the baby was choking. Is there something in her throat?'

'It's a kind of membrane. I tried to clear it but it keeps forming.'

He took a wooden spatula from his bag. 'Open her mouth for me. Hold her still while I . . . Yes, you're right.' He put the spatula into a glass bottle. 'I'll have some tests done, but I'm afraid it may be diphtheria. There have been some cases reported. You'll have to stay in the cottage and keep Joe away from school. We don't want it to spread.'

'What can I do for her?'

'There's not very much you can do – except what you've been doing already. Keep the obstruction clear. Keep her warm. Give her water to drink if she can swallow.'

'Shouldn't she be in hospital?'

'I'm not sure it would be the best place for her, Betty. She would have to be in isolation and she's so young – I think you will nurse her as well as anyone. I'm sorry, but I'm not sure I could find her a place even if I tried.' He smiled apologetically. 'We haven't yet got all those new hospitals the government has promised.'

I felt close to despair as he went out. What was I going to do now? I felt so useless, so ignorant. I'd never had to cope with real illness before. Little Joe was standing looking at me silently, his eyes dark with guilt. I knew he was blaming himself for bringing home the infection.

'Why don't you try and get some sleep?' I suggested. 'You won't be able to go to school I'm afraid . . .' I

323

suddenly realised what that would mean for him. 'The football match – I'm sorry, Joe.'

'It doesn't matter,' he said, blinking hard. 'She will be all right, won't she, Betty?'

'Yes, of course,' I said, smiling at him. 'Go back to bed now, love.'

As he turned reluctantly towards the bedroom door, I looked at Dorothy Ann. I wasn't at all sure that she was going to pull through.

Chapter Thirteen

Dorothy Ann seemed to be a little easier. I changed her clothes and put her back in her cot. Joe was asleep. He seemed to be peaceful enough. Maybe he hadn't got it. Maybe it wasn't diphtheria after all. I kept praying that the doctor was wrong.

While the children were resting, I made up the fire and snatched a bite to eat. Before I could finish my toast, Dottie was choking again. I hurried back to the bedroom. Joe had begun to toss restlessly. He opened his eyes and looked at me.

'Can I have a drink of water, Betty? My throat feels sore.'

I laid my hand on his brow; he felt hot. Panic ran through me. Not Joe. Oh, please not Joe as well!

I gave him a glass of water and he settled. The doctor had told me to keep them warm, but he looked as though he had a fever. I poked my finger in Dottie's throat, clearing the horrid mucus. It seemed to be getting tougher, more difficult to break.

My brother got steadily worse throughout the day. My father came to the door but I chased him out.

'Stay away, Dad,' I said. 'I can't nurse you, too.'

'I only wanted to help.'

'You can help by shopping, but otherwise stay away.'

'I want Joe,' my brother moaned. 'Why won't he come?'

'Joe doesn't know you're ill,' I said. 'He'll come soon.'

I made warming drinks and a thin soup. My brother managed to swallow a little, but I couldn't get anything down Dottie's throat. Maybe it was wrong to try. I just didn't know. She was only comfortable when I was nursing her, but I couldn't hold her all the time. Joe needed attention, too.

It was a long, terrible night. Dottie was hardly moving at all now. She just lay still and the choking sounds were very feeble. I was afraid for her. She didn't seem able to fight it. I wondered about sending for the doctor again, but what could he do?

Daylight came and little Joe had begun to make the same horrible choking noises. I laid Dottie down to see if I could clear Joe's throat. The membrane was so leathery I couldn't break through it at first. Caught up in my desperate task, I didn't hear the door open and I jumped as someone spoke.

'Let me see if I can do it, Betty.'

'Oh, Joseph,' I cried. 'You shouldn't be here. The doctor said no one was to come in. I sent Dad away so he wouldn't take it – he hasn't has he?'

'No, he seems all right. He came to fetch me.'

'You mustn't stay.'

'You don't think I'd leave you to cope with this alone? I'd have been here sooner if I'd known.'

'I don't want you to catch it.'

'What about you?' He looked at my strained face. 'You've been up all night. Leave them to me and get some sleep.'

'No – you shouldn't be here.'

'I'm going to be angry in a minute, Betty. You need sleep if you're to look after them when I've gone.'

There was no point in arguing with him. Besides, I was almost dead on my feet. As I moved towards my room, he was lifting little Joe from his bed. He shouldn't be here, but I was relieved to have the burden lifted from my shoulders for a while.

I slept for several hours. When I woke it was to find Joe sitting by the fire still nursing my brother. The child's face was stained with tears, but he seemed to be sleeping.

'I'll get us something to eat.'

Joe nodded. 'I'll put him back for a while.'

I filled the kettle and put it on the fire. Then I started to slice some bread. I was spreading it with butter when I heard an odd sound. Turning round, I saw Joe standing in the doorway. He had a terrible expression in his eyes and it sent a chill of fear through me. I started towards him.

'Dottie . . .'

'She's gone, Betty.' His face creased with distress. 'I looked at her an hour ago and she seemed better. I thought she was past the crisis. The boy was restless so . . .'

'An hour! You left her for an hour?' My voice was sharp with accusation. 'You know she never cries.'

'I'm sorry, Betty. I didn't think. The lad seemed the worst.'

'I shouldn't have left her. It was my fault.'

'It was mine and we both know it.'

He looked so guilty. 'No, it wasn't,' I said, tears stinging my eyes. 'She was slipping away from me anyway,' I went past him and bent over the cot, taking the tiny body in my arms. 'She was so vulnerable. She never stood a chance – that's why the doctor left her with me. He knew it was hopeless.'

Joe moved towards me, holding both me and Dottie to his chest. 'Don't cry, love. You did all that could be done.'

'No.' I moved away to sit by the fire. 'I should've done more. There should be something to cure it. Why did she have to die? Why do they let innocent babies die?'

'I've heard they give penicillin for it,' Joe said.

'What's that?'

'A new drug that fights germs. I'm not sure, Betty.'

'Why didn't the doctor give it to Dottie then?'

'It causes more harm than good sometimes, so they say.' Joe looked upset. 'It's very new, Betty. Maybe he thought the child would react badly to it.'

'Perhaps I should have sent for him again.'

327

'We'll fetch him today,' Joe said. 'Sit by the fire while I get the tea.'

'I couldn't eat anything now.'

'You must try. A cup of tea anyway.'

I stared down at Dorothy Ann's face. Through the mist of my tears, I could see that she looked as serene and lovely as ever. The pain tore at my heart. She was dead before she'd had a chance to live.

'Let me put her back in her cot, lass.' Joe set a mug of tea beside me. 'I'll see if the boy's resting.'

I could see he was still blaming himself. I let him take my sister and I made an effort to drink the tea. I knew it wasn't Joe's fault. Dottie was dying even before he came.

'He's asleep at the moment.'

I looked up as Joe came back. 'Drink your own tea, and eat some of that food.'

'You should eat something too.'

'One slice of bread and butter then.'

I made myself swallow the food. I knew I had to keep going.

'Your Dad came when you were asleep. He wanted to know how you were.'

'He wanted to help look after Dottie. He'll blame me now she's dead.'

'Of course he won't, Betty.'

'He must get some of that stuff,' I said. 'What did you call it?'

'Penicillin,' Joe said, frowning. 'There's no guarantee it will work. It's just something I read somewhere.'

A choking cry came from the bedroom. We both jumped to our feet at once. Then I saw the look on Joe's face and I let him go. Little Joe had always been his favourite. He couldn't have loved the boy more if he'd been his own son.

He was back again in a few minutes. I could see my brother was desperately ill and I knew that I must go for the doctor at once. If there was something that might save his life, I had to try it. I grabbed my coat and started for the door.

'I'm going to fetch the doctor,' I said. 'If that stuff works for some people I want it for Joe.'

'Go on then, Betty. I'll try and clear his throat.'

I had never run so fast in my life. I was panting when I arrived at the doctor's house, gasping for breath as I pounded frantically on the door. It was opened by his wife. She looked startled and then concerned as I gasped out my errand.

'I'm terribly sorry, Betty,' she said. 'The doctor's out at the moment. I'll tell him the minute he gets in. He's been called to a difficult delivery, so it might not be for a while.'

'Tell him my sister is dead and little Joe is really bad. I want some of that penicillin for him.'

'Yes, my dear,' she said. 'The moment he comes in.'

I ran home again, tears of frustration trickling down my cheeks.

Joe was still nursing my brother, talking to him gently. As soon as I saw his face I knew the child was worse.

'I was thinking mebbe you'd like a pony of your own. I could teach you to ride it. Next summer we'll go to the seaside for a holiday, and we'll go on the river in a boat. You'd like that, wouldn't you?'

The child was too sick to answer. I could see the tears slipping down the man's face, and my heart contracted with pain.

'The doctor's coming soon,' I said.

'Did you hear that?' Joe said, cradling the boy. 'Hold on, son. Don't let go.'

He had fought so hard to save little Joe, but it was no use. I stood watching as the life drained out of my brother, the bitterness twisting inside me. If there was a drug that could have helped him, it should have been tried. Something should have been done! I was angry and bitter. We had a National Health Service now, things were supposed to be better, yet my brother had still died.

It might have been easier if little Joe had gone quickly and quietly as Dorothy Ann had, but he fought hard. It was agony watching as he choked, the colour slowly leaving his face.

I saw my Joe age ten years in as many minutes. He wept as he saw that it was over. I let him cry for a while, then I took the boy from his arms. We laid him on his bed, next to Dottie.

'I had such plans for the lad,' Joe said brokenly. 'I can't believe he's gone.'

'You did all you could,' I said. 'You need some rest. Come and lie down for a while.' I took Joe to my room and made him lie down on my bed. Then I lay down beside him. He made a slight protest but I placed my finger against his lips.

'Don't say anything,' I whispered. 'Just hold me. I love you, Joseph. I didn't know it until today, but it's true. Hold me close.'

Joe's arms closed around me. For a long while we simply lay there together, and I think we both slept. When we woke again it was the most natural thing in the world to be together. Our lips touched, seeking, needing the comfort that men and women have always found in each other's bodies.

The touch of Joe's hand stroking my breast seemed to ease the terrible pain inside me. I quivered and trembled, clinging to him with a fierce need. For a few minutes I was able to forget the aching loss I had experienced during the day.

Joe's loving was slow and gentle. His kisses did not arouse the same trembling excitement in me that Nathan's had but they were a comfort and a solace to me. When it was over, I cried in Joe's arms.

We were in the kitchen having tea when the doctor finally arrived. He was concerned and distressed when I told him that both the children were dead.

'I only received the results of the tests today,' he said. 'I thought the baby was too young to risk giving her penicillin. I didn't know your brother had it too.'

'You should have sent them into hospital,' I cried, my voice loud and accusing. 'You're responsible for their deaths.'

'Now then, Betty,' Joe said. 'It wasn't the doctor's fault. You can't blame him.'

'I've been trying to find a bed in an isolation ward.' The doctor's eyes were sad. 'I can't tell you how sorry I am. It was very quick . . .'

'Because they've had years of deprivation,' I said. 'I know the last year has been better, but they were neither of them strong.'

'I'm afraid you're right,' the doctor agreed. 'But they aren't the only ones. A good many people are under-nourished these days – and will be until things get better.' He glanced at his watch. 'I must go now. Be sure to contact me if you feel ill yourself.'

'So that you can let me die, too?' I asked bitterly.

'Now then, Betty,' Joe said again. 'That wasn't called for.'

They had come for the children. I said a silent farewell to my brother and sister, the tears rolling down my cheeks. They were so young. Once again I was wracked with bitterness. Why? Why should it happen to them? I brushed away my tears as Joe told me it was time.

Two men came in with tiny coffins. Dad followed them. He frowned as he saw me.

'I'll see to it, Betty.'

I went into the kitchen and sat down. My father carried the coffins from the bedroom one by one. I looked at Joe, tears running down my cheeks.

'Do they have to go so soon?'

'It's best. The funeral will be on Sunday.'

'I'll see to it now,' Dad said as he carried the coffins out to the waiting hearse. I realised that he was completely sober, and I knew that he was suffering too.

331

When he had gone a silence fell between Joe and me. We looked at each other, then he took hold of my hands.

'You don't regret what we did?'

I knew he was talking about the time we had spent in my bed. 'No, of course not. I'm glad it happened that way, Joe.' I put my arms around him, laying my head against his shoulder. 'I'm glad we're to be married.' And as I said it, I knew it was true. Romantic dreams were all very well, but this had more substance.

He stroked my hair. 'You don't want to change your mind?'

I gazed up at him, suddenly quite sure that I wanted to marry this man. 'Are you still sure? I know you loved my brother like a son.'

'I loved him and the little one – but it's you I want, lass. I never dared to say much, but now I think maybe you're ready to hear it?'

I experienced a surge of happiness. What a fool I'd been to feel that I was being trapped into marriage. Joe was a man I could always rely on. The feelings I had for him might not be the romantic love I'd once dreamed of, but I did love him. I had discovered a sweet pleasure in his arms, and it made me feel good to know that we should soon be wed.

'I'm ready, Joe,' I said, smiling. 'You go home now. You must have work to do. I can manage.'

'Are you sure, love?'

'Yes. I want to scrub this place from top to bottom.'

Joe looked into my eyes. He knew I had to work my grief out. I had cried until my eyes felt gritty, now I needed the physical relief of work.

'Shall I come back tonight?'

I shook my head. 'No, not tonight. Last night we needed each other, Joe, but it can't happen again. Not until we're married. I won't give the gossips the satisfaction of knowing they were right all the time.'

He chuckled deep in his throat. 'It's as well I'm a patient man, Betty.'

'Go on, Joseph Morris!' I cried. 'Just you make sure you're in the church when the time comes. I'm depending on you to make an honest woman of me.'

'Mebbe I will . . .'

We smiled at each other. The tears were close beneath the surface, but we had to try to put our shared grief behind us.

It was harder when Joe had gone. The silence was all-enveloping, but I couldn't bring myself to put a record on. Music was for happy times.

I went to strip the beds. As I pulled the covers off my brother's bed something fell out with a chunk. It was the little wooden train I'd bought him years before. His first real toy. He'd had such a short, hard life, and now when things were getting better, he'd had to die. The waste of it appalled me. A rush of grief came over me. I picked up the toy and suddenly the tears I'd thought had all dried up were pouring down my face.

I cried until I ached, then I bundled the sheets into the copper full of water in the wash-house and lit the fire under it. I carried out all the children's soiled clothes and put them on the fire. Then I started to scrub the place clean. I washed the floors, the furniture, the windowsills and the walls. I cleared everything from the larder and scrubbed the shelves. The whole house smelt of carbolic and my hands were red and raw. Yet I could not stop.

I was scrubbing the kitchen table for the second time when the door opened. I didn't look up. I was concentrating on one spot in the pine table top. I was determined to scrub it away.

'Stop it, Betty! That's enough!'

My father's voice broke my concentration. I realised I'd been trying to scrub out a knot in the wood. Drying my hands, I was aware of the sting of tortured flesh, and of the ache in my back.

I slumped down in a chair by the fire. 'I haven't cooked anything. Will some bread and cheese do?'

'Mrs Brown sent you a pork pie and a loaf.' He pressed me back as I made to rise. 'Sit where you are, girl. I'll get the food for once.'

'I can do it, Dad.'

'Stay there. You're exhausted. Do you want to kill yourself too?'

I stared at him, my eyes dark with pain. 'So you do blame me. I knew you would.'

'Don't be a fool, girl, I know you did all you could. I'd only have been in your way.' He choked back a sob. 'I've not given you much cause to trust me.'

I couldn't say anything and he turned away. I knew I had given the knife another twist, but I was too exhausted to help him.

'I'm going to bed,' I said. 'We'll talk tomorrow.'

We did not talk the next day. When I awoke it was to feel a terrible soreness in my throat. My body was throbbing all over and I could barely stagger into the kitchen. Dad took one look at me and ordered me to bed.

'I'm not ill,' I croaked. 'It's just tiredness.'

Even as I said it, I was swaying on my feet. Dad caught me and carried me back to my bed. From then on I was aware of very little. The fever had laid me senseless and I barely felt the cool hands on my brow. I thought it was Joe who tended me, and I cried his name often, but when the day finally dawned when I could see clearly again, my father was sitting beside the bed.

'Feeling better?' he asked when I croaked his name. 'There's some soup made if you fancy it.'

'Have I been ill?'

'The doctor said you had it mildly. He gave you injections, Betty. He saved your life.'

My body felt as if it had been beaten all over, but I knew I'd been lucky. I couldn't have suffered as badly as the children. I'd survived.

'How long have I been here?'

'Ten days. You were stronger than the others, Betty. You fought back.'

'Has Joe been looking after me?'

'Some of the time.' He stood up. 'I'll get the soup.'

His manner seemed strange, but I was too exhausted to wonder at it for long. I might not have been as sick as the little ones, but it had left me feeling very weak. I could barely swallow the soup when he spooned it into my mouth.

'That's enough,' I muttered. 'Have you been ill?'

Dad shook his head. 'Seems I'm immune to it. It must be all that alcohol. My insides are pickled!'

'Don't joke,' I sighed wearily. 'I must look a sight.'

'You don't look as pretty as usual.'

My hair felt sticky and I could smell the stink of sweat on my body. 'When is Joe coming? I have to wash my hair.'

'Stay where you are, girl,' he said gruffly. 'Joe's too busy to be running after you all the time. He'll come on Sunday. You'll be feeling better by then.'

'Yes, I suppose you're right.'

I sighed and lay back against the pillows. Almost without realising it, I drifted into sleep.

Sunday came and went, but Joe didn't arrive. I was weaker than I'd realised. I couldn't manage to get up just yet. I asked Dad why Joe hadn't come, but he only told me not to be so impatient.

'Joe has done enough for this family. Maybe he wanted some time to himself for once.'

I felt instinctively that something was wrong. It wasn't like Joe to miss coming on a Sunday. It wasn't like Dad to stay sober all this time.

A week passed. By the next Sunday I was strong enough to wash and dress myself. I made my way unsteadily downstairs. The kitchen was untidy, but Dad had obviously done his best. He was just filling the kettle at the sink.

'Should you be up?'

'I can't stay in bed for ever. Besides, I had to make an effort for Joe's sake.'

He put the kettle on the range. 'Joe's not coming . . .' As he turned to look at me, I saw the expression in his eyes and fear clutched at my heart. 'He won't be coming any more, Betty.'

'What do you mean?' I stared at him wildly. 'Of course he'll come. We're going to be married.'

'I'm sorry, Betty. Joe's dead.'

His words stunned me. I stared at him in disbelief, feeling the sickness begin to swirl inside me.

'Joe – dead?' I shook my head. 'No! He can't be. It's impossible. Joe is so strong. He can't be dead.'

'He had it real bad. No one realised he was ill. They all thought he was here with us. When one of the labourers went into his cottage they found him. He'd been dead for several days.'

'No . . .' The scream was building inside me. The thought of Joe lying untended was unbearable. *Unbearable!* He had nursed my brother so tenderly. He was so good and kind. It broke my heart to think of him dying alone. 'Oh, please, no. I should never have sent him away. If he'd been here the doctor might have saved him. It's my fault. I never thought Joe would get it.' I looked at my father in desperation. 'How could Joe die when I survived?'

'I don't know, Betty.' He shook his head sadly. 'Why didn't I get it? Only God knows the answer.'

It was strange to hear Dad talking of God. I realised that he had nursed me through my illness alone. Joe hadn't been there at all. Joe had been alone. Dying.

It was cruel. So terribly cruel. Joe had always helped everyone. No one had been there to help him. It was like a knife twisting in my heart. I wanted to cry but the pain went too deep. I just sat, as if turned to stone, staring at my father.

It was another two weeks before I felt well enough to go

out. I went to the churchyard, spending some time looking at the graves of my mother, my brother and my sister. Then I knelt down on the grass beside Joe's grave. It was hard to believe that a man as strong as he had gone so quickly. I wished I hadn't sent him away. Perhaps if we had been together he would have lived. At least he wouldn't have died alone. It was so cruel and so useless. Joe was such a good person. I didn't know how I was going to manage without him.

'Oh, Joe . . . Joe . . .' I whispered, the tears beginning to slide down my cheeks. 'Why did you have to die? I'm going to miss you so much.'

I hadn't realised how much he meant to me. He was a dear friend and his death had left me numb and empty. What was there to look forward to now?

As I got to my feet, I became aware that someone was watching me. Turning round, I found myself staring into the glittering eyes of Zac Jarrold.

'So you're alone now then?' he said jeeringly. 'Old Joe upped and died on you, did he? Now what are you going to do?'

'Just leave me alone, will you?'

He came closer and I caught the stink of beer on his breath. 'You always thought you were too good for the rest of us, didn't you? Vera said you changed when you went to The Willows.'

'What do you know about Vera? Why did she go off like that? Was it because of you?'

He leered at me. 'You'd best ask your father about that.'

'What's that supposed to mean?'

'Your father's a right bastard, Betty Cantrel. If you want to know why Vera ran off, ask him.'

'I shall,' I said, glaring at him. 'Now just get out of my way or I'll scream so loud the whole village will hear.'

He gave me a nasty look but stood aside.

I didn't say anything to my father. I wasn't in the mood

for quarrelling. I just felt numb and dazed. I needed time to come to terms with what had happened.

Throughout the winter Dad did what he could to take Joe's place. He helped to dig the garden, but he could only manage a few minutes at a time. The pain in his guts was so bad that he couldn't hide it from me now, and he often brought up blood when he vomited.

I hated to see him wasting away. He was a pale shadow of the man he'd once been, and I did what I could to make him comfortable. He slept downstairs in what had been the children's room. I was no longer afraid of him. We didn't bother to argue. We both knew it couldn't be long before the end.

'What will you do when I'm gone, Betty?' he asked one night as we sat by the fire. 'You'd have been a rich woman if you'd married Joe. They say he left more than ten thousand pounds. It should have been yours. He would have wanted you to have it, not that cousin of his.'

I shrugged and shook my head. 'Joe never thought of dying. It didn't occur to him to make a will. If we'd married it would have been mine, but I don't care about the money. I just wish I could have Joe and the little ones back.'

'There's no use in crying for the moon – so what will you do?'

'I don't know. I don't want to think about it yet.'

'Don't stay here, Betty,' he urged. 'You're a clever girl. Use your brains. Make something of yourself.'

'I'm not sure I want to any more. It seems so pointless.'

'People die but the world doesn't end. Don't let it break you, girl. You've got more guts than that,' he said harshly. 'I've wasted my life – don't you dare waste yours.'

'I'll think about it when the time comes.' I got up and yawned. 'I may as well go to bed now. Oh, I'd better fetch the wood for the morning.'

'Leave it until tomorrow.'

'No. I'll do it now. I hate a cold grate first thing.' I

slipped on my coat. 'It won't take long. You go to bed. There's no need for you to wait.'

There was a bright moon. It was freezing and the wind almost pulled the door from my hand as I opened it. I nearly changed my mind, then I made a dash for the wood shed. It was cold enough for snow.

I bent to gather the logs. I'm not sure whether I heard a sound or whether instinct alerted me, but a prickling sensation started at the nape of my neck. As I whirled round, I saw the shadow of a man.

'Is that you, Dad?'

The man came at me and I saw his face clearly in the moonlight. It was Zac Jarrold. I gave a cry of alarm as I saw the expression in his eyes.

'What do you want?'

He laughed mockingly. He was so close that I could smell the whisky on his breath. It was very strong. He had been drinking heavily. The look on his face frightened me, and I sensed what was in his mind.

'Don't you dare.' I cried.

'I've waited a long time for this, Betty Cantrel,' he muttered thickly. 'You've made a fool of me, acting the high and mighty lady when you were giving it to him all the time – now I'm going to get me some.'

I screamed and backed away, but the shed was behind me and there was nowhere to go. Zac lunged at me, pinning me to the wooden wall. I thrust my knee up hard, but he was too quick.

'You ain't getting away this time, slut!'

He held my wrists above my head with one hand, his wet mouth slobbering over mine in what he fondly imagined was a kiss, while he clawed at my skirt with his other hand. I spat in his face. He hit me across the mouth. I struggled wildly, biting and yelling like a wild thing. I kicked his shin. He shouted in anger and hit me again. I could taste blood in my mouth and I screamed for all I was worth. He knocked me to the ground and flung himself on top of me, his hand going beneath my skirt and tearing at my knickers. I writhed furiously beneath him, bucking and clawing in an attempt to throw him off, but I knew that he was far too strong. Whatever I did, he would have his way.

'Lie still, you little bitch,' he muttered. 'I'll show you what a real man is like . . .'

Even as he spoke, I heard a snarl of rage. Looking up, I could see Dad standing over us. He reached down and grabbed Zac by the back of his coat, hauling him off me.

'You rotten little bastard!' he growled. 'I'll teach you to come sniffing after my girl!'

Suddenly they were fighting, punching each other and grunting like animals. I saw my father land several good blows on Zac's chin, sending him staggering back. If Dad had been the man he used to be, Zac wouldn't have stood a chance, but it was only anger that was keeping him on his feet. His face was wracked with agony.

'Stop it! Stop it!' I cried, scrambling to my feet. 'That's enough Dad. It doesn't matter.'

Zac had caught Dad with a heavy punch. He went staggering back. Zac hit him again, in the stomach this time. My father screamed in pain, dropping to his knees. Sensing his victory, Zac kicked him in his side. I seized a piece of wood and brought it crashing down on the back of Zac's neck.

'Stop it, you fool!' I yelled. 'Can't you see you're killing him?'

Dad was bent over double, blood pouring from the side of his mouth. I saw Zac's eyes widen and he went very pale.

'I didn't hit that hard.'

'He's a sick man. He's dying.' I advanced on Zac with vengeful eyes. 'Run for the doctor. Go get him this instant or – or I'll see you hang for my father's murder.'

Zac shook his head. The words came blubbering out of him, 'I only wanted a bit of fun. I didn't mean to . . .' All of a sudden, he turned and ran as if all the demons in Hell were after him.

A chuckle issued from between Dad's bloodied lips. 'You put the fear into him, girl. Help me up now. Get me inside.'

'The doctor will be here soon, Dad.' I put his arm around my shoulders, taking his weight. 'Zac will fetch him.'

'It doesn't matter, Betty.' Dad's face was ashen. 'If the doctor couldn't save our babes, he won't do much for me.'

I got my father into the house and on to the bed. The blood had slowed to a trickle now. He looked awful. I hovered uncertainly, wondering what to do for him.

'Get me a drink, Betty,' he said. 'There's a bottle of whisky in that drawer.'

I fetched the bottle. He pulled the cork out with his teeth and took a deep swig of it. I watched, flinching as he writhed with agony and cursed. Why must he do it to himself? He must know that he was bleeding inside.

'It's only making it worse, Dad.'

'You let me be the judge of that.'

There was no sense in arguing with him. I couldn't do anything for him and I didn't want to watch him get drunk, but as I turned to leave, he called me back. 'Don't go, Betty. Please, stay with me for a while.'

I sat down on the edge of the bed. 'Thank you for what you did, Dad.'

'I'd have thrashed him once,' he muttered, swallowing another mouthful of the strong liquid and choking. 'I haven't been much of a father to you, have I?'

'What do you want me to say? I won't lie and if I did it wouldn't change things.'

'Sometimes I wonder where you came from. I suppose you take after your grandfather. It's a pity he didn't have the sense to get to know you. It's too late now, the old bugger died a couple of years ago.'

'I didn't know. You never told me.'

'Didn't see much point in it. He left his fortune to a home for dogs.'

'Oh, Dad . . .' I stared at him angrily. 'I would have liked to know, that's all.'

'Well, now you do.' He shrugged. 'Do you ever think of Vera?'

I was surprised. It was the first time he had mentioned her to me since she ran off. 'Sometimes, I wonder where she is – and why she went off so suddenly.'

'It was me,' he said. 'I got at her when I was drunk. I had her, Betty. That's why she went.'

'You raped your own child?'

I stared at him in horror as the silence lengthened between us. I felt cold all over, and the sickness swept up into my throat, making me want to vomit.

'You raped Vera – your own daughter? Is that what you're telling me, Dad?'

He couldn't look at me. His hands were shaking and tears squeezed from the corners of his eyes. 'She was always laughing at me, cheeking me like. She didn't despise me the way you do. I don't know what came over me. I was drunk.' He stared up at me, his face ravaged with pain. 'You never trusted me, did you? Well, you were right. I am a bastard through and through.' He drank deeply again. 'I did it to her and I've paid for it since, but I don't want you to pity me. Don't stay here and don't mourn me, Betty. Go somewhere new – and if you ever see Vera, tell her I'm sorry. It was the drink that made me do it. I'd never have . . . Well, I don't have to tell you, do I?'

I felt sick. I could hardly bear to look at him. He had raped his own daughter! If ever I had felt any sympathy for him it died right then. He was a drunkard, a wastrel and a brute.

'There's someone at the door,' I said, standing up. 'I expect it's the doctor.' I turned away. I never wanted to see him again.

He died in his sleep that night. Perhaps the drink helped. I don't know. I was glad it was over. If he had lived I wasn't sure that I could have gone on looking after him now that I knew the extent of his beastliness. He'd saved me from Zac Jarrold, but he'd ruined all our lives.

When the funeral was over, I put flowers on all the graves, lingering the longest over Joe's. As I approached Dad's grave, after everyone else had gone, I saw the lone figure of a young woman standing there. She turned as I drew near and I saw that it was Vera. Her eyes were hard as she looked at me.

'So you came back then,' I said.

'I wanted to be certain the bastard was really dead,' she said bitterly.

'Vera . . .' I was shocked by the hatred in her. Then as I looked at her more closely, I saw the thick make-up and the cheap, skimpy dress she was wearing. I moved towards her, suddenly angry. 'What have you been doing with yourself – and why did you never let us know how you were?'

Her laughter was shrill, almost hysterical. 'As if any of you would've cared,' she said. 'Mum let him dominate her . . .'

'He told me,' I said quickly. 'I know what Dad did to you. But Mum couldn't have known.'

'Oh, she knew all right. She knew and she didn't care.' Her head went up and her eyes glittered. 'Look at me, Betty. You don't need me to tell you what I've been doing.'

'Vera . . .' I frowned. 'He's dead now. Why don't you come home? We could . . .'

'Come back to this dump?' She laughed mockingly. 'I'd rather be dead. I'm an actress and one day I'm going to be famous. I've got friends now. You'll see.'

'An actress,' I said. 'That's not what I'd call it.'

Her cheeks flushed but she faced me defiantly. 'It's all right for you to be so high and mighty. You've always had everything. So I do a few favours for friends of a certain gentleman who's been good to me. He's promised he'll get me a part in a film one day . . .'

'Don't you know he's using you? Turning you into a . . .'

'Go on, why don't you say it?' she asked angrily. 'You always were a selfish bitch, Betty. You could've got me a job with your posh friends, but you didn't want me there, did you?'

I stared at her helplessly, knowing that there was some truth in her accusation. She laughed as she saw I was lost for words, then began to walk away.

'Where are you going?' I called after her. 'When shall I see you again?'

'When Hell freezes over,' she replied with a sneer. 'And that will be too soon for me.'

I watched sadly as she walked away. We had never been friends but I hadn't wanted to be her enemy. I knew that I would probably never see my sister again.

I went to see Mrs Jackson once more before she left to live in Cornwall with her friend.

I asked her what she thought I should do with my life now and she looked at me oddly, not speaking at once.

'You could train to be a secretary or something,' she said. 'But I always thought you might marry Nathan Crawley.'

'Marry Nathan? What on earth gave you that idea?'

'Is it so impossible? He fancied you, Betty.'

'He wanted to get me into bed, that's all.'

'Well, you should know,' she said. 'What are you going to do then?'

'I'm going to try for a job as a singer.'

'So you're off to London then?'

'Yes,' I said. 'There's nothing to keep me here now.'

PART THREE

Chapter Fourteen

Laurence was here again today. He says that unless I allow him to appeal they will hang me. He repeats it over and over again, as if he thinks I don't understand what it means.

For a moment today I saw him with fresh eyes – as a man and not just as my lawyer. He has black, straight hair, a jutting chin and thick sensuous lips. It occurred to me that his mouth was made for kissing, and I smiled.

'Why the smile?' he asked. 'You intrigue me. Most women would be begging me to try for the reprieve – aren't you afraid of dying?'

'It's not the fact of dying I fear, but the dying itself . . .' My hand crept to my throat as I felt a spasm of sheer terror. 'Will it hurt? Will it be over quickly?'

A nerve began to jump in his neck. 'Let me help you. For God's sake, tell me the truth. I know you're not the cold-blooded murderess they make you out to be. I know it! The mood of the Press has begun to change. They were against you to a man, but now people are beginning to say that hanging is barbaric. They're calling for mercy. If I just had some new evidence . . . something to go on . . .'

How his voice rings with conviction! Just as it did in the courtroom. People watching from the gallery were moved to tears by the brilliance of his oration in my defence, but without any testimony, he has no hard evidence.

'If anyone could have saved me, it's you,' I said.

'Then let me help you!'

His fist struck the table as he spoke. One of the women

in black turned disapproving eyes on him. I touched his hand. He seems so young and vulnerable to me, and I know he is a little in love with me.

'Forgive me,' I whispered. 'I didn't mean to hurt you.'

'Betty,' A groan broke from him. 'You're so beautiful – surely you can't want to die! There's still time. I swear I'll save you if you'll just tell me . . .'

'You don't understand.' I smiled, but already his face was fading from my mind. Other faces crowded in on me. 'You don't know how it was . . .'

Once again I felt the pace of the city; the roar of the traffic was like a heart pounding with excitement and I knew that I'd been right to come to London. I was determined to put all the sadness behind me, to take all that I could from life. I'd been hurt, but I was young and resilient. As I gave my ticket to the collector and passed out of the station, I felt wonderfully, tinglingly alive.

My first priority was to find somewhere to stay. I'd given this some thought and asked Mrs Jackson what I should do.

'My advice would be to find a bed-sitting room,' she'd said. 'A flat of your own would be too expensive. When you've been working for a while, you might find a friend to share with you.'

It struck cold as I left the station. The sky was dark and dull, a typical day for late February, and there was rain in the air. Pulling up the collar of my coat, I ran towards the line of taxis. It wouldn't hurt to be extravagant for once.

'Where to, miss?' the driver asked.

I hesitated, then smiled at him. 'You'll think I've got an awful cheek, but I've just arrived in London and I wondered if you could recommend a decent lodging house, please? I want somewhere clean and respectable.'

He gave me a broad grin. 'Bright girl. Some of them haven't got the sense they were born with; they come up here thinking the streets are paved with gold and fall into the hands of the first pimp who smiles at them. I know a place. She's a crusty old thing and her rooms aren't the cheapest, but if you want respectability, Mrs Stiggly's the one for you.'

'Mrs Stiggly?' I stifled my urge to laugh. 'She sounds like someone out of Dickens.' I said as I climbed in the back.

'You've hit the nail right on the head!' He chuckled, eyeing me in the mirror. 'This your first trip to London then?'

'No. I came up a couple of years ago for a visit. This time I'm hoping to find work.'

'What do you do?' His brow arched. 'I'll bet you're a model – haven't I seen your photo in the papers?'

He was chatting me up. I smiled slightly as I shook my head. 'Sorry. It wasn't me, but maybe you will one day; I want to be a singer.'

'I thought there was something about you,' he said. 'Well, here we are then.'

The streets we had been passing through had a dull greyness about them, the windows dirty and the paint peeling from doors and frames. We had halted in a little cul-de-sac, in front of a dreary brown brick house. It wasn't particularly impressive but a second glance re-assured me; there were spotlessly clean white lace curtains and the windows sparkled.

'That was a short ride,' I remarked. 'Mrs Stiggly, you said?'

I could easily have walked it if the driver had directed me. As I paid the fare, I realised I'd probably been overcharged, but it was better than wandering the streets on a damp evening. I paid up cheerfully, adding a shilling tip.

'Tell the old witch Harry sent you,' he said and winked. 'Good luck with the singing.'

He drove away, leaving me standing on the pavement. I knocked at the door, appreciating the gleam of the brass plate. At least I could be sure of clean sheets here! The door opened so quickly that I was sure my arrival had

349

been noted from behind the lace curtains. The woman who answered it was tall and thin with a sharp, fox-like face and suspicious eyes. She wore a black dress that buttoned all the way up to the neck, and her hair was set in crisp waves with ridges that looked as if you might cut your fingers if you touched them.

'Mrs Stiggly?' My heart sank as I saw the disapproval in her face.

'Yes. What do you want?'

'I was wondering if you might have a room to let?'

'I might and I might not. It depends.'

'On what? If you want a reference, I have a letter from my local vicar.'

'Have you indeed?' Her eyes narrowed. 'Who told you to come here?'

'A taxi driver. He said his name was Harry.'

She was silent for a moment, then: 'You'd better come in then. I charge fifteen shillings a week and I'll want two weeks in advance. I'll want to see that letter, too, though you could have written it yourself.'

'And I shall want to see the room before I decide whether or not it will do.'

She seemed surprised by my challenge. For a moment I thought she was about to throw me out, then she nodded. 'I think you'll be quite satisfied, Miss . . . What did you say your name was?'

'Cantrel. Betty Cantrel.'

She nodded but made no further comment, merely indicating that I should follow her upstairs. The room she showed me was about the same size as the one I had shared with Polly, but it looked smaller because of the cumbersome furniture. The bed was a generous single; there was a table with a lamp to one side and a small chest the other. A large wardrobe took up most of one wall, and there was a wash-basin in the corner. Mrs Stiggly showed me the gas meter in the cupboard underneath, warning me to keep a supply of shillings handy.

It was a dark, depressing room, but I could see that

everything was very clean. It was as good a place as any to begin. Once I knew my way around, I could look for somewhere more cheerful.

'Yes, I think this will be satisfactory,' I said, opening my purse. 'Thirty shillings for the first two weeks, I think that's what you said?'

She nodded, accepting the money grudgingly. 'There's a gas ring to heat a kettle,' she said with a little frown. 'But I don't allow cooking in the rooms – and no men. If I catch you sneaking a man up here, you'll go out faster than you came in.'

'I understand. You needn't worry, I've no intention of bringing a man here.'

'They all say that.' Her mouth twisted. 'You'd be surprised at some of the things that go on. Brothers, uncles, cousins; I've heard every excuse under the sun.'

'I don't have any male relatives. Nor do I have a boyfriend.'

She laughed harshly. 'Maybe you haven't yet, but you will. Well, you've been warned.' She gave me the key. 'I can do a hot meal in the evening for an extra ten shillings a week.'

'Thank you. I'll think about it.'

As the door closed behind her, I heaved a sigh of relief and turned the key in the lock. I'd thought Mrs Jackson was hard when I first went to the farm, but my new landlady was made of granite. I didn't think I would be staying here for too long. And with any luck, I wouldn't need to. I already knew exactly what I was going to do.

I wasted no time in setting out the next morning. Thelma Blair had told me to contact her when I was ready; she knew many influential people in the world of show business, and she had promised to help me.

My hopes were high as I caught the bus and then walked the short distance to the Blairs' house. I wanted to sing and I was sure that my voice was as good as many of the female vocalists I'd heard on the radio, but I had no idea how to begin. Did you just attend auditions, or did you need a theatrical agent? How did you find out when they were holding auditions? It would be much better to seek advice. I was confident that Thelma would help me.

Was that the only reason I felt so excited? My heart was beating wildly as I stood outside the house, and I knew that at least a part of it was due to my hopes of seeing James. I had thought never to see him again; I had resigned myself to being a country housewife, but now the world had suddenly opened out to me and anything was possible.

It was several minutes before the door was answered. The girl looked at me, frowning slightly.

'Don't you know me, Maisie?' I asked, laughing as I saw her expression change to one of incredulity. 'It's Betty. Betty Cantrel.'

'Of course I remember.' Her face lit up with pleasure. 'Well, I never! What are you doing here then?'

'I came to see Mrs Blair. Is she in?'

Maisie's thin face creased with sorrow. 'No, Betty, she's not living here at the moment. Not since Mr Blair died . . .' She broke off as I gasped.

'James is dead?' For a moment the world seemed to crash around me.

'Bless you, no,' Maisie said. 'Mr Blair senior. You remember he was poorly when you were here?' I nodded and she frowned. 'Well, he died last summer.'

'Oh, that's awful,' I said as the world steadied and my breathing returned to normal. 'He was still a young man.'

'Yes.' Maisie opened the door wider. 'Why don't you come in and have a cup of tea with me, and I'll tell you all about it.'

'I'd like that very much.'

Maisie led the way down to her domain. A cheerful fire was burning in the kitchen grate and I sat in the chair beside it, warming my hands as she made the tea.

'I'm sorry it was such a shock for you,' she said as we

sipped the strong, hot liquid. 'You went as white as a sheet just now.'

'I was hoping to see the family.' I tensed as I looked at her. 'You said Thelma was away – will she be coming back soon?'

'I really can't say. She went down to the country for a while, but now she's living in Spain, in a little village called Mijas. It's in the mountains; she sent me some lovely photos.'

'Oh . . .' I felt disappointment sweep over me. 'But you've kept the house open, so does James still live here?'

'He was here until last week,' Maisie said. 'You've just missed him. He's gone to America – for three months I think.'

The second blow was too much. I swallowed hard. 'I thought he was a partner in his father's firm?'

'So he was. When Mr Blair died he left fifty-five per cent to Mr James, thirty per cent to his wife and the rest to his daughter. Mr James was very clever; he sold the company for a lot of money. Now he's gone to America to talk about investing in a new company – something to do with aeroplanes, I think. He was always keen on flying.'

'Yes, I know.' The disappointment was so great I could hardly hide it. 'You said he was coming back to England in three months?'

'As far as I know.' Maisie finished her tea. 'Miss Christabel – or Mrs Harding as I should call her now – she pops in on a flying visit now and then. She'll probably come for Wimbledon, and Mr James will be here then.'

'Will Mrs Blair come home soon do you think?'

'She might – though she says she adores living in Spain, because the light there is so good for her work.'

I put my cup down. 'Well, thank you for telling me, Maisie. I suppose I'd better go now.'

'Would you like Mrs Blair's address? She writes to me every now and then, just to ask how things are.'

'No, I don't think so. I wanted to ask her something –
but it doesn't matter. Perhaps I'll see her in the summer.'

'I'm sure she'd be pleased to see you. She used to talk
about you, you know. I'll tell her I've seen you, shall I?'

'Yes, if you like.' I stood up to leave. 'Thank you for the
tea, Maisie. It was lovely to see you again.'

'You come again if you want to – come for a meal. My
aunt's still here. It's her day off today. She'll be sorry to
have missed you.'

'Give her my love,' I said. 'I must go now.'

Maisie let me out of the basement door. I ran up the
stone steps to the street. It was a pleasant day, mild for the
time of year and sunny. I walked, deep in thought, not
really appreciating the elegant houses and the sound of
birdsong in the garden at the centre of the square.

What was I going to do now? All my hopes had centred
on Thelma Blair. I felt lost and bewildered. I was really on
my own now. There was no one I could turn to . . .
Except Nathan. But if I went to Nathan for help, I knew
what it would mean.

I shook my head. I wasn't desperate, not yet. I still had
over half the money Joe had given me to buy a wedding
dress, and there were a few pounds I'd raised from selling
the contents of the cottage. No, I wouldn't go to Nathan.
I could find a temporary job in a shop of some kind, and I
could start looking for adverts for auditions in the
papers. I wasn't helpless. I'd wait for a while, anyway.

Somewhere deep inside me, the hope that everything
would be solved when James came home was still alive.
Three months wasn't so long to wait.

Within a few days I'd begun to know the area around
Mrs Stiggly's house as well as I'd known my own
village. I explored Houndsditch. I walked down Lime
Street and Leadenhall Street, admiring the fine
buildings. The city and its history fascinated me and I
was always eager to learn. They were talking of rebuild-
ing on the bomb sites, and some people thought it was

354

too soon, but it made me sad to see derelict ground where homes had once stood.

So many people had died in the war. Sometimes I wondered what it would be like to die, but mostly I was too busy exploring to have morbid thoughts.

I hadn't yet started to look for a job. I saw cards in windows advertising work for waitresses and barmaids, Woolworth's wanted salesgirls, but I wasn't in a hurry. I wanted to take my time, get to know my way around the city.

I went now and then to the theatres and cinemas in and around Hammersmith. I was still fascinated by the laughter and music I found in these places, and I longed to be a part of that other world. The world I'd glimpsed when I'd stayed at the Blairs' house. James and his family symbolised respectability, the respectability that my mother had lost when she married Robert Cantrel.

It might have been better if I could have forgotten that my maternal grandparents were gentlefolk. Maybe if I'd never gone to The Willows, I would never have realised how much I'd lost, but the past could not be changed. I had seen, heard and tasted another way of life, and it was this I hankered after. If James could only see the real me, I believed he would love me as I loved him. If I could find fame as a singer, he would forget that I had once been a servant to Frances Crawley.

Frances was often in my mind these days. It was because of her that I had met James – and Nathan. I wondered if she was well now, and if she ever thought of me.

I came out of the theatre. It was a dull afternoon and the light was already fading. I had been to my first audition. Singers were wanted for a new musical that was soon to begin rehearsals. I'd seen the advertisement in a paper left on a café table the previous day and I'd arrived early to be sure of being one of the first, but there were fifty other girls there before me. I wasn't even given a chance to sing.

A smartly dressed woman cast an experienced eye over us, choosing twenty. 'The rest of you can go,' she said.

Most of the other girls turned away with a groan, but I went after her. 'Why won't you give us a chance?' I asked. 'We've all been waiting for ages.'

'I picked the most suitable,' she said.

'But you haven't heard me sing.'

Her eyes flicked over me scornfully. 'I don't need to. If you're serious about this business, get some professional advice. You're attractive but you need to smarten up. Get your hair done, buy some decent clothes and learn how to present yourself – otherwise, go home. You're wasting your time coming to auditions looking like that.'

She walked away, leaving me staring after her resentfully. I might not be as well dressed as some of the girls, but I didn't look that bad.

'Silly cow!' One of the other rejects grinned at me. 'Don't take too much notice of her. Mind you, it helps to look right. Have you been to many of these?'

'This is my first.'

'Lucky you. This is my tenth rejection this month.'

I stared at her, amazed at her cheerfulness. 'How can you stand it?'

'Oh, you get used to it, and sometimes it works out.' She smiled and held out her hand. 'My name is Tina. I'm a singer and a dancer.'

'Betty Cantrel,' I said. 'I'm hoping to be a singer, but if no one will let me try . . .'

'Don't give up too soon. Look, Betty, there's a place some of us meet in the evenings. Everyone goes there, all the big names: Danny Kaye, Ella Fitzgerald, Max Bygraves . . .' She paused as I stared. 'Have you heard of the Stork Rooms?'

I shook my head. 'No. Is it a theatre?'

Tina laughed. 'No, though it's the next best thing. It's a nightclub run by Al Burnett, and all the stars go there after their own shows. You need an escort to get in, because when the owner ran previous clubs the police were always trying to close him down, and a woman on her own could be – well, you know. The thing is, Al's a decent bloke. He might give you an audition if he likes the look of you, and if you're any good, you'll soon be on your way.'

'Thank you for telling me,' I said. 'But I don't have an escort.'

'A bright girl can always find someone,' Tina said, winking at me. 'I must dash now. I'll see you around sometime.'

'But you haven't told me where . . .' I shrugged as she dashed away. It didn't really matter. I couldn't go to this nightclub alone anyway.

I often found myself thinking about Frances and I realised I was lonely. I spent too many hours brooding on the past, because I'd nothing else to do. Polly had sent me a card the previous Christmas with a new address, and I decided that I would go and visit her. It was just possible that she might know of someone who could help me to find work as a singer.

The address Polly had given me was in Clerkenwell, an area well known for its goldsmiths and clockmakers. The house itself was in a narrow lane running at right angles to one of the main streets. It was a tall, four-storey building of faded red brick, its windows screened by thick net curtains.

I crossed the road, dodging between the cars and lorries. For a moment I hesitated, wondering if I'd come to the right house. It didn't look like a lodging house, but the number was the same as in Polly's letter so I rang the bell. In a matter of seconds the door was opened by a girl of about sixteen. She looked a little surprised to see me.

'What can I do for you?'

'I should like to see Polly Baxter, please.'

'Who sent you? You're not one of those interfering church women, are you?'

I blinked. 'Do I look like one? My name is Betty

Cantrel. I used to be a friend of Polly's – before she came to London.'

She looked at me doubtfully. 'I suppose you'd better come in. You can wait in the parlour while I ask Polly if she wants to see you.' She ushered me into a small room to the left of the hall. 'You'd better not be one of those busybodies. You just stay here and don't move until I come back. Do you hear?'

'Yes,' I replied meekly. 'I ought to have written to Polly instead of just turning up.'

'Just stay where you are.'

As the girl went out, I heard a burst of laughter from upstairs. There was the sound of more than one voice, both male and female. It sounded as if Polly had guests.

I glanced round the room. The furniture was good quality, but there was too much of it. A big sofa, chairs, tables, cabinets stuffed with china figures and a rose-patterned tea-set. The mantelpiece was crammed with ornaments and photograph frames. On top of the wireless was a pretty silver frame with the picture of a baby of about six months. I picked it up and saw that it was a little girl.

'What are you doing?'

I turned as I heard the voice, the photo still in my hand. 'I was just looking – Polly! Are you ill? Did I get you out of bed?'

She was wearing a dressing gown of crimson satin, her thick hair hanging on her shoulders. She blushed and touched her hair self-consciously.

'I was having a rest,' she said. 'I often do in the afternoons. I work late some evenings.'

'Oh, I see.' I stared at her foolishly. 'I'm sorry if I disturbed you.'

She'd looked angry when she came in, but her expression softened as I put down the frame and moved towards her. She smiled suddenly.

'So it is you, Betty. I could hardly believe it when Nora told me you were here.'

'I hope it isn't too much of an intrusion? I – I thought perhaps you had guests?'

'What do you . . .' Polly stopped as the door opened and a man came in. Grey-haired, middle-aged and slightly overweight, he was wearing his trousers and shirt, but he had no socks on and he was carrying his shoes.

'Damn!' He smiled at her foolishly. 'I've lost my socks, Polly.'

'Don't you always?' Polly's look of annoyance changed to a laugh. 'You'll get me hanged yet, Charlie.' She looked at me. 'Betty, this is Charlie. As you can see, he's a good friend of mine.'

'Sorry for barging in,' Charlie said, his eyes twinkling. 'But I have to get back to the office.'

'Ask Nora to look for your socks. I expect they're under the bed as usual.' As he went out, Polly smiled ruefully. 'It's just as well you've seen him, now you know the truth and I shan't be tempted to lie.'

'Is he your lover?'

'He's one of my very good friends.' Polly frowned as she saw my look. 'I'm not a prostitute, if that's what you're thinking. I have a few friends I oblige now and then. They look after me, and I look after them.'

'Do you enjoy living like that?'

'Why shouldn't I?'

'I don't mean to criticize, Polly. I was just surprised.'

'It's better than scrubbing floors.' Her expression was challenging. 'Do you want to leave now that you know? Or will you stay for some tea?'

'I'll stay, Polly.' I smiled at her. 'It will be good to have a friend to talk to. I've been very much on my own since I came to London. Mrs Stiggly's other lodgers are all so much older. We speak on the stairs but that's all.' As Polly rang the bell for Nora, I picked up the picture of the child again. 'What a beautiful baby! Does she belong to one of your friends?'

Polly's face clouded. 'That was my Violet. Eben

359

Crawley's child. She died of German measles just after that was taken.'

It took a few seconds for what she'd said to sink in. 'I'm sorry,' I said at last. 'What a terrible time that must have been for you. You never mentioned it in your letters.'

'Well, I didn't want Mary Crawley to know I'd had the kid.' Polly blinked fiercely. 'Funny thing is, I'd have given back every penny of that money to save Violet. You were right, Betty. When it came to it, I couldn't kill my own child.' She choked on a sob. 'Even though I only had her for a little while, it was worth it.'

'I'm glad you feel like that, Polly,' I said softly. 'I know how it feels to lose a child you love.'

'What do you mean?'

I explained about the children and Joe. She stared at me in silence for a moment, then reached out and squeezed my hand.

'You've had a rough time, but . . .' She broke off as the door opened and Charlie poked his head round the corner. He was now fully dressed.

'I was wondering whether you'd like to bring your friend to the party tonight, Polly?' He smiled at me. 'Come if you like, my dear. We've always room for another pretty girl. You might do yourself a bit of good.' He winked significantly. 'I must dash now.'

I looked at Polly as the door closed behind him. 'What did he mean by that?'

She looked a bit embarrassed. 'Well, you know . . . Charlie has some generous friends. If you picked the right one, you might even get yourself a nice little house like this . . .'

'No thanks, Polly,' I said hastily. 'I'm not condemning you, but it's not what I want. We can still be friends, can't we?'

'Of course. I didn't expect you would want to be a part of our crowd,' she said easily. 'Not right off – but if you change your mind, you only have to say.'

Nora brought in the tea tray then, and I was saved from

replying. Polly changed the subject and we got to talking about the old days. Soon we were laughing and giggling, just as if nothing had happened in between.

I stayed with her for over an hour, and it wasn't until I was walking home afterwards that it really hit me. My money was running out fast, and Polly was my only friend in London. If I didn't want to end up like her, I'd better start looking for a job!

Chapter Fifteen

I found a job in a high-class dress shop in Oxford Street. It was called Trés Chic and the clothes were expensive. Taking Polly's advice, I'd had my hair trimmed and I now knew how to dry it in a long, sleek pageboy. It suited me and it made me look smarter. I'd also invested six pounds and fifteen shillings in a good suit. I was wearing it for my interview, and I could see the manageress was impressed.

'Your references are excellent, Miss Cantrel,' she said. 'Unfortunately, you have no experience of selling. I'm prepared to train you. But it does mean that you'll be doing all the odd jobs for a while, and of course, you'll be paid accordingly, with a rise and commission once you've got the idea.'

'Thank you, Miss Browne,' I said meekly. 'When would you like me to start?'

'Next Monday,' she replied, her mouth relaxing into a smile. 'We open at nine, but I like my girls to be here by half-past eight.'

Working at the dress shop was all right. I was on the go all day, fetching and carrying gowns from the workshop downstairs, holding pins while Miss Browne pinned up hems and lifted shoulders, brushing the clothes and straightening the rails after the customers had been through them. I made tea, dusted and hoovered the carpets – and all for two pounds and fifteen shillings a week. By the time I'd paid my rent, bought food and budgeted for bus fares, it left me very little, but at least it would preserve my dwindling savings for a while. One perk was that I got a big discount on any clothes I bought for myself.

I rather liked Miss Browne. She was in her mid-thirties, but she wasn't in the least old-maidish. She was strict about working hard and being polite to the customers, but when we had the shop to ourselves, she enjoyed a bit of a joke. When I'd been working there for a month, I told her about my ambition to sing. She was enthusiastic.

'If you want some time off to attend a special audition, just tell me,' she said. 'I'll let you off if I can – but I won't stand for unexplained absences.'

'I wouldn't do that,' I said. I was glad of her understanding and besides, I needed all the help I could get.

Now that I'd been in London for more than three months, my thoughts began to turn towards James Blair once again. Was he back from America? And if he were, could I call at his house, or would it seem too pushy?

It was a warm summer day. We had been very busy all morning and I'd been up and down to the workrooms a hundred times. I was on my way back to the showroom, my arms full of evening dresses, when I heard Miss Browne talking to someone.

'I hope you'll be pleased with your dress, Miss Crawley. Not everyone can wear that shade, but it certainly suits you.'

'Thank you. It's very pretty. I'm wearing it to the theatre this evening.'

For a moment I was turned to stone. That was Frances's voice. I couldn't be mistaken. It was her. It had to be! I hurried up the stairs, almost tripping over the trailing skirts of the dresses I was carrying in my haste. A woman was at the door, her hand on the door knob. I called to her, my heart beating with excitement.

'Frances! Is it you?'

She turned her head and looked at me, her eyes meeting mine. I waited for some sign of recognition, a smile or a cry of pleasure. For a moment there was nothing, then her eyes went cold. She said nothing, but it was all there in her expression; anger, contempt, rejection. She had not forgiven me for deserting her. I felt chilled, my pleasure in seeing her dying as swiftly as it had flared to life. As I stood dumbly, unable to speak, she opened the door and went out. I was left staring after her, my cheeks on fire as the manageress looked at me.

'Miss Cantrel,' she said sharply. 'You're creasing those dresses. Hang them on the rails properly please.'

'Yes, Miss Browne,' I whispered.

I obeyed at once, glad to have something to do. Frances had deliberately snubbed me. She'd known me just as I'd known her, but she was unwilling to acknowledge me. I felt mortified, desperately hurt. I'd been so glad to see her. I hadn't dreamt that she would still be angry with me after all this time.

Miss Browne came up to me as I finished hanging the dresses. She was frowning. 'Do you know Miss Crawley?' she asked.

'I thought it was someone I once knew,' I said, avoiding her eyes. 'But I was mistaken,' I lied instinctively, hiding my hurt.

Miss Browne seemed relieved. 'Good. I don't particularly like that young woman. She seems to have money but . . . Oh, well . . .' She smiled. 'Put the kettle on, Betty. I could do with a coffee.'

I went for an audition for a new show. Miss Browne let me have a smart dress, though I couldn't pay for it. It was still ten pounds after my discount was deducted.

'You can pay for it weekly,' she said. 'If you get this job, you'll be so rich you can buy a dozen more.'

'You're a brick,' I laughed, crossing my fingers. 'Wish me luck?'

'Lots of it.' She smiled. 'You look pretty, Betty. I'm sure you'll get picked this time.'

I don't know whether it was the dress or the new hairstyle, but I was one of the lucky ones who actually got to sing. I'd practised songs from *Oklahoma* and *Kiss Me Kate*, but when it came to it, I sang, 'This Is My Lovely Day'.

A man with glasses pushed up on top of his head and a worried frown came up to me afterwards. He looked at his list of names.

'Who are you?'

'My name is Betty Cantrel,' I said, my pulses racing.

His eyes went over me critically. 'What experience have you had?'

'None. Except for the church choir.' My heart sank. That was sure to be the end of it.

'Thought so – you've got talent, though. Leave your telephone number as you go.'

'I'm not on the phone, but I could ring in.'

'Ring tomorrow.' He smiled and patted my bottom. 'You're in with a chance, Betty Cantrel.'

For once I didn't mind the gesture. It had been friendly rather than predatory. Besides, he'd said there was a chance!

I was walking on air as I left. The sun was shining and the world seemed full of promise. Miss Browne had told me that I needn't go back that afternoon, and with a surge of new confidence, I decided to call at the Blairs' house. It couldn't do any harm, could it? I would ask Maisie if Mrs Blair had returned – and if James happened to be there . . .

Feeling extravagant, I hailed a taxi. It was just five o'clock when I knocked at the door. Maisie opened it, looking surprised and then pleased.

'Well, fancy it being you,' she said. 'Come in, Betty.'

'Is Thelma back?' I asked, stepping into the hall.

She shook her head. 'No, but Mr Blair is in. If you'd like to wait in the downstairs parlour, I'll tell him you're here.'

'Thanks, Maisie.'

I went into the room she indicated, noting that everything was just as it had been. I glanced at the pile of records on a table behind the door, wondering if there were any new ones. As I began to examine them, I heard hurrying footsteps and then voices.

'She's in the front parlour, sir.'

'Did you tell her I was in, Maisie?' A pause and then, 'That's a pity. I really haven't time — I suppose a few minutes . . .'

I almost ran to the other side of the room. I was staring out of the window when James entered, and I didn't turn immediately.

'Betty . . .' He sounded impatient. 'Maisie told me you asked for Mother . . .'

I turned then, giving him a cool smile. 'It was just an impulse. I wanted to tell her something.'

His expression was that of a stranger, but then his eyes widened in surprise. 'You look wonderful. How are you? Are you visiting friends?'

'I'm living and working in London now.'

'Really?' Interested, he took a step towards me, then stopped and looked at his wristwatch. 'I have to go. Look, leave your address with Maisie. I'll get Frances to ring you. We can all meet for lunch or something.' He flashed a meaningless, insincere smile at me. 'My meeting is important. Excuse me.'

I stood absolutely still, listening to his hurried footsteps in the hall and then a door slamming. I felt chilled. Despite his momentary interest, I was of no real consequence to him. I forced a smile as Maisie came in.

'Always in a rush, that's Mr Blair these days.' She pulled a face. 'Meeting one of his American friends I suppose. Big money men.' Her eyes worked expressively. 'Have you got time for a cup of tea, Betty?'

'Why not?' I asked, brushing away the hurt James's indifference had given me. 'I can always find time for a friend . . .'

Who said that when your dreams die, a little bit of you dies with them? Perhaps no one said it, perhaps I made it up.

*

It was a time for the death of dreams. When I rang the number I'd been given the next day, I was told I'd been unlucky.

'You were on our shortlist of six, Miss Cantrel,' a woman said brightly. 'Never mind, you'll probably make it next time. Our Mr Rogers was most impressed with you.'

'Not impressed enough to give me a job,' I said to Miss Browne later. 'I really thought I stood a chance this time.'

'Don't take it too much to heart,' she said. 'It's a pity you don't know anyone in the business. It always helps to have a friend.'

'Yes,' I said. 'I had hopes but they didn't work out.'

'Well,' she comforted, 'keep your chin up, Betty. Something will turn up. You'll see.'

What turned up a few days later was the boss and his nephew. They paid one of their flying visits, something that happened only a few times a year. The nephew trapped me in the staff-room as I was making tea. Immediately, I sensed he was trouble. I tried to escape, but he spread his arms across the doorway, grinning.

'You're not going?' he said. 'Stay and talk to me, Betty.'

'Miss Browne and your uncle want their tea.'

'Damn Miss Browne,' he said and made a grab for me. 'Come on, darling, give me a kiss.'

Forgetting the manageress's warning to treat him with extreme caution, I hit him as hard as I could. I was wearing my mother's wedding ring on my right hand and it caught his lip, making it bleed. I saw the dismay in his eyes as he tasted blood and I laughed. It was the wrong thing to do. Dismay turned to fury.

'You little bitch,' he muttered. 'I'll teach you to laugh at me.'

All hell was about to break loose when Miss Browne came in. She saved me from his anger, but she couldn't save me from the sack.

'I'm so sorry, Betty,' she said as she paid me my wages. 'I don't want to lose you, but I have no choice.'

'I couldn't stay here now,' I replied. 'He'd make me suffer for it one way or another.'

I was thoughtful as I walked home that night. It seemed to me that men were all the same; they all wanted only one thing from a woman, and it didn't matter much whether you encouraged them or not. They believed they had a God-given right to take what they wanted. I'd thought that perhaps James was different, but he wasn't interested.

I felt tired and depressed as I went to bed that night. I'd been so full of hope when I came to London, but now it all seemed to have gone wrong. I'd lost my job and I would have to start all over again . . . Unless I went to Nathan.

All thought of sleep had deserted me. I sat up in bed, hugging my knees. I'd held out for as long as I could, but there were more important things in life than pride.

The address Nathan had given me was in Leicester Street. On one side was a theatre and a restaurant, at the south-eastern corner a grammar school standing on the site that had once been the great artist Hogarth's house. I read the inscription on a bronze plaque in passing as I looked for the number on the card Nathan had given me.

I stood outside for several minutes, wondering if I dare go through with it now that I was here. Supposing he rejected me, too? My courage faltered and I was about to turn away when a young man came out of the shop next door.

'Have you come about the flat?' he asked. 'Mr Crawley isn't here at the moment, but I could show you round if you like. He leaves the key with me in case anyone comes while he's out.'

'I don't understand. I thought Mr Crawley lived here?'

'Well, he does and he doesn't.' The man smiled. 'He has moved into another flat – bigger than this, I think –

and he wants to rent this one. He calls in every now and then to see things are as they should be.'

'Oh, I see. Will he be calling in today?'

'I don't know. Can I give him a message?'

I took an envelope from my pocket. I'd brought a letter just in case Nathan was out. 'Could you see he gets this?' I asked. 'Or should I put it through the letter box?'

'No, give it to me. Letters sometimes fall behind the door and he doesn't see them. I'll give it to him; he's sure to come into the shop and have a word.'

'Thank you,' I said, giving him the envelope. 'Do you think he may come today?'

'If he doesn't, I'll ring him tomorrow and tell him there's a letter waiting for him.'

I thanked him again, and he went back into the shop. I turned away, at a loss to know what to do with myself. It was strange not to have to work. I decided to spend the day exploring the city. There was still so many places I hadn't been.

It was dark when I got back to my lodgings. I saw the curtains twitch, and I knew Mrs Stiggly had been watching for me. The rent was due any day now, and she was probably waiting for me to pay her. She pounced on me as I let myself in.

'I'll have that key if you please.'

I stared at her. 'What do you mean?'

'I want you packed and out of my house tonight.'

'Why? What have I done?'

'A person called today. She said she was a friend of yours.' Mrs Stiggly's lips narrowed. 'I wouldn't have her in the house. And you can go, too. I thought you were too good to be true . . . Putting on your airs and graces as if butter wouldn't melt in your mouth. Well, I know a whore when I see one, and out you go today!'

'Because I have a friend who . . . It doesn't mean I'm the same.' I glared at her furiously. If she didn't want me here, I would leave. 'It doesn't matter to me. I was going

369

soon anyway. You charge far too much for your rooms – and your cooking is awful.'

She gave a snort of indignation, but didn't reply. I was smarting as I hurried upstairs. The woman was impossible. I was glad to be leaving her depressing house. She came to the door, watching as I collected my things.

'You needn't worry,' I snapped as I flung them into a bag. 'There's nothing you have I would bother to steal.'

'Oh, I knew you were a bad one. The minute I saw you, I knew.'

'Then why did you take me?' I laughed harshly. 'Don't think I don't know. It was because I was foolish enough to pay your prices.' I tossed the key of my room on the dressing-table. 'I hope the next tenant has more sense.'

'Good riddance!' she called as I ran down the stairs.

I didn't bother to answer. I was seething with anger as I burst into the street. The old witch had no right to tar me with the same brush as Polly.

Angry, my eyes smarting with tears, I didn't notice the car until it screeched to a halt outside Mrs Stiggly's front door. I began to walk briskly. I heard shouting behind me but even then it didn't occur to me to look round. Feet pounded the pavement behind me, and then someone caught my arm, swinging me round.

'Where do you think you're going? Why are you running away?'

'Running away?' I blinked as I gazed up into the man's furious eyes. 'Why should I run away?'

'That's the way it looks to me. You left me a note and when I got here . . .'

'Oh, Nathan!' Sheer relief made me giggle. 'I wasn't running away from you.'

'Where are you going then?'

'I've no idea. My landlady just threw me out.'

'Threw you out?' He glanced back down the road to where Mrs Stiggly was standing in her doorway, and from the look on his face I knew he was planning to go back and do her some injury. 'Why did she do that, Betty?'

I explained about Polly and he frowned. 'Mrs Stiggly never did like me. She thinks I'm bad,' I said.

'Polly's not your sort, Betty.' He looked at me oddly. 'Thank goodness I came as soon as I got your letter. I might have missed you.'

'It was lucky for me,' I said. 'I have to find somewhere to sleep tonight.'

'You could stay at the flat – if you'll let me take you there?'

'I should be grateful. I need your help, Nathan.'

He gazed at me in silence, then he smiled. 'I'm glad you came to me, Betty. Come on, give me your bag. Get in the car and I'll take you out for dinner. We can talk: it sounds as if we've some catching up to do.'

'I'm not starving, Nathan. Things haven't been good, but they're not that bad either.'

'They're not that good,' he said grimly. 'Save it until we're at the flat. I want to hear everything.'

He opened the car door for me. Mrs Stiggly had gone in, but she was watching from behind the curtains. I waved to her as Nathan drove off.

'Silly old witch,' I said. 'I never should have stayed there as long as I did.'

Nathan grinned but made no comment. He didn't say much until we were seated in the small restaurant, then he looked at me seriously. 'I couldn't believe it when I got your note, Betty. How long have you been in town?'

'Since the middle of February. I've been working in a dress shop but I got the sack.'

He looked thoughtful. 'The last I heard, you were going to marry Joe Morris. What happened?'

I was surprised. 'Who told you that?'

'I had a letter from Aunt Hilda.'

'I see.' I frowned. 'Did she tell you when Joe died?'

Nathan shook his head, his face registering shock. 'My

God! Joe's dead? How did it happen. Was it some sort of an accident?'

'He died of diphtheria . . . My brother and sister died, too. I was ill but my father nursed me through it.' I took a deep breath. 'He died earlier this year.'

Nathan's eyes narrowed, a little nerve jumping in his cheek. 'It sounds as though you've had a rotten time, Betty. You'd better tell me exactly what happened.'

We talked as we ate. I told him how I'd nursed my little sister and brother, and how Joe had died alone in his cottage. The expression on his face was grim as I went on but he stayed silent, not interrupting until I came to the part about getting the sack from my job.

'I didn't see why I should put up with him mauling me so I hit him,' I said.

Nathan laughed then. 'Good for you,' he said. 'I see you haven't changed. I'm glad about that.'

'So then I came to see you,' I said.

'You should have come before.' He grinned. 'But better late than never, kiddo.'

'You don't change either.'

We lingered over the meal for some time, then Nathan drove me to the flat. I remembered the bright light in the hall. Then we were upstairs and it was just as it had been the first time. I sat on the sofa and Nathan dumped my bags in the middle of the floor. I looked at the fur rug and smiled as I recalled dancing on it barefoot.

'The man next door told me you're going to rent this place. You don't live here any more then?'

'I've bought somewhere bigger. I'll make us a hot drink. I've got powdered milk in the kitchen if that's all right?'

I nodded and Nathan went into the kitchen. I kicked off my shoes and curled my feet up on the settee, sighing. It would be wonderful to live here.

'There's tea or Camp coffee, but only condensed milk.'

'Tea without milk would be fine. I often have it that

way.' I closed my eyes, breathing deeply. 'Can I stay here for a few days?'

'I'd be insulted if you didn't.' He came back with a tray and set it on the table. 'There's some biscuits in the tin but they might not be fresh.'

'After that meal? I couldn't eat another thing.'

'Why didn't you come to me as soon as you arrived?'

'I thought I could find work as a singer myself.'

'Same old independent Betty!' He grinned. 'Have you seen Frances at all?'

'No,' I said quickly, wondering why I lied, though I knew it was because that incident in the shop still hurt. 'Is she in London?'

'She comes and goes. She and Mary spend most of the winter in France, but Frances likes London in the summer.'

'Oh . . .' I said. 'Is she better now?'

'She was very well when I last saw her,' he replied with a slight frown. 'I always knew she would be when she got away from the fens.' He looked at me thoughtfully. 'I hope you haven't been seeing too much of Polly. You do know she's a call girl, don't you?'

'Well, yes, sort of,' I said. 'I know about her work. I'll have to look for a job soon.'

'You've got me to look after you now.'

'A kept woman?' I raised my eyes to his. 'Nathan, I . . .'

'As stubborn as ever, I see. You'll stay here until we sort out your life. If you run away, I warn you, I'll find you and bring you back.' He grinned. 'I was always your friend, but you couldn't see it. I want to help you and I shall – if you'll let me?'

'I'm tired of struggling alone. I'll accept your help, Nathan, but I can't stay here for ever.'

'We'll talk tomorrow,' he said. 'Get some sleep and make yourself at home. I'll be back with breakfast.'

I smiled as he left. I hadn't expected him to leave me alone, but perhaps he no longer wanted me the way he once had. It was strange the way things had worked out.

Nathan had always pursued me and I'd run away, but now I'd come to him of my own accord. If James had acted differently, it might have been another story. I wondered what Nathan would say if he knew that I'd gone to James first, but I would never tell him.

Four days later I stared in surprise as Nathan carried in a huge box. Every day he'd brought me something: food, flowers, sweets, newspapers, a record player and stacks of new records for my use while I was at the flat. I'd accepted everything gratefully, but I felt a little flutter in my stomach as I stared at the box.

'What is it, Nathan?'

'Open it and see.' He grinned at me. 'Go ahead, it won't bite you.'

I removed the lid carefully, a gasp of surprise breaking from me as I lifted the layer of tissue inside. Underneath was the most stunning dress I'd ever seen. It was black, cut on long, sleek lines like something Marlene Dietrich might have worn in *The Blue Angel*, and the back dipped alarmingly.

'It's shameless,' I said as I held it against me. 'Nathan, I can't wear this.'

'Don't be such a prude,' he said, his eyes glittering with determination. 'You're going to wear it this evening. I'm taking you out.'

I held the dress against me again, looking in the mirror above the fireplace. I'd never be able to wear a bra with it, and it would show every line of my body.

'Where are you taking me?'

'To a nightclub,' he replied, smiling as I continued to preen in front of the mirror. 'I want you to meet someone. Someone who may be able to help you get started as a singer.'

'Nathan! What are you up to?'

'Just wait and see,' he began, but as I pulled a face, he laughed. 'Always so impatient, Betty. I told you I knew someone who might help you once before, didn't I? Well,

374

his name is Richard, he's a distant cousin of my mother's and he runs a nightclub in Mayfair . . .'

I gave a little scream of delight, dropping the dress and launching myself at him. 'Oh, Nathan,' I cried. 'Do you think he'll like me?'

'I'm sure he will. We'll have dinner at the club tonight and by the end of it, he'll be begging me to let you audition for him. I've told him I'm your business manager.' Nathan's tone was slightly odd, but I was too excited to wonder at it.

'I can't believe it!' I glowed as I looked up at him. 'I should have listened to you when you offered to help me years ago.'

His mouth twisted in a strange smile. 'I wish you had, Betty.' For a moment his expression was so peculiar that it made me pause, then he caught me to him, brushing his lips over mine in a light, passionless kiss. 'Go and get ready. I have something to do, but I'll be back in an hour. Why don't you try those new bath crystals I bought you yesterday?'

'Yes, I will.'

I smiled at him shyly as he left. I was floating on air as I ran the water and sprinkled the perfumed crystals generously. I felt as if I were dreaming as I soaked in the water, reflecting on how my life had changed in a few short days – and it was all due to Nathan. He was so good to me!

I wondered now why I had tried to keep him at a distance for so long. A bubble of happiness surrounded me as I dressed in the fabulous gown he had given me, relishing the feel of the silk against my skin. It clung to my body so seductively that I could wear only the finest silk briefs underneath it and nothing else. Staring at myself in the long mirror in the bedroom, I saw a total stranger. That woman was too elegant to be Betty Cantrel! She was beautiful . . . beautiful, and something more. I had a certain something . . . a look in the eyes that I'd seen in my heroines of the big screen . . . I realised why I'd had so much trouble with certain men in the past. It gave me a feeling of power and I laughed, twisting and turning vainly in front of the mirror as I marvelled at the transformation.

Hearing Nathan come upstairs, I was tempted to rush and greet him, but I wanted to make a grand entrance. I wanted to test my new-found confidence. I waited until I heard him calling me, then I opened the bedroom door and walked slowly towards him. I moved with the grace my new image demanded, feeling a surge of triumph as I saw the surprise and pleasure on his face. I halted a few paces in front of him, lifting my eyes to his.

'Well, Nathan, will I do?'

'Fantastic,' he breathed. 'I always knew it, but that dress is perfect for you. Now you look what you are, a seductive, passionate woman. Richard will be mad to get you. Especially when he hears you sing.'

'Do you really think so?' Underneath my new image, I was still the uncertain little village girl I'd always been.

'Yes, I really think so.' He grinned and offered me his arm with a flourish. 'Your carriage awaits, Miss Cantrel. The future is before you . . .' I took his arm, hoping that he wouldn't notice I was trembling. 'Just leave everything to me, Betty. Don't be nervous. I know what I'm doing. All you have to do is smile and agree with whatever I say.'

From the moment we walked into the club, I was aware of people watching us. We looked well together; Nathan distinguished in his black silk evening suit and me in that startling gown. The back dipped so low that I felt half naked, but somehow I didn't care any more; I was too excited.

I never knew what we ate or drank that evening. When the floor show came on, I laughed at the comedian's jokes and applauded the male singer, but it all seemed muted, as if it came from a distance. It wasn't until the show was over that a man approached our table. Tall, stout, with a florid complexion and greying hair, he terrified me. Supposing he didn't like me!

'So this is the girl you've been hiding from me,' Richard Warren said, his sharp eyes assessing me. 'I can see why. She's everything you promised, Nathan. If she can sing I'll be happy to give her a job.'

'Oh, she can sing,' Nathan said chuckling. 'She hasn't had any training, but she has the voice of an angel – or maybe a siren.'

'When can I hear this angelic voice?' There was an amused look on Richard's face.

'Now, if you like,' I said, my fear of him evaporating.

His eyes began to twinkle. 'So she can talk. I was beginning to wonder.'

'She can talk and she can sing,' Nathan said, 'but at the moment she wants to dance.'

'There speaks the voice of a manager,' Richard replied good-humouredly. 'Enjoy your evening then – but bring her to me tomorrow morning.'

I glanced at Nathan, hardly able to contain my excitement. Richard liked me!

Nathan smiled, taking my hand to pull me to my feet as the musicians began to play a waltz. I melted into his body as he held me close; the excitement and the wine we'd had at dinner was going to my head. I wasn't used to champagne; it sent bubbles up my nose and my head seemed to be full of bubbles, too. Dancing with Nathan was like being in heaven. I closed my eyes, leaning my head against his shoulder, and I felt the touch of his lips against my hair. I wanted this evening to go on and on forever.

It must have been two or three in the morning when we left the club. I was walking on a cloud, still swaying to the music, happy, relaxed. Nathan drove us home. I blinked in the bright light of the hall, then we were upstairs and Nathan was holding me, kissing me.

'You're not intoxicated tonight, are you, Betty?' he asked. 'It's not like the last time?'

377

I shook my head, moving towards him and sighing gently. 'No, it's not like the last time, Nathan,' I said softly.

As he reached out for me, I went willingly to his embrace. It seemed right and natural. My arms folded about his neck as he kissed me, gently at first and then with increasing passion. I swayed against him, surprised by the sudden urgency of my own response, and then I knew. I knew that I had been waiting for it to happen again ever since the first time, and that I wanted it. I wanted Nathan to make love to me.

'Let me stay with you tonight,' he whispered huskily. 'Let me love you, darling.'

'Yes. Yes, stay with me,' I cried, clinging to him. My body was crying out for love. I wanted Nathan, I was on fire for him, my senses clamouring impatiently. 'Don't go. Stay with me, Nathan. Love me. I want you so much . . .'

He groaned deeply in his throat, bending down to catch me behind the knees and sweep me off my feet. I clung to him as he carried me through into the bedroom, returning his kisses with an eagerness that surprised even him.

'You want me this time, don't you, Betty?'

'Yes. Yes, I want you,' I cried. I felt again the breathy excitement of my first seduction, but this time I was not afraid.

'I promised you I would be patient the next time,' Nathan said as his lips moved softly against my throat. 'I want to make you happy, darling.'

I was sleepy but not tired. I felt wonderfully relaxed as I lay with my hair spread out on the pillow, smiling up at him. He did everything slowly, removing my dress and panties a little at a time, his hands stroking and caressing me so that my flesh began to tingle with the delicious sensations he was arousing. He seduced me with his eyes, with the lingering touch of his hands and lips, with his tongue and the soft whisper of his breath against my ear.

He whispered words of love so sweet that I could feel my limbs melting and the moisture begin to run between my thighs. Yet still he did not touch me there.

'Nathan . . . Nathan,' I moaned, arching towards him as the desire moved in me hotly.

'Patience, my love,' he murmured. 'If I must wait so must you. Undress me now. Let me feel your hands on my skin. Make me know that you want me.'

My fingers trembled as I fumbled with the buttons of his shirt. He laughed at my eagerness, refusing to help me as I thrust it back over his shoulders, my hands moving feverishly over his firm, satin-smooth skin. He had such a hard, lean back with taut muscles that flexed at my touch. I ran my hands over his chest, down to the obstruction of his trousers, pushing at them impatiently, but still he made me wait. I had to unfasten every last button before he would help me to thrust them down over his thighs.

Then we were both naked and lying side by side. In the light of the lamp Nathan's body glistened with little beads of sweat. His skin was several shades darker than mine, making my arm look creamy white as it lay across his thigh. I thought that now he would possess me completely as he had done the first time, but he continued to kiss and caress me until I was moaning with frustration.

'Nathan . . . Nathan, please now,' I begged, straining towards him. 'Oh, please, I can't stand it . . .'

Only then did he part my legs and slide between them. As I felt the hot, hard thrust of him inside me, I gasped with pleasure. I had not expected it to feel quite this good. Even now he was moving with a slow deliberateness that had me moaning, my nails digging deep into his flesh as I cried aloud, but then he gave a groan and suddenly he was driving into me so deeply that I thought I should die of pleasure. My head turned from side to side on the pillow and I called his name wildly as the climax came with a suddenness that had me jerking spasmodically. My legs closed around his body, hugging him to me.

Nathan lay still at last as I held him to me. For a while neither of us moved. His weight was crushing me but I was too exhausted to protest. I just wanted to hold him and feel the sweet contentment of perfect peace. I had never felt this way before, and when he rolled away onto his back, I protested.

'Hold me,' I whispered. 'I just want you to hold me.'

'Come here then.' He turned on his side, his hands on my bottom as he pressed me against him and then held me trapped with one leg. His hands slid up my back and he began to stroke the nape of my neck. 'Happy now?' he asked with the indulgence of a satisfied male.

'Yes, Nathan. I . . .'

'Hush,' he murmured against my ear. 'There's no need to say anything. Go to sleep now.'

It was as if I no longer had a will of my own. He told me to sleep and I obeyed, my eyes closing as I snuggled up to his warm body. It felt so good not to be alone. I sighed with contentment, letting my mind empty itself as I slipped away into a dreamless sleep.

When I woke much later, Nathan had gone. The bed felt cold and empty as I slid my hand across the sheets. I felt cheated and bereft. I wanted him to be there. My mind was crystal clear now, though my temples throbbed. I'd drunk a considerable amount of wine at dinner, but I was too honest to blame what had happened on that. I'd known that if I came to Nathan it was bound to happen, and perhaps that was exactly what a part of me had always wanted.

Nathan returned with some hot rolls for our breakfast, and another large box, which he deposited on the end of the bed with a huge grin.

'I ordered this a couple of days ago,' he said. 'And picked it up this morning.'

This time I felt no qualms, opening the box eagerly to exclaim in delight as I saw the dress inside. It was a pale grey silky material with a full skirt over stiff petticoats, and there was a white jacket that fitted into the waist to go with it; also a big straw hat and white gloves.

'You'll spoil me,' I said. 'It's lovely.'

'I intend to spoil you,' he replied, taking my hands to pull me to my feet and into his arms. 'I want you, Betty. I've always wanted you. I knew one day you would understand that you belong to me. Now I have you and I don't intend to let you go again. You're mine and I'll take care of you. I'll give you everything you could possibly want.'

'I won't be a kept woman,' I said, frowning. 'I'm going to work for my living – but I'll stay with you, Nathan. If there's one thing I've learned since coming to London, it's that I hate living alone.'

'Just as long as you know that you have to be with me.' He looked down and I was frightened by the intense expression in his eyes.

'Don't look at me that way,' I said. 'Sometimes you scare me, Nathan. You're so intense.'

A little shadow passed across his face. 'I'm sorry, Betty. I don't mean to be. It's in my nature. I think all the Crawleys are inclined to brood. Frances was much the same.'

'Yes,' I said. 'Sometimes she was – but with you, it's that little devil on your shoulder.'

He laughed. 'So that's what you think, is it? Maybe you're right. It's these black moods . . .' He shook his head. 'You don't want to hear this. Don't be afraid of me, Betty. I never want to hurt you. I promise I'll do my best to make you happy.'

'You have.' I smiled, sliding my arms up around his neck. 'I've never felt so wonderfully alive . . .'

'This is just the start, my darling. One day you'll be rich and famous. You'll have fabulous jewels, more clothes than you can wear – anything you want.'

'At the moment all I want is to be with you.'

'My sweet Betty.' He drew me against him, his eyes on

381

fire as he gazed down at me. 'I wish we could stay here, but you have to get ready. Richard is waiting.'

I left his arms reluctantly to change into my gown. It fitted me perfectly. Nathan had a good eye. The dress he'd chosen for me years ago had been right for the girl I was then, just as this was right for the woman I'd become.

In the light of the morning, the club looked empty and a little garish with its crimson and gold decor; it needed the softness of subtle lighting to make it into the paradise of my dream world. Richard was sitting at one of the tables, smoking and talking to another man. They turned to look at us as we approached, then Richard stood up and the other man did the same.

'Betty,' Richard said, kissing my cheek. 'You look wonderful. I've been looking forward to this immensely.' He turned to the thin, slightly tired-looking man beside him. 'This is Tim Reynolds; he plays the piano for us. He'll be helping us this morning.'

'Hello,' I said, feeling nervous again. 'I've never sung anywhere except in church or at home. I do know some of the popular stuff, but I may make some mistakes.'

'Don't worry, Betty, I'll cover for you.' Tim smiled lazily. 'Shall we try out a few keys and see what's right for you?'

Richard nodded at us approvingly. 'If you have a voice I shall teach you to sing like a professional. Just relax and pretend that you're at home in the bath, my dear. For this first time, I should like to hear you sing without accompaniment.'

Nathan grinned at me. 'She doesn't need the music, it's in her head.'

'What are you going to sing?' Richard asked.

'I'd like to try "Stormy Weather" – if that's all right?'

'That's fine by me.'

I walked over to the tiny stage. Nathan and Richard were sitting at their table, Tim was at the piano, his hands in his lap. I felt their eyes on me and my knees shook. This was it, my big chance at last! Supposing I made a mess of it? The palms of my hands were damp with sweat and I felt sick. What was I doing here? I was an ignorant village girl, what made me think I could follow in the footsteps of people like Judy Garland and Elizabeth Welch? I closed my eyes for a moment, wishing the floor would open up and swallow me. I was sure I wouldn't be able to sing a note. Then my courage began to return. I wasn't just Betty Cantrel, from a village in the fens, I was *me*. I could do whatever I wanted to do with my life. It was up to me.

The music flowed out of me. I forgot who I was. I forgot the men watching me. I just sang for the pleasure of it. I began with a hymn, then something from *Kiss Me Kate*, and finished with the deep, throbbing notes of 'Stormy Weather' — a song from a film I'd seen some weeks previously. When I'd finished there was for a moment complete silence. I came back to earth with a bump, feeling anxious. Why did no one say anything? Had I been that awful? My worst fears were realised as the terrible silence continued. I walked to the edge of the stage area, looking at the two men. I was vaguely aware that other people had suddenly arrived from nowhere. I could see white faces with eyes peeping at me from behind the bar and the doorway.

'Was I all right?' I asked anxiously. 'Do you want me to try something else?'

Richard stood up. He was smiling. He began clapping, and then I could hear a babble of excited voices. People came towards me, all talking and laughing together.

'Wonderful!'

'A natural.'

'Never heard anyone do that before.'

I heard the voices but I couldn't take my eyes from Richard's face. He came up to me. He embraced me, kissing first one cheek and then the other. I stared at him, my heart beating so fast that I thought I should faint.

'Was it what you wanted?'

'It was terribly amateur,' he said and my heart sank. 'But you have a voice. Undoubtedly, you have a voice.'

'Nathan . . .' I looked at him, bewildered. Was I hired or not?

Nathan grinned. 'Take no notice of him, Betty. You were wonderful, believe me.'

'Will he hire me?' I turned from him to Richard. 'Will you take me on?'

'You have a great deal to learn . . . but I'm sure we can do something with you. You'll have to work hard . . .'

'I don't mind work.' I gazed at him eagerly.

'Of course she'll work hard,' Nathan said. 'Stay here and talk to the others, Betty. Richard and I have business in his office.'

I felt deserted as he and Richard walked away, but then Tim called me over and began to introduce me to the others. 'This is Bill, he works in the bar – a wizard with the cocktail shaker, but watch out for him when he's experimenting.'

Bill was tall and dark, with a thick moustache and a friendly smile. He grinned at me and offered to make a new drink in my honour as long as I promised to try it. I laughed and said I would. Behind him were two girls called Julie and Liz, who I gathered worked as hostesses in the club. Also a plump, cheerful woman called Maggie who looked after the cloakroom.

'We don't usually see any of this lot at this unearthly hour,' Tim said. 'But they've turned out to have a look at you.'

'It's very kind of you all to welcome me,' I said. 'Especially as you must have been up very late last night.'

'Don't kid yourself,' the girl called Julie said. 'We all wanted to see what Nathan's new woman looked like. Liz has been making eyes at him for months . . .'

'Bitch,' Liz said. 'You're the one who's had her nose put out.'

'Liz, pretty pussy,' Bill said. 'Don't you two ever ease up?'

'Go and stick your head in a Tom Collins,' Liz said, but without any real malice. 'We're the best of friends, though you'd never know it. Welcome to our merry band, Betty. How long have you been in London?'

'Three – no, nearer four months now.'

'That song "Stormy Weather", it gives me the knee trembles,' Liz said. 'I like to hear Frank Sinatra singing it. I saw him in *The Kissing Bandit* three times. Did you know he was coming to Britain soon? He's doing a European tour and then coming here for the first time.' She rolled her eyes. 'I just love that man.'

'I'd like to see him in concert,' I said. 'I should think it would be difficult to get tickets, though.'

Liz winked at me. 'It depends on who you know. Do you want to come if I can swing it?'

'Yes please . . .' I broke off as I saw Nathan returning with Richard. Both men looked pleased with themselves.

'It looks as if our Nathan has twisted Richard's arm a little,' Liz whispered.

'I still can't believe it's happening.'

'You're a lucky girl. I wouldn't have minded having Nathan as my . . . manager . . .'

The expression in her eyes was distinctly wicked. I blushed and glanced away. She couldn't know that Nathan and I were lovers, why should she assume it was so? Was it taken for granted in this new world I'd entered? Surely Nathan had meant it when he said he wanted us to be together always? I'd believed him last night, but now I was uneasy, recalling his determined pursuit of Polly and then his sudden lack of interest in her. What if that happened to me?

'Well, kid, we're in business.'

His words and the excitement in his voice swept all the doubts from my mind. My heart beat wildly as I gazed up into his eyes. 'Is he going to take me on?'

'You start rehearsing tomorrow. You won't sing for the customers until he thinks you're good enough, then you'll be performing five nights a week.'

'Nathan!' I squeaked with delight. 'It's like a dream come true.'

'It's just as well I didn't take you with me just now,' he said, grinning. 'You'd have taken whatever he offered.'

'You're looking very smug,' I said, slipping my arm through his. 'Just what have you been up to?'

'I'll tell you in the car. Come on, my girl, we've got work to do.'

'What do you mean?'

'You need clothes. Lots of them. We're going shopping.'

'But I'm wearing a new dress now.'

'Do you want the rich women who come here at night to look down their noses at you?' One brow rose. 'You're going to be the best, Betty Cantrel. That means you have to look the part, and that means clothes. Wardrobes full of them.'

'But, Nathan, you can't keep buying me things. It must be costing you a fortune.'

He laughed. 'Let me worry about that. It won't be long before you're earning a great deal of money. I'm your manager, remember. Consider it an investment.'

I stared at him, then nodded. 'You promise me you'll take your percentage from what I earn, and the money you're spending on me now?'

'Don't worry about money, Betty. I can afford it, I give you my word. My father made his fortune from the retailing business. I discovered that when I was given control of my trust fund. A lot of his money is still tied up in property, shops, houses, things like that – though Eben sold some of the best when he was in control. I can't understand why. The money didn't do anywhere near as well in the investments he made.'

I didn't answer. I could have told him why his uncle had chopped and changed the investments, and why he hadn't earned all the money he should have, but I kept quiet. The past was dead and buried. Let it lie. The farm had been sold now and the money would eventually pass to Frances. My loyalties were still divided between them, despite the way she had behaved towards me. And there was the mystery of Eben's death. I should never be quite sure what had happened that day in the barn, or how much Nathan knew about his Uncle Eben's death.

I gazed up at Nathan curiously. 'Are you very rich?'

He smiled, amused. 'It depends on your viewpoint. I'm not as rich as I intend to be one day – then I'll cover you with diamonds from head to toe.'

'No!' I cried sharply. 'I don't want that, Nathan. I should feel as if you owned me. I'll accept your help – on the understanding that we're partners.'

There was an odd look in his eyes. 'If that's the way you want it. Don't be too proud, Betty. Pride only gets in the way of other things.'

'Like what?' I asked. 'We both know our relationship isn't permanent. It may last for a long time, it may not . . .' I paused so that he could contradict me if he wanted to but he didn't so I went on: 'I'm grateful for what you've done for me, but don't imagine that's the only reason I want to stay with you. I hate living alone. I'm comfortable with you and last night was . . . was wonderful. So as long as you want us to be together, Nathan, I'll stay with you, but I want to earn my living and I don't want you to be forever spending money on me.'

He shrugged his shoulders. 'Well, at least I managed to get fifty pounds out of Richard as an advance on your salary. So you'll soon be able to afford to buy your own clothes.'

'Fifty pounds?' I was shocked. 'How long will it take me to earn that?'

'Not long. He offered thirty for a start, but I got him up to fifty.'

'Fifty pounds a month?' I gasped. It was a fortune.

'Good Lord! Do you want to work for nothing? It's fifty pounds a week, but it's not enough. We'll have a hundred out of him as soon as you start drawing the customers – and you will. Julie and Liz earn twenty-five pounds a week. I think you should get at least twice that – you're worth it. Once word gets around, we'll have standing room only in the club. Everyone will want to come to the Purple Moon to hear Betty Cantrel.'

'Oh, Nathan,' I said, laughing. 'You make me feel like a star. I shall be rich . . .'

'You certainly will.' He grinned at me. 'This is the first step, kiddo. The next thing is a recording contract and then maybe a movie . . .'

My knees began to shake. 'Don't, Nathan. You frighten me. I'm not sure I want to be that famous.'

He gripped my arm, looking at me intently. 'Then what *do* you want, Betty? Make up your mind now, there's no going back once you start. You can reach for the moon or you can run away and hide. Come on, what's the matter with you? I thought you had more courage than this!'

I wasn't sure what I wanted at that moment. It was all going a little too fast for me. Singing had always been something I did for pleasure. The shining future Nathan was holding out to me seemed unreal.

'I'm not a coward, Nathan. I just want to be happy, that's all.'

He gave a harsh laugh. 'Happiness is an elusive dream, kid. I can't guarantee you that, I'm afraid. With me you won't be hungry and you won't be cold – but happiness is something you have to find for yourself.'

What did I want him to say? Did I hope that he would say he loved me and wanted to marry me? Would I have married him even if he had? Whatever was in my mind at that moment, I knew that he was offering me far more than I'd ever dreamed of. I was a fool even to question it. There was no point in even thinking about the future too much. I must just take what I could from life and make the most of it. I must learn to trust Nathan. My father had made me bitter, but Nathan wasn't Robert Cantrel. Maybe there was a little bit of my father in most men, but it was the way they shaped up to life that made the difference. I must try to forget the past and live for the present.

'I thought this was what you wanted.' Nathan was looking at me intently. 'If it's marriage . . .'

'No!' I said quickly. I'd wanted to be James Blair's wife, and where had that got me? In my heart he would always be the perfect man, but I had to face reality. James wasn't interested in me. Nathan was, but if I demanded too much from him, I might lose him too. 'No, this is what I want,' I insisted. 'I'm not ungrateful, Nathan. It's all a little too much for me to take in.'

His grip tightened on my arm. 'You wouldn't leave me?'

There was an odd note in his voice and he looked so strange that my heart jerked. Had I misjudged him? Could he really care for me? Suppose he was in love with me? I wasn't sure how I'd feel about that. The idea was so new and amazing that I rejected it instinctively. I'd be a fool to believe that. Besides, what was love? My father had said he loved my mother, but he'd never given her anything but pain. No, far more sensible to carry on as we were. Smiling, I touched his cheek with my fingertips.

'Don't look so cross,' I said. 'I've nowhere to go. Besides, I need you, Nathan. We're partners, aren't we?'

'Then we'll go on as we planned?'

'Of course.' I tucked my arm through his. 'Didn't we have some shopping to do?'

Richard was a hard taskmaster. I had always sung for pleasure, but now I discovered that I did not know how to sing. I made mistakes all the time, but Richard was patient with me. I was allowed to try and try again until I learned to do it his way.

'No. No,' he would cry. 'I've told you before, Betty. You're not breathing properly. Pause at the end of that phrase. Move your arms, move your body.'

'I can't sing and dance at the same time.'

'I'm not asking you to dance. I just want you to move.

You're not in church. You're a pretty girl flirting with your audience. Look at those people out there – they've paid to come and see you. That man over there thinks you're wonderful, make love to him with your eyes. Make him think you're singing just for him.'

'He'll think I'm a harlot!' I laughed at the frustration in Richard's eyes and blew a kiss to his imaginary audience. 'Is that better?'

'Well, it's a start. Let's go back to the beginning, shall we? Remember to breathe this time.'

So it went on. Gradually, I made progress. I learned to think about what I was singing instead of simply enjoying the music. It was much harder than I'd imagined. I had to work long hours in those first few weeks and sometimes I was so tired that I wanted only to sleep when I got back from rehearsals. Yet I loved every minute of it. My life was so exciting. I spent the morning and some afternoons at the club, but my nights were spent with Nathan. He took me to quiet restaurants where we could dine alone or mix with men he knew. The women with those men were never their wives. They were like me. Pretty, bright young women who laughed a lot, but never smiled with their eyes.

I wasn't unhappy. I was conscious of my status as Nathan's woman, but I wasn't ashamed. I enjoyed being with Nathan, though I couldn't have said exactly what I felt for him. I knew that he excited me, that his love-making could bring me intense pleasure, but I didn't look too deeply into my heart. Sometimes he went away for several days at a time, and he rarely spent the whole night in my bed, but I accepted the situation. It was perhaps not what I would've chosen, but it was better than being alone. I was content with Nathan, and I needed him. Had I ever really thought about it, I should probably have said that I was happy. I was on the verge of achieving everything I'd ever wanted. The world was opening before me. But I was greedy; I wanted the moon and the stars as well! Despite all I had, I hankered after James. I couldn't quite put him out of my mind even when I was with Nathan . . .

One of the women in black has begun to like me. She is younger than the others and she comes at night. I see her watching me sometimes when she thinks I'm asleep, and I see sympathy in her eyes. I think she wonders how it feels to be waiting for death. Once, when she looked at me, I asked her if she was happy. She looked startled, then shook her head.

'I'm a widow, see. I have to do this job to live.'

'That's not what I meant,' I said, but she didn't understand me.

I'd once asked Mrs Jackson if anyone was ever happy.

'The trick is knowing when you're happy,' she'd said.

I think that was the wisest thing anyone ever said to me.

I went to visit Polly, even though I knew Nathan wouldn't approve. She was pleased and surprised to see me after her visit to Mrs Stiggly's.

'You look wonderful, Betty,' she said. 'That dress must've cost a fortune.'

'Yes, I suppose it did. I bought it from a friend of mine at a discount.' I laughed at the curiosity in her eyes. 'So much has happened since I was last here. I met some-one . . .' I paused, then, 'I'm singing in a nightclub, Polly. You must come and see me. I'll arrange for you to be a temporary member.'

'Singing in a nightclub?' She looked surprised but pleased. 'Well, I never . . . Our Betty singing in a nightclub.'

'It was because of Nathan . . .' I paused, waiting for her reaction.

'You don't mean Nathan Crawley?' Her smile faded. 'Oh, Betty . . .'

'Richard Warren is the owner of the club.' I lifted my

chin. 'Yes, I do mean Nathan Crawley. He – he's my lover.'

'I don't know what to say.' She frowned. 'Is he good to you?'

'I know what you're thinking, Polly, but it isn't like that. Nathan has been wonderful to me. He's always buying me things, and he introduced me to Richard – they're distant cousins. Without him I should probably be working in Woolworths or somewhere similar.'

'Is he going to marry you?'

'We haven't discussed it. I'm not sure that I want to marry him – or anyone. I don't want to be like Mum.' I frowned. 'I used to think that all men were the same.'

'And now?'

'So far I've no complaints. Nathan takes care of me. He would give me even more if I'd let him.'

'Then I'm glad for you.' She smiled at me. 'Maybe you'll be luckier than I was. Maybe Nathan will stand by his word . . . Anyway, I'm glad you've come. You will stay for tea, won't you?'

'Yes, of course.'

She rang the bell, then looked at me. 'What does Frances say about you and Nathan?'

'I'm not sure if she knows.' I frowned. 'I haven't seen her. Nathan told me she had gone to France the other week. I believe Mary was still there. Why?'

'Oh, I just wondered. She always seemed to think Nathan was her private property.'

'She wasn't in love with him,' I said. 'I know there was someone else.'

'No, I didn't mean that exactly . . .' Polly shook her head. 'Take no notice of me, Betty. She was always such a jealous little madam, but if you never see her . . .'

'No, we don't.' I dismissed her fears as nonsense. 'Have you ever written to your brother George? He asked me about you several times, you know.'

'I daren't, Betty. If he ever found out what I'm

doing . . .' Polly sighed. 'I've burnt my boats. It's no good looking back.'

'No, I suppose not. I try not to, but I can't help it sometimes. When I think of what my father did to Mum . . . and Vera . . .'

'You're too proud, Betty. Look what Eben did to me. I got over it and so will you, if you let yourself.'

'Yes, I expect so. I'll have to go soon. Nathan is coming this evening.' I stood up, then remembered something. 'Did you want anything important when you came to visit me at Mrs Stiggly's, Polly?'

She frowned, then shook her head. 'It was just to ask you to a party – you could come with me tomorrow if you like? It's at Charlie's house.'

'No, I'd better not,' I said quickly. 'Nathan wouldn't like that. But we'll meet again soon, Polly. We'll go shopping together.'

Chapter Sixteen

There had been an accident in New Coventry Street. A beer lorry had spilled its load into the middle of the road, causing chaos. Seeing that there would be a long delay, I left the bus and ran the last few streets, but I was still late. Nathan was waiting for me. I saw the look in his eyes and braced myself for the storm.

'I'm sorry,' I said breathlessly. 'I was caught up in the traffic. There's been an accident . . .'

'There are always accidents.' His eyes went over me, and they held suspicion, anger and something else I couldn't read. 'Where have you been?'

'To visit a friend. Polly Baxter. I told you I'd seen her.'

'You've been to her house? Good Lord, Betty! Do you want to ruin your reputation?'

'What do you mean?' I flinched at the scorn in his voice. 'Polly is my friend.'

'Then visit her somewhere else. I don't want you going to that house.'

'None of her friends were there, if that's what you're worrying about.' My chin went up. 'Don't tell me what to do, Nathan. You don't own me.'

'I don't want to own you. I'm telling you for your own good, can't you see that?' He gave a sigh of exasperation. 'Do you always have to fight me? Can't you believe I'm on your side.'

I'd done it again, provoked a quarrel when all I wanted was to be in his arms. I was sorry for a moment, then, when I saw the look of frustration in his eyes, it made me smile.

'Don't glare at me like that, Nathan. I do know you're right, and I'll arrange to meet Polly somewhere else in future.' I moved towards him, gazing up at him provocatively. 'I'm sorry I was late, and I'm sorry I was prickly. You know I can't help it. Don't let's quarrel. It seems ages since you were here. I missed you.'

'I had to go to Portsmouth to sort out the customs forms for some goods I'm importing. I didn't get back to London until one in the morning. It was too late to come to you then.'

'You could have woken me; I wouldn't have minded. It was lonely in that bed without you. I hate it when you go away. Why couldn't someone else have sorted out the forms?'

'Because I like to see to it myself.'

'You seem to have your fingers in so many pies,' I said sulkily. 'I don't really know what you do, Nathan.'

'There's no need for you to know more than you do,' he said, frowning slightly. 'I don't want you involved.'

'But I am involved – I want to know everything about you.'

'Everything?' Nathan drew a deep, shuddering breath. He moved towards me, his arms going round me with sudden urgency. I saw the shadows leave his eyes and then he was smiling. 'Sometimes you almost drive me to the brink, kid. One day you'll push me too far – and then we'll both be sorry.'

'I don't know what you mean.' I pouted at him.

'Don't you?' He traced the line of my cheek with one finger. 'Why do you make me feel this way? You're like a fever in my blood that won't go away.'

'So now I make you sick.' I opened my eyes wide in innocence as he frowned. 'That's what you said, isn't it?'

'You know it isn't.'

I laughed and slid my hands up over his shoulders, stroking the nape of his neck the way he liked it. 'So what did you mean then?'

'Stop that, Betty, or you won't get any dinner. Where do you want to go tonight?'

'I'm not hungry . . . for food.' My eyes were inviting him to make what he would of the words. 'There's enough food and wine in the kitchen for later. I thought I would take a bath and go to bed early . . . with you.'

'Betty . . .' he breathed huskily. 'No wonder I adore you . . .' His mouth went loose and his face creased with a kind of pain; then I was in his arms and he was kissing me, lighting a fire that was soon raging out of control. 'Let's forget about the bath,' he muttered. 'God, how I want you!'

I pushed him away, glancing up at him wickedly as he protested and tried to take me back in his arms. 'Don't be so impatient, Nathan. I need a bath – why don't you share it with me?'

'You little wanton!'

At first I thought I'd shocked him, but then I saw the gleam in his eyes and I felt the laughter bubbling up inside me. 'Come on,' I said, taking his hand. 'Whatever I am, you've formed me. You taught me all I know.'

'Show me,' he said. 'Show me what you've learnt, my little temptress.'

I made no reply, smiling as I led him into the bathroom. As the steaming water cascaded into the porcelain tub, I sprinkled liberal amounts of the perfume he'd bought me into it. It rose in the steam, surrounding us in a haze of fragrance. Then I began to unfasten my clothes. I was looking at Nathan all the time, my eyes never leaving his, seducing him with each movement and making the removal of a stocking something that he found tantalising to watch. I could see the heat in his eyes and I knew he was loving it. When at last I stood naked before him, he began to unbutton his shirt, but I stopped him.

'Let me do it, Nathan.'

He smiled but said nothing as I pushed away his hands. As each button gave way, I kissed the spot revealed, flicking his skin with the tip of my tongue. When I had finished with his shirt, I turned my attention to his trousers, kissing him and licking him as before. I could see what effect it was having on him, and he groaned as my tongue stroked his blood-engorged penis and then my lips took it into my mouth.

'Betty! You're killing me. I've taught you too well.'

I laughed as he drew me up into his arms, crushing me against him, and I shivered with delight as I felt the heat of his flesh scorching mine. 'No, not yet, Nathan,' I whispered. 'Let me bathe you.'

'Witch!' he cried as we almost fell into the water together. 'I didn't teach you this.'

'Give me some credit for imagination,' I murmured. 'You wanted me to be a courtesan, didn't you, Nathan? Well, now you've got your wish.'

I began to soap his body, rubbing it into the smooth, firm skin with the tips of my fingers, massaging gently so that his flesh quivered and jerked with exquisite pleasure. There wasn't much room in the bath for two, so I had to sit with my legs opened and around him as I stroked his back and shoulders. Suddenly, he grabbed me round the waist, lifting me to bring me down hard on top of him. I gave a little scream of laughter as I felt the thrust of him and the water went splashing all over the floor.

'Careful, Nathan,' I cried. 'You'll drown us both.'

'To hell with the water,' he moaned. 'You asked for this and you're going to get it.'

I was laughing as I bent to kiss him, gasping with pleasure as he lifted and drove frantically. His need was urgent and he climaxed swiftly, leaving me wanting more, but I did not have to wait for long. He was by no means satisfied yet.

'You've had your fun,' he murmured as we dried ourselves on warm, fluffy towels. 'Now it's my turn.'

'That sounds ominous,' I said, my breath quickening as I anticipated the long, sweet loving that I knew would follow.

He took his revenge in a way that made it seem more

397

like a reward. As I lay on the bed, my skin tingling from the freshness of the water, he turned me over on to my stomach and straddled me, pouring a little perfume into his hands; then he began to massage my back with firm, strong fingers that eased my muscles, relaxing me. I could feel the sting of the perfume in my open pores; it made me tingle with a delicious coldness, and I moaned with pleasure. Then he put his arms around my waist, pulling me up to my knees and I felt the burn of him as he slid into the wetness of my vagina. A little shock went through me; this was the first time he had entered me in that way. His hands encircled my breasts, squeezing and caressing as he moved with a slow, satisfying rhythm. When he had had enough of that for the moment, he moved me over on to my back and began to kiss my stomach and my breasts, then the moist patch of dark hair between my thighs. By this time I was arching uncontrollably, crying his name feverishly as I begged him to come back inside me. When he did, we moved gently in perfect harmony, our bodies in unison as we reached that far distant shore at exactly the same moment, letting the soft waves wash over us as we lay in total exhaustion.

It was a long, long time later that I looked up at him and smiled. 'Is it sinful to feel so much pleasure, Nathan?'

'Why should it be a sin?' he asked, his hand idly stroking my breast. 'You were made for love, Betty. God would never have given you this beautiful body if he had wanted you to feel ashamed.'

'Am I really beautiful?' I gazed up at him, wanting to know, but he only shook his head and laughed.

'You know exactly what you are, and what you do to me, don't you?'

I stared at him as he rolled away and began to dress. How could I know if he never told me? He seemed to imagine I had more confidence than I had. From the way he spoke, it was as though I had him where I wanted him, but that was nonsense. I should never feel entirely sure of Nathan. There was always a part of him that remained aloof even at times like these. I frowned as I watched him button his shirt.

'Do you have to go? Why don't you ever stay the whole night with me?'

'I thought you wanted it this way? You're the one who doesn't want to get too involved.' There was a certain cruelty about his mouth as he smiled. 'You ask too much, Betty. You want your independence, but you want to be protected and loved, too, don't you? One of these days you're going to have to make up your mind.'

'Don't scold me, Nathan.'

'I'm not – I'm merely telling you the truth. Anyway, I'm not going yet. Get up, woman, and get me something to eat. If you want me back in that bed, I need to keep my strength up.'

'Nathan!' I laughed as he dragged me from the bed. 'Sometimes I think I love you.'

'Only sometimes?' He pulled a face. 'Then I'll have to do better, won't I?'

I was so nervous the night I was to sing at the club for the first time. When Nathan came to the flat to fetch me, I clung to his hand, my eyes wide with fright. 'I can't do it, Nathan, I can't go on. My throat's dry. I won't be able to sing.'

'Of course you can do it.' He bent to kiss me with unusual gentleness. 'You're going out there and you'll sing like an angel. You have a wonderful voice and you're beautiful. They'll love you. Take my word for it.'

'Hold me for a moment. Kiss me.'

I was trembling as he took me in his arms. He kissed me lingeringly and with great sweetness. 'Don't be frightened, Betty. Just sing to me. I'll be at my table. Sing for me, darling. No one else matters.'

'Yes.' I took a deep breath, inhaling the perfume of the huge bouquet of roses he'd brought me. 'Yes, I'll sing for you.'

As we walked into the club, Nathan saw some men

talking at the bar. One of them gave him a significant look and he frowned, turning to me.

'You go and get ready, Betty,' he said. 'I have to talk to someone.'

I glanced at the men, not liking the look of them. There was something almost sinister about them. What business could Nathan have with men like that?

The waiting was the worst. Once Richard told me it was time, I felt better. I walked on to the stage; I looked across at Nathan and began to sing. At first the people at the tables carried on eating and drinking, but then I sensed a change. They began to look my way, they began to listen. I could feel them warming to me. My nervousness fell away. I was enjoying myself. Everything Richard had taught me came naturally. I flirted with my audience, teasing them a little. I gave them smiles and caressed them, and they loved it. I entreated them to love me . . . and they did. Right from that very first night, they adored me.

The applause just went on and on. They would not let me leave the floor. I sang again. They called for more. A single red rose fell at my feet. Tears slid from beneath my lashes. I felt the warmth of their affection surround me. And I knew I had finally found myself. It was for this moment I had waited all my life – and it was all due to Nathan. I looked across to his table, intending to blow him a kiss. I looked and he was not there. He had missed my moment of triumph. Where was he? I felt a coldness inside me. He had promised, but he was not there.

As I turned to return to my dressing-room, Richard came and caught my arm. 'You can't leave just like that,' he said. 'You were a success, Betty. People want to talk to you. Some of the customers have asked to meet you.'

I knew that Liz and Julie often sat with the customers, especially men who came in alone. It wasn't part of their job exactly, but they got commission if the customers bought champagne, and I knew that Julie at least sometimes went home with a man if she liked him.

'Why not?' She shrugged when I asked her about it once. 'I can get double my week's wages from the generous ones.'

Richard saw my face and laughed. 'Nothing like that, Betty,' he said. 'Nathan would kill me if I even suggested it. No, there's a man I'd like you to meet, and a party of mixed company want you to join them for a drink. But come and meet Al first. He's absolutely green that you've signed up with us.'

He took me to a table in a corner. A man stood up and smiled. He was dark haired and attractive with an engaging smile. He held out his hand and I gave him mine.

'I'm glad to meet you, Miss Cantrel,' he said. 'I'm Al Burnett. I run the Stork Rooms – I don't know if you've heard of me?'

'Yes. Yes, I have,' I smiled. 'A girl I met once told me I should ask you for a job.'

He grinned and winked at Richard. 'You wouldn't like to ask me now, would you?'

I laughed, liking him at once. 'No, not at the moment. I'm very happy here.'

'I was afraid you would say that. Never mind, you'll know where to come if Richard doesn't pay you enough.'

'Hark at him,' Richard scoffed. 'Everyone knows Al doesn't like to pay much – he prefers it when the stars get up and do their turn for free.'

'I'm no mug.' Al grinned again. 'Would you like some champagne, Miss Cantrel?'

'Sorry, Betty has to circulate.' Richard laughed. 'Nice try, though, Al.' He steered me away towards the other side of the room. 'Al's all right, Betty. We go back a long way.'

I was laughing as I followed Richard. If all his customers were as nice as . . . Then I saw where we were heading and my heart missed a beat, beginning to race wildly as I saw the man and woman sitting together. Why hadn't Nathan warned me they would be here tonight?

'Now,' Richard said. 'This is Mr Blair's party. They would like you to join them for a drink, Betty.'

For a moment I felt as if I might faint. My mouth was dry and I could only stare as James got to his feet, smiling.

'You were wonderful,' he said. 'Won't you join us?'

'James . . .' My lips were too stiff to smile. I turned slowly to face Frances, feeling strange. 'Frances . . . I – I had no idea you were coming. Nathan didn't . . .' I stopped, realising that I was making a fool of myself. 'It's nice to see you.'

'Didn't Nathan tell you?' Her laughter was a little shrill. 'How very naughty of him. We wouldn't have missed it for the world, would we, James?'

'No,' he agreed. 'I should say not.'

Richard had signalled for a chair for me and I sat down, still feeling as though the ground had been cut from beneath my feet. The last time I'd seen Frances, she'd cut me dead, now she was here and smiling as if we were the best of friends.

'You were wonderful, Betty,' she said. 'When I saw you come on stage I couldn't believe it was you. You look so different.'

I glanced at her, detecting a hint of spite beneath the words of praise. 'I couldn't have done it without Nathan's help,' I said. 'No one would give me a chance.'

'I wrote to Mother,' James said. 'She told me she'd promised you an introduction to Noel Coward. Is that why you called at the house?'

'It was one of the reasons,' I said. His smile still had the power to charm me, but I had no right to feel this way. I belonged with Nathan. James must never be more than a friend to me now. I owed Nathan too much in every way.

'We must celebrate,' James said, handing me a glass of champagne. Our hands touched and I almost jumped. 'We were so delighted when we heard you were singing here tonight. Frances wrote to your last address inviting you to dinner, but the letter was returned with 'gone

402

away' written all over it. We had no idea you were still in London until quite recently, had we, Frances?'

'No, of course not,' Frances said, smiling at him. 'You know how much I wanted to see Betty. I've told you so many times, haven't I?'

'Have you been wanting to see me, Frances?'

She was smiling as she looked at me, but her eyes were cold and I felt that she was still angry with me, though she wouldn't allow James to see that.

'Frances often speaks of you,' James said. 'She was so upset when you were forced to leave her . . .'

'Please don't,' Frances said, laying her hand on his. 'Betty doesn't want to be reminded of that. It was all so long ago – and look at what she's done with her life. She's going to be rich and successful now, aren't you?'

Was that jealousy I saw in her eyes? I couldn't be sure, but I felt something . . . something hidden. I was sure she hadn't forgiven me, and I believed the only reason she'd come here this evening was to see for herself if I were a success or not. Perhaps she'd hoped to see me fail – or was I being unfair now?

I turned away from the resentful glare in her eyes, looking at James. Something in the way he was looking at me turned my knees to water. I was no longer an inexperienced child, and I knew what that expression meant. James wanted to go to bed with me! I felt a rush of breathless longing, and my heart raced. Then I dropped my eyes, feeling regret. If only I'd waited just a little longer! If only he hadn't been in such a hurry the day I called at his house.

'We're going down to the country next weekend,' James said. 'I don't suppose there's any chance of you coming down on the Sunday?'

I saw the question in his eyes and my head whirled. I wanted to go, oh, how I wanted to say yes, but Nathan would kill me.

'I don't finish here until the early hours . . .' I began, but I was interrupted.

'Don't let that worry you, Betty.' Nathan's voice was like cut glass. 'You don't work on Sunday or Monday nights. I could drive you down for Sunday lunch and bring you back Monday morning.' His brows rose as I stared at him. 'Always supposing that I'm invited?'

I was aware of tension as James and Nathan stared at each other and I thought that if looks could kill, one of them would fall dead at any moment, then Frances laughed, her voice shrill as she cried,

'But of course you are! Betty couldn't come without you, could she? After all, you are practically living together – aren't you?'

If she hadn't known where to find me, how did she know that we were lovers?

Nathan ignored her taunt. 'That's settled then. Now, if you will excuse us, I'm going to take Betty home.'

As I was propelled firmly from their table, I glanced at Nathan, noticing a tiny cut on his lip. He looked as if he might have been involved in a fight. His shirt was not as immaculate as usual and there was a spot of blood on his collar.

'What happened to you?' I asked. 'You didn't stay to hear me sing.'

'You were doing fine,' he said, his mouth grim. 'You didn't need me – and I had some business to attend to.'

'What kind of business? You look as if you've been fighting.'

'There was a misunderstanding; it's all been cleared up now.'

'Was it to do with those men you spoke to earlier?'

Nathan frowned. 'That's none of your business, Betty. You don't need to know.'

I glared at him. 'They looked like gangsters. Just what are you mixed up in, Nathan?'

He smiled as if amused. 'You've seen too many Hollywood films, Betty. They're friends, that's all I'm going to tell you. I know they look tough but in their business they have to be.' He shook his head as I frowned. 'Leave it, kid.'

I hated it when he shut me out like that. It had happened before when I'd asked about his business. I was certain that though much of his money came from legitimate sources, there was something hidden, something not quite legal. I glanced back at James's table and saw Frances watching us, a gleam of satisfaction in her eyes. I shivered, turning back to Nathan.

'Don't let's quarrel. Not tonight. We should be celebrating. I was a success.'

His expression softened slightly. 'Didn't I tell you it would be all right?'

'Yes, you did.' I smiled at him, feeling ashamed because he had given me so much and I had betrayed him in my thoughts. 'Shall we go? We'd better say good-night to Richard.'

'Going so soon?' Richard said as he came up to us. 'I thought we might have some champagne to celebrate?'

'I have a little headache,' I said. 'I think it's all the excitement. I'll see you tomorrow.'

'That will disappoint some of the customers; they've been asking me if you'll sing again – especially the men.' He grinned at Nathan. 'You'll have your work cut out fighting them off, my friend. I think our Betty is going to be very popular.'

I saw the little muscle twitch in Nathan's neck and cursed Richard for his foolish jokes. I supposed he had meant to flatter me, but I could see Nathan was angry again, and I knew he had one particular man in mind. I was sure he knew that his only real rival was James Blair. His hand tightened on my arm as he took me outside. He hardly spoke as we drove home and I sensed that a storm was building. Nathan had such a temper when he relaxed his guard. When we got in, he went straight to the drinks cabinet and poured himself a brandy. I walked into the bedroom and began to undress. I was at the dressing-table, brushing my hair, when he came in.

'Don't look at me like that,' I said. 'Richard was teasing you. If you'd been there . . .'

'I can't be with you all the time.' He looked at me broodingly. 'You'll have to learn to cope with your success. I may not always be around.'

A chill went through me. Was he saying he was getting bored with our relationship? My nails curled into the palms of my hands. I couldn't let Nathan suspect that I was afraid of losing him. I turned to look at him, my eyes challenging.

'I had to manage this evening, didn't I? Where were you, Nathan? Do I have a rival?'

'Don't be a bloody fool. You'll know soon enough when I've finished with you.'

The hairbrush clattered to the floor. I stood up, my body rigid with fury. 'Damn you, Nathan Crawley! I won't be treated like this. I'm not some harlot you can toss aside when you've had enough.' I threw myself at him in a sudden fit of temper, striking him with my fists. 'I hate you, Nathan. Sometimes I really hate you!'

He caught my wrists, holding me until I ceased to struggle. For a moment his eyes were hot with temper, then he seemed to relax. 'That's better, Betty. If you must know, I had to collect some money that was owing to me – or rather to some friends of mine. They called in a favour – and when that happens, you do what they ask. If you want to survive.'

The anger drained out of me and I shivered, feeling a chill at the base of my spine. 'They *were* gangsters – what are you mixed up in, Nathan?'

'It was a little favour, Betty. Nothing for you to worry about, I promise. It's done now and they won't ask again.'

'Until the next time.' I was suddenly frightened for him. 'You're a fool, Nathan. Those men are dangerous.'

'So am I.' He smiled and came towards me, touching my cheek. 'You're too tense, my sweet. You should learn to relax. Just let things happen. Everything will turn out right in the end.'

I felt a coldness inside. Tonight I had caught a glimpse of Nathan's other life, the life he did not share with me, and it worried me. How much did I really know about him? Could I really trust a man who had friends like the men I'd seen at the club that evening? Just who was the real Nathan Crawley?

I turned away from him, my nerves grating. 'I have a headache. I told you that.'

'Poor kid.' He bent to kiss my neck. 'Shall I make it better?'

I pulled away from him. 'I'm tired, Nathan. I just want to sleep.'

He stared at me for a moment, then he shrugged his shoulders. 'Have it your own way. I'm going out of town for a couple of days. I'll see you when I get back.'

I didn't turn round as he left. After he'd gone, I couldn't move for a while. I was frightened and confused. Why had I deliberately provoked a quarrel with Nathan? Was it because of the way James had looked at me? If that was my reason, I was a fool. I had risked everything just for a smile.

Feeling lonely, I rang Liz the next morning, asking her if she would go shopping with me. She agreed at once and we spent a couple of hours indulging in a fit of extravagance in the West End stores.

'Isn't it lovely not to have to worry about clothing coupons any more,' Liz sighed as we came out with our arms full of bags.

'I still think I'm dreaming sometimes,' I said. 'When I remember the way things were.' I laughed suddenly. 'Come on, Liz, I'll treat you to lunch at the Savoy.'

'Really?' Her eyes gleamed with excitement. 'I've only been there once.'

'I've only been a couple of times,' I said. 'But I'm in the mood for some spoiling today.'

'I should think so after your success last night.'

Liz grinned at me. I didn't tell her that my big night had ended in a quarrel with Nathan. She would think I was the world's worst fool.

We were lucky enough to be given a table straight away, the waiter leaving us to look through the menu. Liz nearly fainted when she looked at the prices, but grandly I told her to choose whatever she wanted.

'Don't forget I'm going to be a big star,' I said and she giggled.

We gave our order, talking and laughing excitedly as we waited. We had asked for white wine, but when the waiter came he had brought champagne. He smiled as he saw our puzzled look.

'It is with the compliments of the gentleman over there, Miss Cantrel.'

We both looked in the direction he had pointed out and my heart missed a beat. It was James. I felt a shock run through me, but before I could say anything, Liz was speaking.

'Won't you ask him to join us?' she said, smiling delightedly. 'Please bring another glass.'

The waiter went off obediently and I gripped my fingers under the table. My pulses raced as I avoided looking at James until he was at the table.

'What a pleasant surprise,' he said, smiling at us. 'Frances has gone to the hairdressers. I arranged to meet her for lunch but she seems to be late – which gives me time for a drink with two beautiful ladies.'

Liz was wriggling with pleasure under his flattery. I glanced up, my palms moist with sweat as I saw the look in his eyes.

'It was kind of you to send the champagne, James.'

He sat down, lifting his glass in a salute. 'This is a celebration, of course.'

'Oh yes,' Liz said. 'You were at the club last night, weren't you?'

James nodded. 'We could have made a party of it if it

408

weren't for those ridiculous licensing laws. They're much more sensible about these things in America, you know.' He looked at me and I wondered what was in his mind when he said, 'Your type of singing would be very popular over there, Betty.'

'What's it really like?' Liz asked, her eyes glowing. 'I've always thought I'd like to go.'

'It's a good place to work,' James replied seriously. 'America went straight back to its old ways after the war. They didn't have the shortages and rationing we had here. I'm sure you would like it – some of the clubs are fantastic.'

He described various clubs he'd visited in Las Vegas, and Liz's eyes lit up. So did mine when he began to talk of meeting people like Humphrey Bogart, Marlon Brando and Sammy Davis Junior.

'You make me envious,' Liz cried. 'I feel I want to go home and pack a case straight away.'

James laughed, his gaze moving to me. 'What about you, Betty?' he asked. Somehow I felt there was more in his question than it appeared.

'I don't know,' I said, looking away. I saw Frances staring at us from across the room. 'Oh, isn't that Frances? I think she's waiting for you, James.'

Frances looked annoyed. From the expression on her face, I could tell that she was angry because he'd joined us for a drink. She made no attempt to come over to us, and James frowned as he put down his glass.

'I mustn't keep her waiting,' he said apologetically. 'It was nice seeing you both. Perhaps you'd have lunch with me one day soon, Betty?'

'Perhaps,' I said. Frances was frowning. 'You'd better go.'

Liz looked at me as he walked away, her eyes sparkling with amusement. 'Well, well,' she said. 'You certainly know how to pick your men.'

'He isn't mine,' I said, blushing. 'He's just a friend of Nathan's.'

'His companion wasn't very pleased about it.' Her brows went up. 'You've been getting some very dirty looks, my friend . . .'

I hadn't expected to see James again until Nathan drove me to the country, but the morning after I'd had lunch with Liz, he came to the flat. I stared in surprise as I saw him standing outside the door.

'What are you doing here, James?'

'I rang Nathan about something and I was told he was out of town,' he replied. 'So I thought you might be lonely, and as Frances is going to be busy all day, I thought I'd take you to lunch.'

I felt the disappointment run through me. 'I can't make lunch today,' I said. 'We're rehearsing a new song.'

'That's a shame,' he said, giving me a persuasive smile. 'Couldn't you manage just an hour or so?'

'Well . . .' I felt my resolve ebbing as I looked into his eyes. 'I might be able to have tea if you picked me up at the club later.'

'Four o'clock?' His brows went up.

'Yes,' I said, my heart missing a beat. 'Don't come to the club. I'll meet you just down the road, outside that bookshop.'

'If that's what you want,' he said.

'Four o'clock then. Now, I really do have to get ready.'

After James had gone, I experienced pangs of guilt. I shouldn't have agreed to meet him – and yet, what harm could it do?

I felt rather like a naughty schoolgirl as I left the club after rehearsals. I wasn't actually doing anything wrong, but I knew Nathan wouldn't see it that way. As I saw James waiting for me, I experienced a thrill of excitement and I ran to meet him.

We had tea at a small, old-fashioned hotel where the waiters all wore black coats and bow ties. Munching freshly baked scones with raspberry jam and cream, we talked and laughed as we watched some of the hotel's rather odd customers, in particular an elderly lady who looked like a Victorian martinet and kept calling the waiter to bring her hot water to top up her tea.

'Where is Frances?' I asked James. 'You said she was going to be busy all day.'

'Oh, she's meeting her Uncle Henry,' he said. 'I believe you know him?' I nodded and James smiled. 'Frances has always been very fond of him. Well, he's in town for the day and she'll be with him all the time.'

'She'll enjoy that,' I said. 'I think she was happier that time we stayed at his house than I'd ever known her.'

James looked at me. 'And you, Betty?' he asked. 'Are you happy?'

'Yes, of course,' I said quickly, dropping my eyes. 'I have so much to look forward to.'

'I've been wondering . . .' He reached across the table to touch my hand. 'What's the matter?' he asked as I withdrew it quickly.

'I've just seen someone I know,' I said. 'She works at the club. Not Liz, someone else. Her name's Julie and I don't think she likes me that much. I think I'd better go.'

'But why?' James frowned. 'Oh, I see . . . Nathan . . .'

'And Frances,' I said. 'I don't think she would be all that pleased if she knew – do you?'

'We're only having tea, Betty.' He sighed. 'But perhaps you're right.'

It was almost five o'clock when I got back to the flat. I was due at the club at nine, so I had plenty of time to have a bath and change. As soon as I ran upstairs, I knew someone was there, and I gave a glad cry when I saw Nathan sitting reading a paper.

'You're back,' I said, feeling a pang of guilt because I'd just come from having tea with James. I fought my guilt, smiling as I went towards Nathan. 'Have you been here long?'

'Not long.' He folded *The Times* and looked at me.

'I'm glad you're home,' I said. 'I missed you.'

'Did you? That's good.' He smiled and stood up, opening his arms. I went to him, hugging and kissing him fiercely as I smothered my guilt. 'Steady, I was only gone for a couple of days.'

I gazed up at him. 'I thought you might not come back after the way I behaved the other night.'

'You had a headache.' He shrugged as if it was nothing. 'Is it better now?'

'Yes, much better. Are you coming to the club tonight? I've been rehearsing a new song all day.'

'Of course I'm coming.' There was a teasing look in his eyes. 'And I'm bringing you home, if you want me to?'

I pushed all thoughts of James out of my mind. Nathan was here and I needed him. 'You know I do. I hate it when you're not here.'

He looked at me thoughtfully. 'I was thinking perhaps we could be together more often . . .' He waited for my reaction. 'How would you like to live in a house, Betty? A house with a garden . . .'

'Do you mean it?' I stared at him uncertainly. 'Would you live there, too?'

'Yes. I see no point in carrying on as we are. What Frances said the other night made me think. Everyone knows we're lovers – so why not live together openly?'

'You – you're not asking me to marry you?'

'No. Not yet. I don't think either of us is ready for that yet. Let's take things slowly, Betty.'

I was silent as I thought about his suggestion. It would make our relationship more binding, making it even more impossible for me to spend time with James. I still felt guilty because I'd had tea with him, though that was silly. I'd done nothing wrong, nothing at all. Yet I knew that Nathan would be angry if he guessed. If I agreed to share a house with him, I would be even more committed to Nathan than I was now – and there was still a part of me that longed for James.

'Can I think about the move for a while?' I asked.

'If you feel it's necessary. You said you were lonely – so

412

I can't see what the objection is.' He gave me a long hard look. 'Don't think about it too long, Betty. I've seen the house I want for us.'

I felt that he was warning me he would not wait for ever.

The woman who has begun to like me showed me a newspaper. There was a picture of me on the front page and big headlines. A huge campaign was going on to get me a retrial. They were saying that it was a crime of passion and that the reason I hadn't spoken was because I was protecting someone else.

'Why don't you tell your story?' she asked, her eyes dark and anxious. 'I'm sure that nice lawyer could get you . . .'

'You are not to speak to the prisoner, except to ask if she needs anything.' The other woman frowned. 'If you persist I shall have to report you.'

'Don't get into trouble because of me,' I said.

'But if it's true — if you really loved him as they're saying . . .'

'Love?' I smiled at her. 'But what is love? Tell me, what would you do if a man you loved let you down — would you kill him?'

She shook her head, looking unhappy. 'Is that what you did? Is that why you killed him?'

'I wish I knew the answer,' I said. 'But there were two of them you see . . . I was too blind to see the truth . . .'

She looked at me, her eyes pleading with me to tell her more but I only shook my head. How can I explain what I do not understand myself?

Nathan drove us down to James's family estate. I wasn't sure what I'd expected, but I wasn't surprised when I saw the size of the house. I suppose it wasn't huge, not by country house standards, but it had twenty or so bedrooms and several reception rooms. Set in large, attractive grounds with a lake, woods and a little stream, it had been built in the days of elegance. It took my breath away, and I felt a twist of envy as I saw Frances walking towards us across the lawns, her arm linked with James's in a way that I could only describe as possessive. She looked so at home, so sure of herself as she smiled at us.

'We've just been for a walk. Isn't it a lovely day?'

'Yes, beautiful,' I said. 'Your home is magnificent, James.'

'I'm glad you like it.' He smiled, but it was guarded. 'Lunch will be ready soon. Come and have a drink. I'm not sure if Frances's mother will be joining us for our meal or not.' He looked at Frances enquiringly.

'She's resting at the moment,' Frances said. 'I think she would rather have her meal in bed, James.'

'Oh,' I said, looking at Frances. 'Is Mrs Crawley ill?'

'She's had a nasty attack of influenza,' Frances replied. 'It's the first time she's been back to England for months – and she's gone and caught a bug.'

'Oh, I am sorry,' I said. 'Perhaps I could see her later?'

'I'll see how she feels,' Frances replied, frowning. 'It's usually me who catches everything going, isn't it?'

I looked at James. 'Is Thelma still in Spain? Maisie told me she loves it there.'

'She does. I doubt if she'll ever come home to live again, though she did say something about a visit in the spring. If you still want that introduction, Betty . . .' He stopped as he saw my expression. 'Sorry . . .'

Nathan was aware of something. He looked at James and then me, frowning. 'What's all this?'

'Oh, nothing,' I said quickly.

'Didn't you know?' Frances cried, her eyes glinting. 'Betty went to see James just after he got back from America. Thelma had promised to introduce her to Noel Coward, or so she said . . .'

Nathan frowned. I hadn't told him about the visit, now he would think the worst. And the way Frances had come out with it hadn't helped. She was smiling now, a hint of triumph in her eyes. A little nerve was ticking in Nathan's temple, and I expected an angry outburst, but he said nothing. In a moment he began to talk to James about general affairs. They discussed the war in Korea, in which correspondents from two national newspapers had recently been killed, and the final test match at the Oval, won by the West Indies by an inning and fifty-six runs, then the conversation turned to business.

'When are you going back to America?' Nathan asked. 'Are your negotiations complete yet?'

'We've hit a problem,' James replied, grimacing. 'There's some difficulty with the design of the tail section.'

'All these delays must be expensive?'

'Bloody expensive,' James said with a wry laugh. 'Father would turn in his grave if he knew how much of his money had gone into research, but I'm convinced it will be worth it in the end. Travel in the future is going to be in the air, and the Americans will be masters of the skies . . .'

'I wouldn't mind betting de Havilland's will have something to say about that . . .'

Frances and I had dropped behind the men as we went into the house. She pulled a face at me. 'I hate it when they start talking business, don't you?'

I looked at her warily. Her tone was friendly, but I had the feeling that I was very much on trial. 'I don't really mind. I sometimes wish Nathan would talk about his business more.'

'Oh, Nathan. He never tells anyone anything.' She shrugged her shoulders. 'Have you been to the cinema recently? I know you used to love it.'

'So did you,' I said. 'I saw Olivia de Havilland in *The Heiress*, did you? She was voted the best actress of 1949 for that.'

'Was she?' Frances wasn't interested. Her eyes narrowed as she looked at me. 'Are you in love with Nathan?'

I blushed, caught off balance by the question. 'I'm not sure . . . Why do you ask?'

'I wouldn't play fast and loose with him if I were you, Betty. He's the jealous type, and he has a nasty temper. He can be quite violent if he's upset. Don't you remember how he used to argue with my father?'

There was something odd about her manner at that moment. I wondered what was behind the warning.

'Yes, I remember. But . . .'

Frances caught my arm, the pressure of her arm silencing me as Nathan looked round. 'Just be careful,' she said in a low voice. 'Don't make him jealous.'

I had the feeling that Frances was jealous, not only of my success but of my relationship with her cousin. He had made so much fuss of her when she was younger that she had come to think of him as her property.

'I know Nathan has a temper,' I said. 'But he would never hurt me, Frances.'

'Don't be so sure of that,' Frances replied. 'He's a Crawley, isn't he?'

Now what did she mean by that?

I tried to explain to Nathan when we were alone. Maybe I should have let it rest, but it was nagging at me and I had to say something.

'I went to see Thelma,' I said. 'She told me to – and I thought . . .'

'Leave it, Betty.' Nathan's lips were bloodless. 'I'm not a complete fool.'

'I saw James for a few minutes. That's all . . .'

'That's hardly the point, is it?' His voice had a deceptive lightness. 'Forget it, kid. There's nothing I don't know about you.' For a moment his eyes blazed and I shivered. 'You can't hide from me. I know you too well.'

'Nathan . . .'

'I'm going riding. I'll be back for tea. Enjoy yourself.'

I watched helplessly as he strode from the room. I'd been looking forward to this weekend, but it was all going wrong. For a while I sat staring out of the window, feeling miserable, then I jumped up. If Nathan was going to be like that, I'd take him at his word!

I went downstairs and out into the gardens, passing the open french windows where I could see Frances at a writing desk. I waved to her but didn't stop. The gardens were glorious, and I meant to make the most of my time there.

I spent a pleasant hour wandering in and out of the little winding walks between the shrubberies before finding a seat in a sheltered rose arbour. I sat there for quite a while, thinking about life in general and wondering why things always had to be so difficult. Why couldn't I be happy now that I had so much? Why must I keep hankering after a man who . . .

I looked up as James came towards me, my heart hammering. Somehow I wasn't surprised. It was almost as though I'd expected him to find me.

'Where are the others?' I asked.

'Frances went up to see how her mother was,' he replied. 'I've no idea where Nathan is, I thought you might know?'

'He went riding,' I said. 'Isn't he back yet?'

'I haven't seen him.' His brows rose. 'Have you two had a row?'

'No,' I lied, turning my head. 'Why should we?'

James laid his hand on my arm. 'What's wrong, Betty?'

'Nothing.' I blushed, keeping my eyes averted. 'I expect Nathan just wanted to take advantage of the chance to ride. It's difficult in town.'

'I wasn't talking about Nathan.'

I turned to look at him then, catching my breath as I saw the look in his eyes. 'James . . .'

'Betty . . .' He leant towards me. 'You seemed angry with me the other day – did I do something to offend you?'

'No, of course not.'

He touched my cheek and I recoiled as if I'd been stung.

417

'You do like me a little, don't you? I've never been sure . . .'

'Yes, I like you . . .' I broke off as he lowered his head and I knew that he was about to kiss me. I sprang to my feet, agitated. 'No, James,' I cried. 'Nathan will be waiting.'

'Can't you stay for a few minutes? I had to make all manner of excuses to get away to be alone with you.'

'Then you shouldn't have,' I said. 'Not here, not now. This is the wrong time and the wrong place.'

I walked away before he could stop me.

We returned to London the next morning. Nathan seemed pleased with himself. I think he believed the weekend had served its purpose, which was to make it clear to everyone that I was his property. My own feelings were confused. James was interested, but what did that mean? He and Frances were clearly still on intimate terms, though she hadn't been wearing an engagement ring. She'd talked of going back to France with Mary for the winter, and James was planning a trip to America.

Even if James was really interested, I wasn't sure what I could do about it. I'd taken so much from Nathan, it would be a terrible betrayal to leave him for another man – and in a way I was happy . . .

My life was busy. I rehearsed with Richard most mornings, and I performed at the club five nights a week. Liz and I had become firm friends now, and we often went shopping together. Now and then I visited Miss Browne, who had somehow found the money to start her own little shop. I took Liz and Julie to buy from her and she gave them discounts. I bought a lot of clothes from her, and I could afford to indulge myself. Richard had decided I was worth the salary Nathan had demanded, and more.

I wrote to Hilda Jackson, telling her all about my life and asking how she was, and I went to visit Polly a couple of times.

One evening after I'd stayed to have tea with her, I hurried home, knowing I would have to be quick or I would be late for the club. Nathan was waiting for me impatiently.

'I had tea with Polly,' I said. 'And a friend of hers brought her baby for Polly to see. She was such a sweet little thing, Nathan. I'm afraid I stopped longer than I should have done.'

'Since when have you been interested in children?'

'That's unfair,' I said, forgetting that there had been a time when I'd resented the birth of yet another Cantrel. 'I've always liked babies, Nathan – and she was such a dear little thing.' I looked at him, suddenly wistful. 'Sometimes I wish that I – that we had a child . . .'

'You want my child?' His look was so intense that it scared me.

'Only sometimes,' I said. 'It can't be, of course. What would Richard say if I couldn't sing for months?'

'Damn Richard!' Nathan caught me by the shoulders, his eyes burning into mine. 'Have you thought about that house, Betty? It has a big garden – big enough for children to play in.'

As I looked up into his eyes, I was tempted. For a moment the idea of being Nathan's wife and bearing his children was appealing, but then I remembered James.

'I'm not ready to start a family yet,' I said. 'It was just an impulse.'

Anger flared in his eyes then. 'Don't play games with me, Betty,' he warned. 'Not about something like that.'

Frances called in at the club while I was rehearsing. She stayed until I'd finished, then asked me to have lunch with her. I was surprised, but I agreed at once. She seemed friendly and we talked about fashion, films and France. Only after we'd eaten did she mention what was really on her mind.

'I'm sorry you didn't get to see Mother the other week,' she said. 'She really was too ill to see anyone.'

419

'I understood that,' I said. 'Is she better now?'

Frances frowned. 'Yes and no. She hasn't been really well for some time now.' She pulled a face at me. 'Isn't it strange? I always used to be the invalid, now I have to look after my mother.'

'What's wrong with her – apart from the influenza?'

'It's her nerves, I think.' Frances shrugged. 'Oh, I don't know. Anyway, she'll be happy now. We're going back to France tomorrow.'

'You don't seem very happy about that?'

'James is going to America. I shan't see him for months.'

'I see . . .' I tried not to look at her. 'You're not engaged or anything then?'

'Mother won't hear of it.' Frances sounded angry. 'She still thinks I'm too delicate, though I'm perfectly well now.'

'Oh . . . I'm sorry.'

'Are you?' Her eyes met mine as I looked up. 'Don't forget that James is mine, Betty. We may not be engaged yet, but one day I'm going to marry him. You would be unwise to forget that.'

As I looked into her eyes, a little chill went down my spine.

It was a week later. The club was very full. I had to sing all the old favourites, and people kept calling for more. Finally, Richard insisted that they let me leave and I went to the little dressing-room I used, to have a cool drink before my taxi arrived to take me home. I always ordered a taxi on the nights when Nathan didn't come to the club. He'd gone away on business again and wouldn't be back for a week, something I bitterly resented.

I didn't feel like going home to an empty flat. Nathan had only been gone two days, but already I was lonely. I slipped into a thin silk robe and cleansed my face of the heavy make-up I wore when performing. Someone knocked at my door. Thinking it must be Liz, I called out that she might enter as I went behind a screen to put on my street clothes.

'I'll be with you in a minute,' I said. 'Where shall we go for lunch tomorrow?'

'Anywhere you choose.'

My heart jerked and then stopped beating for one frightening moment as I heard James's voice. I came round the screen and stared at him, suddenly breathless.

'I didn't know you were here tonight – are you alone?'

'Yes,' he said, smiling. 'I'm quite alone, Betty.'

'Why have you come?'

'To visit a friend, I hope?'

I gazed into the deep blue of his eyes and felt my heart flutter. He had scarcely changed since that day at the farm when I'd first seen him. If anything the years had improved his looks. There was something distinguished about him, an air of wealth and power – and respectability. There were no disturbing questions about James, no mysteries, nothing slightly dubious or frightening. He was a gentleman.

'I thought you were off to America?' I said, needing time to recover my control.

'I am, at the end of the week.'

'The end of the week – that's in three days.'

'Yes,' he said and smiled. 'So, I'm free for lunch tomorrow, if you'll take pity on me?'

'I thought it was Liz when I said that . . .'

'Does that mean you won't?'

I stared at him, knowing that I ought to refuse, then I smiled. 'I'd love to have lunch with you, James.'

'Good, that's settled. Now, can I take you home?'

I hesitated, thinking of my lonely flat, wanting to say yes, then I shook my head. 'I've ordered a taxi. It will be here at any moment.'

He looked disappointed, but accepted my decision without protest. 'Then I'll just have to wait until tomorrow, won't I?'

'Yes, I . . .' I paused as Liz put her head round the door.

'Oh, sorry,' she said. 'I didn't know someone was with you.'

'This is James Blair,' I said. 'You remember we had a drink with him at the Savoy?'

'How could I forget?' Liz's eyes sparkled with mischief. 'I just popped in to see if it's still on for lunch tomorrow?'

'No, not tomorrow. Sorry, Liz.'

'Not to worry,' she said cheerfully. 'Another day will do. Oh, your taxi is here, if you want it?' Her tone implied that she would understand if I didn't.

'Yes, I do,' I replied, picking up my jacket. 'I'm sorry, James. I must go.'

'Of course,' he said. 'I'll see you safely inside.' He took my coat, placing it around my shoulders. I trembled as his fingers touched my neck, glancing away quickly as he looked into my eyes.

The taxi was waiting. James opened the door for me.

'I'll pick you up tomorrow,' he said.

I closed my eyes as the car drew away, my pulses racing. It was just lunch, I told myself, nothing more. A meal in a restaurant, perfectly innocent. It hardly constituted a betrayal of Nathan – so why did I feel guilty?

James took me to the Ritz for lunch. The elegance of the cream and gold decor matched the dreamlike quality of the occasion. Nathan had never taken me there and I was glad; I wanted no memories to disturb my conscience.

'What will you have?' James asked. 'I believe the trout is very good – or would you prefer guinea fowl?'

I chose chicken in a white wine sauce and James had trout with almonds. He ordered a very expensive champagne. It was much too dry for my taste, but I drank it. Nathan would never have chosen it. He knew I had no palate and he always ordered a sweet wine for me, whatever we were eating. But the food was not important, I scarcely tasted mine.

For the first time I didn't have to rush away. I had James's undivided attention, and I loved it. He was such an interesting man. I'd never really understood how knowledgeable he was, but then, I hadn't spent much time alone with him. He'd travelled widely, and he told me about the countries he'd visited, thrilling me with his vivid descriptions of a sunset in India and an African dawn. We talked and talked for hours, about politics, art, books – he was still a keen collector – music and aeroplanes. His love of anything to do with flying made him lose all reserve as he talked, and I caught his enthusiasm as he spoke of his plans for the future.

'One day there will be planes flying regularly to every destination you can think of,' he said. 'Not just for the wealthy, but for the man in the street. It will be cheap enough for families to take their children for a fortnight's holiday in France, Spain or Greece . . .'

'Do you really think so, James?'

'I'm sure of it – and much sooner than you'd imagine.'

I was fascinated by his stories of the people he worked with. Being with James was a new experience for me, and I was beginning to realise that there was another, wider world outside the one I'd found. He had time to talk to me, to explain things I didn't understand. Nathan was always so busy. When we were together, he was usually only interested in one thing. Nathan shut me out of his business life, James enjoyed telling me about his triumphs.

The waiters were hovering. We were the only ones left in the dining-room. James laughed and signalled for the bill.

'I think we've outstayed our welcome,' he said. 'We'd better go before they throw us out.'

He drove me back to the flat. We sat talking in the car for a while, and I knew he wanted me to invite him in, but I was afraid of what might happen if I did. I wanted to make love with him, and I knew he wanted it too, but I was terrified of what Nathan might do if he found out.

'Can I see you again, Betty?' James looked at me and

my heart somersaulted. 'Can you get some time off from the club?'

I shook my head. 'No. I can't let Richard down.'

'Lunch tomorrow then?'

I hesitated, knowing I should refuse, but also knowing that I wouldn't. 'Yes, all right. Will you pick me up again?'

'Yes. May I come to the club tonight, Betty? May I bring you home?'

'I don't think that would be a good idea.'

He looked disappointed and I almost weakened, then he smiled. 'Tomorrow then,' he said.

I stood on the pavement, watching as he drove away. Inside I felt a kind of desperation. Nathan could be back at any time, and James was leaving for America in two days – why hadn't I agreed to let James bring me home that evening? Why wasn't I in his arms now? It was an impossible situation. I was in love with one man and the mistress of another – what could I do?

'I thought you might change your mind,' James said when he picked me up the next day. 'Where would you like to go?'

'I almost did,' I said smiling wryly. 'Could we find somewhere quiet? Perhaps outside London?'

'Of course. What time do you have to be at the club?'

'Not until nine this evening.'

'Then if I have you home by eight?' I nodded and he looked pleased. 'We'll go to a place I know. I think you'll like it.'

'I'm sure I shall.'

I settled back in my seat. The sun was warm through the car windscreen, even though it was autumn now. James was silent for a while, but as the noise of London was left behind and we began to see green fields and trees, he glanced at me.

'Are you angry with me for rushing off when you came to the house, Betty? I know I was abrupt with you.'

'Angry?' I thought for a moment. 'No, not now. I was hurt at the time, though.'

'My meeting was important. I've regretted it since – a thousand times.'

'Have you?'

'Yes.' James pulled the car into a lay-by and stopped the engine. As he turned to look at me, my heart pounded wildly. 'You must have some idea of how I feel about you?'

'No. No, I don't. I thought you might be in love with Frances.'

'She is very special to me,' James sighed. 'I know I've no right to say this to you, Betty, but I can't get you out of my mind. I want . . .' He broke off and leaned across to kiss me.

I was shaking when he moved away. 'You shouldn't have done that, James. Nathan . . .'

'Are you happy with him, Betty? Really happy, I mean? If I thought that he . . .'

'He has been good to me. I'm grateful to him – and yes, I am happy, most of the time.'

'Are you going to marry him?'

'I don't know . . . No, I don't think so.'

James hesitated, then: 'There's a spare seat on my plane, Betty. I could arrange it. Come with me. Come to America with me.'

I stared at him, stunned by his suggestion. 'Leave Nathan and come to America with you? What are you saying, James? Are you asking me to marry you?'

The eagerness faded from his eyes. 'I'm asking you to live with me, Betty. Marriage isn't a part of my plans, at least, not yet.'

'I see . . .' I turned away, hiding my disappointment. James said marriage wasn't a part of his plans, but what he meant was marriage to me. What he was offering me was the kind of relationship I had with Nathan. 'I don't know,' I said slowly. 'You'll have to let me think about it.'

'I didn't expect an answer now,' he said. 'Think about it tonight and tell me tomorrow.'

'Don't come to the flat again,' I said. 'Nathan could be back. We'll meet somewhere – if I'm there it will mean I've decided to come with you.'

'I hope you'll be there.' James smiled. 'Now we'll have our lunch. This place was a sixteenth-century coaching inn. I believe the food is excellent . . .'

'You were wonderful tonight,' Richard said as I went through to my dressing-room. 'I was talking to someone earlier this evening – I think he's going to offer you a recording contract.'

'A recording contract?' I looked at him. 'Are you sure?'

'Well, he said he would be in touch as soon as Nathan gets back.'

'Oh . . .' I bit my lips. Would I be around when Nathan returned? 'We'll talk about it then. Will you excuse me? I have a headache.'

Richard looked at me, clearly puzzled. Obviously he had expected me to be very excited, and a part of me was. I wanted to go on with my career, but I could do that in America, couldn't I?

The excuse about a headache wasn't entirely false. I felt tired for some reason and I'd been sick that morning. It was probably only nerves, but it had happened a couple of times recently. Usually, I was refreshed after a performance, but that night it had left me drained. It had to be nerves. I'd been on edge ever since James asked me out, and now I was so tense that it was making me dizzy.

James's proposition had been so sudden, so unexpected. I was confused and frightened at the idea of leaving my secure little world for new horizons. In America I would be safe from Nathan's anger – he'd hardly follow me there – but had I the courage to make the break? And could I do it to him?

I was in love with James. He was my ideal man, but

Nathan was . . . It was too difficult to define my feelings for him.

Chapter Seventeen

'Hi . . .' Liz popped her head round the door. 'I wondered if you'd like to . . .' She broke off and frowned. 'What's the matter, Betty? You look awful.'

I blinked as I looked at her. 'I don't feel all that great,' I said. 'It must be a bug of some kind. I was sick this morning, and yesterday . . .'

Liz raised her brows. 'You know what that could mean, don't you?'

I stared at her, not realising what she meant for a moment, then I shook my head. 'No. No, it can't be that, Liz. I'm sure.' I gave a little shiver. The last thing I wanted at this moment was another complication!

'Well, what's wrong then?' She smiled at me. 'Come on, you can tell Auntie Liz.'

I drew a deep breath. 'James has asked me to go to America with him.'

Liz pursed her lips in a soundless whistle. 'You're not thinking of going?'

'I – I don't know.' I looked into her eyes. 'I'm in love with James. I have been for years. I think I'm going to tell Nathan the truth.'

'Are you sure you want to do that?' She looked worried as I nodded. 'He'll go wild.'

'I know he'll be angry, but . . .'

'Angry?' she laughed mirthlessly. 'Nathan is obsessed with you, don't you know that? I heard him threaten to kill one guy who was saying what he'd like to do with you. I think he'd rather kill you than let you walk out on him.'

'That's made me feel much better.'

Liz smiled ruefully. 'Me and my big mouth. Honestly, Betty, I think you should be careful. Nathan is a good friend – but I think he'd make a bad enemy . . .'

'Then – what am I going to do?'

She frowned. 'I don't know. You haven't seen Nathan tonight, have you?' I shook my head and she looked concerned. 'Only I thought I saw him in the club earlier . . .'

'You couldn't have done. He wouldn't leave without speaking to me.' I met her eyes. 'Unless someone told him . . .'

I paid the taxi driver and got out. Looking up at the flat windows, I could see they were in darkness. I'd thought that perhaps Nathan would be there. It wasn't like him to come to the club and not wait for me. And if Liz had seen him earlier . . .

'Nathan, are you there?' I called as I ran up the stairs. 'Nathan . . .'

Switching on the lights in all the rooms, I saw that the flat was empty, yet I had the strangest feeling that someone had been there a short while before. It seemed that things had been moved, and there was the faintest trace of cigar smoke in the air.

Feeling uneasy, I began to look for a note. Something to tell me why Nathan had been and gone without waiting to see me. It was so unlike him. I felt a flutter of nerves. There was something odd about this.

He knew! He had to know I'd been seeing James. Someone had told him. Liz had seen James. Would she . . . No, not Liz. It must have been Julie. She had always been jealous; I knew she wanted Nathan herself. Yes, I was sure Julie would have enjoyed telling him I'd been seen leaving the club with another man. James had come out to the taxi with me. To anyone inside the club it might have looked as if he was taking me home . . .

It still didn't explain why Nathan hadn't waited for

me. I would have expected him to be angry. I was prepared for a furious quarrel, but not for this. It made me uneasy.

Perhaps he didn't know. It might be only my guilty conscience nagging at me. There could be many reasons why he hadn't stayed. Yet it wasn't like Nathan. I was nervous. I was restless. I spent the night dozing rather than sleeping, jumping at every sound. Nathan did not return.

In the morning I wrote Nathan a letter and left it on the table where he could see it. I could only carry a small bag with me, but clothes were not important now. Perhaps if Nathan still hadn't returned I could collect a few more of them later.

The sun was shining as I walked through the streets. I had left early because I was afraid Nathan might return and stop me. I had arranged to meet James in the park, and my pace quickened as I saw it ahead of me. Would James be waiting? I was still a few minutes early.

My anticipation faded as I saw the bench was empty. James had not arrived. But I was early. It was foolish to feel disappointed. If I had been less eager I should not have arrived too soon. The wooden bench was shaded by the branches of a chestnut tree. I could wait in comfort. Yet it might look as if I had been waiting too long.

I decided to walk a little further into the park. It was a lovely autumn day. Some boys were cycling along the paths and a woman with a child was feeding the pigeons. Somewhere in the distance a band was playing.

Enough time had passed. I returned to the bench. It was still empty. I glanced at my watch. James was two minutes late. It was not much. It was my own fault for being early. I sat down to wait, reading a headline in a newspaper that had been discarded on the seat. Sir Stafford Cripps had resigned and his place was to be taken by Hugh Gaitskell.

The sun was very warm for the time of year. I watched people hurrying by. Time passed and I was unaware of it.

I waited patiently. Trustingly. James would come. He had been delayed but he would come eventually. He must come! The church clock struck twelve times. It was noon. I had waited for two hours. James was not coming. I got to my feet feeling numb. I could not believe it had happened. Why? Why hadn't he sent me a message? Why had he not kept our appointment?

Perhaps he'd had an accident? My heart raced for a moment. He might be ill. Perhaps he had received bad news . . . Perhaps he had simply changed his mind. My steps were heavy as I left the park. I walked slowly, my eyes blinded by unshed tears. I was a fool. I had always known I would be a fool to love him. I could never be more to James than a casual lover. I should have learned that years before. I blinked away my tears. Crying wouldn't change a thing. I had to face the truth. James had changed his mind. He'd wanted a casual affair but because I wouldn't go to bed with him, he'd made his offer on the spur of the moment – regretting it as soon as the words left his lips, no doubt.

I felt very bitter. Were all men the same? Wasn't there even one you could trust?

I let myself into the passage to the flat. An envelope was lying on the mat. Picking it up with trembling fingers, I saw the unfamiliar writing. My heart leapt as I tore it open. Perhaps James had made another appointment?

'I know what your answer must be. I'm sorry. Forgive me, James.'

It had been waiting for me all the time. If I hadn't left early, I should have saved myself a journey.

For a moment the pain was so intense that I thought I should die, I choked back my emotion. I wasn't going to cry. It was my own stupid fault. I should have known better than to love any man. Love was a myth. A beautiful shining butterfly with the sting of a wasp.

I stuffed the crumpled paper in my pocket and walked upstairs. The sharp aromatic smell of cigar smoke reached my nostrils. I tensed, a quiver of fear going through me as I halted on the landing. Nathan was sitting in the chair by the window, smoking. I stared at him, unable to speak. For a moment his eyes seemed to glitter and I sensed that he was angry, then the glitter faded and he smiled.

'It's a lovely day for a walk. Did you enjoy it, Betty?'

Why did I feel that he was like a cat waiting to pounce on an unsuspecting bird? I glanced towards the table: my letter was still there, unopened. Why hadn't he opened it?

'I went to meet someone but . . .'

He got to his feet quickly. I hesitated, fearing what he was about to do. Before I could speak again, he put his arms round me, catching me to him and kissing me with an intense passion. I stood unresisting in his arms until he released me.

'I've missed you so much,' he said. 'I know you're angry because I wasn't here last night, but I had something to do. Before you say anything, Betty, I've something to tell you . . .' I looked at him in surprise as he paused. 'I've bought that house I was telling you about. It's all ready for us to move in. In future we're going to be together much more. I shan't have to leave you alone at night. We'll be together all the time.'

I was stunned. It was the last thing I'd expected. Why wasn't he angry? Could it be that he knew nothing of my meetings with James? If so, I had to tell him now before someone else did.

'Nathan . . .' I drew a deep breath. 'I have something to tell you.'

'I don't want to hear. It doesn't matter.'

The look in his eyes told me that he did know. He just didn't want to talk about it. He was going to shut it out, pretend that it had never happened, but I couldn't do that. Everything was different now. I had to tell him. 'Nathan, while you were away . . .'

'I know.' He put his fingers to my lips. 'I was told – but it's over now. It is over, isn't it, Betty?'

I turned away, closing my eyes. I knew I must end our relationship now, but I couldn't when he looked at me that way. 'I've changed, Nathan. I don't love you.'

'You do love me,' he said and I felt the touch of his lips on the back of my neck. 'You think you love someone else, but he would only have hurt you. He could never love you the way I do. You love me in your own way and you need me. You can't bear to be alone. I shouldn't have left you. In future I shall take you with me wherever I go. It doesn't matter about the club. You're mine and I'll take care of you. I'll take you away, to Italy and Greece. You'd like that, wouldn't you?'

He was trying to dominate me again, to control my life and make me do what he thought was right. I tried to deny him, but I couldn't speak. My throat felt tight and I was close to tears. This pain inside me was almost too much to bear. How could I bear it alone? Nathan's arms went round me and his lips moved seductively from my neck to my ear. He knew so well how to arouse me! I shivered, trying to avoid his searching kisses, but he held me tight. I knew I should be strong. It was not fair to either of us. I should send him away now.

Tears were stinging my eyes. My body shook with the force of the emotion I had tried to keep inside. I hadn't expected such tenderness from Nathan. I could have coped with his anger more easily. I was crying now.

Nathan turned me round, kissing my wet cheeks and smiling with a kind of sad triumph. 'Don't cry for him,' he said softly. 'You still have me. You always will have me.'

Then he picked me up in his arms and carried me through into the bedroom. He undressed me gently as though I were a child, then he began to kiss and stroke my body in the way that only he knew. For a while I tried to resist him, but as his kisses moved down over my quivering flesh and his tongue began to stroke the delicate flesh between my thighs, I could no longer hold back. I gave a cry of pleasure, arching to meet him as the desire

433

moved in me. He made a sound of triumph in his throat, and then his body was covering mine as he possessed me. He possessed me utterly and completely, bending me to his will as always.

Nathan had reclaimed me. I belonged to him. He owned me now and he knew it. I hadn't been strong enough to break away. He was more sure of me than he had ever been, and it began to show in little ways. He was not always so gentle now. Sometimes when we lay together he would just take me swiftly, without bothering to arouse me, as if he needed to show his mastery over my body.

A few days after he returned, I signed a recording contract with Columbia. I was to go on singing at the club two nights a week, but most of my time would be in the studio now. In a way it suited me better. I'd been sick several times and I was beginning to wonder if Liz had been right. When I missed a period, I decided to visit a doctor. What he told me frightened me. I kept my secret to myself.

Nathan had begun to buy me expensive jewellery, fastening a diamond bracelet round my wrist as if it were a trinket. He was always with me now, and I wondered if his business suffered because of it, but I didn't ask. It no longer mattered to me what he did or where his money came from. I was living in a dream world, because that was the only way I could bear to live. I came to life only when I sang. Only then would I let myself feel anything. For the rest of the time, I was Nathan's beautiful doll.

We had moved into a house in a secluded square. It was a large house and we had servants to run it. It was funny but I'd achieved at least the outward show of the respectability I'd always craved. Nathan even hired a personal maid for me. He didn't consult me. She simply arrived one day. I thought that perhaps he'd hired her to watch over me on the rare occasions he was absent.

*

I could bear the weight of my secret no longer. The worst had happened: I was carrying Nathan's child. I hadn't told him yet, because I knew he would use it to bind me to him even more completely. He would insist on marriage – and then my dream of becoming James's wife would be gone for ever.

I knew I was a fool to cling to the remnants of that dream. James had made it clear that I meant nothing more than a casual love affair to him – so why couldn't I accept my fate? What was it that made me struggle against it still? Surely I could not still be remembering my parents' unhappy marriage? Nathan wouldn't treat me the way my father had treated my mother . . . And yet there was a little streak of cruelty in him.

I went to see Polly. She was the one person I could talk to freely. She had known Nathan in the old days. She had carried Eben Crawley's child. She was the only one who could even come close to understanding how I felt.

'I thought this might happen,' she said, looking at me anxiously. 'But why are you so upset about it, Betty? You said Nathan was good to you . . .'

'He is . . .' I stared at her. 'How can I explain? I feel trapped . . .'

Polly smiled. 'You're not the only woman who's ever felt that way, Betty. It's frightening, knowing that you're carrying a new life inside you, especially in your situation. Once you've accepted it, once you're married, you'll feel better.'

'Do you really think so?'

'Yes, I do.' Polly kissed my cheek. 'My advice is to tell Nathan as soon as possible. But you need something to cheer you up. Why don't you stay to dinner this evening? Charlie is coming but no one else.'

Nathan wouldn't be pleased if I stayed, but I wasn't going to let him dominate me all the time! I felt a spurt of rebellion. If I was going to marry him, he would have to realise that he didn't own me. Suddenly, I was feeling better than I had for ages.

I smiled at my friend. 'I'd love to stay with you this afternoon,' I said. 'But I must be at the club by nine.'

'Charlie likes to eat at seven,' she said. 'You'll have plenty of time to go home and change afterwards . . .'

It was a quarter past eight when I let myself into the flat. I was late and if I didn't hurry, Richard would think I wasn't coming. I needed a bath.

'And where do you think you've been?'

Nathan was at the top of the stairs, his face tight with anger. I blinked, feeling stunned.

'What's the matter?' I asked. 'Surely you're not angry because I wasn't here? You didn't say you were coming this afternoon.'

'Do I have to make an appointment to see you now?'

'Of course not. Don't be silly, Nathan,' I sighed. 'I went to see Polly and I stopped to have dinner with her, that's all.'

'Liar!' The bitterness in his voice shocked me. 'You've been with a man, haven't you?'

He reached out and grabbed me by the shoulders, his fingers biting into my flesh. I was stunned by the fierceness of his attack. He was a stranger. A man with glaring eyes and a pale, sweating face. He seemed half out of his mind.

'I told you, I was with Polly . . .'

'And no one else?' His eyes burned into me.

'Charlie was there but . . .'

'And who else?' He shook me. 'Tell me the truth, damn you!'

'I've told you. I was with Polly and . . .'

'No doubt she'll confirm what you say is true.' The sarcasm in his voice stung me like the lash of a whip. 'I can just see the pair of you laughing at the story you've dreamed up. You're no better than she is. You've been with a man and now you've come crawling back like the last . . .'

'How dare you!' I lashed out at him, catching him

436

across the face. 'How dare you say that to me? I've never been unfaithful to you.'

'Not with your precious James? You were with him for at least one night while I was away. Oh yes, I knew who you'd gone to meet; I knew that you were planning to go away with him.' He was so full of bitterness that he almost choked on the words. 'Do you expect me to believe that you didn't sleep with him? He always wanted you, even when you were at the farm . . . Perhaps he had you even then?'

'Stop it! Stop it, Nathan. I've had enough. I'm in a hurry. I can't take any more of your stupid jealousy. I'm going to have a bath and get ready for the club.'

He tried to grab my arm, but I shook him off. His attitude sickened me. I'd been ready to tell him that I was having his child, but now wild horses wouldn't have dragged it out of me.

I walked past him into the bathroom, turning on the taps. I began to undress, feeling tense and on the verge of tears. Why did he have to be so insanely jealous? How could I marry him when he was so suspicious? I should be afraid even to look at another man. I was about to get in the bath when the door was flung open and Nathan came in. Startled by the rage in his face, I reached for a towel to cover myself.

'It's too late for false modesty,' he muttered, snatching the towel from me. 'I know you for what you are.'

'Nathan, I don't want to argue with you.'

'I didn't come to argue. It's time you learned who's the master here. I'm sick of you mooning after that fraud.'

'What are you talking about? James is the most sincere man I know.'

'You think he's some kind of a bloody hero, don't you? Well, let me tell you, you're wrong. That story of his having saved his crew's life in the war was a lie. It was the other way around . . .'

'That's a lie — and even if it isn't, it doesn't matter. I

love James because he's a gentleman – something you wouldn't know how to be.'

'I'm as much a gentleman as you are a lady, you little slut . . .'

'James is in America,' I said wearily. 'Even if I wanted to . . .'

'He flew home a few days ago. Don't pretend you don't know. You've been with him, laughing behind my back . . .'

I saw the strange glitter in his eyes and I felt a shaft of fear strike through me. 'You're crazy, Nathan. Crazy and sick if you think . . .'

He grabbed hold of my shoulders, shaking me until I was dizzy. 'Don't you say that to me. Don't you dare to think it!'

His manner was so threatening that I was really scared. 'Nathan,' I whispered. 'Please listen to me. I was with Polly.'

'I don't want to hear your lies. You're a deceiving little bitch and I'm going to make you pay for what you've done.'

The hatred in his voice made me flinch as though he had struck me. He was staring at me blindly as if he could not really see me, but only the blood-red mist of rage in his mind. I tried to dart past him, but he was too quick for me. He seized my wrist, twisting the skin so that I whimpered with pain. Terrified of this new Nathan, I strained against him, kicking and struggling. He stamped on my bare foot, his shoes crushing my toes. I screamed in agony and his mouth curved in a cruel smile.

'That's just the beginning,' he spat the words out. 'You'll beg me to forgive you before I'm finished.'

'Never! I'll hate you for this, Nathan.'

'Have you ever done anything else?'

He was trying to drag me into the bedroom. I wriggled and strained, catching at anything I could to hold back, but he was much stronger than me. I lost my footing on the slippery bathroom floor and stumbled, falling to my knees. He dragged me across the floor for several feet, not caring that I hit my legs against the doorpost, then he bent down and caught me beneath the arms. I was half carried, half dragged into the bedroom.

'For God's sake have some pity,' I cried as he pushed me across the bed. 'I'm exhausted.'

His only answer was to slap me across the face three times. His eyes were glittering and there was a film of sweat along his top lip. He seemed to have lost control. He was half crazy, beyond the reach of reason. As he came at me, I went for his face, scoring a line on the lower half of his cheek. He hit me hard in the mouth, almost knocking me senseless. I tasted blood in my mouth. After that I could only push at him feebly as he forced his knee between my legs, then threw himself on me fully clothed, thrusting at me with a savagery that made me want to scream in pain. Only pride kept me silent as he raped me. The buttons on his coat dug into my bare flesh, bruising me as he vented his anger on the body he had always loved to caress. Once he had gloried in stroking and touching, now he sought to hurt me in every way he could, biting my lips and my breasts, humiliating me in all manner of ways.

It was a punishment for all the pain he believed I had caused him. It was to punish me for not loving him. All his anger, all his frustration, came pouring out as he called me every vile name under the sun. I was a bitch, a whore, a cheat, a liar and many other things that made me want to vomit. He used the language of the gutters, as if by doing so he could somehow defile what he had once desired.

When at last he had finished with me I lay still, my face turned to the pillow. I felt so bruised and torn that I was almost beyond pain. There was not one part of me that had escaped his assault. There was blood on my lips, in my mouth and between my thighs. Numbed, too weary to cry or even protest, I lay like a rag doll as he turned my face to look at him.

'You deserved that, Betty,' he said. 'I had to teach you, but I won't hurt you any more.'

I didn't speak as he lifted me in his arms. He was gentle now as he carried me to the bathroom. I lay in the water unprotesting as he tenderly bathed the flesh he had earlier abused. The soap stung the cuts and bruises but I didn't cry out. He washed and dried me as though I were a child, removing all traces of the blood that had trickled between my thighs. I was a broken doll he had lovingly restored. His possession once more. I looked at him as he placed me in the big bed and pulled the covers over me.

'Go to sleep now, Betty,' he said. 'I think you've learned your lesson. I shan't need to hurt you again.'

I closed my eyes. He left the room, shutting the door softly so as not to disturb me. A single tear trickled from the corner of my eyes. I was too weary to wipe it away.

I awoke to the sting of bruised flesh and aching limbs, but the draining tiredness had gone. My one thought was to escape. Dressing quickly, I stuffed some money into my purse. The rest of my possessions could wait for another time. I had to leave now, while I had the chance. I'd finally woken from my state of apathy. Nathan thought he'd broken my spirit by imposing his will on me so brutally, but what he'd actually done was to awaken it. I'd been a fool to let him take over my life, but that was all over.

I was nervous as I left the bedroom. I wasn't sure where Nathan was, but if he challenged me, I should say I was on my way to the club. Fortunately, there was no sign of him as I made my escape. I was going to Polly. I needed a friend. Someone to advise me how to disappear. Perhaps I could stay with her for a few days.

As I was getting out of the taxi, I saw Nathan leaving her house and I shrank back out of sight. What was he doing here? Had he come to ask Polly for the truth? It was a bit late for that now.

I waited until I was sure he'd gone, then I ran across the road. Polly opened the door herself. Her hair was straggling down her neck and there was a cut on her lip.

'Oh no!' I cried. 'Did Nathan do that? I saw him leaving just now.'

Polly shook her head. 'No. It was lucky for me that he came when he did. It was my brother, Betty. It was George.'

'George?' I stared at her in dismay as she drew me inside the house. 'But why? How did he find out where you live?'

'Someone told him,' she said, shuddering. 'He wouldn't say who it was – but he knew what I was doing . . .'

'Oh, Polly . . .' I looked at her. 'You don't think it was me, do you?'

'Of course not.' She pulled a face. 'I think I can guess – I had a visit from Frances Crawley a few weeks ago. She told me I was the cause of her mother's illness. Apparently Mary's nerves are bad and she drinks, and she said she would see that I got what I deserved.'

'Frances said that?' A chill went down my spine, but I knew she was right. It had to have been Frances.

'So what are you going to do?' I asked.

Polly shrugged. 'Nothing. George won't come here again. He knows there's no point.'

'I'm so sorry, Polly.'

'It doesn't matter,' she said. 'But what about you, Betty? Nathan asked me if you were here yesterday. He seemed very odd . . .'

'He raped me, Polly. I'm leaving him.'

She gazed at me with horrified eyes. 'Nathan did that to you?'

'He beat me and then he . . .' I swallowed hard. 'I can't stay with him now.'

'But the child – didn't you tell him?'

I shook my head. 'He would probably think it was James Blair's. There's no point in telling him now. It's over.'

'But Nathan won't let you go that easily, Betty.' She frowned. 'I've never told you, because you said he was good to you, but . . .'

'Go on, Polly.'

'This house belongs to Nathan, Betty. He set me up in it after my baby died. He introduced me to Charlie and the others – as a favour to them really . . .'

'No – I can't believe it!'

'Nathan is mixed up with some powerful people, Betty.'

All those things Nathan had said about Polly being a whore! No wonder he'd been uneasy about our friendship. I felt sick at the hypocrisy of it.

'I would've told you before, but I thought . . .'

'He lied to me, Polly. It was all a lie . . .'

'I wanted to tell you, but one word from him and the police would have had me picked up on some charge or another,' she said.

'The police – I don't understand.'

'Why do you think Nathan's clubs never get raided?'

'His clubs?'

'He's a partner in the Purple Moon – but he owns several less respectable places, Betty. Where do you think his money comes from?'

'My God! He's ruthless. That settles it, I'm leaving him.'

'But where will you go?'

'I don't know. I thought I could stay with you . . .' She had no need to say anything. It was obviously impossible. 'I'll speak to Richard. He might help me.'

Polly looked at me anxiously. 'Be careful, Betty. Nathan's a Crawley. Don't forget that.'

'What do you mean?'

'All the Crawleys . . .' Polly sighed. 'Eben was very violent at times . . .'

'I'm not afraid of him,' I said, but in my heart I knew I was lying.

'You'll let me know when you get settled?'

442

'Yes, of course,' I said, embracing her. 'Don't worry, Polly. It will be all right.'

Outside in the street, I stood and wondered what to do next. The wind was rising. It looked as if we were in for some rough weather. I shivered, turning up my collar. I'd always hated the wind. My first thought on waking had been to run away, but now I realised it was the worst thing I could do. If I were ever to be free of Nathan, I had to stand up to him. I had to tell him that it was over, face to face.

I was dressing for the evening when Nathan came in. He looked at me, his eyes brooding.

'Where did you go this morning?'

I stood up, taking a deep breath. 'I don't see that it's any of your business. In future I shall go where I please and with whom I please. It's over, Nathan. Either you can leave this house or I will, but I refuse to go on living with you.'

He was surprised. It was the last thing he'd expected. There was a gleam of anger in his eyes.

'It's no use thinking you can beat me into submission,' I said coldly. 'That was your worst mistake, Nathan. I was prepared to stay with you despite your stupid jealousy – but not after last night. I hate you for what you did. I shall never forgive you. You proved to me what I'd always suspected – you're just like my father.'

I saw the shock register in his face. This was the old Betty talking and he didn't quite know what to do. He'd thought I was a wax doll he could mould as he pleased. 'Betty,' he said in a strangled voice. 'You can't mean that? You know I love you. I'm sorry for what I did. I was out of my mind . . .'

'My father was forever saying he was sorry. You were jealous. You were angry and you just took it out on me without pausing to look for the truth.' I looked at him scornfully. 'I know you now, Nathan. You're a bully and a hypocrite . . . I know your dirty little secrets. You said

443

Polly was a whore but you're worse than she ever could be. You live on the earnings of the women you profess to despise. Your clubs are little more than vice – '

His face blanched with shock. 'No, that isn't true. I helped Polly, I'll admit that, and I do run some sleazy clubs – I'm not proud of it – but I'm not a pimp. I don't charge the girls who . . .'

'Whatever your motives were, it amounts to the same thing. You condemned Polly, but you got your pay-off one way or the other.'

'That's business, Betty. A lot of dirty things go on in the real world. You have no idea. You've been cushioned and protected . . .'

'Well, I don't want to be a part of your world, Nathan. Either you leave, or I do. I never want to see you again.'

'So you don't want to see me again.' His mouth twisted cruelly. 'You put up with me while you needed my help, but you don't need me now. You're the famous Betty Cantrel. You think you can just cast me aside and walk over my broken body . . . Well, you're the one who's made a mistake . . .'

As he advanced threateningly, I feared for my life. I wasn't sure what had happened to Nathan. He seemed to have lost control. He was so strong that he could break my neck with his bare hands if he tried. I felt the panic rising and I knew I had to get away. I tried to run past him, struggling as he caught my arm. I struck out at him, managing to wrench myself free, and then I fell. Somehow I tripped and fell against the edge of a mahogany chest of drawers. As I lay on the floor, looking up at him, I felt the first searing pain in my belly. For a moment I just gasped, the room spinning round me. Then, as the pain intensified, I realised what was happening. I stared at Nathan in horror. History was repeating itself! I was having a miscarriage. I was losing our child . . .

'Nathan,' I cried hysterically. 'Oh, Nathan, help me.' I screamed with the pain and clutched at myself. 'For God's sake help me.'

He saw at once that something terrible had happened. His face went white. 'What is it, Betty? Oh, my Lord! What have I done now?'

'It's the baby,' I whispered, gasping as the pain lanced through me. 'I'm losing our child, Nathan.'

'Our child . . .' The horror crept into his eyes. 'You were having our child! Why didn't you tell me last night? For mercy's sake, why didn't you tell me?'

'Would it have made any difference?' I asked bitterly. 'Would you even have believed me?'

'I don't know,' he admitted. He moved towards me, bending down to scoop me up in his arms. 'God forgive me for what I've done – for I never shall.'

He laid me down on the bed. I looked at him with hatred in my eyes. 'Nor shall I,' I said. 'You've killed our child, Nathan – I can never forgive or forget that.'

'No, I don't suppose you can,' he said in a flat voice. 'I'll get the doctor.'

'You can get him if you like,' I said wearily, the tears beginning to trickle down my cheeks. 'But it's too late, Nathan. It's much too late . . .'

Nathan fetched the doctor. I saw him hovering in the doorway as I was examined, his eyes bleak, but the blood soaking my clothes and the sheets was evidence enough of what had happened. Nothing anyone could do would bring back my child. The doctor wanted me to go into hospital, but I refused. The bleeding had stopped now. All I wanted was to be alone.

After the doctor had gone, Nathan came to the bed, looking down at me in silence. I turned my face aside, refusing to meet his gaze.

'You should have gone into hospital,' he said.

'I'll be all right,' I said. 'My maid will look after me.'

'Megan isn't a nurse . . .'

'Leave me alone, Nathan. Go away!'

'I have to talk to you.'

'We have nothing to say.'

'I know you don't want to hear this now,' he said. 'But I would do anything if I could undo what I've done. I'll live with this for the rest of my life, Betty. If it's any consolation to you, I shall be in hell from now on.'

I wouldn't answer. I was remembering my father and the way he'd tried to make me forgive him for his crime against my mother. I hadn't forgiven him, and I wouldn't forgive Nathan now. I hoped he was suffering. I wanted him to be in hell! I closed my eyes, shutting out the sound of his voice. Why wouldn't he just go?

'In a few minutes I shall leave,' he said. 'You won't be troubled with me again, Betty. I give you my word. This house will be yours. I'll have it transferred into your name first thing tomorrow.'

'I don't want the house.'

'Don't do this to me, Betty,' he cried despairingly. 'You're going to have the bloody house whether you want it or not. I owe you far more than that – but it will be some compensation for what I've done.'

I didn't want compensation. Nothing could bring back my child. I shook my head, willing him to go away and leave me to my pain. There were no tears now. The hurt went too deep.

'Betty . . .'

I heard the note of agony in his voice, but I wouldn't look at him as he stood by the bed, staring at me in silence. Perhaps he was hoping for a sign of forgiveness, if so he looked in vain. My heart had hardened against him. I'd sworn long ago that no man would ever treat me the way my father had treated my mother. There was no forgiveness in me.

Chapter Eighteen

I'd been offered a new recording contract, and I'd been asked to sing on television. Television was still very new, and I didn't even own one when I was approached to appear.

Despite the emptiness in my heart, time raced by. It was now 1951 and everyone was talking about the Festival of Britain and the pavilions that were being built on the south bank of the Thames, between Westminster and Waterloo. A wonderful new building to be called the Royal Festival Hall had been erected especially for the occasion, besides all the temporary pavilions which would contain the many marvels of science and new technology Britain was creating.

It was a celebration of the new era. Petrol rationing and the points system for food had finally been abolished in 1950, and though even now the shops were still short of some goods, there was a feeling that we were at last beginning to recover from the war – and the exhibition would show our achievements to the rest of the world.

Concerts and celebrations were going on all over the country. I was surprised to receive a letter from Hilda Jackson, asking me to visit her for a couple of weeks in June. After thinking about it for a few days, I decided to go.

She and her friend ran a small boarding house near the sea, and they both made me very welcome. It was good to get away from London for a while, and to be with old friends.

'I was sorry about the baby,' Hilda said as we sat in her garden one day. 'Do you see anything of Nathan now?'

'I haven't seen him since . . .' I blinked hard as the memory brought sudden tears to my eyes. Even now I still had days when the pain was almost unbearable.

'What about Frances?'

'The last I heard she was in France with Mary. I believe Mary hasn't been too well.'

Hilda nodded. 'Frances writes occasionally, more to Henry than to me. She said Mary suffers with her nerves, but she was very vague about it – I think it all stems from that time just before Eben died . . .' She frowned and looked at me oddly.

'What are you thinking?' I asked.

'I wondered . . . but it's a long time ago.'

'What did you wonder?'

'I thought that perhaps Mary might have pushed Eben herself.' She nodded to herself as I gave a cry of surprise. 'Well, who could have blamed her? The way he was treating her . . .'

'I'd never even thought of that,' I said. 'Is that what you thought at the time?'

'I wondered if you were covering up for her, Betty?'

'No.' I bit my lip. 'No, I wasn't.'

'Well, it's all water under the bridge now.'

'Yes,' I sighed. 'Are you coming up to London next month for the opening of the Exhibition?'

'No, I don't think so. We're very busy and there'll be plenty going on here, but you'll write and tell me all about it, won't you?'

'Yes, of course.' I smiled. 'It's good to have a friend.'

'Are you still singing at that club? I hear you on the radio all the time – and I've got every one of your records.'

I laughed. 'You sound like a fan, Hilda. Don't forget I'm still only that Cantrel girl.'

I returned to London and life went on as before. It was the

summer of 1952. We had a young, as yet uncrowned, Queen of England. I remembered how beautiful the Princess Elizabeth had looked on her wedding day, and I wondered how she felt about taking her father's place. It had been a terrible shock for the whole nation when the King died in February. The Queen's Coronation was not to be until the following year, but already our young monarch must know how it felt to bear the weight of sovereignty. I wondered if it made her feel lonely sometimes.

I was now twenty-one, a rising star in the world of popular music and very much alone. Oh, I still had my friends: people I met while I was working and Polly, Liz, Hilda and Miss Browne, but I was desperately lonely. No one could fill the huge gap Nathan had left in my life, and I carried a constant ache inside me. I was still mourning for the child I'd lost, and I could hardly bear to look at proud mothers as they walked with their babies in the park.

I'd met other men, of course. When performing at the Stork Rooms one night, I'd received a proposal of marriage from the drummer of a famous jazz group, and he was only a little drunk at the time. I'd met many personalities at the Stork Rooms: Elizabeth Taylor, Ava Gardner and Lena Horne were just a few of the well-known names who had become real people to me. I'd been on television and appeared at the Palladium several times, and there was vague talk of an American tour and maybe a film in the near future. So my life should not have been empty – but there was something missing.

That particular June morning, I'd been to see Polly. It was the last time I would see her for a while. She was going abroad on an extended holiday, and I knew I was going to miss her very much.

I was thinking wistfully of the day James had asked me to go to America with him. Supposing I'd said yes straight away? Supposing I'd gone with him before Nathan came back? But it was foolish to let my thoughts dwell in the past. I shook myself. I was young and the future was before me. I must shake off this morbid longing for something I could never have.

Perhaps it was a kind of premonition. Perhaps I should have been warned that the past was about to come back into my life with a vengeance, but I suspected nothing as I let myself into the house. I could hear Megan talking to someone, and I was a little puzzled – that sounded like a woman's voice. I walked towards the sound, entering my small back parlour. A woman was standing at the window, looking out.

'Oh, there you are, Miss Cantrel,' my maid said. 'I was just telling Miss Crawley that I thought you wouldn't be long.'

For a moment I was shocked rigid. Frances turned to look at me, smiling, a hint of malicious amusement in her eyes that reminded me of Nathan.

'I'm not surprised you're speechless,' she said. 'I know this is an awful intrusion, coming unannounced . . .'

'You can go, Megan,' I said, and my voice was harsh. I began to peel off my gloves, feeling annoyed. 'What do you want, Frances?'

She looked at me reproachfully. 'I was just admiring your garden, Betty – and the house. Is it still just as it was when Nathan gave it to you?'

'Frances . . .' I said. 'Why have you come?'

'That's not much of a welcome, Betty. I thought you might be pleased to see me?'

'I would've been pleased to see you if you'd called on me when I lost the baby.'

'I was so sorry about that.' She took a step towards me. 'I thought you would be too upset to see me.'

I acknowledged the truth of that with a shrug. 'So you're back in England then. I thought you were still in France?'

'I was until a couple of weeks ago. Mother . . . she wanted to come home.'

'I see. That doesn't explain why you're here.'

'I thought it was time to heal old wounds. I hoped we could be friends again, Betty.'

'The last time we met you made it pretty clear that you didn't want to be my friend.'

She had the grace to blush. 'I know, I was a bitch to you.' She gave me one of her persuasive smiles, and again I was reminded of Nathan. 'I suppose I was angry with you for not replying when I wrote to you – I don't mean the letter inviting you to lunch when you were living in Hammersmith. I'm talking about the letter I wrote you years ago, when you were at the cottage. I missed you so much in those early years, Betty, and I wrote you a long letter of apology – but you never replied.'

I stared in disbelief. 'I certainly never received it.'

'Oh . . .' She pulled a face. 'It must have gone astray. I ought to have written again, but I was angry because I thought you didn't want anything to do with me.'

Somewhere lost in the mists of memory I had a vision of my father at the gate, talking to the postman. Had he taken and destroyed the letter from Frances? I should never know for certain, and it didn't matter. It was all so long ago.

'I was angry with you sometimes,' I admitted. 'But mostly I missed you.'

'Don't be angry any more,' she said, holding out her hand to me. 'I need you, Betty. I've never had a friend like you.'

I was aware of being manipulated. I knew that look of old. In the past Frances had used it against her mother. I knew it would be wiser to keep her at a distance; she had dominated my life once, but I was free of her now. I was free of all the Crawleys. I would be a fool to let even one of them back into my life.

I took off my jacket, playing for time. 'How long are you home for?'

'I'm not sure.' She smiled again. 'I've seen you on

451

television. You're very famous now, aren't you?' Was there a faint hint of the old jealousy in her voice?

'I'm getting there. I'm at the Palladium for a special show next week. Would you like tickets?'

'I'm not sure if I'll be able to come.' She sighed and her eyes misted with tears. 'Mother is ill, Betty, that's why we've come back. I can't get out much. In fact I must go soon, but I was determined to see you. Oh, Betty, you don't know how miserable I am. I've no real friends. It's impossible with Mother the way . . .' She choked back a sob. 'But I mustn't bother you with this.' A single tear ran down her cheek.

'What's wrong with her?' I felt the barriers begin to crumble. Once she'd been the centre of my world and I felt the tug of old loyalties.

She blinked her tears away. 'I shouldn't have mentioned it. I just wanted to see you. I hoped . . . that we could be friends. But you wouldn't want to visit me now. You must have so many friends . . .'

'Of course I want to visit you,' I cried impulsively. 'I'm lonely too, Frances. I do have lots of friends, and I am busy – but there has never been anyone like you.'

I saw a sudden gleam in her eyes. She was triumphant but she was doing her best to hide it. I'd walked neatly into her trap, but I didn't care. Frances wanted something from me, but I wanted something, too. It was still there, that old need to be a part of her world . . .

Richard took me to dinner that night. He came to pick me up and in the taxi, he asked me if I would go back to the club for a few weeks. 'If you could just help me out,' he said. 'Things haven't been that good recently.'

'Of course I'll come,' I said. 'I've got that show at the Palladium and then I'm free for a couple of weeks.'

Richard smiled and kissed my cheek. 'You're a good friend, Betty. Thank you.'

'You gave me my start, Richard.'

He nodded, looking at me awkwardly. 'Do you ever

think about Nathan. He was the one who really gave you a start.'

'I know.' I bit my lip. 'I'd rather not talk about him.'

We were given a discreet table in the corner of the restaurant. I looked through the menu, vacillating between the lobster and the Dover sole.

'What do you think?' Richard mused. 'I'm going for the beef myself . . . What's wrong, Betty?'

For a moment I couldn't answer. My mouth had gone dry and I was shaking. I'd seen a man come in, with a beautiful blonde model clinging to his arm. I hoped they hadn't seen us.

'Nothing's wrong,' I said. 'I'll have the sole please.'

Richard had seen them. 'I thought you were over him, Betty?'

'Nathan means nothing to me, Richard. It was just the shock. I haven't seen him since . . . Oh no!'

Nathan had seen us. He was steering his lovely companion towards us. I'd seen her picture in the papers and I knew she was sought after by the fashion magazines. Why was he bringing her to our table? Was it to show me that he had completely recovered from our affair?

'Good-evening, Richard. Betty. It's good to see you again. You're looking very well.' Nathan might have been a stranger, so polite and cool was his manner. 'I don't think you know Helga, Betty. Helga — this is an old friend of mine, Betty Cantrel. Richard, you know, of course.'

The girl simpered and smiled at Richard, but her eyes were cold as she looked at me, and her hand tightened on Nathan's arm. She was making her position quite clear, as though she sensed a rival.

'We saw you at the theatre the other week,' she said. 'You were wonderful, Miss Cantrel.'

Her smile was so false that I knew she hated me, but she needn't have worried. I had no intention of spoiling anything for her.

'Betty, I should like to see you some time,' Nathan said, surprising me. 'May I call on you tomorrow?'

'I'm visiting Frances,' I said, my pulses racing. 'Is it important?'

My hands were shaking. I clasped them in my lap, startled by the effect this meeting with Nathan was having on me. It brought back such vivid memories, memories that filled me with searing pain, blinding me. Perhaps he sensed that I was barely keeping my emotions in check, because he frowned.

'It will keep,' he said. 'Forgive me for disturbing you, Betty.'

As they walked away, Richard looked at me. 'He's still in love with you, Betty.'

I was trembling all over. 'No,' I said. 'He was never in love with me. Not in the way you mean, Richard. Besides, it's over.'

'Is it?'

As his eyes met mine, I had to look away. There was still something between Nathan and me – I'd felt the pull of it as he stood there gazing down at me.

I didn't sleep much that night. Tossing and turning in my bed, I went over and over the last terrible scene with Nathan. I'd been so bitter then. I hadn't been able to forgive or even to try and understand how he felt. I'd believed I hated him, but now I wasn't so sure . . .

I was apprehensive about the visit to Frances. After she'd gone that morning, I'd wondered if I was a fool to agree. The Crawleys had been such a big influence in my life, and mostly they'd brought me pain. Perhaps it would have been wiser to stay away from Frances, and yet I was excited at the prospect of seeing her again. Like Nathan, she had a special charm of her own. I had never been strong enough to resist her.

Dissatisfied with my appearance, I changed my clothes three times before settling for a pale blue wool dress I'd bought at Hardy Amies' salon a few weeks previously. As

I climbed into the taxi, I smiled to myself. I was rich and successful, but my legs felt like jelly and my mouth was dry. My fine clothes were just a sham. Underneath, I was still the child of a wastrel father who had gone to work at the big house because her family was close to starving.

I travelled everywhere by taxi these days. When I'd first come to London I'd used the trolleybuses or sometimes the trams. The last tram in London was due to cease running in July; it would be the end of an era.

When the taxi drew up outside a modest, brick house in a quiet cul-de-sac, I was surprised. It looked small and rather dark and dreary, tucked away behind the high hedges as though the occupants had something to hide. I wondered if Frances enjoyed living there after all her travels abroad. She'd told me Mary preferred the climate of France, so why had they come back to live in England?

There was a face behind the nylon curtains at the window, as if I had been eagerly expected. Then the door was flung open and Frances came out to meet me.

'I was afraid you wouldn't come,' she said and there was a breathless catch in her voice. 'I don't really deserve it, Betty.'

'Oh, Frances,' I cried. At that moment she looked so much like the girl I'd idolised that all my doubts vanished. This was the Frances who had shared her books with me. It was she who had sat beside me as we watched the mysteries of life unfold on the glittering screen of the Rex Cinema. She was changeable, spiteful and unpredictable, but she could still command my affection. 'How could I stay away? Did you imagine it was easy for me to go back to the cottage and leave you?'

'No. I knew it was even worse for you, having to go back to that awful place.' She looked at me through a mist of tears. 'I was such a selfish brat. I was so angry with you for leaving me. I wanted to hurt you – but I hurt myself more.'

'Did you?' I longed to believe her. 'I thought you would soon forget me.'

'I've never forgotten you. You may not have known where I was, but I always knew where you were, and what you were doing.'

'Oh, Frances . . .'

I smiled as she led me into the sitting-room. It was in many ways almost a replica of the house in the fens with its dark furniture and tables crowded with bits and pieces. I lived amongst the spacious elegance of furniture crafted more than a hundred years earlier. Nathan had taught me about style.

'We can be together again now,' she said. 'We can be friends.'

'Yes, we can be friends.'

'You don't know how much I need you, Betty.'

I smiled at her. 'Then, why don't you tell me?'

Frances stared at me. 'Nathan didn't say anything to you then – about my mother?'

'No – nothing. Hilda said Mary's nerves were bad.'

'If only that was all of it,' Frances sighed. 'She drinks, Betty, and it's making her ill. She pretends to give it up, but she hides bottles of gin in her room and pours lavender water all over herself to mask the smell. Poor Mother. It started when Father began abusing her. I've sometimes wondered if she . . .' She shook her head. 'No, she couldn't have . . .'

I was shocked. Mary an alcoholic! Like Hilda, Frances seemed to be suggesting that Mary had had something to do with Eben's death. Surely neither of them really believed it? Of course neither of them knew that I'd found Nathan in the barn, but even so . . . Yet Mary had seemed to be waiting for bad news that night . . .

'I'm sorry,' I said. 'Isn't there anything you can do about the drinking?'

'She won't admit that she drinks to excess, Betty. Her mind wanders now and then, and she'll go for weeks at a time without leaving her room . . . Oh, Betty, I'm so worried! She won't eat . . .'

'Don't cry, Frances,' I said as the tears gathered in her eyes. 'Is there anything I can do?'

'She often speaks of you. I think she would like to see you – if you can bear it?'

'Of course I can. Shall we go now?'

Frances got to her feet, her manner agitated. 'You needn't stay long. I'll tell her lunch is ready – you will stay for lunch?'

'I should like that.'

I smiled and followed her from the room. We walked upstairs together.

'You'll find her much changed, I'm afraid.' Frances paused outside her mother's door.

I understood that she was warning me not to show any shock I might feel at Mary's appearance, and I nodded.

The warning was very necessary. My first reaction was one of dismay when I saw the woman in the bed, propped up against a pile of pillows, and it was all I could do to stop myself gasping.

Mary Crawley looked shrivelled and grey, years older than she should. Her eyes had sunk into their sockets so that she seemed to peer through folds of wrinkled flesh. Her cheeks were hollowed and her skin had an unhealthy yellow look. The once-dark hair was thin and completely white, falling about her shoulders untidily. Her pretty silk bedgown hung on her emaciated frame, and it was stained down the front. As I moved towards her, I could smell lavender water.

'Mrs Crawley,' I said, smiling cheerfully to hide my horror. 'Frances said you would like to see me. I hope I'm not intruding?'

Those eyes that had once seemed to show such intelligence peered at me dully. Her hands plucked at the patchwork quilt, and I noticed that the skin on the back was blotched with ugly brown marks. She was like a woman twenty or thirty years older than her true age.

'Who are you?' she asked suspiciously. 'Not another of

those wretched nurses? I won't have them prying into my affairs. Meddling in what doesn't concern them!'

'It's Betty, Mother,' Frances said. 'Betty Cantrel. I told you she was coming today.'

Mary's eyes gleamed suddenly. She straightened up, looking at me intently. 'You've grown up, Betty,' she said, and it might have been the old Mary talking. 'I'm glad you've come back to us. I could always trust you, couldn't I? You'll look after me now. Frances doesn't need you, but I do . . .'

'Betty hasn't come to work for us.' Frances shot an apologetic look at me. 'She's a famous singer now. You know that.'

There was that odd note in Frances's voice again. Just a hint of the old resentment. Resentment that I had a busy, interesting life, while she was forced to look after Mary.

'We must go now,' she was saying. 'Lunch will be ready.'

'It was nice to see you, Mrs Crawley . . .' As I turned to leave, Mary caught my sleeve. I stopped, surprised by the expression in her eyes. She looked frightened.

'Come and see me before you go,' she said in a low voice. 'Please, Betty?'

'Yes, of course I will.' I smiled at her and followed Frances from the room. She closed the door before turning to me with a sigh.

'I'm sorry. She was so much brighter this morning. I thought . . .'

'Don't apologise. Her mind wanders sometimes, that's all. She's ill. She can't help it. Dad was like that – just at the end.'

Frances pressed a shaking hand to her lips, choking back a sob. 'Sometimes I can hardly bear it. Why does she do it? She's killing herself. The doctor says she won't live much longer if she doesn't stop drinking.'

'I don't know why. It's like a sickness with them. Dad did try but he could never stop for long.'

Frances dabbed at her eyes with a lace handkerchief.

'Let's talk about something else. It depresses me to think of Mother.'

I slipped my arm about her waist as we went downstairs. 'Why don't you come to the club tonight? I'm making a special appearance – and it's Liz's birthday. She's a friend of mine, and we're going to have our own party when the club closes. It would do you good.'

Her face lit up. 'I'd love to,' she said. 'I should have to get a nurse in to sit with Mother. She hates them, but just for once . . .'

'I'll talk to her about it before I go.'

'Oh no!' Frances was alarmed. 'Don't do that; she'll make such a fuss. It's better if I just slip away.'

'Perhaps it would be better if I didn't go up to her before I leave?'

'That might upset her more. She would be sure to say I'd stopped you visiting her. She says the oddest things, Betty. She accuses me of standing by and letting someone try to poison her. As if I would! No one wants to hurt her except herself. She's destroying her own body without any help . . .' Frances looked at me, her eyes wild with pain. 'Oh, do let's talk of something else. I can't bear it!'

We talked and talked for more than three hours. Frances's cook had prepared a splendid luncheon: thin clear soup, succulent fish, chicken and asparagus in aspic, and a dish of brandied peaches and whipped cream. We picked at each course, swallowing a few mouthfuls as we laughed and gossiped, catching up on all the years.

'What a sinful waste of food,' I said. 'People would have killed in the war for what we've left – and after!'

'Thank God that's all over,' Frances said. 'The food situation was much better in France and Italy than here, you know. I think half the time it was the government's fault.' She smiled at me. 'We went to Greece the first year, Betty. You would have loved it.'

I listened to her stories, bewitched. The old magic was there. I still wanted to be a part of her world. The bonds we'd forged in childhood were as strong as ever.

'I wish I'd been there. My life has been full, but there's never been anyone like you.'

We sat on at the table, sipping a light sparkling wine and enjoying ourselves. It was as if the years between had never existed. I was surprised when I glanced at the clock.

'I must be going. I'm due at the club at eight tonight.'

'Oh, must you go? I haven't enjoyed myself this much in ages.'

'Why don't you lunch with me tomorrow?'

'I'd love to but the doctor is coming. I should be here. Why don't you visit me again?'

'Why not?' I smiled. 'I might not be able to stay as long, but I shall come. Now, I must go and say good-bye to Mary. Will you ring for a taxi for me, please?'

I went upstairs. I thought I must have been mistaken in the look Mary had given me. She couldn't have been pleading with me to help her. Frances had warned me that her mind wandered.

Opening the door to Mary's room, I saw that she was lying with her eyes closed. I was about to go away again when she suddenly opened them and looked at me.

'Am I disturbing you?'

'Is it you, Betty?' she said in that harsh, whispery voice. 'Are you alone?'

'Yes.' I went in as she beckoned urgently. 'Is something the matter, Mary?'

'Are you sure you're alone? There's no one listening at the door?'

She was frightened! I walked over to the bed, sitting on the edge. Her hand reached tentatively for mine and I could see the fear in her eyes. I took her hand, holding it tightly as I felt her tremble.

'There's no one there. What's wrong? Why are you so frightened?'

Her skinny fingers curled about mine, and she glanced at the door. 'I'm being poisoned,' she said, clutching at me in a pitiful, eager way. 'They put it in my food, that's why I send it away. They think I don't know, but I'm not

460

as mad as they think I am. I only eat the fruit. The fruit is safe.'

A chill ran down my spine. I knew it couldn't be true. No one in this house could possibly want to harm her, but it was still dreadful to hear. She believed the threat was real, so for her the pain and the terror *were* real. Instinctively, I knew there was no point in trying to comfort by denying it.

'Who is it, Mary?' I asked. 'Tell me who is trying to harm you and I'll stop them.'

'But you know.' Her eyes gleamed. 'You always knew everything, didn't you, Betty? Now that you've come back I shall be safe. They won't dare . . .' Her voice dropped and she put a finger to her lips. 'Shush . . .' Her hand trembled in mine.

Then the door opened and Nathan came in. My heart skipped a beat, just as it had done the previous evening when he came over to Richard's table, yet I wasn't quite as shocked as I had been then. I fought for calm, squeezing Mary's hand reassuringly.

'It's all right,' I said. 'It's only Nathan.' Only Nathan! When my mouth was dry and I wanted to get up and run from the room.

Nathan's face had a concerned, anxious look as he came towards us, and I saw pity in his eyes. Then he turned to me and he seemed to lose all expression, as though he too was hiding his emotions.

'Frances said you were here. Has Mary been asleep all the time?'

I glanced down and saw that her eyes were closed. She was pretending, but I decided to play along with her.

'Most of it,' I lied.

'She sleeps a lot. It's a mercy really.' He looked at me. 'Shall we leave her to rest?'

I followed him from the room. He closed the door softly and then turned to me.

'Frances tells me you've invited her to a party at the

club. That was kind of you. She doesn't get out as often as she should.'

He looked at me expectantly, as though he were waiting for me to invite him, too. I frowned. 'Last night you said you wanted to speak to me about something, Nathan?'

'I can't discuss it here. When can I see you alone?'

'I'm not sure.' His eyes darkened. Those odd chameleon eyes that had always fascinated me. 'Perhaps tomorrow morning early? I've promised to visit Frances again.'

'Thank you for that, Betty. I promise you, it is business.' We had reached the bottom of the stairs. He stared at me, hard. 'Frances wants to bring James with her this evening. I thought I should warn you.'

For one awful moment I couldn't breathe. 'James Blair,' I said with studied carelessness. 'Why should I mind?'

'Be careful, Betty,' he said. 'I don't want to see you hurt again.'

Before I could reply, Frances came into the hall. 'Are you leaving?' she asked.

'My taxi is waiting,' I said. 'I heard it arrive. Shall I see you this evening?'

'Yes, I'll get a nurse in.' She glanced at Nathan. 'Have you been up to Mother? I thought she seemed better today.'

'She was asleep.' There was an odd look in his eyes. 'I think she should go into a nursing home, Frances. It's not right for you to be tied to her like this.'

'It can't be helped,' she said. 'She was always so good to me when I was ill. I can't desert her now – can I?'

The years had improved Frances's disposition. I could remember when nothing would have been allowed to interfere with her pleasure. She'd used and tormented Mary shamefully in those days. I admired her for her devotion to her sick mother, but felt sad that her life was now so difficult.

Appearing at the Purple Moon was like coming home. The customers were as enthusiastic as ever, especially as I gave two performances. Some of the regulars had been invited to stay for Liz's party, and because it was a private occasion we were served free champagne. Because of the licensing laws, we couldn't sell drinks after a certain hour, but we could give it away to our friends. Richard had bought a huge surprise cake for Liz and we all had presents for her. So I was feeling happy and excited as I went to freshen up.

I was removing my stage make-up when Liz came in. She was looking especially pretty in an expensive new dress one of her admirers had given her, and her eyes were shining. Liz was one of those people with the capacity to really enjoy her birthday, and I felt a thrill of pleasure as I handed her a small box wrapped in silver tissue and saw her face light up. I knew her taste for expensive trifles, and I thought she would like the gold scent bottle I'd bought her.

'I adore presents,' she cried, hugging me. 'Especially yours, Betty. You always choose such unusual things.'

We linked arms and went to join the others. There was a large three-tiered cake with pink and white icing decorated with sugar roses and silver balls. The champagne was already opened and glasses were being passed from hand to hand. I took one and saluted Liz.

'Happy birthday,' I said. 'Let's all drink a toast – what shall it be?'

'To old friends?' a voice suggested at my elbow. I gasped and swung round, gazing breathlessly into a pair of vivid blue eyes. James touched his glass to mine, smiling in a way that made my head whirl. We hadn't met for more than two years, but his smile could still turn my knees to water. 'Frances had to stay with her mother. I hope you don't mind my coming alone?'

My hand trembled slightly as I sipped my drink. 'Is Mary worse?'

'Not worse exactly. She plays on Frances's nerves. She wouldn't accept the nurse, so Frances had to stay with her.'

'I'm sorry. It must be so difficult for Frances.'

He smiled wryly. 'It can be hell. Frances is a fool to put up with it. She should put her mother in a private hospital where she can be properly cared for. I've told her that and so has Nathan.'

I was only half listening. My heart was racing wildly. James was the same as ever; his lean face had a sensitivity that was lacking in so many men, fine dark brows accentuated by the silver-blond of his hair, an aristocratic nose and sensuous lips – a face that had always had the power to set my stomach churning. I felt a rush of choking desire. Just to see him was to start the longing up again. How I wanted to be held in his arms. And I believed I could see an answering desire in his eyes.

'Do you want some cake?'

Liz's question startled me. I was aware only of James, and the clamouring for physical contact with him. I had lived alone too long! 'Just a small piece,' I said. 'Then I must go. I have a slight headache.'

'Then perhaps you will allow me to take you home?' James offered.

It was what I had wanted, what I had hoped for. I smiled, trying to still my racing heart. 'Thank you. It will save me waiting for a taxi.'

'Then we'll leave when you're ready.'

We stayed for another half an hour, just to see Liz open her gifts. Then James took me home in his car. He pulled into the drive, stopped the engine and turned to look at me.

'How's your headache now?'

'Much better, thank you.' Headache – what headache? My pulses raced wildly.

'It's been a long time, Betty.'

'Yes,' I said. 'A long time.'

'Are you happy now?'

I shrugged. 'What is happiness? I have everything I need. My life is busy and . . .'

'But what about you?' His eyes seemed to pierce me.

'I – I'm lonely sometimes. You knew Nathan and I had parted?'

'I know . . .' He couldn't quite meet my eyes. 'I meant to meet you that day, Betty, but Nathan got to me first. He asked me if we'd been lovers and – and he said he was going to marry you. He told me I would ruin your life if I took you away from a successful career . . .'

'He had no right to do that.' I looked into his eyes. 'I went to the park that day, James. I waited for over two hours.'

He drew his breath in sharply. 'What a fool I was to listen to him! You know how I've always felt about you, Betty. I've always wanted . . .'

'Wanted me?' I finished for him. 'You don't have to pretend, James. I know I was never the kind of girl you could marry.'

'Betty, I . . .'

I leaned towards him, touching my fingers to his lips. 'Kiss me, James. Just kiss me.'

He made a deep, growling sound in his throat, then he caught me to him. Our lips met eagerly, hungrily, as we released the pent-up desire we had suppressed for so long. My hands moved urgently over his shoulders, my fingers tangling in that thick, pale hair as he crushed me to him. I wanted that kiss to go on and on until our bodies, hearts, minds and souls fused into one. We were both shaking as we drew apart.

'May I come in?' James asked as we looked at each other. 'I'd like to stay with you tonight.'

I breathed deeply. Every nerve in my body was alive and tingling. I felt almost sick with the need to feel his naked body close to mine, to twine myself about him like a vine about a tree and take him deep into myself.

'Just try leaving me,' I whispered huskily.

Megan, my faithful maid, tried not to show her

surprise as she let us in. It was the first time I'd brought a man home since Nathan left me. I made a pretence of taking James into the dining-room, where a cold supper was laid in case I was hungry, but food held no appeal for me now. I was starved of only one thing. I wanted James. We crept upstairs, holding hands and laughing like excited children. I saw my own hunger mirrored in James's eyes. We undressed each other hurriedly, straining at buttons and zips with impatient fingers. We were in such a state of urgency that it was all we could do to keep from falling to the floor fully-clothed.

At last, at long last, we were in each other's arms. Our swollen lips devoured each separate part of the other's body, kissing, tasting, drinking the droplets of sweat. The first thrusting penetration was over far too quickly to satisfy either of us. It didn't matter. We had all night. We laughed and drank from the wine bottle James had thoughtfully snatched from the supper table, looking at each other as if we had suddenly been cured of blindness. As if we could see for the very first time.

'You have no idea how often I've thought of you like this,' he murmured, his hand stroking me from breast to thigh. 'Thought of you, wanted you . . . wondered where you were and who was with you.'

'No more than I've thought of you,' I said, laughing up at him. 'There has been no one else since Nathan. When I was a child I could never understand why women enjoyed being with a man like this. I heard my mother and father through the bedroom walls and I thought it was dirty and ugly, but if she felt the same as I do . . .'

I got no further. James's kisses stopped my mouth from uttering senseless words. There was nothing to be said, nothing that mattered. We were aware only of our mutual need.

James pushed me back into the bed. This time he made love to me slowly, enjoying each sensuous movement and caress. His tongue teased my nipples, making them swell and stand up as I felt desire moving inside me once more.

This time it was not so urgent, building little by little until it was once again a raging fire that swept me out of control. I cried out as James penetrated me, turning my head from side to side on the pillow as he plunged deeper and deeper, carrying me on to unknown realms of pleasure.

It was a long night. We were young and greedy for love, and James was strong. When at last we fell asleep in each other's arms, it was from sheer exhaustion.

I awoke reluctantly. My dreams had been too sweet to leave behind. I stretched out my hand and felt the bed cold and empty. As I turned my head, I saw a sheet of my own pink notepaper on the pillow beside me.

'I'll see you this evening, before you leave for the club. James.'

I read the brief message aloud, and a little pain caught my heart. It was a curt, almost cold message, so unlike his kisses the night before. I lay looking at it, frowning as I read it again, trying to put some warmth or feeling into the words. Then I suddenly remembered that Nathan was coming to see me. Leaping out of bed, I showered hastily and pulled on a pair of denim jeans and a fluffy jumper, feeling guilty. It was as though I had betrayed him — but that was stupid. It was ages since we'd parted.

Nathan was waiting for me downstairs. He looked at me, his eyes narrowing, and I blushed. I was sure that he knew I'd spent the night making love, but all he said was,

'Jeans, Betty?'

'I wear them at home sometimes,' I replied defensively. 'Lots of women do these days.'

'I wasn't criticising you. They suit you.'

I turned away to pour myself a cup of coffee. 'Would you like one?'

'No, thank you,' he said stiffly. 'I forfeited that right a long time ago, didn't I?'

I glanced at him. He was unsmiling, obviously under

tight control. 'Is something the matter? What was it you wanted to discuss?'

'When I bought this house it was a part of a property deal for which I had a large bank loan. I cleared that loan recently, and I wanted to give you the release from the bank, that's all.' He laid an envelope on the table. 'You were never in any danger of losing the house – I would have taken care of it.'

'I never wanted you to give it to me, Nathan.'

'Do you still hate me, Betty?'

I was silent for a moment, and I could see the little nerve jumping in his throat. 'No, I don't hate you, Nathan. I did for a while, but I don't now. You were good to me – except for . . .'

'How many times I've wished I could undo what I did!' His face was white and strained. 'I must have been out of my mind. I was angry, Betty. I've always had this terrible temper. God knows, I've suffered for it!'

I turned away from the naked, pleading look in his eyes. It hurt me to see him like this, but it was too late for there to be anything more between us.

'If that's all, Nathan, I have to get changed. I promised Frances I'd be there by eleven.'

'Don't let her use you, Betty.'

'What do you mean?'

'You've always been so loyal to us, Betty, and we've all used you in our way: Frances, Mary and me. Be careful. We're dangerous people to know. I don't want you to be hurt again.'

'That's the second time you've said that – what are you trying to tell me?'

'I'm not sure I know myself.' He gazed at me in silence for a moment, then reached out to touch my cheek. 'I know you never believed it, kid, but I always cared for you a great deal. I still do.'

He hadn't called me kid like that for a long time and it brought a lump to my throat. Suddenly I was remembering the good times.

'Nathan . . .' I whispered.

He shook his head. 'You don't have to tell me,' he said. 'Do you think I don't know, Betty? Do you think I don't know James was with you last night? I saw it in your face as soon as you came in. There's a look in your eyes and your mouth . . .' He shrugged. 'So you got what you wanted . . .'

I dropped my eyes, unable to meet the accusation in his eyes. 'You've had other women – don't tell me the beautiful Helga is just a friend!'

'I won't deny that there have been others – too many.' He smiled ruefully. 'But no one but you will ever have my heart . . .' He turned as he spoke and walked from the room, leaving me to stare after him with the tears streaming down my face.

Frances had almost given me up. She looked at me resentfully. 'I thought you weren't coming.'

'I overslept.' I couldn't tell her that it had taken me half an hour to stop crying after Nathan left.

'Were you up late last night?' Her eyes were suspicious.

'No. I didn't stay at the party long.' I avoided her eyes, feeling guilty. 'I was sorry you couldn't come. How is Mary?'

'She wants to see you. It was because you weren't here that she made so much fuss. She expected you to take her supper up and when you didn't . . .' Frances looked at me wearily. 'I can't leave her, Betty. She won't eat anything unless I share it. We've lost more servants . . . Oh, what's the use! Sometimes I wish she would die!'

'I know you don't mean that. You look worn out.' I smiled at her. 'I can spare an hour or two. Why don't I take her tray up while you go for a walk or something?'

'I have some shopping I want to do.' Frances eyed me hopefully. 'Could you stay that long?'

'Well, I have to go to the studio this afternoon, but I'll make time. Just tell your cook that I'll see to Mary's tray so that she doesn't throw a tantrum. You don't want to lose her, too.'

Frances was relieved. We explained to the cook, and then she hurried away.

'Mrs Crawley never eats anything we send up,' the cook said with a sniff. 'Nothing but fruit – and that with the skin still on or she won't touch it.'

'Would you mind very much if I prepared her food myself? I thought something light – like a scrambled egg and toast.'

'You're welcome to try, but you'll be wasting your time.'

I felt like an intruder in her kitchen, but I tried to be diplomatic as I prepared a tray very carefully, the way Mary had always liked it. A lace mat on the tray, shining glass and cutlery, and the bread sliced very thinly. The care I took raised some eyebrows, but I had good reason for what I did. Mary was not a fool whatever else she might be. She knew how I did things, and she would know I'd prepared everything myself.

I was surprised to find her out of bed and in a chair by the window. Her hair had been brushed and swept up into a knot on top of her head, and she was wearing a dark burgundy dress fastened at the neck with a cameo brooch. Nothing could disguise the ravages of illness in her face, but she looked better than the previous day.

'Ah, there you are, Betty,' she said. 'I'm glad you've brought my tray today. Where were you last night?'

'I only come mornings now, ma'am. I can't manage the evenings.'

'Why couldn't Frances have said so? She treats me as though I were a child.' Mary looked at the tray with interest. 'What have you brought me?'

'I thought you might like some soup, ma'am – and I've scrambled an egg the way you like it, all soft and fluffy.'

Her eyes went over the tray. 'You prepared this yourself, didn't you?'

'Yes, ma'am. It's quite safe to eat it. I made everything myself.'

'Will you stay with me while I eat? The way you used to with Frances?'

'Yes. If you want me to.'

Her hand trembled as she raised the soup spoon to her mouth, spilling half the contents. Some of it reached her mouth, however, and a look of such joy came over her face that it brought a lump to my throat. She could eat because she trusted me. She knew I wouldn't bring her poisoned food.

It was terrible to see her struggle to eat. She had lost the habit and she had so little strength. Again and again I wanted to help her, but I knew I must not. She had to do it for herself. Only by making the effort could she begin the long climb to recovery. She swallowed most of the soup and a few mouthfuls of the egg. It wasn't much, but it was a start.

'That was very nice,' she said, touching the white napkin to her mouth. 'Thank you.'

'I'm glad you enjoyed it, ma'am. Shall I take the tray away now?'

'No, not yet. Stay and talk to me . . . please.' She tipped her head to one side. 'Is it true that you sing in a nightclub?'

'Yes, ma'am. That's why I can't come in the evenings.'

'I'm not sure I approve of that. Still, I suppose I can't stop you. I expect you need the money for that wretched family of yours?'

She must know what had happened, but for reasons of her own she was pretending not to. It was a little game we were playing, and I decided to go along with her. Perhaps it was easier for her to pretend than to face the truth.

She stared at her hands, then looked up. 'I had to send Polly away, you know. I couldn't let Eben's bastard have what belonged to Frances.'

'It doesn't matter. It's all over now.'

'You knew Eben stole Nathan's money, didn't you?

471

You were under the table and you heard it all, but you haven't told Nathan, have you?' I shook my head. 'That's good – Nathan has such a temper. He might kill Eben if he knew . . .'

Her mind was wandering in and out of the past. She knew Eben was dead, but for some reason she wanted to pretend that he wasn't. What was in her mind. What did she know about that day in the barn that she couldn't bear to face? I was certain that she knew something . . . that she had seen something . . .

'Would you like to rest now, Mary?'

She made a faint movement with her hand, which I took to mean yes. 'I'll come tomorrow if I can,' I said. 'Don't be frightened, Mary. I'll take care of you now.'

I thought she smiled, but I couldn't be certain. She might have been asleep.

I returned the tray to the kitchen. No one commented but their eyes flicked disbelievingly towards the almost empty dishes. As I went through into the front hall, Frances came in. She was loaded with parcels and her cheeks were glowing from the fresh air. She smiled as she saw me.

'Have I been too long?'

'No, of course not.'

'How was Mother?'

'She had most of her soup and a little of the egg. It's going to take a while to get her eating again.'

'Does that mean you'll be coming regularly?'

'I'll come every morning for an hour or so. It will mean some rescheduling, but I'll manage.'

'Oh, Betty, I do love you! I feel much better already. Do you have to go or can you stay for a drink?'

'I'll have some fruit juice,' I said. 'I think I had too much champagne last night.' I followed her into the sitting-room, glancing at the parcels she dumped on the table. 'Have you been buying something nice?'

'Most of it is for James,' she said, her eyes glowing. 'It's his birthday soon.'

472

I felt a sharp pang of guilt as I saw the pleasure in her eyes. In James's arms I'd blotted out all thought of Frances, but now, face to face with her, I couldn't hide from myself. I'd always known that Frances was in love with James. I called myself her friend and yet last night . . .

'I've just remembered something,' I said. 'I don't think I'd better stay for that drink.'

'You will come tomorrow?'

I owed her that at least. 'Yes,' I said, forcing a smile. 'I'll come every day — but if one day I can't make it, tell Mary that it's my day off. She won't make a fuss then.'

'You're so clever, Betty.'

It was difficult to behave naturally. I smiled and talked until my taxi arrived, then I just climbed in, closed my eyes and let the shock waves wash over me. Frances was obviously still in love with James, she still thought of him as the man she was going to marry. I remembered the day she'd invited me to lunch to tell me that James was hers. I was well aware of her jealous nature. If she ever discovered the truth she would never forgive me . . .

Chapter Nineteen

I've counted every brick in the wall, every crack in the ceiling, every line in the floor. I do not want to remember any more. It is too painful – how I wish it were over!

She whispered to me that her name is Sally, my friend in the black dress. She is a little afraid of her companion, but she tries to make my life more comfortable in any way she can. She smuggled in a bar of my favourite chocolate the other day.

Yesterday, when we were alone for a short time, she asked me again why I had killed the man I loved. I smiled at her and shook my head.

'You wouldn't understand why it happened,' I said. 'Your husband was a good man. You loved him – how can you know what it's like to be betrayed by the man you love?'

I don't want to think about that day. I don't want to remember. But the thoughts keep crowding in on me, forcing me to feel the pain . . .

I was tortured by my guilt as I waited for James to come that evening. I'd always loved him, but Frances was my friend. She was almost a part of me . . .

'What's wrong?' he asked, as I moved away when he tried to take me in his arms.

I looked at him. 'What is Frances to you, James?'

He frowned. 'I don't understand, what has she said to you?'

'Nothing . . .' I drew a deep breath. 'I just had the feeling that she thought you were her property . . .' The blue eyes darkened to violet. 'You're not engaged to her, are you?'

He looked relieved. 'No, I'm not engaged to her,' he said. 'I am fond of her, we're good friends.'

'That's all?' I felt relief flood through me. 'She was always my best friend . . .'

James moved towards me and this time I didn't resist as he took me in his arms. 'Frances needs all her friends,' he said softly. 'But she has nothing to do with us, Betty; there's no need for her to know anything.' He raised his brows. 'Is there?'

I hesitated, sensing that he wasn't telling me the whole truth. In my heart I knew that I should send him away, but when he looked at me that way . . .

'No . . .' I breathed. 'There's no need for her to know anything . . .'

His mouth covered mine and I clung to him dizzily, returning his kiss hungrily and blotting out the look in Frances's eyes that morning. Frances was my friend, but James was my lover – and for the moment that was all that mattered . . .

I was happy to be singing at the club that night, and I'd planned to try out a new song. It was called 'Soliloquy' and it came from the hit musical *Carousel*. I'd wanted to try it since I'd heard Frank Sinatra sing it at the London Palladium, but it was difficult and I'd been practising for a long time.

'I'd just started my second number when the disturbance started somewhere at the back of the club. At first it was just shouting, then a fight broke out and there was a lot of crashing as furniture was smashed. Feeling stunned by the sudden outbreak of violence, I stopped singing abruptly, standing there for a few minutes, wondering what to do. Then Richard took hold of my arm and urged me from the stage.

'You'd better get out of here,' he said. 'It could be very nasty.'

'But what's wrong?' I asked, puzzled.

'It's that young fool I threw out of here the other week when he was drunk and making a nuisance of himself. I gave orders not to let him in again, but somehow he slipped in – and he brought a few of his friends to help him break up the place.'

'And he's the grandson of an earl!' I said disgustedly. 'You'd think he'd have learnt better manners at that fancy school of his.'

'They're sometimes the worst,' Richard said grimly. 'I'm sending both you and Liz home in a taxi before the police arrive.'

Liz was angry about the riot at the club. 'I'm sure they're out to ruin Richard,' she said as we drove home. 'Things have been pretty bad for him recently.'

'Can't the police do anything?' I asked.

She pulled a face. 'All they'll do is blame us and close the club!'

'Let's hope it doesn't come to that.'

'If it does, I'll be out of a job.'

'Something will turn up,' I said to cheer her. 'If you're in trouble with money, Liz, I can help.'

She laughed and shook her head. 'Don't worry about me, Betty. I'm just in a mood, that's all.'

The taxi drew up outside my house. I got out and walked to the front door, moving my feet restlessly as I waited for Megan to open the door. It was chilly tonight! A shadow moved from behind some bushes, giving me a fright, then I saw that it was James.

'I thought you weren't coming tonight?'

'I couldn't stay away from you,' he murmured throatily. 'I had to see you, Betty.'

Megan opened the door and we went in. A cold supper had been laid in the dining-room, but as soon as we were alone, James swept me into his arms. I slid my hands into the hair at the nape of his neck, caressing him. He groaned as I arched against him, and then we moved as one towards the stairs.

It was only much later that I wondered why he had waited in the garden instead of coming to the club.

James came to me every night for the next two weeks. I gave him a key to the house so that he could let himself in. I didn't ask why he hadn't come to the club that night, but he said it was for my sake.

'You seemed worried in case Frances was jealous,' he said. 'I thought it was better if we were discreet.'

I accepted his explanation. We both knew how jealous Frances was. It would be better if she didn't know we were lovers. I eased my guilt by doing all I could to help with Mary. And it seemed that Mary was getting better. She still ate very little, but she was improving. We spent many hours together, talking of the past.

So, though my conscience wasn't clear, I could live with myself. Frances loved James, but she wasn't engaged to him. She wasn't his lover – so I wasn't really deceiving her, was I?

The police advised Richard to close the club for a few weeks after the riot. During this time I worked in the studio, but I was disinclined to accept contracts for theatre work. I wanted my nights free for when James came to me. Then Richard told me he was reopening the theatre and asked me to appear.

'I promise there won't be any trouble this time,' he said. 'I spoke to Nathan, and I don't think we'll be getting any more aggravation from that particular source.'

I remembered the night Nathan had disappeared from the club and come back with a slight cut on his lip, and I nodded. 'He usually manages to take care of that sort of problem, doesn't he?'

'It comes in useful to have friends sometimes,' Richard said cryptically, leaving me to fill in the spaces for myself.

I was a little nervous as I walked out into the spotlight that first evening, but immediately the customers began to clap and cheer. The regular crowd were in, and I felt my tension ease. Glancing towards Nathan's table, I saw that he, Helga, Frances and James were all together.

I'd never sung better. Frances blew me a kiss when I'd finished and Nathan smiled as my performance was greeted with enthusiasm. I had to sing again and again before the customers would let me leave the stage.

Afterwards, we all celebrated with champagne. It was a wonderful evening. Richard was very relieved that his club was open again, and packed with regular clients; they seemed to have turned out especially to show their support. I promised Richard that I would make a guest appearance at least once a month, more if I could manage it.

The one sour note for me was when I had to watch James take Frances home. My bed would be empty without him, but he would not come to me that night.

Richard took me home, seeing me to my door. 'It was marvellous tonight,' he said, holding my hand for a moment. 'I'm so relieved it went so well.'

'Thanks to Nathan,' I said.

Richard looked at my face and frowned. 'I think he's still in love with you,' he said. 'Good-night, Betty.'

For a moment I stared after him, stunned. Nathan still in love with me? Tossing restlessly in bed, I found myself thinking about the bitter quarrel that had driven us apart, and wondering if perhaps I'd been almost as much to blame as he. Angry with myself, I asked what was the matter with me? I'd got what I'd wanted since I was fifteen years old. James was my lover . . . So why was I thinking about Nathan?

Do any of us ever know what we truly want out of life? I watch the women in black playing cards in the fading light of evening, wondering about their lives. Are they happy? Have they ever known true contentment – and if they have, why am I different?

I've been thinking about my feelings for James as I lie here on this hard prison bed. It is because of him that I am here, because I wilfully made an idol out of him. For years I convinced myself that he was the perfect man. I told myself that if only he were mine, I would be perfectly content.

And I should have been happy. I had everything any woman could want. I was a famous singer. I had money. The man I'd always wanted was my lover. Frances was my friend. What more could I possibly want?

Perhaps the ending to my story was written long ago in the stars. Perhaps there was nothing I could have done to change what happened. And yet, I'm torn by guilt and despair when I remember.

Oh, God . . . Oh, God, is there no mercy? Must I go through it all again?

Mary didn't seem quite as well when I next visited her. Her hands were restless and she plucked endlessly at the bedcovers. I caught them, holding them firmly.

'What is it, Mary? Can't you tell me what's wrong?'

She looked at me, her eyes dark with fear. 'They want to put me away,' she said. 'They want me locked away in a madhouse – then they'll leave me to die.'

'Who, Mary? Who wants to lock you away?'

I felt so sorry for her. Her mind wandered sometimes, and she did drink whenever she could get her hands on a bottle of gin, but she had seemed to be improving. She wasn't mad, just a little disturbed at times. I couldn't believe that anyone would want to have her committed.

'They do,' she said, her eyes suddenly sly. 'I heard them talking when they thought I was asleep.'

'But who?'

'All of them,' she said. 'You know who I mean.'

Did she think that all her family wanted her shut away? I remembered both James and Nathan saying that she should be in a nursing home. She had misunderstood them.

'No one is going to shut you away in a madhouse,' I

said. 'Rest now, Mary. I promise you I won't let them do that to you.'

I felt very sad about the deterioration in Mary's condition. When I discovered Nathan sitting by her bed a few days later, I asked him what he thought of her health. He put his finger to his lips and beckoned me to come outside.

'I think she's worse,' he said. 'She thought I was Eben this morning. She says some very strange things, Betty – and it isn't the drink. Frances has all the cabinets locked now. The doctor says that one more overdose of alcohol could kill her.'

'She seems so frightened, Nathan,' I said. 'She's terrified of being shut away. She thinks everyone wants to have her committed to an asylum.'

Nathan frowned. 'She must have heard me say she should be in a nursing home. I think she might be better if she had proper nursing care . . . Not that you haven't done your best.' He smiled. 'I really thought she was going to pull through when you got her to start eating, Betty.'

'So did I.' I looked at him. 'She seems to have changed suddenly . . .'

'Yes . . .' He looked thoughtful. 'Yes, you're right.'

'I'd better go . . .'

Nathan caught my arm. 'Don't go, not for a moment. I wondered if you'd have dinner with me tonight?'

I stared at him, not knowing what to say. His concern for Mary had got through to me. This was the old Nathan, the Nathan who had followed me when my mother was ill, the Nathan who had given me my first pretty dress . . . the man he had been until I drove him out of his mind with jealousy.

'For old time's sake,' he said. 'Just to show that you don't hate me . . .'

How could I refuse when he asked like that? 'Yes, I will,' I said. 'Come to the house at seven.'

*

James was angry because I'd agreed to go out with Nathan. 'And what am I supposed to do?' he asked. 'Hang about like a thief, in the gardens, waiting for him to leave after he brings you home?'

His attitude annoyed me. 'You don't own me, James. I'm only going to dinner with him. He's concerned about Mary's health, just as I am. I think he wants to talk about her.' I was lying but I thought it would placate him. I was surprised when he scowled.

'Frances should have her put away,' he said harshly. 'She's as mad as a hatter.'

'James!' I stared at him in dismay. 'You can't really think that? Mary is terrified of being shut away.'

He saw that he had upset me. 'I was just thinking of Frances,' he said. 'She'll never have a life of her own while Mary's alive.'

As I looked into his eyes, I was chilled. Could he really be as uncaring as that? I'd always thought he was kind and gentle, but I didn't like what I was seeing now.

Nathan took me to a quiet, discreet restaurant that evening, ordering all my favourite foods, and the light sparkling wine I liked best. He knew my tastes so well, and he was obviously determined to spoil me. His mood was relaxed and he went out of his way to charm and entertain me, making me laugh. It was as if that terrible night had never happened. This was the Nathan who had teased me unmercifully at the farm, and I was so glad to have him back. Suddenly, he reached across the table and touched my hand.

'Are you happy, Betty?'

'Yes. Why do you ask?'

'I don't mean just tonight.' His eyes were serious. 'I don't like the way Frances is using you. You shouldn't be acting as Mary's nurse.'

'I don't mind, Nathan. Really. I feel sorry for her – and I'm helping Frances.'

'Guilty conscience?' His brows went up. 'He'll marry her when Mary's dead, Betty. He wants the money.'

I felt a chill go down my spine. 'What do you mean?'

'The American firm he invested in so heavily?' I nodded as he paused. 'It ran into difficulties over design problems. At the moment de Havilland's are way ahead with their four-jet Comet, and Vickers had the first propjet airliner. James should have cut his losses long ago, but he was either too proud or too blind . . .'

'That's a rotten thing to say, Nathan.'

'He lost a lot of money when the company folded.'

'But most of the Crawley's money is tied up until . . .' I stared at him. 'You think he's waiting for Mary to die before he marries Frances – but that's despicable!'

'Yes.' Something flickered in his eyes. 'Shall we change the subject? I've sold my clubs, Betty. All of them. From now on I'm strictly legitimate.'

'I'm glad.' I tried to put what he'd said out of my mind. James couldn't be that mercenary – could he? 'It used to worry me when I thought of you mixing with men like the ones I saw at the club that night.'

'I've started a new venture now,' he said. 'Plastics. That's the thing of the future, Betty.'

'How will you find the time? You're always so busy.'

'Managers. I'm going to delegate, Betty.' He smiled regretfully. 'That was one of my mistakes, leaving you alone so often. I wouldn't make that same mistake.'

I fiddled with the stem of my glass. 'Why didn't you talk to me like this when we were together?'

'I was in a rotten, dangerous business, Betty. I didn't want you too involved. I've learned my lesson. It's all going to be different now.'

'These plastics,' I said. 'What will you be making?'

'Everything.' He grinned at me. 'From food packaging to boats, from washing-up bowls to the new recordings – we've only just seen the tip of the iceberg as far as plastics are concerned.' He talked about his new factory and I listened, absorbed by this new Nathan. 'You can't be interested in all this, kid?' he said, laughing.

'I was always interested in many things, Nathan. I can even talk reasonably intelligently about politics. You just didn't have the time, or the inclination, to find out.'

'It wouldn't be like that the next time.' He looked at me pleadingly. 'I know I promised I'd never bother you again,' he said, 'and I won't pester you, but I must just ask once. Please, Betty, give me another chance?'

'It wouldn't work, Nathan. We would just destroy each other again.'

'You don't know that. I've learned. I'm different now.'

Tears gathered in my eyes. 'Please, don't,' I whispered. 'I can't bear it.'

'I won't press you now, but think about it, Betty. Please?'

I hesitated, not knowing why I did so, and he smiled. Soon he was making me laugh again.

I slept alone that night. James was sulking because I'd gone out to dinner with Nathan. I was glad to be alone, I needed the chance to think.

I had learned many things that night, about myself, and about Nathan and James. I couldn't help thinking about what Nathan had said. Once I would have dismissed it as nonsense, but now I wasn't so sure. James's attitude towards Mary had shocked me. Was it possible that Nathan was right? Could James be waiting for Mary to die so that Frances inherited her mother's money?

It was a horrible thought. If it was true, James wasn't the man I'd always believed him to be – but I couldn't believe it! James had just been thinking of Frances when he'd said her mother should be put away. Nathan had said something similar . . . but in a different way.

Suddenly, I remembered something – the look on Maisie's face that morning she'd muddled up James's book collection. She'd been really upset, afraid that she would lose her job because of it. It hadn't struck me at the time – because I was too besotted with James to think straight – but any man who would sack a maid for such a little crime had to have an unpleasant streak in his nature.

Yet I couldn't let myself accept it even now. If I did, it meant that my whole life had been based on a lie . . .

I was awakened by Megan shaking my shoulder. I blinked stupidly, only half awake.

'What is it, Megan?'

'I'm sorry, Miss Cantrel, but there's an urgent message for you from Miss Crawley . . .'

As soon as I saw Frances's face, I knew I was too late. Mary was dead. My frantic dash in a taxi through the early morning mists had been in vain.

'It was very sudden at the end,' Frances said, choking back a sob. 'I gave her her sleeping pills as usual last night but . . .' Frances stared at me wildly. 'Somehow she'd got hold of a bottle of gin . . .'

'But you keep it locked away. Nathan told me.'

'How she got it, I don't know,' Frances said. 'It was the combination of the pills and the alcohol, Betty. She vomited in her sleep and choked.' She gave a little cry of grief. 'I came in to check her when something woke me and . . .'

'I'm sorry,' I said. 'So very sorry, Frances.'

'The doctor said she couldn't have suffered,' Frances said, dabbing at her eyes with a lace handkerchief. 'But what made her do it, Betty? She knew it was dangerous to drink on top of the pills. I'd told her several times.'

'She must have forgotten,' I said. 'You know her mind wandered, Frances. At least she's at peace now.'

Frances looked at me gratefully. 'Thank you, Betty,' she said. 'You always make me feel better.'

There was relief in her face, and I had the feeling that she was glad her mother was dead, despite the tears. She had often felt like a prisoner these past few months. Now that Mary was dead she was free to live her own life . . . Free to marry James.

'Is there anything I can do for you?' I asked.

'No.' She smiled oddly. 'James is here. He stayed here last night because he knew I was worried about my mother.'

'That was good of him,' I said. Obviously she had no idea that James had only been with her because he was angry with me.

'You go home now,' she said. 'I'll be all right with James to look after me.' She was barely controlling her excitement. 'It was good of you to come, Betty. You've been wonderful to Mother. I shall never forget it.'

Guilt lanced through me like a sword. 'You will tell me when the funeral is, won't you?'

'Of course.' Frances smiled again. 'You must lunch with me soon, Betty. I've got something to tell you.'

From the look in her eyes. I could guess what she meant. So Nathan had been right after all!

Mary was decently buried and prayers were read over her grave. Frances insisted that I stay for the reading of the will.

'You must be here,' she said. 'Apparently Mother left you something.'

I didn't want to stay. From the way she'd been clinging to James's arm, I guessed that their engagement must be official, though she still wasn't wearing a ring – but that might have looked too obvious.

When Frances was with the lawyer, James came up to me. 'I must see you tonight,' he said. 'It's important, Betty.'

'I'm not sure . . .' I began, then as Frances turned. 'All right – at eight.'

He moved away, sitting next to Frances. I saw her smile up at him. He squeezed her hand and an intimate look passed between them. I felt a flicker of anger. I was beginning to know James Blair for the man he was.

'Did you hear, Miss Cantrel?' the lawyer asked. 'Mrs Crawley bequeathed all her personal jewellery to you.'

I blinked at him in surprise. 'But that should be for Frances – surely?'

'No, Betty,' Frances said. 'Mother wanted you to have it – and there's nothing really valuable, you know. It's just a few trinkets.'

'Then I can only say thank you.'

'Shall we continue?' The solicitor frowned as he looked at the will. 'Mr Crawley, your aunt has left you the sum of ten thousand pounds. She states that it is owed to you, and I have a letter she left which should explain her wishes in this matter . . .'

The lawyer paused significantly, looking at Frances. 'This will was made about two years ago. I have no reason to suppose that Mrs Crawley was not in her right mind when she signed it.'

Frances looked puzzled. 'Why – is something wrong?'

He cleared his throat. 'After various small bequests, Mrs Crawley's estate is divided into two equal parts. One half is to go immediately to the church in Sutton . . .' I heard Frances gasp and James looked startled. 'The second half is to be put in trust, the income to go to Miss Frances Crawley for her lifetime . . .'

'But that's ridiculous!' James ejaculated.

'The capital to go to Ely cathedral in the event of Miss Crawley's death . . .'

'No . . .' Frances whispered. 'She can't do that . . .' She got to her feet. 'That isn't fair. I've looked after her. I've kept my part of the bargain. She promised . . . She . . .'

'Is there anything we can do?' James asked, standing beside her. 'Surely we can contest the will?'

'If you could prove she wasn't of sound mind . . .' the lawyer shrugged. 'If Mr Crawley were to support you . . .'

'Yes, I can see what you mean.' Nathan rose. 'We shall have to discuss it, of course. We'll let you know what we decide, sir.'

Nathan went to the door with him. James poured

himself a drink from the decanter on the sideboard, and Frances went to stand beside him.

'It can't be right,' she said. 'Nathan will help us . . .'

She broke off as Nathan came in. He was carrying a small leather jewel case that I recognised, and he held it out to me.

'This is yours, Betty. No matter what we decide about the will, I think we all want you to have this.'

'Yes, of course,' Frances said, but there was an odd note in her voice. 'You deserve something – this doesn't concern you.'

Her look and her tone told me I was being dismissed. I was the faithful servant who had served her purpose, but I wasn't a part of this family. I never had been.

'I'll go then,' I said. 'Perhaps we can have lunch one day, Frances?'

'Yes, we must arrange it soon,' she said brightly, insincerely.

'Don't bother to see me out. I know you must have lots to talk about.'

I glanced at James, but he wasn't aware of me. He looked shocked, dazed even. Had the money meant so much to him?

'I'll see you out, Betty,' Nathan said.

'No, please don't,' I said. 'I'd rather go alone.'

When I got home, Megan told me there was a message from Liz.

'She phoned a couple of times,' Megan said. 'It seemed urgent.'

'Thank you. I'll ring her now.'

The phone shrilled several times before Liz picked it up. Her voice was thick and choked and I knew she'd been crying.

'What's the matter?' I asked. 'Is there something I can do, Liz?'

'I – I'm in trouble, Betty,' she said. 'I – I didn't know who else to turn to.'

487

'You sound really upset. Tell me what's wrong, Liz. You know I'll help you – if I can.'

She was silent for a moment, then: 'I – I'm having a child, Betty.'

'Oh, I see. Is he married?'

'No . . . but he won't marry me. I know he won't.'

'Have you asked him? Does he know about the baby?'

'No, not yet. I – I'm afraid to tell him.'

A little chill went through me. 'It isn't Nathan, is it, Liz?'

She laughed hysterically. 'I only wish it was – but you're nearly there. I know I shouldn't be telling you, Betty, but I need money for the abortion. I can find a doctor to do it, but it costs a fortune.'

'Think about it first, Liz,' I said. 'If you need money I can let you have some, but you've got to tell me who the father is. He might marry you.'

'It's James Blair,' Liz said. 'I'm sorry, Betty. I never meant to get involved with him, but he was so persuasive . . .'

'James . . .' I was stunned. 'How long have you been seeing him?'

'Oh, ages, off and on . . . It started the night he came to the club and you went home in a taxi alone. Do you remember?'

'Perfectly.' I felt sick. 'Look, Liz, I can't talk to you now, but I'll help you with money whatever you decide to do.'

'Do you hate me?' she said. 'I know you must.' I heard a sob over the line.

'No, Liz,' I said. 'I don't hate you . . .'

Putting down the receiver, I stared blankly into space. James Blair was the father of Liz's child. He had been seeing her, sleeping with her occasionally, for years . . . even during the time we had been lovers. He had lied to me, lied to Frances, and probably to Liz as well.

The walls were tumbling about me as all my illusions

shattered. I'd believed that James was the perfect man, but I'd deceived myself. He had betrayed us all . . .

I was waiting when James came that night. I'd never felt so angry in my life. He came towards me eagerly, expecting to take me in his arms. I moved away sharply, barely controlling my temper. He looked at my tight face and frowned.

'What's wrong, Betty?' he asked. 'Have I done something to upset you?'

I laughed bitterly. 'Where would you like me to start?'

He looked shocked, wary. 'Has Frances said anything to you?'

'You mean – has she told me you've asked her to marry you? Or has she told me you're not quite sure now that she isn't the wealthy heiress you thought she was?'

His face blanched, and he seemed to wilt under the scorn in my eyes. 'That's not fair,' he faltered. 'I – I haven't said I won't marry her . . .'

'You want to see if the will can be overturned, I suppose,' I said. 'I expect Frances will try if you tell her to, James. I think she'd do almost anything for you. She's nearly as big a fool as I was . . . and Liz.'

'Liz?' He stared at me. 'If she's been telling you lies . . .'

'No, you're the one who's been lying, James. To me, to Frances, to Liz . . .'

'I can explain about her. She threw herself at me . . .' He shrugged his shoulders. 'It was only a couple of times, Betty. You know it was you I really wanted, don't you?' He moved towards me and I retreated.

'I only know I was a fool to love you,' I said. 'But it wasn't really you I loved, James. It was the man I thought you were – and that man doesn't exist.'

'Betty . . . don't look at me like that. I know I've been a fool, but . . .'

'Don't make excuses,' I said. 'I know you now, James. I know you for what you are and I want you out of my life.'

He stared at me. 'Are you going to tell Frances?'

I smiled scornfully. 'You'd like that, wouldn't you, James? You'd like me to do your dirty work for you. It would save you having to tell Frances that you can't marry her because all you ever wanted was the money . . . the money she doesn't have.'

'You little . . .' He raised his hand to strike but I lifted my head proudly.

'Do that and you'll answer to Nathan.'

He stared at me, then his hand dropped to his side. 'So you're going back to him,' he said bitterly. 'I suppose he told you my company has gone bust?'

'Don't tar me with your own brush,' I said. 'I've made mistakes in my life. At the moment I'm not very proud of myself, but at least I'm honest enough to admit that I was wrong.'

James's eyes glittered. 'So you want me out of your life, do you? You think you can drop me the way you dropped Nathan – but I'm not that easy to get rid of. I'll be back . . .'

A chill went through me as I looked into his eyes. For a moment I was frightened, then he pushed past me and went out of the door. I breathed deeply, trying to keep calm.

My obsession with James was over. I was free at last. Free to get on with my life . . . And yet that look in his eyes had made me afraid. I knew that it would haunt me when I was alone. It would rob me of my peace of mind . . .

Chapter Twenty

Freedom! Was I ever foolish enough to believe that I could be truly free? Was I so blind that I couldn't see the trap was closing in? Yet if I had known, what could I have done?

Sally is not here tonight. There are two new black crows to preside over my last hours . . . The time is coming soon now. I can feel it . . . Perhaps when it is over I shall find that freedom after all.

When James left me that night. I should have done something. I should have talked to Nathan or Frances – or even Liz. I did nothing. I was tired and depressed. So I did nothing.

I did nothing and because of it I am here in this cell. But the end is near now. I have just a little further to travel. I wish that they would come for me now so that I didn't have to live through that terrible day again, but there is no escape. I must continue my journey for just a little longer . . .

Nathan came to the club that night. He asked me to have a drink with him after the show and I agreed. I was pleased to see him, and I felt that it was almost like old times again. Now that I no longer believed myself in love with James, I could see that the best time of my life had been while I was living with Nathan. I wondered what we might have made of our lives if I hadn't been obsessed with my dreams of the perfect man . . . a man who didn't exist outside my imagination.

'You look thoughtful, Betty,' Nathan said with a smile. 'I'll give you a penny for them?'

'I was thinking it was nice to be with you again.'

'Do you mean that?' His face was suddenly intent. 'Have you thought about what I asked you the other night?'

'It's too soon to decide.' I took a deep breath. 'I'm not saying no. Only that I want a little time to think about it.'

'Is it over between you and James?'

'Yes. Completely. It was a dream, Nathan – all tied up with my wanting to be like Frances – and I've finally woken up.' I smiled at him. 'I believe I've finally come to my senses. I think I may be able to put the past behind me. I'm going to try.'

His eyes glowed as he looked at me. 'If you decide to give me that chance, I won't let you down. I swear it.'

'Don't promise too much too soon. Let's take it slowly this time.'

'Betty, I love you,' he said, his hand reaching for mine across the table. 'I know you've never believed it. You've never trusted me – but please believe me now. If you take me back it will be for always.'

'If I come back – that's the way I want it to be.' I looked into his eyes. 'What about Helga?'

'She knows it's only a casual affair, Betty. I'm not the only man in her life. I wouldn't want to be.' He touched my cheek. 'You're the woman I love, Betty.'

It was very late when Nathan drove me home. As we got out of the car, he pulled me into his arms, kissing me with a passion that sent my senses reeling. 'Don't send me away, Betty,' he pleaded huskily. 'Let me stay with you tonight. I need you so much.'

I'd planned to take my time, to be certain that the decision I came to was the right one, but with Nathan's arms around me and his lips on mine, I couldn't think clearly. My body was clamouring for his with a new-found urgency. Weakly, I gave way to his pleading.

'Yes, Nathan,' I whispered. 'Stay with me.'

I wasn't promising anything, yet even as I told myself that, I knew that Nathan would take my words as a binding commitment. As we walked up to the bedroom, our arms about each other, I realised there was no going back. Nathan would never let me go now. I was his totally . . . And I was content.

Our loving that night was beyond anything I'd ever known, even at the beginning of our relationship. This was the first time I'd given myself to him without reserve. I was his, body and soul, and as our bodies moved in slow unison, I knew that I'd never felt such exquisite pleasure. We were one person, one being, in a way we had never been before. I knew that Nathan loved me – and I loved him. Not blindly as I'd loved James, but with my eyes open, accepting him as a man with all his faults.

Afterwards, I lay nestled in his arms.

'Was it like this with him?' he asked, and I heard the jealous pain in his voice. 'Did he make you happy?'

I leaned over him, seeing the anguish in his face, and I shook my head, letting my hair brush across his face. 'To be honest,' I said, a wicked smile on my lips, 'he has no imagination and not much staying power. Too often, James satisfied only himself. He isn't and never was half the man you are.' It wasn't strictly true; James had been almost as satisfying a lover as Nathan, but I wanted to salve his pride and ease his jealousy.

A gleam of triumph entered his eyes as he caught me to him fiercely. 'I wanted to kill him, Betty. I threatened to when I thought you were leaving me for him. Sometimes I even wanted to kill you.'

The glitter in his eyes was a little frightening.

'Why didn't you?'

'Because I'd no right to hold you after what I did that night.' His arms tightened about me. 'I deserved to be cast into the wilderness for what I did to you and our child. But now you belong to me, Betty, and if you ever betray me again, I'll break that adorable little neck of yours . . .'

For a moment I was startled, but when I looked up into his eyes, I saw that he was laughing, teasing me in the old way, and I knew that I had come home at last. Nathan loved me. He loved me more than anything in the world . . .

'I'll never leave you again,' I vowed. 'Only death will part us and not for long, my darling. Without you, I wouldn't want to live . . .'

The bed was cold and empty when I woke. I was disappointed that Nathan had gone so early. But even as I slipped from the warmth of the sheets, he came into the room, carrying a tray with breakfast and a single red rose.

'You're not getting up yet, are you?' The tone of his voice filled me with delight and I grabbed him and pulled him down to me as he set down the tray. 'Wait for it, kid,' he said. 'Breakfast first.'

'No,' I said, beginning to cover him with kisses. 'I want you . . .'

It was a long time afterwards that we sat together, drinking our cold coffee and eating toast. He stroked my arm lazily with the tips of his fingers, sighing heavily.

'What's wrong?' I asked, suddenly anxious.

'I was thinking how much I'd like to stay here for the rest of the day – but I have an appointment I can't break.'

'Oh, Nathan . . .' I pouted at him. 'Do you have to go?'

'Unfortunately, I do. We have the rest of our lives, Betty. I want to get my affairs settled, then we'll go on that trip I once promised you. Our honeymoon. Where would you like to go? Italy? Greece?'

'I don't mind – Venice!' I gazed up at him excitedly. 'I've always wanted to visit Venice.'

He laughed and kissed me again. 'We'll go everywhere. Everywhere you ever wanted to go – but now I have to keep that appointment.'

After Nathan had gone, I bathed and dressed in a new suit of emerald green. He'd always liked me in bright colours. I'd preferred the more subtle shades I believed a real lady would wear, but now it no longer mattered. I was Betty Cantrel, the daughter of a wastrel, and nothing would ever change that, but I no longer cared. Nathan wanted me the way I was.

I spent all morning shopping. I bought freely, indulging in an orgy of spending just because I felt so good. I bought presents for all my friends, but mostly for Nathan. He'd always given me so much, now I wanted to give him the earth. I wanted to shower him with my love, to make him happy . . . I wanted to make up for all the pain I'd caused him by my wilfulness in the past.

When I got back to the house, the telephone was ringing. I snatched it up, breathlessly. 'Nathan . . .'

'Betty, it's me,' Frances said, a note of hysteria in her voice. 'I have to see you. I have to see you straight away . . .'

'Frances . . .' I looked up as Nathan came in. He bent to kiss me. 'Frances, I can't talk to you just now,' I said. 'I'll ring you later.' I put down the receiver and Nathan took it off the hook.

'That's the first time you've ever refused her,' he said. 'And a good thing, too. We've all danced to my cousin's tune far too often.'

I didn't say anything. I couldn't, because I was in his arms, clinging to him as he kissed me hungrily. 'I missed you,' I said. 'I went shopping – but I missed you.'

'I missed you,' he said. 'From now on, I'm never going to leave you again . . .'

I took his hand, tugging at him, laughing excitedly. 'Come on,' I cried. 'Come and see what I've bought for you – it's all upstairs . . .'

Nathan grinned. 'Presents, too? You'll spoil me, Betty. I shall think you really do love me if you're not careful.'

'But I do,' I said. 'I always have, but I didn't know it until now . . .'

Nathan gathered me to him. I pushed him away, teasing him. 'Not just yet. I want to show you. Come on!'

'Impatient brat,' he said, but he gave way.

Upstairs, I began to open boxes and packages, holding up the expensive silk shirts, dressing gown, and pyjamas I'd bought for him.

He grinned at the pyjamas. 'I don't expect to be wearing those much . . .'

'Oh, you,' I said, pulling a face at him. 'They're for when you lie down on the bed in the hotel.'

'Well, as long as that's all . . .'

'Look at this,' I said excitedly. 'You can open this one yourself, Nathan.'

His eyes danced with amusement as he took the box from me, looking at the name of the expensive jeweller. 'What's this then? It's too big for cufflinks . . . My God! That's fantastic, Betty. You must have paid the earth for it.'

Inside the box was an Eastern-style dagger with a jewelled handle. As he took it out, I hastened to warn him. 'Be careful, Nathan. I was told the blade is very sharp. Mind you don't cut your fingers.'

He took the dagger out, examining it carefully. 'It's beautiful,' he said. 'But don't start buying me presents like this. It's you I want, my darling.'

'You've bought me loads of things,' I said, pulling a face at him as he laid it on the dressing table. 'Now don't be silly, Nathan – thank me nicely for it.'

He reached for me then, drawing me tight against him. This time I didn't resist. We tumbled to the bed together, kissing feverishly. There was something almost desperate about the way we made love then – could we have guessed that destiny was waiting to sweep us away with the wind?

Afterwards, we lay entwined on the bed, talking idly. Nathan ran his finger down my spine.

'Do you want children, Betty?'

I rolled over to look up at him. 'Your children? Yes, of course I do – but it's you I want most, Nathan. The children will come when they're ready.' I frowned. 'Do you want a child?'

'Yes . . .' He was silent for a moment. 'Once I would have been afraid to say that . . .'

'What do you mean?'

'For years I wondered if there was something wrong with me. My temper . . . I thought I might be unbalanced or something. I felt so guilty about Edward . . .'

'Your cousin? But that was an accident – wasn't it?'

'Yes, of course. I did push him because I was angry . . .' Nathan frowned. 'But I was always jealous of Edward. He was the son of the family, while I . . . I suffered hell for that, Betty. Then my temper betrayed me again. I killed my own child . . .'

'Don't, Nathan!' I caught his hand. 'That's over now. I've forgiven you, my darling. It was as much my fault as yours. I drove you to it. I knew you were jealous and I – I went on thinking about James, robbing you of the love you should always have had. It was my fault as much as yours.'

'Jealousy is a terrible thing. All the Crawleys are jealous, Betty, and we all have violent tempers when roused – including Frances.'

There was something in his eyes then. 'What do you mean?'

'I've never been certain, but Mary said something . . .'

'About that day in the barn?' I stared at him, a little shiver running down my spine. 'What did happen, Nathan?'

'I saw Frances run from the barn,' he said slowly. 'She looked terrified. When I went in, I found Eben lying there. I went up to the loft to look – and I saw there had been a struggle . . .'

'You don't think Frances pushed him?'

'I don't know. It could have been an accident. Why would she want to kill him?'

'Because he wouldn't let her become engaged to James,' I said, shivering. 'I was obsessed with James, I'll admit that – but Frances is even more obsessed than I was. I think – yes, I think she might kill if it meant getting James.'

'But you've ruined my chance of that, haven't you, Betty?'

Neither of us had been aware of her until that moment. We looked towards the doorway and then at each other, both of us horrified at what had happened. She must have heard every word we'd been saying.

'Frances . . .' I jumped up, hastily pulling on my dressing gown. 'Who let you in?'

'I used this.' She held up a key. 'It's the one you gave to James, isn't it? I took it from his pocket the other night. I thought I knew where it would fit – and today he told me everything . . .' Her eyes glittered with fury. 'He told me that you and he were lovers . . .'

Nathan was pulling on his trousers. 'It's over,' he said gruffly. 'Betty is going to marry me. We're going away. She won't be seeing James again, Frances. I give you my word.'

Frances ignored him. She was looking at me, hatred in her face. 'So you'll have everything, just as you always did,' she said bitterly. 'You were free to live your own life while I was a prisoner. You could have had anyone – any man you wanted. I only ever wanted James, you knew that. You knew that!'

'I know you'll never forgive me,' I said. 'I wish it had never happened. If I could, I would go back to the night I first slept with him and . . .'

'But you always wanted him,' she screamed. 'You always wanted what was mine. I told you he was mine, Betty. I warned you . . .'

'He'll come back to you now . . .'

'No!' It was a cry of despair. 'He told me that he was going away because you threw him over for Nathan. He said he can't bear it and he's going back to America. It's because of you . . .'

'He's not worth breaking your heart over, Frances.

498

Even while he was with me, he was seeing someone else . . .'

'Liar!' she cried. 'Liar!'

'He always wanted the money, Frances,' Nathan said. 'If you're honest, you'll admit that.'

She didn't even turn her head to look at him. Her eyes narrowed to menacing slits. 'It was you, Betty,' she said. 'You've ruined my life – and now I'm going to have yours . . .'

Before I could take in what she was saying, she picked up the jewelled dagger I'd bought for Nathan. As she rushed at me, I gave a cry of alarm but I couldn't move. I was frozen to the floor. Then, suddenly, Nathan launched himself at her and they were struggling for the knife. I stood, turned to stone, doing nothing.

Oh God, why didn't I scream for help? Why didn't I throw myself on Frances, pull her hair, hit her . . . anything? I did nothing because I was incapable of movement. I watched as they struggled desperately for the knife, then I saw Frances draw back her arm and drive the knife deep into Nathan's stomach. I heard his scream of pain – and then I moved. I ran towards them, catching him in my arms as he fell. Frances backed away, staring at us, her eyes wide with fright.

'Oh, Nathan,' I cried desperately. 'I love you. Don't die . . . Please don't die.'

The blood was pouring from the wound. I pressed my hands against it, trying to staunch the flow. Then I looked up at Frances.

'For God's sake get a doctor,' I said. 'Go on!'

As she ran from the room, I looked down at Nathan.

He smiled at me so sweetly. 'I waited so long for you to realise you loved me,' he said. 'Why couldn't we have had just a little time? Why were we cursed?'

'Don't leave me,' I begged, the tears streaming down my face. 'Please don't leave me alone, my darling. I need you so.'

'As I always needed you,' he said. 'You do believe me,

499

don't you? You know that I loved you – right from the beginning?'

'Yes, yes,' I said feverishly. 'Don't talk, my dearest. Save your strength. Frances will bring the doctor soon.'

He shook his head. 'I can't hold on, Betty. Not even for you . . .'

I saw the colour fading from his cheeks and I held him tighter, sobbing wildly. 'You mustn't die! You can't. I won't let you . . .'

He smiled once more. 'Here's looking at you, sweetheart,' he said, then his eyes closed.

I sobbed as I held his lifeless body to me, rocking him as the blood soaked into my dressing gown and the ice entered my soul. I knew what I'd done by my wilfulness. I'd killed the only man I'd ever truly loved. Because of my blind stupidity, I'd aroused Frances's jealousy – and it was as if I had driven the knife into my lover's heart with my own hands!

I kissed the face of my dead love, wetting it with bitter tears. As I held him to me tightly, my heart broke into a thousand tiny pieces. I held him until he was cold and stiff in my arms – and then Frances walked into the room, followed by someone else I could not see through my tears.

'It's too late,' I said. 'He's dead.'

'And you killed him,' she said, her eyes dark with hatred. 'You killed him, Betty . . .'

I gazed into the bitter eyes and I said nothing. She was right. I had killed him.

There will be no reprieve. They will come for me very soon now. This morning one of the women in black cut off my hair. She was almost in tears. A priest has been to see me. We prayed together. I think it was a comfort to him. I don't know whether or not Heaven exists, but I think perhaps I shall very soon know. My heaven will be to be with Nathan again.

I've been trying to remember a nursery rhyme I used to sing to Dorothy Ann. How did it go?

'Rock-a-bye baby in the treetops . . .
When the wind blows the cradle will rock . . .'

I'm not sure if that's right. Have I missed out a line?
The door of my cell is opening. Four men are waiting outside. They want me to go with them: it is time. If only I could be sure that I will see Nathan again.
They all look so solemn: the prison governor, the priest and two wardens. Strong men. I suppose they need to be strong in case I struggle. The woman who cut off my hair is crying. The men look grim, their faces white and strained. This must be a terrible ordeal for them. I pity them. Even the governor looks ill. Poor man.
How does that rhyme go? Dorothy Ann loved it so.

'When the bough breaks
The cradle will fall
Down will come baby
Cradle and all . . .'

I think that's almost right. I wish I could remember.
The first day of the trial was the worst. All those people waiting outside the courtroom to jeer at me. All the eyes staring at me, waiting to hear me plead for my life. They waited in vain . . . A few friendly faces in the gallery. Hilda, Richard, Liz.
Hilda came to the prison to see me. She asked if there was anything she could do, but I shook my head. No one can bring back Nathan, no one can give him back his life.
Frances didn't come. I didn't expect it. She had known right from the start that I would not betray her. Hadn't I promised on pain of death?
It wasn't because of a child's oath that I'd kept silent. I

*simply had no wish to live. I want to die. I want them to
take my life. I did nothing to save Nathan and so he died.
His blood is on my hands. I want someone to punish me
for doing nothing. Death is so much easier than this living
hell.*

'You're that stubborn and proud, Betty. I only hope
you don't end up as bitter as your grandfather.'

'I'm not bitter, Mum.'

*The men have stopped walking. Why have . . . oh!
There is nowhere else to go.*

*Please God, don't let me be afraid. But I'm only afraid
of never seeing Nathan again. I can endure anything if
only I can be with him once more. Just once more . . .*

*The wind is rising. It's so cold that it will snow before
nightfall.*

'Let's go home, Mum. I'm so cold. Please take me
home.'

Mum can't take me home. She's dead.

I wish the wind would stop. I do hate the wind.

'Don't cry, little Joe. Big Joe is going to buy you a pony
and we'll all go on the river in the summer. We'll all be
together very soon . . . If God is merciful . . .'

*Forgive me, Nathan, forgive me for wasting all the
years. Please be waiting for me. You know I can't bear to
be alone. I love you so . . .*

*Somehow I shall find Nathan, whether it be in Heaven
or in Hell or in another life. I shall search for him through
all eternity until I am given a chance to put right the
wrong I have done.*

*Oh, Nathan, Nathan, my love. I robbed you of the
happiness we should have known. Forgive me. Forgive
me. Nothing can be as bad as the agony I am enduring
now. Oh, God, take my poor wretched soul and give it
peace . . .*

*There is no more wind. Only a lovely calm. I believe
that God is with me. God is merciful. I am not afraid. I
just wish that I could remember that rhyme. Dorothy
Ann did love it so.*

502

I am not afraid.
I'm coming, Nathan. Wait for me . . .

Epilogue

They hanged Betty Cantrel. I did everything I could to save her, but I failed. I failed because she would tell me nothing, but I knew she was innocent . . . I knew because Mrs Charles Kingston told me the story of her life.

It was just after Betty was sentenced that she walked into my office. 'Mrs Kingston,' I said, offering my hand. 'It was good of you to come. Won't you sit down?'

She shook my hand and smiled. 'I've been travelling with my husband or I would have come sooner,' she said. 'I couldn't believe it when I read the headlines. Betty would never kill Nathan. I know her too well. She just isn't the type. It couldn't have been her.'

'You know her well then?'

'We were in service together.' She laughed as she saw the surprise in my eyes. 'I haven't always been Mrs Charles Kingston. My name was Polly Baxter then.'

'Can you tell me about Betty?' I said. 'She won't tell me a thing.'

'Betty was always one to keep things to herself,' Polly Kingston said. 'She was as stubborn as they come, and proud – but a good friend. I'll tell you, if you'll tell me exactly what happened?'

'It's a deal,' I said. 'Would you care for some coffee while we talk?'

'That's nice of you,' she replied, a twinkle in her eye, 'but I'd rather have a tot of the good stuff, if you know what I mean? Just to keep out the cold.'

'Certainly,' I said, getting up to pour her a drink. I was going to like Mrs Polly Kingston!

'Now,' she said, drinking her whisky in one go. 'You first. You tell me what they say she did – and I'll tell you what really happened.'

'Have you seen Betty?'

'I don't need to – I've seen someone else. She lied to me, but I know her. I know her right through to her rotten little core . . .'

We talked for a long time, Mrs Kingston and I. When we had finished I knew that what she had told me was the truth. There was no way I could prove it, of course, not without Betty's testimony – and I knew now that she would never speak. But I was going to do something. I had to!

I agonised over what I should do for days. I wanted to go to the police, to tell them what I knew, to force them to arrest Frances Crawley, but without proof I could not hope to be believed. The evidence against Betty was too damning. She had bought the dagger herself. She had blood all over her. Surely Frances had some on her, too? But that was explained easily. She had testified in court that she had struggled with Betty, trying to stop her attacking her cousin. She had wept as she gave her evidence. Everyone felt so sorry for her.

At last I knew what I had to do. I called on Frances Crawley an hour after I'd seen Betty for what I knew must be the last time.

She came into the room, dressed all in black.

'You asked to see me?'

'Yes, Frances,' I said. 'I've something to tell you.'

She stared at me, affronted because I'd dared to use her first name. 'Do I know you?' she asked.

'Not yet,' I replied with a smile. 'Not yet, but you will. In time you will come to know my face better than you know your own, because it will always be popping up in front of you. In the shops, in the cinema, in the street . . .'

She gasped, her eyes wide. 'I do know you – you're . . .'

'Laurence,' I said. 'The lawyer for the woman you condemned to death, Frances. Yes, I know you killed

Nathan. I suspect you killed your own father – and maybe even your mother . . .'

'You're mad!' she cried. 'This is all lies! No one would believe a word of it.'

'If that were not the case, you would be taking Betty's place on the gallows, Frances. I can't prove any of it – but I know it. In here and in here.' I touched my head and my heart. 'I know it and one day I'm going to make you pay for what you've done.'

She shrank away from me, fear in her eyes. 'If you touch me I'll . . .'

'Oh no,' I said, smiling pleasantly. 'I'm not going to kill you, Frances. That would be too easy. You might even welcome death. I'm going to wait, that's all. I'm simply going to wait.'

'What do you mean?'

'One day you'll make a mistake. You've killed more than once if I'm not mistaken. One day you'll do it again – and when you do . . .'

'You – you don't frighten me.'

'Perhaps not yet, but I will, Frances, I will . . .'

I saw a look of terror in her eyes and I knew that I'd got through to her. She herself was capable of murder, she would naturally believe that I too was capable of carrying out my threat. She would never know an easy moment again. Whether I ever managed to bring her to justice or not, she would serve her sentence – and it would be for life.

ROWAN BESTSELLERS

OLD SINS
Penny Vincenzi

An unputdownable saga of mystery, passion and glamour, exploring the intrigue which results when Julian Morrell, head of a vast cosmetics empire, leaves part of his huge legacy to an unknown young man. The most desirable novel of the decade, *Old Sins* is about money, ambition, greed and love... a blockbuster for the nineties.

GREAT POSSESSIONS
Kate Alexander

A wonderful saga set in glamorous between-the-wars London that tells the story of Eleanor Dunwell, an illegitimate working-class girl who comes quite unexpectedly into a great inheritance. Her wealth will attract a dashing American spendthrift husband – and separate her from the man she truly loves.

THE WIND IN THE EAST
Pamela Pope

There were two things Joshua Kerrick wanted in the world: one was money to buy a fleet of drifters; the other was Poppy Ludlow. But Poppy and Joshua are natural rivals. This vivid historical drama traces their passionate story among an East Anglian community struggling to make their living from the sea.

FRIENDS AND OTHER ENEMIES
Diana Stainforth

Set in the sixties and seventies, the rich, fast-moving story of a girl called Ryder Harding who loses *everything* – family, lover, money and friends. But Ryder claws her way back and turns misfortune into gold.

THE FLIGHT OF FLAMINGO
Elizabeth Darrell

A strong saga unfolds against a backdrop of marine aviation in its heady pioneering days before the Second World War. When Leone Kirkland inherits her autocratic father's aviation business, she also inherits his murky past, and Kit Anson, his ace test pilot. She needs him; she could love him, but he has every reason to hate her.

THE QUIET EARTH
Margaret Sunley

Set in the Yorkshire Dales during the nineteenth century this rural saga captures both the spirit and warmth of working life in an isolated farming community, where three generations of the Oaks family are packed under the same roof. It tells of their struggle for survival as farmers, despite scandal, upheaval and tragedy, under the patriarchal rule of Jonadab Oaks.

ELITE
Helen Liddell

Anne Clarke was a ruthless, politically ambitious, beautiful and brilliant woman... passionately committed to the underground workers militia of Scotland. But did her seemingly easy rise to the post of Deputy Prime Minister and her brilliantly orchestrated, perfectly lip-glossed public face conceal a sinister secret?

THE SINS OF EDEN
Iris Gower

Handsome, charismatic and iron-willed, Eden Lamb has an incalculable effect on the lives of three very different women in Swansea during the Second World War that is to introduce them both to passion and heartbreak. Once again, bestselling author Iris Gower has spun a tender and truthful story out of the background she knows and loves so well.

OTHER ROWAN BOOKS